INTERNATIONAL TEAM OF MYSTERY

WHISKEY WITCHES PARA WARS BOOK 4

S.S. WOLFRAM

F.J. BLOODING

WHISTLING BOOK PRESS

Whistling Book Press

Alaska

Printed in the United States of America

Published by Whistling Book Press

Whistling Book Press
Alaska
Visit our web site at:
www.whistlingbooks.com

❀ Created with Vellum

Shifting Heart Romances

by Hattie Hunt & F.J. Blooding

Bear Moon

Grizzly Attraction

Here's the reading order to make it even easier to catch up!

https://www.fjblooding.com/reading-order

Other Books by F.J. Blooding

Devices of War Trilogy

Fall of Sky City

Sky Games

Whispers of the Skyborne

Discover more, sign up for updates and gifts, and join the forum discussions at www.fjblooding.com.

WHISKEY MAGICK & MENTAL HEALTH

S ign up to learn more about our books and receive this free e-zine about Whiskey Magick and Mental Health.
https://www.fjblooding.com/books-lp

THANKS

We have to say a huge thank you to Thomas who has really stepped up and does his absolute best to tell us about typos as he's reading the ARC. Thank you so much! You're the best!

Auto-incorrect to the resc…

No. No. That's not a rescue. That's what he's rescuing us from!

Right! Thank you for healing our broken heels.

Dexx's running footfalls echoed through the cobblestone tunnel. Rain dripped from his coat and his hair. He had the thumb drive in hand. The mission was complete and a success, and now it was time to get out of there. Getting the thing had been easy—a little too easy, so he was keeping his eyes and ears open for trouble as he left the area to return to his team. There was no sense in getting even more information on DoDO—hopefully, to take them down once and for all—only to get caught getting out of there.

The rain had started up from nowhere. Not exactly nowhere. He'd felt the magick forming it.

An elemental had to be in the area, but whose was it? DoDO or someone else? Foe, bigger foe, or potential friend?

The wet cobbles reflected splintered light everywhere. Dexx's enhanced vision didn't help much in that environment.

Got any ideas who's following us? Having Hattie back was like regaining use of an arm or leg after an injury. It sure was nice when the connection worked.

No response. Contact had been spotty at best since regaining his memories, and he still had to release her, release them both, or they would die. But not yet. He'd find a way. She was the other half of him.

So maybe she was on the injured reserve list and not very useful to the team.

A slightly darker patch resolved into a tiny alcove that might fit him. The space barely covered him enough to slink into.

His super-hearing picked up the sounds of two sets of running bootsteps. The jingle of full DoDO combat equipment gave their identities away.

So the anonymous source was a trap. Was the info on it a trap, too?

Dexx willed himself deeper into the slot, not wanting to be discovered by the enemy.

They had ways of finding him, but they didn't have a lot of time to cast a spell. Sometimes regular vision trumped magick. This time it backfired on them.

They ran past and continued on.

Dexx's infra-red vision followed their trail around the corner and beyond his ability to see.

He counted to five, and just as he made a move to leave, he heard something else.

Bigger.

Slower.

Less easily tricked.

Maybe he didn't hear it as much as he felt the soft concussion of footfalls through the ground.

He pulled in a deep, slow breath, calming his heart. The exercise didn't do a lot, but it *did* help a little.

Ten more seconds and the water dripping from the archway at the end of the tunnel fell in a sheet in time with the footsteps.

The demon that'd just manifested had to be massive.

Was this thing after him? It had to be. DoDO agents arrived on his tail, then *this?*

Coincidences were one thing. This had the feel of a sting.

Can you answer me? Hattie just wasn't around a lot, but sometimes she broke through enough to talk. *Any information here would be helpful.*

Stay. Hattie's voice sounded distant. Her normally soothing voice had desperation in it.

No shit. I need more, like what is it? Or how to kill it fast and quiet would work, too.

Nothing. Hattie wasn't there.

Damn.

The beast blocked off the tunnel opening with a body bigger than an elephant and wings to make a pterodactyl jealous. Hot, glowing eyes made the air feel hot.

That blurred Dexx's heat vision, so he tried regular sight. That caught refracted light, making details impossible, but Dexx knew that was a fucking demon. There was no special skill required to see that *just fine.*

One was more than enough. Shit, this one might be able to take on an angel.

Or not. Angels were tough too.

Please, oh please, just pass by. Nothing interesting to see here. Hattie, where are you?

Suddenly, the demon looked up over the tunnel. With one leap, and with a swish of his too-huge wings, it left.

Could Dexx really be that lucky? He made a slow count to sixty before twitching so much as a finger.

Let whoever had him trailed think he wasn't there —all quiet.

Dexx crept forward and poked his head around the corner. Nothing in the color spectrum or infra-red. Nothing out of the ordinary, anyway.

One more pass of the outside and Dexx broke cover. He ran to the rendezvous, silent as possible. Shifters ran quietly even when not shifted.

Who would bring in the elemental and why? To drive bystanders away while closing off escape. Smart.

Dexx stretched his senses out, smelling the air, listening for suspect sounds, and looking for anything out of the ordinary.

The way out looked clear, but caution was the word of the day. Two steps, then something made his hairs stand on end, though all he sensed was a dark sense of *nothing*.

Dexx pulled his *ma'a'shed* but held it inside his coat. The blade wouldn't reflect light, but he didn't need anyone freaking out because he had a scary knife.

He poked his head out from the tunnel and searched the area, including the path over him.

Trees in the distance occluded buildings further on, but the near area looked cl—

Dexx felt the magick forming a ranged attack. He leapt to the side as hard as he could.

The ground exploded into a boiling crater of lava for an instant, and the thunder echoed across the night-dark grounds.

He missed the biggest part of the blast, but it still rang his bell pretty good. A bright green after-image splotched out the world, and his ears rang so loud they felt like they were stuffed with cotton.

Wait there, cub. Be dead. Hattie's voice came through clear as a summer sky in the Sahara.

He didn't ask questions. He just obeyed. If she was back, he'd take the win.

Dexx lay on the ground in the most awkward position, waiting.

A minute passed. Two.

A cramp formed in his back, but he didn't move.

On the far edges of his hearing, Dexx heard stealthy footsteps.

Those weren't a bystander investigating the sudden explosion. Those were the steps of a hunter checking on the kill to confirm the death.

Dexx risked opening his eyes a crack, but he faced the wrong way.

The smell of ozone faded enough to smell the fear of the killer. They knew who he was. *What* he was.

Hard to kill, but easy enough to put down for a while. Bussemi had proved that multiple times.

Dexx slowly tightened his grip on the hilt of the *ma'a'shed,* readying himself for the attack.

The second set of footsteps came in from the other direction, one where he could see but not clearly.

Shit. Shit, shit, shit. Dead people don't have closed eyes. He let them open a little more. Hopefully, these two wouldn't notice.

"Is he dead?" The DoDO agent on the far side let his hesitation to get close filter through his voice.

He got points for not being stupid.

"You didn't cast a detection spell?" Brooks said behind Dexx, his voice irritated. "Are you on a pisser? That's why you pulled this detail. Check him."

They were too far apart to take down together, but the one he could see closed the gap, seeing his dead, staring eyes.

"Wait. What was that?" Brooks looked skyward.

Another sound in the distance. Heavy wingbeats. The massive woosh of air announced the demon was coming back.

Fuuuuck. These two idiots deserved this.

Dexx flung the *ma'a'shed* at the far DoDO, planting the knife right between his eyes.

Instant death was better than Brooks deserved. Way better. The death caster fell to the ground without surprise or anything.

Mr. Not Stupid pulled a wand from the pouch on his vest. He began a spell, waving the stick back and whipping it forward, crackling energy glowing at the tip.

Too late. Dexx had a powerful shifter spirit pushing him forward. He jammed one hand to the DoDO agent's throat as the other caught his wand hand.

The man's wrist popped with the breaking of bones. The man had a good scream trying to get past the constricted windpipe, but instead, his eyes bulged out, making him look like a surprised frog.

More bones popped in his neck, and he became dead weight but not dead.

Dexx ripped the wand from the man's hand and pulled the gun from his holster. Dexx didn't have time to get the extra mags with the wingbeats closing hard.

With another leap, Dexx landed next to Brooks. No wand, he was a finger mage. But he still had a gun. And a *ma'a'shed* between his eyes.

The knife slipped free without catching on a bone. It went way beyond being merely sharp.

Dexx turned to flee and skidded to a stop.

The demon landed thirty feet away. Like maybe two steps for him. Too many for Dexx.

"*Shedim Patesh,*" the demon said in a raspy voice. "I've always wanted to meet you."

Oddly polite. What was *this* guy's deal? "Well, now you have." Nothing like pushing the envelope. "This is the part where you kneel down and swear your eternal devotion to me."

"They said you had a way with words. But you're hurt. I will end you forever."

9

Really? *"I will end you."* Dexx enjoyed a good mock whenever someone said something over the top stupid. "Do you even hear yourself? Why don't you bring it up a few millennia at least and say something like, 'Yy name is Inigo Montoya. You killed my father. Prepare to die.'"

The *Princess Bride* would always be a classic.

The demon roared, spraying a furnace-blast of air across the short distance, crisping grass into smoke.

"Or maybe *Mentos, the fresh maker*." That breath was fearsome. "You need a mint, man."

"I will kill you."

"That's more like it. Simple. Direct." Dexx wasn't ready for this. He needed more time. "But why? *If* I was in as bad of shape as you think, wait until I'm better. *Then* you could say you bested me when I was in top form. Whadaya think?"

The demon rushed him in a classic move with his head down, arms out to the side, and wings flared.

Dexx pulsed a thought to the demon knife and transformed it into a *mavet ma'a'shed*, the demon sword. He brought it up and twisted, catching the demon in the side and ducking under as it went by.

The move mostly worked. The sword cut deeply into the demon's flesh, but he lost his grip on the sword as the demon drove his knee into Dexx's side.

The demon fell to the ground on his other knee.

The *ma'a'shed* flew away into the bushes, slicing leaves and branches.

Dexx groaned on the hard cobblestones of the path, holding his ribs as he tried to catch a non-painfilled breath.

At least the rain had stopped.

The demon roared into the sky. It stood up, favoring the leg on the slashed side.

Dexx dropped his head to the ground and pushed himself up. If the demon could keep going, he could too. "Had

enough? Cuz I'm prepared to say you beat me in a fair fight."
He was pretty sure he had some broken ribs.

"You are only human."

"A human that flayed you open like a fish. I don't give this chance often, and I suggest you take it. You won. You go to your corner. I go to mine." Dexx meant to motion someplace vague behind him, but the sharp pain stopped him.

Something was definitely broken.

"I'm taking your head back with me. The great *Shedim Patesh*, reduced to begging for his life."

Rule number one of demon hunting. If it's talking, it's lying. Rule number two. If it's talking and lying, it's trying to buy time or bluffing.

The demon moved his hand, and some of his intestines spilled onto the ground. The demon spared a glance to the injury, then back up to Dexx.

"I slashed you once." Yeah. That demon wasn't making it too far this way. "I swear to fucking Pete, you come at me again, and I'll make two of you." Without that sword. "A top half and bottom half. Won't be much to talk to, but you'll be an interesting conversation starter on my mantle." Rule number three of demon hunting. Out-bluff the bluffers.

"You lost your *ma'a'shed*. Without that, you are just a human. I can take you as my meat suit."

"'Bout that—" Dexx held up his arms, they still hurt, but he was mending fast. "I've taken special precautions. You try possessing me, and you'll be so sorry."

Dexx might be healing quickly, but the demon had to be healing up too. Maybe faster. Probably faster.

"I'll still take your head." The demon produced his own *ma'a'shed,* and it lengthened into a sword.

As scary as Dexx's sword was, all black with two blades split down the middle with blood-red edges, the demon's blade took scary to a new level. It still had two dead black blades and crimson edges, but it also had curling spikes and skulls etched into the flats.

Fantasy swords *wanted* to be that thing.

The wound in the demon closed, and the innards fell to the ground with a wet splotch.

Feeling came back into Dexx's arm with the pins and needles of mending, but the demon looked ready to go again.

"Last chance, big guy. Go now in one piece or go home in several." Dexx really hoped he could follow through with this bluff because he did not for one minute think the demon was buying it. "Final answer." Dexx just needed Hattie to heed his call and come out because she was better than *any* knife.

The demon laughed. A deep rumble that rattled Dexx's teeth and tickled his feet through the ground.

Dexx pushed.

He leapt toward the demon, his hands clawed, and called to Hattie.

Dexx woke up on the wet ground, shivering to beat all.

Naked.

Fuck.

The demon wasn't anywhere. Mostly. A severed clawed hand still gripped a *mavet ma'a'shed*.

Dexx rolled over, grateful to be alive. He gathered the remains of his coat and pants. They might work as a cobbled-together covering, but he'd look funny as hell until he had proper clothing. "Hattie? Is that you, girl? Please, if you can talk, I need to hear from you. You're all I have right now."

Nothing.

Damnit all to hell.

Dexx pried the hand from the demon blade, which immediately shrank into a knife. The thing wasn't like any other blade he'd seen. Still scary, though. He set the blade on his shredded shirt on the ground.

The bush his own knife went into gave it up easily, and he

added his to the demon's. He almost draped his coat over his back. Then he spied the DoDO agents.

One of them looked about his size.

Yeah, now *that* what was he was talkin' about.

He stripped the bigger guy and dressed. He left the vest for last and held it out in front, facing him. "You get that?" he said into the hidden camera. "I'm gonna fuck you up next. I'm coming, and Hell's coming with me."

He crushed the camera and snipped the feed.

He piled the equipment on the other vest after disabling the feed and rolled the bodies for anything they could use. Not bad for an evening.

Last, he dug a small stone from his own rags. His little piece from a life gone.

It was complete silence in his head, though, and he didn't like it. "Hattie, where are you?"

Nothing.

Paige. Home. He had to get home.

2

Dexx dropped the bundle of rags that had been his clothes on the small table in the motel room.

The place hadn't seen a decent cleaning in decades. With the dirt, though, came privacy. And that's what they needed most.

Alwyn and Rainbow sat on the furthest bed, talking quietly.

Of his old team, only she and Ethel ever talked to Alwyn. The others either didn't trust him or his motives, seeing him only as a DoDO agent. Fair, considering not even Dexx understood why Furiel's spell had brought him along.

"What's that?" Frey snarled at the package of Dexx's clothing, but her eyes popped at his DoDO uniform. "What the fuck are you wearing? What the fuck happened out there? I thought you were going to get a simple drive so we could get the hell out of here."

Yes. That had been *her* plan. Get the drive, get the info, and get out. "Funny thing about life. Nobody cares about your plans except you." He was *really* getting tired of Frey's attitude. "A trap. Care to comment?"

Dexx picked out his *ma'a'shed* from the rags of his clothes. "I don't understand." She looked genuinely shocked. "Don't go out again. Tell me what happened."

"Got picked up on the way back. Two DoDO agents and one demon. It might have been a demon, but I haven't seen anything like that one before. I don't know if he was working with DoDO or tracking them. But hey, I brought presents." He pulled the guns out and gave one to Frey and one to Michelle. He split the mags between the two.

"What am I supposed to do with this?" Frey inspected the pistol, then field stripped it and put it back together.

Almost as fast as Dexx could have. Maybe. "Thought you could use some self-defense of your own. I got mine." He hefted his demon knife.

"So do I." Frey patted the back of her neck.

"I'll take them both *without* complaining." Michelle held her hand out and made the "gimme" motion.

"Maybe I'll just hold on to it." Frey tucked the pistol away behind her back. "Still doesn't tell me what the hell you were doing. How did they find you? And why are your clothes ripped up like you shifted?"

Dexx really didn't appreciate this newfound demanding nature. "Because I did."

Everyone snapped to attention, staring at Dexx.

They were seriously overreacting. "Well, mostly." Okay. No, they weren't. "I can't remember doing it or what happened, but I was just about to be eaten by the demon. Then I woke up naked. The demon was gone, but he left a parting gift." Dexx nodded to the shirt. "It's a *ma'a'shed,* but I've never seen one like that before. Didn't want to leave it laying around either, so here it is."

Frey didn't look at the shirt. She stared daggers into Dexx. "I thought we had some sort of magickal cover. What happened to that?"

How many times did he have to repeat himself? "That was for electronic devices, not good ol' sleuthing."

Frey glared at Dexx, reminding him silently that this was all his fault. If he hadn't been kidnapped and forced to work with DoDO, none of them would be across the ocean and being hunted.

She was bucking to challenge for the lead, was what she was doing, and it was irritating him.

"Can I look at the knife?" Ethel's small voice broke the silence and the contest.

Dexx stood aside and flicked a finger at it. "Sure. But I don't think I have to tell you how sharp it is."

"You don't, but thanks for your concern." She picked the knife up, carefully examining the blade. She had run Dexx's first *ma'a'shed* through a battery of tests when he'd first found it. "This is not the same as yours."

"Pretty much got that when it was being swung at my head."

"No," she said, giving him a saucy look. "I mean, there are different properties to this one than yours. Can I see the other one?"

Dexx rolled his neck as the silent clock ticked in the back of his head where Hattie should have been. They were running out of time to sit around and look at pretty knives.

Frey obviously agreed because she locked onto his gaze and held it, challenging him.

That was going to get old real quick.

Rainbow scooted off the bed to join Ethel.

Michelle sighed in heavy disgust as she leaned against the wall, breaking up the staring contest between Frey and Dexx. "But did you get the information you went out to get?"

"Yeah." Dexx knew that Frey's idea of information gathering and retreat wasn't a bad one, and he really had been simply trying to figure out if it was even safe for them to leave.

It was. But only for a short time.

"May I talk with you for a moment, Dexx?" Tarik was polite. He was *always* polite.

Talking with Tarik could get him away from Frey, but he also didn't have to back down. She would continue to press until she had the upper hand. When she did, things would go pear-shaped in a hurry.

Tarik pulled him into another corner.

They were going to run out of corners soon.

The djinni spoke softly. Apparently, this was a private conversation. "We are going to current day Egypt, yes?"

"Yeah." Furiel had told them to start at Tarik's origins. That was Egypt. So, yeah.

"There are things about me and my home that you should know."

This didn't sound good. "Okay."

"I think I should go alone. There is more than a chance that I won't make it from there alive."

That sounded a little dire, actually. "Probably just as well we all go together. Strength in numbers, you know." Dexx couldn't afford to lose part of his team. The rest of the world needed them to be done with all of this and able to go back home.

"I am not like the rest of my people. I have been stripped of what made me a djinn, and even more, was taken at the facility. I can no longer relate to my people."

Dexx understood that he was trying to share something big, but Dexx was *over* big. He had an ancient brother who wouldn't give it a second thought to kill Paige and the kids if it meant getting closer to him. "Sure, but think of all the cool stories you'll get to tell at the reunion. Look. None of us here are what we were before we joined up. Life changes us all the time. You've got to hang in there, bud. We're all here together, and there's no bunch of assholes I'd rather be with right now."

Except for Paige. And the kids. And Hattie. And Jackie. But no other people. Leslie would be awesome to have around. So would the rest of the Whiskeys.

So maybe the team had some things to work on. But this is what they had, and come Hell or high water, *this team* was going to save Paige and the kids, thereby saving the world. From Dexx's evil first brother. "It's been rough on us all. But we all ended up together, and I don't think you're as different as you want to think you are."

"There are certain... tests I must perform to prove myself. I can do almost none of them."

Like Dexx and Hattie. "But can you do *one*?"

"Yes."

"Then that'll be enough." Because it had to be. "We'll figure out the rest later. Right now, we have a bridge to cross, then another. And what's important is that we'll do it together."

"As you say." Tarik looked far from relieved.

Well, that sucked. "Good talk." Dexx gave him a pat on the shoulder and left the corner.

"How are the wards holding?"

Alwyn's hazel eyes snapped to Dexx with a look of slight terror.

"They *are* still holding, right?" Because with that look, Dexx was getting the feeling they needed to move a little faster. Like... now.

"They are, but I don't think I'm as good as your... as Paige is." Alwyn looked around the room at the people who obviously didn't like him. "I tried to duplicate what you described, but there may be flaws."

"You couldn't tell me this before?" Dexx had known that

was likely, but he let his eyes close and took a deep breath. "For whatever reason, you're a part of us now. They're going to treat you as one of us, too, so you better let us know what's going on with the wards."

"I know I can't do what you described." His nervousness ratcheted up three degrees. "I can't keep anyone out, but I can set alarms. They're vibrating, but nothing is coming through. I think."

"Better to be prepared, then. Ethel, give that to Blu." The *ma'a'shed*. "Blu, hold on to that and don't cut anything off of you that you want to keep. Frey, I need you and the others out patrolling. Take lead and set the perimeter. If something comes in, I want to know about it. I have Ethel."

Everyone got up, preparing to leave.

Frey sat in her chair and crossed her arms. "No. I think I'm good right here."

"Move it." Dexx didn't have time for this bullshit from her. "You've got a chip on your shoulder. I get it. But right now, you're one of the best weapons we've got if we all want out of this." *Had* he been followed? Was he getting sloppy now, too?

"You go. If I'm such a good weapon, Ethel will be just fine until you get back. Demons on your heels or not."

He wanted to punch her in the mouth. What the hell was wrong with her? "We can hit the mats later and discuss it. Go out now. Take the damned lead and make sure they all come back alive and intact. That includes Alwyn."

Frey jumped up and went for her sword.

Dexx grabbed her wrist and pinned it to the wall away from her neck. He twisted to the side and pressed against her, taking away most of her ability to fight. "I said go out and be the second in command. We'll do this later when we don't have millions of bad guys looking to kill us. If I'm not being clear enough, I can tie you up until I am."

"Fine." Frey spat the word like it bit her. "You're going to be *my* last in command. Whatever's under Rainbow."

Oh, for fuck's sake. She wanted the leadership position so bad she'd be willing to jeopardize people's lives? That wasn't the sign of a good leader. That was the sign of a person with a big ego. "We'll see." Dexx let her go. "Stay alive, and you'll get your chance."

Frey snagged her coat and left the cramped room.

"Alwyn." Dexx didn't know what he was going to do about Frey, but he couldn't let this continue.

"Mate?"

"Do you have a use for a wand?" He held one of the sticks out.

"I can use it as a focus and strengthen some of my spells, but those are mostly for lower-ranked."

Any way to make forward motion. "Great. Use it. See if you can make the wards hold out more than our hope. And be careful. Frey doesn't like DoDO at all." None of them did, But Alwyn wasn't DoDO anymore.

"We may be friends yet."

"Maybe." Dexx had to hope so. Dexx turned to Ethel and pulled the thumb drive out of his pocket. What if they could use something on here to diffuse their situation? To buy them a little time?. "We need to know what's on this. And we need it soon." Paige had the other one.

The rest of Red Star filed out the door, Rainbow bringing up the rear.

"I need a few minutes." Ethel cracked open the laptop and waited for the screens to finish loading.

Dexx paced the room while Ethel tapped on the keys. He was out of ideas and didn't know what kind of time they even had. Alwyn said the wards were vibrating. Because people were actively after them? Or was this something less?

"Dexx." Ethel sat back from the screen. "The information is here, I think, but it's garbled. This'll take longer."

"How much longer?"

"Days, weeks."

So, not an immediate save.

"I can't say. There just isn't a reference point to start from, but once I get that, it should take hours to decipher."

"I don't like the sound of that." Dexx pulled the little stone from his pocket and the broken stone bowl from the counter. "See if you can use these to start something. We all of us have to get home."

"What are you going to do about Frey?" Ethel kept her eyes on her work.

Leave it to Ethel to poke at a sore spot to see what happened. "I don't know. She's a part of the team, and I want her to stay, but... I just don't know. What do *you* think?"

"I think I'm not the boss. I'd follow you anywhere. So would Bow."

That touched him a little deeper than he thought it would. "You two are good for the team. We just wouldn't be the same without you."

"That's so sweet of you to say." Ethel threw him a coquettish look. "As it stands, I *know* you wouldn't be the same. There's nobody around like me."

"Nope." He appreciated her words. "Keep going on this. I'm going to circle and keep unwanted guests out."

"May the Lord be with you." She smiled up at Dexx.

"And also with— ha, ha. You got me." Dexx shook his finger, smiling back at Ethel.

"I know you love me."

"Not as much as you think." But he probably did. He left Ethel to do what she did second-best in the world.

As soon as he opened the door, Dexx felt the power in the air. Smelled it. Something wasn't right.

Tiny lines of power crisscrossed the sky in a dome. Those *definitely* hadn't been there earlier.

Dexx inhaled the night air. Something—many somethings—were all around them.

"Ah, shit." Dexx's whisper sounded closed in. He patted his clothes, checking to make sure the feed wasn't operational. He crushed the trackers the DoDO usually used. Didn't he?

No, the cord had pulled just like he normally had it.

He pulled off the vest anyway.

They'd followed him here. Maybe they'd tracked the vest? If so, that was a new trick.

Okay, the first thing Dexx needed to do was to get to the perimeter DoDO had set up and enlarged it, then surprise them where he wasn't supposed to be.

Well, old guys still had a few tricks up their sleeves too.

He skirted the building and went to the roof access ladder. He climbed as quickly as he could while still being too quiet for humans to hear.

When he reached the top, he sprinted to the edge and leapt for the next building over. That distance would have dropped a normie, but Dexx had shifter strength going on even if he couldn't talk to Hattie.

He ran the span of the roof and kept going. Hattie's sight helped him see and judge distances far better than he ever did before her.

The dome followed his progress, marking him at the center. If he got far enough out, Ethel and the rest wouldn't be in much danger—

The crack of a lightning bolt put that thought to bed.

That was another neat trick.

He threw the vest as far as he could onto the next rooftop as he sprinted back the way he'd come. One building back, he turned at a ninety-degree angle and made for the edge of the dome.

Another crack of lightning told him exactly where to find the DoDO mage creating the electricity.

A group of DoDO agents hovered on the roof at the very edge of the dome.

Lucky for him, they had their attention on something at street level.

Too bad for them, the demon hunter extraordinaire had them in his sights.

He leapt from his building to theirs.

3

As Dexx flew through the air to the next rooftop, he pulled the *ma'a'shed* from the sheath and commanded it to change, not even waiting for the knife to turn into a sword.

Wards flared as he passed over the edge of the roof. He hit a solid wall of force. The *ma'a'shed* clanged back into a knife and went flying into the dark.

Shit! He scrabbled against the smooth ward as he fell.

The four DoDO agents rolled back almost as one. They looked at each other surprising flashing across their faces before they advanced on Dexx as he continued to fall against the dome of force.

He fell hard onto a fire escape, but no bones broke.

One of the witches drew back a wand, calling the lightning. Another held up a fist and brought it down sharply, a bolt of fire shooting along the roof and closing on Dexx fast.

He dodged them both by crashing through the window. "Damn, Hattie. Where the hell are you? Could use the help." He sprinted for the door on the far side.

The couple he'd intruded on sat bolt upright in their bed, sleep fuzzing their reactions.

"Sorry, guys." Dexx ran through the apartment to the front door, yanking it open and breaking the chain.

He peered down the hall, searching for the stairwell leading to the roof. He charged to the right, down the corridor to the stairs, and up.

Muffled cracks of lightning urged him up. He *had* to get to those agents before they got anyone else.

Dexx reached for the door to the roof at the same time it swung out, two DoDO agents walking in. He recovered first and grabbed the first one, throwing her over the rail to fall to the ground.

She might survive the fall.

The other one gestured, pulling up a binding spell.

Like hell. Dexx wasn't going to be captured again. He punched forward with as much strength as he had and hit the next one just below his solar plexus.

He felt the internal organs liquefy and pop.

This one wouldn't survive.

Gunshots sounded in the distance.

Dexx made a mental note of triangulation for the team and ran for the DoDO agents still standing.

They were ready this time. The two split apart, keeping Dexx flanked, but not so far they created a crossfire.

He silently groaned. Why would they choose now to listen to his training?

Dexx made for the far DoDO agent, making the man fall back, then changed his direction without warning, crashing into the guy bringing up the rear, knocking him out.

Dexx picked up the senseless agent and held him like a shield. "You got two choices. Make this guy hamburger to get to me or leave. I would choose Option B. Option A gets messy, and the paperwork is boring."

"Give up, Colt."

Dexx didn't' recognize the voice, but why should he? *Everyone* probably knew about him, though.

"Our orders are for you, alive or dead. They'll issue me another partner if I kill this one."

"Wha—" The guy Dexx had been using as a shield shook himself, trying to free himself from Dexx.

The other DoDO agent made the finger gestures for a force spike. Something like that would rip through Dexx and his DoDO shield. He had a few moments, and time was short.

Dexx readied himself to shove his human shield forward and dash away when his *ma'a'shed* sprouted through the mouth of the DoDO in front of him, who fell without a sound.

"Please don't kill me," Dexx's human shield said. "My name is Gary. I have a family, two sisters."

Dexx didn't move. His *ma'a'shed* was wielding *itself*.

Gary was yanked violently away, his vertebrae snapping as he gained distance in a gentle arc over the edge of the building to the ground somewhere far away.

"What the hell?"

Furiel popped into existence. The spiky scent of sulfur filled his nose. Great. Another demon who wanted Dexx for something.

"I can't help more," Furiel said, nervously looking around. "And I can't stay. Take your *ma'a'shed*. Don't lose it again. I went through enough to get it to you the first time. Stay put and I'll get back to you. Don't let them find you again before I get back."

Furiel popped out.

"What the hell just happened?" Dexx scanned the roof for DoDO agents. He didn't see or hear any except the two dead ones on the roof. More would be dead elsewhere.

He pulled his knife from the neck of the dead agent, wiping the blade on the man's vest.

Dexx pulled the gun and the mags but left everything else. He did the same to the other guy as two-toned European sirens sounded off in the distance.

They were still a couple of minutes away.

He went down the stairwell, jumping complete levels until he reached the ground level. He needed to find his team and disappear to the motel.

Dexx cracked the door open slowly. The sirens were closer.

"Dexx."

Frey's voice. He pushed the door open and stepped out. "How'd you know it was me?"

"There isn't a single person alive that can crash as loud as you and still be silent."

Well, when she said it like that... "Oh. Where is everyone? We have to get back to the room."

"No shit. We ran into a little resistance, but now there isn't any."

She said that like it was a bad thing. "Then let's get back."

"Yes. Let's." Frey could have frozen a Great Lake with that tone.

Hattie? You there?

Hattie didn't respond, but there was a weak fluttering against Dexx's mind. More than normal, so he'd take it as a good sign. Maybe she was coming back.

They made it exactly two steps before three demons stepped out of the air in meat suits.

Damn. *Why* did they always show up at an inconvenient time? *Was* there ever a convenient time for bad demons to show up?

They scanned the parking lot, stopping when they saw Dexx. "*Shedim.* You're a very slippery eel."

Dexx stepped in front of Frey. "That's me. The one with all the teeth." He'd shifted once tonight. Maybe he could again. If he couldn't, Frey should be able to handle it.

The demon smiled. "Do you know how to deal with any eel, teeth, or not?

Keep the demons talking. Give the gang time to regroup. He heard their footsteps coming closer. "Why do you keep—"

"Remove them from the water."

Whatever. That was a crappy joke. "—showing up with DoDO? Are you working together, now?"

"What?" The lead demon tilted his head. "What do you mean?" The demon twisted his head and shot his fellows the question. "Find the humans. Kill them all."

That was unexpected but could work in his favor. Dexx took a step back. He whispered himself. "Get ready. This is gonna hurt."

One of the demons disappeared.

If the demons killed the agents, at least one enemy would be dealt with. But the worse ones were still standing.

The lead demon turned back to Dexx, adjusting his baggy jeans. "We have business to discuss."

Dexx just couldn't catch a break. "I already told your buddy. I will *not* date your sister. She has man-hands."

The demon held his arm to the side. A long staff sparkled into existence. He thumped the end to the ground.

The earth gonged with the sound of thunder and rolled like an earthquake.

That was a neat party trick.

"You have not always shown so much bravado. But I have not seen you in some time."

He really did like to talk. "Sure. I would have remembered a colorful type like you. Why don't you let the meat suit go? I'll make your departure quick."

A weave of magic formed behind the demon.

Alwyn. "Not this time." He gestured to the other demon in the universal motion to move forward.

Dexx tried to warn Alwyn to try something besides his normal lightning trick, but there wasn't time. The bolt was ready.

Alwyn released it.

Well, Dexx'd take the bought seconds offered. He charged the lead demon who stumbled, momentarily blinded. With his *ma'a'shed* drawn, Dexx extended the blade and swung into the demon, crashing into the staff the demon carried instead.

The hit violently shook Dexx, and almost dropped the sword, falling to the ground. The pain from the hit started from his shoulders and ended in his hips. Wow. What was in that staff?

Frey leapt over him, swinging her sword, driving the demon back with sharp, precise strokes. She actually had an effect on the demon.

Good for her. Daaaaaamn.

Rainbow, Alwyn, and Tarik took on the other demon, flanking it and using hit-and-run techniques to keep it off balance.

Dexx rose and picked up his blade, extending it again.

Frey drove her demon back.

The others were in a stalemate—no contest who he needed to help. Frey could wait.

Dexx ran forward when another demon landed in front of him, casually holding his hand out in front of him, a blue force enveloping him.

What was that? But it was too late. Dexx was already mid-swing. His sword clanged against the force shield as if hitting something metallic.

The demon shuddered a little, like the attack hurt, but not enough to matter much.

What the heck was going on here?

The courtyard exploded in light, DoDO agents pouring from between buildings slinging spells.

That had an effect on the three demons.

They broke off the Red Star attack and turned their attention to DoDO. The three moved back to back and raised their arms. A ward sprung into place, deflecting spells and elemental attacks.

Rainbow and Alwyn formed up with Dexx. Michelle, Frey, and Tarik formed their own circle.

They could just hightail it out of there. DoDO was there. Dexx and his team could use this moment to save themselves. But then they'd still just have these dumb demons—who were stupid strong—still on their tail. Right. "Okay, guys. I'll draw attention. You go for the soft parts."

Tarik set a magickal barrier while Michelle and Frey lashed out. Michelle took out anything that Frey couldn't reach.

Shit. That *was* a much better plan than an all-out attack.

"On second thought. Let's do that. Alwyn, set as strong a ward as you can. Rainbow, please tell me you can hear the currents."

"Sure do, boss."

Thank goodness. "Get a move on, then."

One demon went into full-on meltdown, flailing and shooting spells haphazardly under the weight of the DoDO agents swarming the quad.

The other two demons vaporized twenty agents without trouble, and Michelle whipped her lithe sapling tentacles, blasting anyone too close.

Frey deflected direct magicks with her sword. She had amazing skills.

Alwyn buzzed with power, then released his ward. It snapped into place just as a lightning bolt cracked from the sky.

Dexx's hair stood on end.

Rainbow didn't do as well. She had called the currents and the water tentacle formed as the bolt hit the ward.

Maybe he shouldn't have asked the electricity mage to work with the water talker.

Rainbow popped like a fuse once and fell to the ground.

"Protect Rainbow." Dexx stepped out of the ward and swung his blade for all he was worth.

They still had two demons to deal with, and a host of DoDO agents

Hattie's power lent him strength, stamina, and grace, but not any skill.

He carved into the crowd agents like he had a club, swinging as far as he could twist one way, then the other.

DoDO agents fell in front of his wild swinging.

Frey and her group moved on from the humans to the demons. Tarik pinned one demon in a flanking maneuver while the other picked himself up from the ground.

Dexx leapt over dead bodies to swing in with the sword and met the demon's neck in a clean slice.

The demon's head fell off with a soft thunk on the ground.

An orange pit of glowing embers opened, and the body of the demon moved with an unnatural pull to the hole.

One down.

No, two down. The horde of DoDO agents had managed to take one out all by themselves.

The last demon standing swung his staff above his head in an arc, wind blasting everything back.

Dexx pulled his sword up just in time to split the torrent in front of him, but he couldn't push forward any closer to the center. It was like walking into a hurricane.

Tarik jammed one hand into the paving stones, and the other held on to Frey, keeping her from flying away. Michelle lashed herself to the ground with her dryad roots. She looked like any tree in a windstorm now.

Alwyn and Rainbow didn't stand a chance. They were being pushed back against the building, Alwyn covering his face with his arm.

Dexx drew his arm back to throw the sword, but the wind pressed against him harder. He had plenty of grip to hold onto the sword, just not enough to move anywhere else.

Tarik began to glow red with heat and magick. The glow began to extend around Frey, and her features changed. She looked sharper, less human for a second. Then she blurred forward, stopping when her sword was buried hilt deep in the demon's chest.

The wind died with the demon.

Frey pulled her sword free, and the Hell hole sucked the demon home.

In the sudden stillness, Dexx looked for any obvious survivors. The cops should have been there already, but nobody had. Demons and DoDO agents all appeared dead.

Dexx ran to Alwyn and Rainbow, his heart racing.

She stirred at Alwyn's gentle tapping on her face. "Five more minutes. I swear I'll pay the rent."

At least she hadn't lost her sense of humor. Dexx knelt beside her and grabbed her hand. "Bow, get up. Five minutes is passed. You're late with rent."

Rainbow sat upright, completely alert. "Oh, no. Molly."

There were a lot of things Dexx secretly liked about the rusalka, but there were a lot of things that just didn't make any kind of sense. "What?"

"We have to go home. Things aren't good."

Yeah. Okay. Well, at least she understood their reality. "We have to clear off the street. Things are way worse right here. Stand up." Dexx reached his hand to her and helped her up. "You okay?"

Brushing herself off, she grimaced at him. "Why do you ask, Pony Boy?"

She wasn't right in the head, but maybe that was her normal. Probably.

"Let's go," Frey growled, looking human again.

Michelle was human again too.

Time to leave. "Yeah. Let's." He had to find a way to get his team out of this mess. And he would. One way or the other. "Come on. There's bound to be more where these came from."

4

E thel greeted them at the door, her body tight and
the rod from the closet in her hand. "Are you guys
alright? I heard a fight."

"Yes, we're fine," Frey said, the room temp dropping
twenty degrees from the chill in her tone." No thanks to our
supreme leader."

What the hell was *wrong* with her? Dexx was going to
have to deal with her sooner rather than later. "DoDO
tracked us somehow."

Frey squared up with Dexx. "I'll bet it had something to
do with you. Am I ringing any bells? I'm fucking tired of
running like a rabbit without any direction. You want to lead?
Lead yourself because I'm walking out."

Good! Because Dexx was done having her breathe down
his neck for... what? Not having his *alpha*? Like that was the
only thing that made him team leader?

"Me and anyone else who doesn't want to go down with
you are gone. You're fucked, and I don't want to get fucked
alongside you. Who's with me?"

Oh, shit. Who *was* going with her?

Michelle rocked from foot to foot and raised her hand.

Tarik nodded slowly.

As in he wanted to go?

Ethel stood next to Rainbow with a hand on the rusalka's arm.

"I'm with you, Dexx." Rainbow gave an open-handed shrug. "I believe in you. I want you to be our leader, but maybe you know, you could take a break? Take over again when you're able."

Frey snorted.

What?

"We're here because of what they did to you. I know you didn't do it on purpose, but I'm so scared all the time that maybe we don't have *all* of you back, you know. What if they broke what keeps us alive? I'm super sorry."

Alwyn's eyes were wide as he looked around the room. He seemed to want to stay small and inconspicuous

Wow. Okay. He exhaled heavily. "You're right." She was? "I'm tired, and I can't seem to get my feet under me." He really couldn't, but he was fighting hard to do exactly that because his team needed him to. "It's just been a ball of shit since they captured me. I just want to go home. Be with Paige again." Have some time before the end.

Dexx sat hard on the closest bed.

Rainbow took a step toward him.

He waved her off. No. If whatever Bussemi had done was really bringing Dexx closer to his end, then he needed to give the team to someone else so he could focus on protecting his family. His kids. Paige. "Frey, you're the leader." It hurt to say those words out loud. "I'll follow your lead. Do what you say. We can't leave yet, though. That demon Furiel said we should wait here."

"Fuck him." Frey shook her head. "How many times have you said all they do is lie? Now you want to just do what it says? We're doing this my way." Frey looked hard. Sounded hard, too. Her smell didn't match.

That's what leadership was, though—projecting strength even if you were scared as shit inside.

At least now, he might be able to just feel like what was he was feeling without having to pretend to be ultra-strong and know all the answers all the time.

Ethel jumped when Furiel appeared next to her.

Frey's hand went to the back of her neck.

Tarik caught her before she could draw her sword.

"He's on our side." Tarik let her wrist go.

"No, he's not. I only trust one of you, and that's *you*. Because I was there. I *helped*. The rest of them? Can go straight back to the hell of their choosing."

Furiel clasped his hands in front of him. "I have missed something." He furrowed his brow. "Dexx?"

Dexx waved the demon off. "She's in charge."

Furiel turned to Dexx and cocked his head to the side. "That can't be. You're my chance to prove I'm— I need your help."

Dexx didn't know what to tell the guy. "It's gonna be nice." He fell back on the bed.

Furiel turned to Frey. "Is there some way I can convince you to let Colt lead you through this?"

"No." Frey snorted. "You're a demon, and as far as I'm concerned *you're* as much to blame as Dexx is. Both of you are trying to play little games, pushing pieces around. I'm not your toy or game piece, and none of this is a game."

"This is…" Furiel bit off what he was about to say, clenching a fist. "…no game, girl. My life is more important to me than yours. Than *all* of you. What I'm doing has many levels you can't even begin to comprehend. I am working to keep you alive, and the best chance you have is Dexx Colt. For you, for me."

Ethel pulled Rainbow forward, hope in her blue eyes.

Frey turned her glare on Dexx, then shifted it to Furiel. "We'll have to discuss it as a team."

Dexx sat up, ready to offer any advice.

"Not you. You and the demon aren't invited."

Furiel pressed his lips together. "Do not be too long. Procrastination has dangers." He vanished.

"You go too. We have to decide if you're important enough to do anything for."

Dexx stood up. "Taking the revenge bit a little too far, aren't you?"

"If I am, you don't get a vote." Frey crossed her arms. "Team business. Low man stands guard."

Wow. She was really taking this too far. He'd never seen this side of Frey, and he didn't like it.

He felt Alwyn's wards go up before he left the courtyard.

All the dead DoDO agents had been removed from the courtyard, probably Furiel doing cleanup to avoid notice. He felt a tingle of the magick used, and it *could* have a demon resonance. Still, he kept a low profile, not wanting to trip anything.

Maybe he *should* stand watch, just to prove he wasn't a bitch. Nine Hells to that. He needed a drink. American, if he could find some.

The team had been around the motel long enough to get to know the area. Good thing Europe had pubs *everywhere.*

A little dive hang-out a little down the street, close enough to stumble home to if he had to. The rain started up again, which fit his mood perfectly.

The *Tiered Crescent* had a single door on a too narrow road, just like lots of places on this piss-ant continent.

Two patrons wobbled their way out as Dexx opened the door. One of them mumbled thanks, and the two used each other to bounce off of as they made their way along.

Dexx went in and sat at the bar, slouching forward until the barmaid gave him a what-you-having look.

"Got anything cold?"

"Jus' mai humor, love." She had a great accent. Scottish, maybe.

"How about anything with hops?"

"American, eh?"

"Yeah."

"Coomin' right oop."

"Thanks."

The barmaid popped the top on a bottle and shoved it at him.

The first glugs hit him like a soft, warm blanket. How long had it been since he'd had a worthwhile beer? Too long.

She moved off, wiping down the bar that probably hadn't had a good disinfecting in years—the perfect place.

The tv over the bar had soccer playing. Ugh. Too much running for too little payoff. Then when they *did* put that tiny ball in that *huge* net, some guy would scream "goal" for as long as his lungs had air.

Not for Dexx.

Hattie, can you answer me? I could really use your help.

Nothing from the spirit. Had it only been hours since he'd heard her voice? Seemed like longer. Forever to put a precise time on it.

Someone squeezed onto the stool next to him.

Damnit. If he'd wanted company, he would have rented some. He turned to the personal space intruder and stopped, his heart melting a little.

"Hey."

Rainbow smiled her big infectious smile. "Hey yourself."

Okay. So, maybe Rainbow was exactly the person he needed. He was feeling emotionally out of sorts, to be sure. "Don't worry about me, little sister. I got this covered."

The barmaid appeared in front of them.

Rainbow stared back.

"Give 'er one of these." Dexx tipped the bottle to the bartender.

Understanding crashed over Rainbow's face. "I don't really drink beer."

"But I *do*. You don't want it. I'll finish it."

The bartender nodded and went back to the end of the bar.

Hopefully, to get another beer. "You're going back to the rest and making plans. Whatever Frey wants. She's going to run things, now."

"Not for me, she won't. I know you'd never hurt any of us if you knew what you were doing. You trusted me when you didn't have to, and I haven't forgotten that."

That's when it really hit Dexx. Frey was pissed because he'd attacked her and Tarik when he'd been under DoDO agents' control. He still only kind of remembered that, but she *really* did. So, now he felt even worse. Great. Suck! "Suit yourself."

"Frey doesn't like me much anyway."

"But you've always had a crush on *her*."

"Things change. I got a new crush."

"Oh yeah?" His heart twisted a little at his ignorance. "I didn't know that."

"You kinda caught us making out. Then you caught me. And put me in DoDO jail."

Ah. That explained it. How many memories had Bussemi taken from him? Would he get them back? "Yeah, sorry about that. Bussemi had me under a pretty strong spell. Still does, I guess." Dexx took a long pull from the beer. That last part scared the crap out of him. How could he—Dexx Colt—outsmart a guy like Bussemi?

"You didn't know." Rainbow touched him on the shoulder.

The bartender came over with another beer, setting it in front of Dexx.

Rainbow's words didn't make it better. "But you *did*." He rolled his bottle along the bottom ridge, making little wet circles on the bar top.

"Not really. You were only gone for a couple of days at that point, and Molly was feeling really low, and so we—"

So, her name was Molly. Okay. Now they were getting somewhere, but Rainbow could tend to overshare. Some details probably should remain private. "So, you wanted to cheer her up. Got it." Dexx set the empty beer down and slid Rainbow's over.

"I want you to know you're still my alpha. I feel it even if the others don't."

Yeah, no. That was gone, and he didn't know how to get it back. He hadn't really had time to process it, but... he didn't feel complete without it. Yeah. Okay. Frey had been combative, and it'd been hard not being able to just put her down with a growl. But it was more than that.

He missed being connected to his pack. "You're a good kid, Bow. But you don't have to lie to make me feel better. I got what was coming, and I'll make it through." He tipped his head to the door behind them. "You should get back."

"I ain't going anywhere without you. You're my bestest attack-cat buddy."

Don't let her go far. Keep her close to you, Cub.

Hattie's sudden appearance poked Dexx like a pin.

"That you girl?"

Rainbow narrowed her eyes. "Of course, it's me. Who did you think I was?"

Yes.

"Not you. Hattie."

I feel the pressure. Something is holding me back. Taking the essence I need from you.

Rainbow's eyes opened wide, and she looked around the bar as though Hattie might be behind her. She shook herself. "Oh, in your head. I knew that."

Why do I have to keep her close?

She is making you her alpha. Like a cub bringing meat to an injured hunter.

He didn't completely understand what she meant, but it felt so good not to be alone in his own head. *Oh, how I missed your riddles. So just keep her close, like a friend or* close friend?

Be her alpha. Let her be your beta.

Got it, I think. So, nothing he'd have to report back to Paige. Got it.

"You talking to Hattie? What's she saying?" Rainbow covered Dexx's hands with hers.

"She says go bring me meat."

"Ew. Why?"

Dexx chuckled. "No, she just wants you to stick close."

"Well, hey, *I* can do that." She sat up straighter on her stool like she was proud she had a purpose.

"Good. I miss her, and I need you. Everything else can be secondary."

Rainbow frowned and slouched forward. "What are you going to do about Frey?"

"Nothing *to do*." Hattie might be back, but not completely, and he still didn't have his alpha will. Also, he had to figure out how to make it up to Frey—well, how to apologize in a way she'd accept, really. "We just be her little toadies. We'll share the low dog on the totem slot." Life wouldn't get any easier, for sure.

Dexx turned back up to the tv just as the camera followed the flight of a long kick. Then the soccer game fuzzed out to a reporter in a studio.

The ticker across the bottom said, "Urgent bulletin from Parliament."

Dexx motioned up to the tv. "Could we hear this?"

The barmaid twisted her head up to look.

"Aye, bu' 'tis borin'."

"I like boring."

She rolled her eyes but turned up the volume.

"...by unanimous vote, the organization calling itself Department of Delicate Operations has been adopted to be the first and last line of defense against the paranormal threat of regular citizens. The operatives of the organization were caught on cameras defending Parliament against... things."

The camera cut to a scene of Cardinal Bussemi and Red Star facing off in the Lower Chambers. DoDO agents lay everywhere, and Dexx and Frey were just about to get their asses handed to them. Right before Furiel showed up to magick them away, the scene cut back to the studio reporter.

"In a frightful attack on our government, the department showed up to drive the creatures away. Under the leadership of the Catholic Church and Cardinal Bussemi, folding into the government should be a quick and easy process.

In related news, the American government has reached out to the Prime Minister, looking into broadening the reach of the paranormal department to their own shores."

That couldn't be good. "There goes the fucking neighborhood."

"Do ye thank those monstehrs d'serve to walk aroun'?" The bartender's fist slammed down on the bar lightly.

Not a good sign. "Not monsters, but regular paranormals?" He knew he needed to tread lightly, but he also needed her to realize they weren't talking about *monsters*. "Why not? I bet you wouldn't be able to tell most of them if they came up and gave you a tip."

"I doubt it. Got a sixth sense, I do. I can smell 'em a mile off. None would dare set foo' in here."

Oh, boy. "Ah." Dexx kept his face straight.

"Can I get a glass of water?" Rainbow perked up, her smile dazzling. "And your name?"

The woman stopped her motion of grabbing a glass. "Veronica." She smiled back. "Did ye wan' my number too?"

Oh, why would Rainbow choose this one who would never accept her for who she was?

"Sure."

Veronica took a napkin and jotted her number down. She slid both over to Rainbow but kept her hand on the glass.

Rainbow covered Veronica's hand, sliding the glass and napkin from Veronica, and held them up.

The water came alive and stretched unnaturally high and waved at Veronica.

The bartender's face went white, and she fell over.

Rainbow took a delicate drink. "Tastes pretty good, actually. Should we go?"

Dexx stood up. "Yup." He left some cash and led them out.

Rainbow giggled all the way to the next bar.

Dexx chose a booth for them both to sit in with as much privacy as a pub had to offer.

Rainbow ordered a drink with Dexx. Then they clinked their glasses together.

Okay. So, maybe the kid was growing up. "Pretty neat trick back there."

"You'd be surprised how many people freak out with that one." Rainbow ducked her head, her brown eyes haunted.

"I've never seen you do that." There was more to this woman than he'd given her credit for. Maybe her optimistic personality was a cover for something else.

"You aren't a creepy guy or a para hater."

"I *was* a para hater. At least, demons." No. He'd hated paras too. "I didn't *know* about this world until a couple of years ago. I knew about witches, demons, and angels, but then I became a shifter. Opened up a lot o' shit I had to deal with in a short amount of time."

"But I don't think you wouldn't have hated first." Rainbow tipped her head to the side and looked up. "Would you?"

Yeah, actually. He had. "The important part is that now I *am* part of that world, and I want to stay in it. This spell Bussemi put on me, keeping Hattie at bay, the one that's literally killing me? I'm not good with it. I *have* to get home. I have to make sure my family—all of you—are safe. Things have been way shitty since I landed on this island."

She grunted in agreement. "You got me, and that's what counts." She beamed a smile at him.

But he saw the lack of light in her eyes. The truth was, that yes. She *did* count. More than the rest of the team. If he wanted to hold on to Hattie. But he'd have to respark that flame of hope she always seemed to have in her. Without it, Dexx didn't know how much further they'd make it.

Furiel appeared in the booth with them.

Dexx only had the shortest time to feel the magick. Maybe his senses *were* sharpening.

Rainbow jumped, sloshing some beer onto the table. "Don't *do* that." She relaxed a little. "You scared me."

"At least you stayed awake." Furiel gave her a wry look.

Dexx pulled his head back. "You were *spying* on us?"

"You must understand. As much as the others don't trust me, *I* don't trust them. I can't do as much as you think I can. I'm showing my hand to too many powerful enemies, and I just can't Thanos them away with a snap of my fingers. I have to stay low and guarded with any help I give you."

It made sense. Dexx didn't do politics, but he *did* do strategy. Sometimes. Rule number one in combat: don't be where they expect. "Did you get an eyeful?"

"Indeed. Your compatriots have voted. Tarik and the new one spoke quite well for you. They've decided to go the way you have indicated."

That was good. "But they won't let me lead."

"The Valkyrie was quite adamant that *you* not."

Dexx *could* be upset, an ego-filled alpha-male need-for-dominance kind of way. Or he could take this time to heal, use this as a break. Frankly, he kinda needed one. "Well, I'll take what I get, I guess."

Rainbow furrowed her brow in a frown as she released a long breath of puffed air. "That's good news, though, right? I mean that we're not going home yet? We're fixing this?"

"It is." Furiel tapped the table with his finger. "I must go." Magick wrapped around the demon, and he was gone.

"Let's go find out what they said." Dexx rose from the table. As much as he appreciated the fact that they weren't going to the one his soul needed him to return to, he knew he needed to get serious about tying up his loose ends. Egypt had to hold the answers. He didn't want to think about the consequences if they weren't there.

5

Dexx and Rainbow stayed in the shadows as much as possible on their way back, so they weren't spotted by magick traps or video cameras or whatever. With his enhanced senses, most people wouldn't even know they passed.

Of course, they weren't avoiding *most* people. DoDO and Cardinal Bussemi had the top spot there.

Rainbow tried to get in touch with the currents, but there wasn't enough water around to help her rusalka side.

Pre-dawn had lightened the sky by the time they opened the door to the motel room.

Frey stood with her arms crossed, leaning against the wall. "I almost didn't think you were coming back. I noticed you didn't take the watch. Dereliction so soon can get you kicked off the team. Is that what you want?"

Dexx bit back his first response, reminding himself that he still had to rebuild their bond. He'd betrayed her trust, but her outright inability to see the world through any eyes other than her own was really starting to just chaff him raw. "Not really."

"Then I suggest you take your watch now and take your buddy along with you."

Yeah, sure. He smelled like beer and hadn't slept in twenty-four hours. This was a great idea. But...building bridges. Maybe she and her team hadn't slept all night either. "Fine. When should we be back?"

"When someone comes to get you."

"Sure thing." Dexx grabbed Rainbow's arm as he walked by.

The rusalka balked, pulling back slightly. "But I thought we—"

"Let's go." Dexx pulled her along behind him.

The door swung shut with a loud slam.

Rainbow dug in her heels. "Hey, she can't do that, can she?"

"Right now, she has the power to do what she wants." Which was fine as long as she didn't get them all killed. Who knew how long it would take a Valkyrie to forgive his level of betrayal, accidental or forced as it was. "We're going to be good little soldiers. She has what I need, and who cares if we have to go see the sights a little."

Rainbow shook her head, her eyes narrowed, her lips compressed. "But she's... she's...*horrible*. She's never acted like that before."

"Yes, and yes." Dexx surveyed the area, trying to determine the best way for two people who hadn't slept to cover the watch without nodding off. "And you want to hang out with that? I don't. So I'll take some time and be outside. I may even watch a little."

She turned her glare on him and followed. "How do you do that?"

"Do what?" Dexx chose a random direction and headed away from the motel, making sure to stay in the shadows still.

"Twist any situation to your side. I just get caught up all willy nilly."

What was she even talking about? "I don't. I just— just forget it. Let's see what we can see."

Daylight crept over the horizon, lighting the city.

"You know—" Rainbow gestured to the street around them as people got up and went about their morning routines. "—this place wouldn't be so bad if we were on vacation. I kind of like the oldness. It makes me think of Grams."

"Your grandma?" For as much as Rainbow talked, she never shared much about her life. "Why?"

"She used to tell stories of the villagers in the old country, and how she—" Rainbow pressed her fingers to her forehead, then took in a deep breath, shaking off the thought. "Well, she used to tell stories."

Probably stories of how young people had died under the rusalka spell. Mythically speaking, rusalkas weren't known for keeping people alive. "There." Dexx pointed to a nearby park and a bench that looked comfortable enough.

They sat on the bench, watching the area grow brighter and busier. The people of this area seemed nice enough, though they didn't show any particular interest in two strange people sitting on a park bench, which was good. Dexx wanted to be overlooked.

The rusalka was showing signs of sleepiness, though, her head occasionally nodding, only to startle herself awake.

Dexx knew he should be tired. Like, exhausted. He hadn't slept well in days, at all in at least one. But his mind was too busy wrapping itself into a pretzel of anxiety, thinking about Paige, about what she was facing, about his kids, the pack, the town, the entire U.S., about Bussemi, and feeling the ward sickness drain him.

Finally, Dexx wrapped his arm around Rainbow's shoulders. "Take a nap. I'll wake you up if something interesting happens."

She released a groaning sigh and sagged into him. "'Kay, boss." Her breathing slowed almost as soon as her head touched his shoulder.

Heartbeat, slow, and soft breathing. Just like Paige. Damn, he missed her something fierce.

Fast-moving feet alerted Dexx to activity, but he spotted a jogger taking advantage of the cool morning air and forced himself to relax.

What was Paige up to now? Knowing her, she probably had six— or a hundred—fires that needed to be put out immediately and more that should have been dealt with yesterday.

He missed his kids. Sure, yeah. He missed the twins, but he didn't know them. They were babies. But Leah? Bobby? Shit, even Tyler, who wasn't his—but neither were Leah or Bobby. Mandy and Kate kept their distance, and that was fine. But... Dexx missed his kids.

Damnit. He wanted to go home. *Talk to me, Goose. You there?"*

Cub.

Relief washed through Dexx at the sound of Hattie's voice. *Sure is nice to hear your voice.*

Rainbow snuggled in against Dexx. His body temp normally ran a bit high. Paige liked to try to soak the heat out from him.

It is nice that you hear me. A feeling of frustration passed along their bond.

Are you recovering?

The sickness isn't from my side. It is from you.

He felt pride and a little accusation from her. The fault was his.

Me? I haven't done anything.

Something is taking what I need from you. That is not in the Time Before.

The spell. Maybe this was how it worked? *Could it be from… him? When he had me?*

Only you can know that. Our connection must be mended, or we could both die.

And be reborn again, but without Paige, without the kids, without this pack, or this Red Star team. *But maybe not?* He had to know. If he failed to fix this—because how in the hell was he supposed to do that?—would she really die? *Look, if I can't fix us, I need to know you'll be okay. You will won't you?*

Does a buck survive a limb torn off?

Is it a little limb? When it hurt too much to be serious, Dexx always went for humor.

Cub. Hattie wasn't in the mood for it.

Yeah. Damnit. He needed to figure out *how* to fix this. *That's what I thought. Do you have any ideas on how to stop it or cure us, or whatever?*

No, cub. Sadness filtered through.

So, this is on me. Again. Well, we've been in tough spots before.

With our prey in our sight. Do you know if it was a thorn or a burrowing insect? Then how will you know how to fix yourself?

I have a good idea of where to start, but… He wouldn't admit to being scared of Bussemi. That guy could go fuck himself. Furiel said to go to Egypt. He wouldn't have just pulled that out of a hat. But eventually, Bussemi would be at the end of the road.

You will have to face the stampede. There was an image of a herd of mammoths trampling through a canyon toward a lone juvenile.

Couldn't hide anything from that fat cat. He still wouldn't admit it out loud, though.

Dexx relaxed, pulling in a breath to clear his mind. Going to Hattie in the Time Before would be preferable to sitting in the park, and he'd be able to keep his "eye" out for bad guys at the same time. It wasn't like he'd be abandoning his post. He'd be killing two birds with one stone, making sure this team was indeed okay, and finding a way to fix himself so he and his team could go back home.

Keeping his physical eyes and ears open, he imagined all-encompassing darkness and a tree in the middle of it all. He didn't know why he called on these images to transition himself from the real world to Hattie's, but it worked.

As the tree grew in front of him, a light fog swirled in the darkness around his mind's feet. He walked into it as light slowly replaced the dark.

A figure stood in his way.

A bahlrok, superimposed of the squat decrepit frame of Cardinal Bussemi. "We've been waiting for you. An interesting place. You will let us in."

What the... No. Bussemi wasn't here. This was a sacred space where only Dexx and Hattie connected.

What if this had something to do with the spell Bussemi had put on him? What if it was a... virus of some sort?

Dexx fled.

He blinked his dry eyes, taking in the morning with a pounding headache.

Holy shit. Was that...

Hattie? Did you see that?

I saw nothing.

Am I possessed? Impossible. His tattoos prevented any sort of demon possession. Many demons had tried. They'd all failed—*everyone.*

So, this wasn't possession. *That was... him. And the demon. They were in my* head. *How are they in my head?*

Hattie stepped forward a little in his mind, butting her big head against a wall of resistance between them. *He has always been beyond me, cub.*

That wasn't what Dexx needed to hear. *How do I fight that? You will have to hunt that prey alone.*

Again, not what he wanted to hear, but... also what he *needed* to hear.

He was a good hunter.

Dexx *thought* he wanted to sleep before, but his heart raced too fast for sleep. He might be awake for weeks.

Rainbow had created a warm spot against him while the other side had cooled. One side comfortable, the other less so. A perfect metaphor. But nothing had set off any alarms in Dexx. Everyone was acting normally.

A cop walked the perimeter of the park, eyeing Dexx and the sleeping Rainbow. He waved a hand to the bobby who gave Dexx a pressed-lip head nod and kept going.

Dexx put Bussemi out of his thoughts for the moment. He was still on watch. People were still trying to get to his team, to him, and he had to make sure they didn't.

Or he tried. Bussemi scared him senseless—what he'd done to Dexx. He still didn't remember all of it, but there were flashes coming back. Him being strapped to a chair and laughing in Bussemi's—the doctor's face. Because the two were the same person. He knew that now. He did. But Dexx'd dared Bussemi to do his worst, thinking he was buying Paige time to find him.

But the time had dragged on. He didn't remember visions, but he remembered the emotions, feeling... abandoned. Feeling... alone. Feeling... betrayed.

How much of that had been Bussemi? He didn't know. And he couldn't be mad at Paige. He just—yes. He could. He'd *needed* her, and she hadn't come. But...

How long had he been Bussemi's prisoner?

One month. Felt like years. Either was far too long.

Dexx took in a shaky breath, staring at a small bird hopping on the ground by one of the trees. One month. Had he broken in one month? He'd been *turned* in mere *weeks*. He'd betrayed his team within *weeks* of having been *captured*.

Dexx *knew* that demons—some demons—had powerful ways of manipulating time. He did. And he knew he needed to let it go. Let it pass. But...

If he hadn't managed to find a way to end Bussemi in the months or years—could it have been years? Was it possible the demons had moved time to years instead of weeks? Did that make Dexx feel *better* for having broken? For having betrayed his team?

What if Bussemi had forced him to betray Paige?

He realized Chuck had been *that* test. He remembered a very... strange version of that take-down that didn't make any sense. But what he'd been able to piece together was that... he'd gone out to take Chuck down—his alpha. He'd been sent to take his *alpha* into custody.

And he'd broken through the constraints on his mind. He'd let Chuck go.

Bussemi must have known then that any kind of—that if he pointed Dexx at Paige, Dexx *would* break free of the mind meld, no matter how strong the spell was.

That had to give Dexx hope. That had to be Bussemi's weakness, but *what was it?* What did that mean?

The bobby came around again, looking at Dexx every few steps.

Dexx put on a mask of a smile and leaned the side of his face against the top of Rainbow's head, stretching his knotted neck. Her hair provided a surprising pillow.

He stayed there not so much for the bobby, but for his soul. It just felt *nice* being close to someone who had no ulterior motives. He squeezed Rainbow's slight shoulders slightly and pressed his lips to the top of her head.

She grunted and snuggled closer.

Dexx missed his family... so much.

The jogger passed by again, apparently making good time around the park, her long ponytail swaying with her steps.

Another walker passed by, followed by more. People were beginning to stir. All of them ignorant of the battles that happened overnight.

Smells came to him. Cooking. Breakfast mostly, but a few scents were fish. Gross.

Two more people materialized, walking together. They had a military gate, walking with purpose.

Ah, shit. Seriously? Why couldn't he just catch one fucking break?

Dexx turned to the footsteps. Two DoDO agents headed up the path toward him. They passed the patrol officer, glaring but weren't looking in his direction.

The jogger had made it around the park again, giving the agents room to walk up the path.

Dexx reached his arm down to wake Rainbow. She'd been sleeping so peacefully, too.

Suddenly, the DoDO agent nearest the jogger whipped out a crackling baton and swung. He hit the young woman hard enough to take her off her feet. She grunted as she slammed into the ground.

The cop turned and rushed to the two agents. "Hey, you can't—"

"Official Department of Delicate Operations business," the first agent said, holding up some sort of badge, glinting gold in the weak sunlight. "Go away, or we'll take you in for questioning."

The beat cop closed his mouth and turned around. He must have had the warning to let DoDO do their thing.

As suddenly as DoDO appeared, the park emptied. Nobody wanted to be around this.

Rainbow jerked awake. She made a noise Dexx'd only heard twice before, each time when the currents had full control of her. "Stop," she said in a voice that held many layers as she stood. "The beasts shall not have our child." Her hand whipped back, then forward, a tentacle of water streaming from everywhere into two thigh-thick bands.

One of the agents looked up in time to see his death. The water hit him like a club wielded by a giant.

The other living tentacle turned into a spear of hardened water like ice and stabbed the second agent.

His eyes opened wide as he tried to gurgle something out, holding a spear as wide as his chest.

The spear splashed to the ground mixed with blood and... stuff that wasn't blood.

Rainbow became a blur of unnatural speed and appeared over the two corpses. Her head turned slowly to the beaten jogger-girl. "Go now and take our revenge on the beasts our child encounters." She gestured to the two dead agents.

"As you command, Mother." The jogger stood and bowed her head. When she raised up, her eyes flashed the same color as Rainbow's, and she dashed from the park at top speed.

Rainbow went to a knee and dipped her hand in the blood, soaking across the ground.

She swirled her hand through the blood, studying it in her hand, pulling it up in long strands that clung to her fingers and drifted like seaweed. The puddle shrunk, but more dripped from the bodies of the DoDO agents.

Rainbow's head fell back in pure pleasure.

Dexx wasn't certain what he saw just now. His Rainbow —his sweet, hopelessly optimistic Rainbow—was dipping her hands in the blood of her enemies. She flared in Dexx's infrared vision, bright as he'd seen anything in the spectrum. She glowed brighter, and the magick around her thrummed in expectation.

Hattie pushed hard and almost shifted them right there.

No, Hattie, stop. We can't do this here. They're hunting us.

The push to shift remained strong for a few seconds then subsided.

The urge was strong, cub. We have not been complete for too long. I feel your presence strongly. We have to shift.

The urge came again, and soft hair sprouted over Dexx's body. His bones reshaped, but he didn't grow large or tear from his clothes.

Pain sprouted in his head, flowing down each nerve all the way to the ends.

Hattie stopped mid-shift and pulled back, regressing until Dexx looked normal.

What happened? They'd *never* done anything like that before. Was this because of Rainbow? The currents?

The same kind of pain flowed from Hattie's end.

Rainbow stood and flowed back toward him. "The Dexx has been our child's champion." Her voice sounded like Rainbow's but with several other voices overlaid on top. She held her arms out slightly. "For a time, *we* shall be the Dexx's champion. The magick wrapped around the Dexx is ancient, as the oldest of us are ancient. Take care of our child, and we will be near."

Rainbow's infra-red aura dimmed.

"Dexx?" Rainbow looked up at him shaking all over. "What happened?" She took one more step and slipped her arms under his jacket in a hug. She shivered against him, freezing cold.

Dexx hugged her back, ignoring the fact that there was blood on her pants and on her hands and probably now on his shirt and the inside of his jacket. What had the currents meant by being her champion? When the hell had he ever been her *champion*?

"I'm pretty sure that was captured on a body cam."

Rainbow nodded into his chest, but she didn't move.

He had to get her motivated to flee. "Probably a hundred more coming right now."

Rainbow nodded again, shivering so hard he was afraid she might break.

"But we'll wait until you can move."

More nodding. She convulsed.

Oh, shit. What the *fuck* was he was supposed to do? Lay her down? Stay close? He kept her close, thinking maybe the convulsions had to do with her temperature. But he kept his eyes peeled for any sign that backup was on the way.

He felt Rainbow's heartbeats tick up a little.

Time to move. He gently pried her away but kept an arm over her as he helped her walk.

The first step seemed to be the hardest, but after a few stumbles, she walked alongside him. She went slow, but at least she was walking.

Sirens sounded in the distance, obviously the *actual* cops with their two-tone wail.

They couldn't be caught up by those bastards either.

Slowly, Rainbow's strides lengthened, and they made it to the motel before the police began to canvas the area.

Dexx pushed Hattie's hearing to get a better sense of just how much trouble they were in. DoDO arrived on the scene as he guided Rainbow to the door to their room.

Dexx sat Rainbow down on the bench outside their door.

DoDO was taking over the scene, but it didn't sound like they were searching wide for Dexx and Rainbow yet. They were after the jogger still. Maybe the body cams hadn't caught Rainbow?

"Lucy," Dexx said in his best Ricky Ricardo interpretation, "I thin' you have some 'splainin' to do." He went back to his regular Dexx voice. "Was that the currents?"

Rainbow's jaw still shivered with cold. "Y-y-y-yes. The M-m-m-m-mother."

"Like Lilith?"

She shook her head. "N-n-n-not her."

If only this was making *any* sort of sense. "Do you want to explain a little further?"

She shook her head.

"You're going to have to." DoDO was still focused on the jogger, or... maybe they were just saying that because they knew he could hear them? "Explain things like how I'm your champion."

"Such a man." Rainbow leaned over and hugged him again. "I wish you were a woman."

Aw. That was so sweet in a my-male-ego-doesn't-hurt kind of way. "No, you probably don't."

The door opened, and Alwyn stepped out. "Oh, hey. I was just looking for you." He cleared his throat. "So, I guess I'm supposed to, ah, you know, take over for you. I guess you should get some sleep. I think we're moving out today."

"Sure thing. There's a thing going on in the park, though. DoDO agents were after a jogger who turned out to be some kind of para. So, keep your eyes open and your wards on high alert."

Alwyn frowned through his nod that seemed to grow more nervous as he moved.

Poor guy. "Thanks for sticking up for me earlier."

"Um, I— how did you know?"

Dexx shrugged as he helped Rainbow off the bench. "I'm may not be the boss, but I still have a few secrets."

"Yank's always got a few."

"Thanks. I mean it."

Alwyn nodded.

Dexx put his hand on the door to the room, ready for a few winks if DoDO allowed it. "Let's go check in with the queen harpy."

6

Dexx and Rainbow walked into a military installation. Maybe not military *exactly*, but Frey had people moving with purpose in the cramped room.

Ethel looked worst off for the experience. Frey stood over her, her arms crossed, while Ethel hunched over her keypad, tapping furiously.

Tarik scuttled through the tiny kitchenette, making food that actually smelled good. Or maybe Dexx just hadn't eaten in a long time.

Michelle didn't move, just like a tree.

Frey cast a cold look at Dexx and Rainbow when they came in. "Catch as much sleep as you can. We move out today."

Dexx was going to fix this—whatever this was—with Frey, but not at the moment. He needed sleep, and he knew he might not get any. "You know when?" Dexx stripped off his coat and hung it on the back of Ethel's chair. He put a reassuring hand to her shoulder but blocked Frey from seeing.

Ethel released a little of her tension but didn't show any other outward signs or signals.

"Let the planning stay with the people in charge."

Ooh. That woman wasn't going to remain in charge for long with that attitude. Dexx'd learned *that* lesson a long time ago.

"Sleep or don't. Your call."

"Don't have to tell me twice. Come on, Bow. Time for some z's." He laid on top of the bed, burying his head deep in the pillows. He desperately needed to cleanse his soul after the past day. He folded the covers over him and drifted off. He had the impression that Rainbow took a few more minutes to fall asleep.

Dexx woke to a poke in his ribs. The sand in his eyes made keeping them open difficult, and the brain fade made thinking even harder. "What time is it?" He sat up in the bed and stretched. He didn't do that often enough. Stretching helped loosen up tight joints and muscles.

Rainbow breathed softly in her sleep.

Frey looked stern but calm. "Time to get up and get out. There'll be something to eat in a minute, and I need your blood flowing. We don't know what we'll be getting into."

That didn't sound good. "What *are* we getting into? Been a little in the dark since last night." Also, how long had he slept?

"If you *must* know, we have a train ride ready in a little less than two hours. Your demon friend guaranteed the same video blackout we had before."

At least she was open to accepting that level of help. "I'll take all the friends I can get."

"Don't forget who's the boss now." Frey narrowed her eyes.

Whatever. If a person had to remind everyone constantly they were the boss, they knew they really weren't. Now, on a typical day, Dexx knew he should be coaching her, helping her do a better job. But he didn't care, really. Yeah. She'd gone through a lot. Yeah. He'd violated her trust according to her, but he'd been fucking tortured, and his head had been screwed with, so if she wanted to ride a pity pony, she was doing it without him. "Haven't forgotten, not that. You da boss, boss."

"Make sure you don't."

But he wasn't sure how much longer he'd have the patience for that. "So... can I be let in on the plan now?" Dexx stood and twisted in place, stretching more. He skirted Frey and sat lightly on Rainbow's bed and gently shook her.

"We grab the train and head south. How that goes will determine if you *need* to be let in."

Ooookay, go fuck yourself, boss. "If that makes you feel snuggly." He shook Rainbow a little harder. The backside of her eyelids must be super interesting.

"Huh, what?" She raised her head and wiped the drool with the back of her hand. "What time is it?"

She seemed so sweet and innocent. Hard to believe she'd just killed people a few hours ago. And soaked up their blood.

"Time to get up. We have a train to catch." Dexx spoke gently. She was his killer. That had to be enough.

Frey made a sound and stalked to the kitchen nook.

"How long did we sleep?" Rainbow asked as she stretched.

"Not long enough." He looked over at Frey's back. "Don't worry about it. We'll outlast her." Maybe.

The extraction from the motel was nerve-wracking.

The trip to the train station had them all swiveling their heads like they were watching different tennis matches. The final wait on the platform until the train arrived had Frey snapping at people until the train came to a slow stop, and the door slid open to admit them.

They grabbed an empty cabin big enough for all of them and sat.

The sitting didn't last for long.

"Alwyn, you still have watch." Frey lowered her head, her ears pulled back. "Dexx, Rainbow, you sleep. The rest of us will stay alert but stand down."

"This isn't exactly the best sleeping arrangements." The two bench seats let them sit mostly comfortable, but sleeping wasn't what the designers had in mind.

"Sleep is where you find it. You don't sleep. That isn't my concern. You'll be on watch, same as the rest of us."

When did they move from a police force to a military one?

"Come on, kid," Dexx muttered to Rainbow. "Let's try to sleep a little more. Gotta keep our thinking tip-top." Dexx shrugged out of his jacket and rolled it up against the window. He leaned as well as he could and pulled Rainbow to him. At least it might be warm.

He closed his eyes and tried to relax, but the outside light was bright. "Can we pull the blinds?"

He heard someone stand and pull a cord.

The light dimmed as Frey's scent whiffed into his nostrils. Why wouldn't Frey make someone else do it?

Dexx chewed that over until he fell asleep to the gentle-ish sway of the train.

In the black of sleep, Dexx felt a tug. The strength of the pull increased. As soon as Dexx gave the feeling attention, he fell.

The fall ended abruptly, but without ground or light.

Cub.

Relief swept over him—fat cat. *Do you have to bother me while I'm sleeping?*

That thing *hunts.*

Not good. *Lots of things do. Could you be a little more specific?* But he had a sinking feeling he knew what she was talking about.

The red one. The demon. It hunts us, but not well. Not yet.

Bussemi is here? He couldn't be. Could he? And hunting *them?*

The way is closed to it, but it might find a way around.

The way to the Time Before, where the shifter spirits lived wasn't something just anyone could access. It was a completely separate realm. He didn't even think the witches with the doors—the Blackmans or whatever—could access it.

But Dexx could. Through his connection with Hattie. How many other shifters had that kind of connection? Not even Paige did. So, what if Bussemi was targeting Dexx in order to gain access to the spirit animal realm? What happened if Dexx let him in? *Is he trying to get to you or what?*

It is hunting. Poking and sniffing like the bear for insects.

So, what does that mean? Is he looking for something to eat? Is he getting close?

What do they always *want? More power. Always more power. Domination. Does it matter?*

Dexx's frustration level hit ten. But he kept his anger in check. Probably not. *So, boil it down for me. How do we kick him out, and how do we prevent him from coming back?*

That is for you to find out. The problem is on your side.

That's what you said last time. Why does it have to be on my side? Because the spell Bussemi had cast was on Dexx, not Hattie. That's why.

How do you catch smoke?

Oh, geez. *What does that mean?*

I cannot catch smoke. That is why you must do it.

You know, for as much as I want you around, you sure can be difficult to deal with. The real question was if Dexx had been trying to find a way to deal with Bussemi for lifetimes, how could he find success this time? What tools did he have in his arsenal he didn't have before? *So, if I stay here*—spirit animal plane—*for a while, what is time doing on the other side*—his side?

Time is different for us all.

Meaning that it could be either way. Since I'm here, can we make things more comfortable? Like with a tree, or—

No. Hattie pounced over Dexx like they were standing on solid earth. *Do not make the bridge. They wait there. They wait for someone to cross, to show them the way.*

Crap. *More riddles?*

No.

So, Dexx *was* the bridge Bussemi was looking for. *Then, is there a way to spy on them while they're spying on us?*

There might be a way, but it is up to you to find it. I cannot see a breath of air.

For fuck's sake! Why couldn't that cat just tell him stuff? *Riddle me this, riddle me that. Who can even figure out the workings of a big, fat cat?*

You speak no sense, cub.

That's what she *said* because neither was she.

Dexx hung out inside his head for a long time with Hattie "resting." He couldn't *see* her, but just hearing her voice did wonders for his soul, up to a point. Boredom took over after a while, and then he needed real sleep.

He actually *got* sleep, and he didn't have to deal with the queen of the... *everything*.

Frey *did* have a legitimate gripe, though. She'd been kidnapped and brought to another country, beat, tortured, and a lot of things that made Dexx pissed, too. But this? The way she was carrying on? This was over the top, even for her. There... had to be something else going on. Maybe this was some part of her Valkyrie coming out? Or...

Yeah. He didn't know what else it could be.

The blackness of his sleep faded, and the dimmed daylight

intruded on his closed eyelids. The warmth Rainbow's body had offered was gone. He remained still, getting a read on the room.

Ethel and Rainbow talked in low voices together. Ethel was talking her down, though the words weren't quite making sense yet as he didn't invoke Hattie's keen hearing.

Frey's scent wasn't in the cabin. Not really, her scent *was* in the cabin, but she wasn't there to keep it fresh and strong. So, she was out. Taking a watch?

Michelle was there, but the strong odor of woodland meant she'd turned into a tree. Or something.

Tarik wasn't in there either. On watch, too?

Alwyn had come back. But his heart was slowed, so he was sleeping.

Dexx picked his head up off the window, his body complaining loudly and reminding him he wasn't nearly as young as he pretended to be.

He opened his eyes as Ethel and Rainbow paused their conversation.

"Hey, boss." Rainbow tipped her head to the side, her brown eyes heavy, her lips curved up in a smile. "Did you sleep well?"

"I don't know yet." He had no doubt that she was freaking out over what had happened in the park. She didn't like being a rusalka. She didn't like taking life or making death happen. But he wasn't going to feed her anxiety, either. "Has it been more than an hour?"

"Uh, yeah. Almost three." Rainbow wore her bouncy chipperness like a mask.

Maybe Dexx was finally gaining emotional grown-upness, but he was starting to see through it. "Then it was so-so." The time he had with Hattie gratified him in a visceral way, but he needed her closer. He needed to shift.

"Good thing you're up." Rainbow rubbed the bridge of

her nose. "Frey was just saying how she was going to poke you awake if you were still 'lazing the day away.'"

Yeah. There was something extra special wrong with Frey. She'd never been this... insensitive? Was that even the right word? "Good to know my timing is still impeccable. Does anyone know where we're headed?"

"I think I heard Monaco." Ethel pointed in the direction the train moved. "She said we're in for a long soak. Whatever that means."

"Means we're getting on a boat." Why wasn't Frey conveying this to her own team? He got that she was mad at him. *This* mad? That was a little hard fathom. She was bordering on unreasonable. But to keep the rest of her team in the dark? "Have any idea what's on the other end?"

"No, not really." Ethel chewed on her thumbnail. "Sorry, Dexx."

"No biggie." Ethel didn't need to be sorry for anything. She was just trying to do her damned job the best she could. "Listen, guys. I want you to do what Frey wants. She says jump, you jump. Just be careful, okay? If she takes things too far..." Then, what?

Rainbow stared obstinately as she nodded at Dexx. "When she takes it too far?"

Dexx scrubbed his face. He needed to deal with Frey. What was her real gripe? She said it was the fact he didn't have his alpha spirit anymore. But was it more than that? Was this because of what he'd done? Could it be that he'd broken some Valkyrie code of honor thing? "Okay. So, let's be ready when they get back. If you think we're almost there, then pack up if anything is out."

Ethel slipped her computer into her backpack.

Rainbow didn't move.

Dexx leaned over and shook Alwyn's shoulder. "Hey, bud. Let's get bright-eyed and bushy-tailed. We might be where we're going soon. Study up your list of spell slots. Dollars to doughnuts, we'll need a few."

Alwyn shook his head, waking up. "This isn't Dungeons and Dragons, Dexx."

"Sure it is." Just real life. Dexx reached over to Michelle's shoulder. Her skin wasn't skin, more like a smooth bark.

She softened, and she looked at Dexx. "I heard. I'm ready." She sat still as a board, though.

The door opened, and Frey stepped in, followed by Tarik. "Look alive. Our stop is shortly."

Dexx watched the passing countryside still blurring by. However, the train *was* slowing down. "Monaco, right?"

Frey's eyes flicked around to everyone. "Yes. Why?"

"Just getting my bearings." Why was she acting so fucking strange? "Not that I have a lot to go on, but they have water and gambling. And a really cool race. Outside of that, I don't know anything about this place."

Tarik stepped away from Frey so they all could see him. "We are close to the borders controlled by the djinn—my people. There are many misconceptions about them, so we cannot treat any we encounter as *enemies*. There will be many who are, but not all."

"We treat any resistance as enemies," Frey said, her tone icy, "and enemies are dealt with extreme prejudice. Am I clear?"

She'd never been one to not listen before. It was like her mind was infected or something. "Just like crystal, boss." Should he be worried? "Just like she said. *Extreme prejudice.*" Yeah. He needed to be worried. About her. About his team, if they followed her lead.

Frey studied him. "Yes."

He borrowed Hattie's senses to see what he could determine about her, to see if there was something wrong with her. Was she sick?

His nose said no.

Was she off in some discernable way?

Other than the fact that she was acting out of character? All of his vision said no. His hearing said no. It seemed she was... fine.

Except that she was on high alert.

Rainbow flicked her gaze to Dexx but went still.

Alwyn rolled through five degrees of confusion, and Michelle went to a soft loamy scent.

Okay. So, he wasn't the only one reading the weirdness coming off Frey. "You got it. Let's get our teams ready. I mean, we *are* doing teams?"

Frey blinked several times as if she was feeling something weird too. Finally. "You take Rainbow. And Ethel. Michelle and Alwyn can take the rear. Tarik and I will take point." She raised her chin, her blue eyes hardening. "Is everyone clear?"

"Sure am." If he couldn't sense what was wrong, then... maybe it was a Valkyrie thing? "Except I don't know where we're going. I'll get them there, but I need to know *where*."

She grunted. "The docks of Port of Fontvieille. I have the contact information for a yacht. From there, we have a two-day cruise. Does anyone suffer from seasickness?"

Rainbow gave a forced laugh. "Not me. The currents are *strong* here." Her eyes lost a little of their deep brown and gained a filmy blue.

"I, uh, don't think so." Ethel glanced at Rainbow several times as if stuck on her eyes.

Dexx grabbed Ethel's gaze and told her nonverbally to stop staring. "I'm good."

"Trees don't get sick." Michelle showed zero emotion. "I'll be fine."

Frey leaned forward to look through the window next to Dexx.

The train slowed to a walking pace. The wide platform

held a few people wandering around who all appeared to be perfectly normal.

Except two. A pair of DoDO agents in full gear prowled the platform near the doors.

"*Shit.*" Frey stood up from the window. "I thought you said you trusted your demon friend."

Dexx's mind scrambled for a solution. "Number one, I never called him my friend. Number two, we don't know if anything went wrong. There aren't a million of those guys out there, so maybe they're not here for us."

"You trust that demon?" Frey curled her lip in a snarl.

Not really. "He hasn't been anything but helpful and cagey. I know that doesn't prove anything, but he's jumped through a bunch of hoops for us. But he's not our problem right now. *Those* are." He pointed to the two riot-geared DoDO agents.

"Then they're *your* problem." Frey looked to Tarik for backup but directed the order at Dexx. "*You* take care of them."

And then he was going to reboot his Valkyrie. "Sure. Can I phone a friend?"

"What?"

"I choose Rainbow." Mainly because he knew what she could do if the currents were talking to her. "You want to help take out the trash?"

Her eyes lit up, the light blue film edging on a glow. "That sounds fun."

Right. Well, this was what he was good for. "Okay, so Rainbow and I are going to clear your way. Port of Fontvieille. Just look for the two American tourists. We'll meet you there."

"Make sure you aren't followed. The rest of you, let's go."

Alwyn cast nervous looks from Dexx to the DoDO agents patrolling the platform.

"Don't worry. We won't kill them unless we have to." Well, unless the currents called Rainbow to do her rusalka thing. "They look like anyone you know?"

"No." Alwyn shifted his weight uncomfortably. "It just feels funny being on this side of the line."

"Your subconscious chose us, pal." That's the story Dexx was going to stick with. "You'll get over it once they *really* try to kill you."

Alwyn's lips thinned. "I—"

"Move it, people." Frey's patience had ended.

"Git. We'll be there soon." Dexx and Rainbow waited for the others to leave and then for a couple more minutes. He slipped his backpack full of *kadu* onto his back and pulled the straps tight.

"Why me, Dexx?" The energy Rainbow exuded vibrated the air.

She was the only one who'd chosen *him*. "You got a good solid contact with the currents?"

"Sure do. It's scrumptious." Her words sounded light, but the semi-haunted look in her eyes said she wasn't stupid. She *knew* he wanted the killing machine, the part of her she walled away.

He didn't know how to help that side of her. They needed to survive. "Do you think you can take these guys down with a complete minimum of cameras from civilians and keep the DoDO agents alive?"

"Why?" All her earlier jubilation gone.

"Because..." He wanted *his* Rainbow to remain as pure as he could keep her for her own benefit. Well, and his. "If we kill them, their monitors'll go crazy, and they'll send backup sooner."

"You don't think they deserve to die?" Her eyes winced and then over-blinked as if she was shaking something off, but her tone was chilly.

"Yeah. I do. But we have to be sneaky, Bow. We got to get them gone and slip the net. Ever seen *Ocean's Eleven,* the remake?"

Rainbow nodded with a deep intake of breath.

There was his girl. "You know how they got out even when the bad guy *knew* something was up? Let's do that."

She puffed her cheeks out and then released her anxiety. "Okay."

Yeah. This was gonna be a cakewalk.

7

The two DoDO agents were in sight, just ahead of them and prowling.

Dexx and Rainbow closed the distance.

Whispering was still important. "Keep them upright. I'm going to knock them out."

"Like how?" Rainbow didn't whisper.

One of them began to turn around.

Dexx pulled a couple of steps in front of Rainbow and right behind the agents.

Tentacles of water slid past Dexx as he grabbed their heads and clonked them together.

Water solidified against the agents as they turned to rag dolls.

"Good move. Thanks, Bow." Dexx grabbed the agents by the back of their vests and walked them forward. Having Hattie back up his strength helped, but Rainbow's water helped way more.

Very few people actually looked their way, but the few who did nudged those around them and made for the exits as quietly as they could.

"What are you going to do?" Her whisper sounded harsh.

"Just keep them moving." Dexx kept his eyes open for anyone who might actually make a fuss. "Hopefully, the monitors aren't watching too closely. Walk them around the corner."

The other side of the building was just as filled with people as the front, but here, fewer people actually paid attention to them. At least the side had solid walls instead of glass doors. A trash can sat a few feet from the corner. *That* looked promising.

They eased the agents down and leaned them together.

"Stay away from anywhere in their front. The cameras point pretty much forward. The vitals sensors won't pick up anything too worrying since they're only out cold. They'll wake up later and won't be able to remember how they got here."

Rainbow glanced around nervously as Dexx propped them together just so.

Making hand motions, Dexx told Rainbow to be quiet and to head the other way.

They made two running steps to the corner, *right into* another pair of DoDO.

Dexx stiff-armed them both.

One slammed into the wall, sliding down like a wet sponge, and the other skidded across the paving stones on his back.

"*Fuck* it all." Dexx ran hard. His backpack slammed against him with every stride. He risked a glance behind him.

Rainbow kept up like an Olympic athlete. Her eyes were wide, but she ran right on his heels.

Okay, so one plan had gone a little sideways. Maybe running hard might work.

Storefronts and houses blurred by as they ran. People got out of their way with little issue. A few were completely oblivious, but Dexx managed to work around them.

In between buildings and along streets, Dexx caught glimpses of the sky, bright blue and beautiful. Paige would love the scenery and all the old-world feel.

The next storefront had clothing in the window. He skidded to a halt, catching Rainbow by the arm as she ran by.

Hauling her around, he guided her into the door and closed it behind them. He hid behind a mannequin and peered through the glass.

The two DoDO agents ran by, one tracing images in the air in front of him, the fatter one laboring to keep up.

Dexx puffed a sigh, then turned to see Rainbow clutching a stitch in her side.

"I think—" He pulled in a big breath. He knew he was fit and, thanks to Hattie, was better suited to running, but it was still exertion. "—we lost 'em." He turned back to the glass, intently watching everywhere at once as he adjusted the bag.

Their breathing slowed, but his heart thudded as they watched for more agents.

A minute passed, then another—no signs of pursuit or discovery.

Dexx turned to grab Rainbow to get moving toward the docks, but he froze in place.

Rainbow had a skirt pulled out, fingering the material. No concern at all on her face.

"What the hell?" Dexx reached a hand up to the fabric.

"Oh." She dropped the skirt. "Well, I thought you would let me know if there was anything important going on, and I haven't seen a store in so long, I thought I might just, you know, let you."

"Bow, please let's get out of trouble. Then, when we're

safe, we can go shopping. Just the two of us." He shifted the backpack on his shoulders.

"Yeah?" Her face lit up with a smile. Her eyes narrowed in slight disbelief.

"Pinky swear."

She gave him a huff of a chuckle, but at least she watched the lane out front.

Dexx let his senses range out as far as he could take them.

His enhanced vision would be useless since DoDO agents' signatures matched regular humans.

Too many scents in the air confused his smell, but at least it had better information than his sight.

His hearing caught way more than he really wanted, but it did the most good. But they were in a city, and he wasn't Superman. "Hey, get the currents to help. Maybe they can tell you the way to go without being caught in a trap."

"Sure." Her eyes flashed blue. "This way." She walked through the door.

He tried to act like he belonged. Just a tourist in the city right out of the stories seemingly unhurried, but had had to slow them down several times. Nobody else shared the path with them, but a surveillance camera could be anywhere.

He glimpsed the harbor between buildings.

They crossed a high, curved bridge with a commanding view of the harbor and ocean. A huge rock jutted up from the beach with an intimidating fortress on top. Trees dotted the side, clinging against gravity.

Or maybe it wasn't a fortress.

Memories of a different time superimposed themselves over the stone. A smaller structure, but impenetrable, sat on top. Tress hung from the side then, too, but smaller. Different. The ocean crashed against the shore a mile out further than it did now. An army of men and women dressed in furs marched haphazardly toward the rock. Tiny men on top looked out over the advancing army, patrolling back and forth. They didn't look concerned, merely interested in the mass approaching.

One man stopped at the base of the rock, shaking a stick at the people at the top, yelling words too faint to hear.

One of the men disappeared into the structure. Soon, more people emerged and shouted back to the fur-dressed people below.

The two men exchanged angry words. At least, they shook fists and sticks at each other.

The man at the top stood and raised his arms to the sky. He chanted in words that *almost* made sense.

A faint dome pulsed into being around the rock until it had the look of solid pink-tinged glass.

The man on the sandy ground raised his stick and made a chant of his own. Those words made no sense. No familiarity at all. A bolt of thick black lightning struck the dome, and the glass cracked. A second strike shattered the wards and lanced into the witch.

He turned into black fuzz and faded away.

The man at the bottom speared his stick into the ground. An earthquake shook the earth, but the rock stood. The land around the rock fell.

The ocean raced in, crashing against the rock and carrying the majority of the army out to sea, *except* the one man at the bottom.

Water washed all around, but nothing touched him. The ocean ran back out, but the new shore stopped at the tall stone.

"Dexx?" Rainbow held Dexx's arm. "Are you there?"

"*Dinya hoght ata Shedim.*" *You lose again, Shedim.*

Rainbow's eyes went wide, and the color drained from her face as she stepped closer. She looked around them, even though they were alone on the overlook. "What did you say?"

The words faded. He *knew* them. But not anymore. "I— I don't know." What was going on? The fortress faded away, and the rock of present became real. Was he losing his mind again?

"You're scaring me, Dexx. I don't know what you are."

Neither did he. "I'm Dexx. No more, no less." Well, maybe more, but nobody needed to know that.

"You said words. You said a *lot* of them. But I only recognized the one. *Shedim*. That's *you*."

But was it? It didn't feel like it. "Yeah. That's me. Sort of. It just means 'demon.'"

"I don't think you meant it that way." She looked past him like she heard a noise but couldn't tell from where. "I think we have company."

"Follow me." Dexx started again, unhurried on the outside.

Rainbow jogged to keep up. "What was that back there? What did you see?"

Dexx kept his eyes on the swivel, making sure they weren't going to get caught. "I saw... I don't know. My past, or someone else's. Doesn't matter." He was sure it did.

"Wow. You can see your past lives?" Rainbow's brow furrowed with what looked like worry while her lips rose in excitement. "How do you do it?"

"I just get glimpses sometimes." Dexx slowed, trying to get a better view of his surroundings. "Bussemi told me I'm really old. I don't know what to believe." Except Alma told him he was magick borne. But that led to a host of questions he couldn't answer. What did it mean? Why couldn't he connect to his magick in this life?

"Hold up." Rainbow stopped walking and stared at nothing, her gaze unfocused. "Something's there."

"Where?" Nothing pinged any of his senses, but the short hairs on the back of his neck rose.

"Shh." Rainbow held a finger to her lips. She backed up slow, crouching further with every step.

Dexx hurried to follow, the backpack shuffling the *kadu* gently as he moved back with her.

They quietly ducked behind the corner of a small shop and waited.

A middle-aged man in a white suit strolled up the street, hands in his pockets, breathing in the open sea air.

Something wasn't right about the man, though. His movements didn't quite fit with natural movement—a small jerk of the head, a twitch of the hand in the pocket.

And maybe he wasn't just pulling in the ocean air. Maybe, he was scenting like a dog with a nose to the ground Dexx did the same thing when he had a scent.

The man dropped his chin and strolled, closing the gap between Dexx and Rainbow.

Damn. They needed to cross the bridge if they wanted to get to Port of Fontvielle before Frey and the others took off.

The man looked up and turned around sharply. He left the bridge at a brisk pace like he'd found his quarry.

"Okay," Rainbow wiggled her eyebrows and bit her bottom lip. "I think it's safe."

Dexx stood slowly, trying to see that the man still kept pace going the other way. So far so good, nobody watching.

They dropped the tourist pretense and slunk along the bridge rails watching everywhere at once.

The huge stone jutting from the beach peeked through the shops and homes along the street. No matter what Dexx did, the rock always drew his attention like it was important. The pull intensified as they drew closer. What could be so important about that stupid rock on the beach?

"Dexx?" Rainbow looked too comical run-squatting.

"That big rock down there is trying to talk to me. Or the currents are. I can't tell."

Strange. "Same. Let's worry about that a little later. Right now, there are more important issues like staying alive."

He stood and shifted his pack behind him as he drew his *ma'a'shed,* lengthening the blade. He had to risk mundanes seeing his magick sword.

The man in the suit strode up the street, confident and slightly amused, his gaze landing solidly on Dexx. He pulled his own sword from the air. "Others have underestimated the great hunter," he said as he got closer. "I do not." He held his arms out and twisted both ways. "See, I even cleared the civilians so we could have some peace."

Dexx felt the urge to shift but couldn't. A thickness like a heavily padded wall separated them.

Come on, girl, break through. How could she break through when he didn't want to and couldn't when it was important?

Cub. She sounded distant, like from behind a door.

But at least she was *there.* That meant one thing to Dexx, though. The pale suit guy was a demon.

Two tactical gear covered men stepped out from between two buildings and closed in on Suit Demon.

Oh, good.

They raised hands and athames, but they never got a chance to sling spells as their heads vaporized in a red spray. Bodies dropped, leaking blood all over the street.

"Pesky little things." Suit Demon chuckled. "Always underfoot."

Well, shit. "Doesn't always make them wrong." Well, it didn't make them right. However, if they showed up to kill the demons trying to kill him, that was always super. "Let the meat suit go, and I'll kill you quickly. Promise."

"I don't think so." The demon tugged on the lapels of his pale suit. "Cultivating the rich isn't as easy as the scum. And there's fewer to choose from. More fun, though." The demon-possessed man walked forward and nodded to Dexx.

No, not Dexx. *Behind him.*

Dexx swung the blade over Rainbow and slashed through the demon slinking up from behind, One arm fell in front of him, and his eyes were wide with surprise but little under-standing of what had just happened. The demon sunk into the demon hole, still surprised.

The air beside him went winter-cold, and the wet thunk told him Rainbow wasn't Rainbow. She felt cold beside him, but her heat signature flared with heat. She pulled her arms backward, and ice crashed to the ground, sliding past Dexx's feet. Rainbow had sliced the guy with an ice guillotine.

The rich demon's meat suit ended midway up his torso, with the demon stuck inside like it had a too-tight wet suit on.

Dexx didn't wait to watch the Hell door to take Suit Demon away. He stowed his knife, then grabbed Rainbow's hand and ran.

Hattie's emotions flowed through the bond, frustration flooding most.

Not now. Dexx loved his cat, but he couldn't let her out right then. *Let's work on the connection later.*

Rainbow kept up with him easily. Too easily. He chanced a look at her, and she *flowed* over the ground. Her feet ended in a fog.

Damn it.

"The caves." Rainbow spoke with the current's voice. "Go to the caves of the lost."

"Hush." Dexx turned forward.

Rainbow pointed to the stone that called them both.

What they *needed* to do was get to the docks and get on the boat to wherever.

Another DoDO agent squad popped up in front of them.

What the *actual* fuck? Dexx moved right with Rainbow still beside him.

A demon appeared in front of them.

Before Dexx had a chance to draw his knife, a wedge of ice split the demon in two. They leapt over the Hell hole that formed to claim it.

The sheer number of DoDO agents and demons popping up as they ran sucked balls. They were being corralled between two factions, and that was never a good thing.

Rainbow lifted her arm and kept pointing in the direction of the rock. Turn after turn, she pointed at the damned stone.

A few times, DoDO had already engaged demons in a fight. They'd learned from their initial contacts and sent more agents to deal with singular demons while tracking Dexx and Rainbow.

They must portals working overtime.

Several demons fell to the onslaught of the undertrained humans, so maybe they were getting better at the whole demon thing. All paras would suffer if they got too good.

Teams of bodies littered a few of the skirmish sites. Maybe they were getting *luckier*.

They found the beach through a small path between storefronts and houses.

The stone emerged from the buildings lining the edge of the beach. It called with urgency, need. Only a small corner of Dexx's mind saw the lines of the spell pulling them forward. The magick wasn't human, or at least nothing he'd seen a human weave.

They tramped into the sand, losing the solid footing of the paved pathway, but Dexx stumbled forward, hoping Rainbow's foggy feet could pull him along easier than he could run in the stuff.

Only four hundred feet of open space separated them

from the stupid rock set at the damned shore of the fucking ocean in fucked-up Monaco.

Between one step and the next, the world went dark and cool. Not the cold and dark of death, but the cool and shade of a cave.

Rainbow fell to the ground like a marionette whose strings had been cut.

8

Dexx pulled out his *ma'a'shed,* turning in all directions. His eyes adjusted quickly, and the dark became a shadow in bright light.

Blue mist swirled from Rainbow into a human-shaped cloud.

He stepped back, ready to run or fight or even scream like a girl if he had to.

The cloud solidified and a woman formed. Not a beautiful woman. She had a died-while-drowning-weeks-ago look about her, which wasn't overly appealing. Her head was slightly bowed like she was expending a lot of effort.

Black tattered rags hung from her deadness. Her hair shifted like she was still underwater, but she still somehow remained dank and clumpy.

Dexx took another step back. *"Fuck me."* That thing was *gross*.

The blue woman with the softly waving hair looked up. "The Dexx." Her voice cracked with disuse, her dead eyes focused.

The Dexx? What was this? "I guess so?" How in the *hell*

was he supposed to talk to a dead, not dead *thing*? Woman. Corpse. She might take offense if he backed up any further, so he planted himself. It didn't stop him from leaning back a little.

"The Dexx has gained our favor." The voice cracked a little less, and her eyes went from a dead film to a soft, glowing blue.

Ah, she must be the currents Rainbow always blathered about. Oops. Talked about.

"This place is thin," the Blue Lady said. "We can take form, offer gifts. We can *do* things."

The way she said that last thing left him to wonder what she was implying. "Hey, that's great. But uh, I'm just going to —" His feet lurched forward on their own.

"Offer boons to the favored." She *changed*. Her sunken face and frame filled, her hair became vibrant although still blue and flowing. Her drawn lips became lush and... supple. The black tatters of her clothes changed to the soft blue cloth, which then morphed into the soft mist rolling from her.

She wasn't terrifying. She was... captivating. She was everything. Dexx took another step and another until all he had to do was lean forward, and he'd be kissing her.

"Tell us, the Dexx. What does your heart desire above all things? We can make them real."

"I—" What *did* he want? Lots of shit. A vat of money to roll around in, a street demon turning low eights, a reliable shift with— "I want Hattie back. Full and perfect and just the way we were. But I want to shift with clothes."

"Is the Dexx sure? Is there nothing the Dexx might like *more*?" She shimmered somehow. She was the same but looked different for an instant. Black hair, slighter frame, deep brown eyes. "We can be anything, *grant* anything. Except the Dexx shifter. That is the Dexx quest. The Dexx journey."

Well then, what the fuck was the dead lady good for except— "I want to see Paige. And my kids." Without bringing his danger to their doorstep. "Safely." Paige, the most beautiful woman he'd ever seen. Leah, just coming into womanhood, and a fantastic mechanic. Bobby, always glowing when he wasn't filling diapers, and the baby twins still all wrinkly and ugly.

"That is ours to give. For a price." The Blue Lady's voice turned sultry. Inviting and lusty and *all* the things that made men weak.

"Price?" Of *course,* there'd be a price. Probably agree to be her love-slave for eternity or kill a thousand Arians, or raise the Titanic, or something else just as crazy. He'd just have to say thanks but no—

"Protect our child."

"Child?" Dexx looked down at her belly, where she would *surely* show signs. "What, am I a witcher now?"

"The Dexx makes humor?"

"Yeah. Kinda lame, I know. Not really on my game here." Stupid as fuck, was what he was. "Sorry."

"This child." Her open hand gestured at the sleeping Rainbow.

"Oh. Gotcha." Didn't he already agree to watch over her? After all, Rainbow was the only reason he could even *talk* to Hattie. "I don't mean to sound... uh, disrespectful or anything, but didn't I already agree to that? I would anyway, but I just have to make things clear."

"We are— will the Dexx agree to watch our child?" The currents rippled, and the dead thing underneath became visible for the briefest moment, and then was back to the enticing blue woman in front of him.

What was really going on here? "Bargain. Yeah. I'll watch over her. You got it. Do I spit in my hand or what?"

"Then, the Dexx must embrace us."

Could she be any more vague? "Embrace, like declare you to be my lord and savior embrace, or a bro hug embrace?"

"Embrace us as a lover."

She was all that and a bag of chips, but the woman in front of him was also *dead*. Or death or something, but she wasn't *alive*, was she? "Lover?" His only lover was Paige because... he didn't want to be eaten alive when he found her again.

The Blue Lady raised her arms to her sides, and the mist that made her covering fell away like fog burning off. She stood before him as beautiful as any woman, with curves in all the right places.

Dexx stepped forward but not close enough to touch her.

She took his hands and placed them on her hips.

Okay. He was perfectly willing to admit he was a guy. A guy who loved his woman, Paige, who was great. But... he could also be turned on by other pretty women too. His heart was Paige's and only hers. But these hips weren't slimy or dead, but they were cold. The Blue Lady's skin was smooth and soft, like any other, but a tingle ran up his fingers and settled in his spine like he held death, and there was nothing he could do to avoid it.

She longed for a lover's touch, and he could give that. But only that. He ran his fingers up to her waist and closed the space between them.

Her breath flowed over his shoulder like a chilled breeze in autumn, but her cheek against his neck felt almost alive. Her hair brushed close to his nose, and the smell of *almost*-life wafted in.

She was as revolting as she was... enticing. He moved his hand higher up her back and pulled with his other hand. He held tighter and whispered. "Paige."

Everything flashed blue, and the cave disappeared.

The currents were gone, and Rainbow, too.

He didn't recognize the room. It looked like a room the Winchesters from *Supernatural* might get out on the road— two beds, one a queen size and the other a full size. The curtains matched the bedding in a late seventies crazy floral abstract pattern with pinks, reds, and oranges fighting greens and gold. Highly disgusting but cute in a retro sort of way.

"Damn it. I got screwed again."

"By who?" Paige's voice came from behind him. "And you better have a good excuse for being gone so long."

Dexx spun at the sound of Paige's voice. His eyes widened. "Pea?"

Paige stepped out of the tiny bathroom. She looked tired but in a good way. Like the twins had her up and feeding in the middle of the night.

"Pea, is that really you?"

"Is that really *you?*"

"You're not an undead blue lady trying to get me to drop my drawers, are you?"

She looked super confused. "No. It's just me." He wasn't going to enlighten her. "Fuck it. It *has* to be you." He rushed her and wrapped her up in a fierce hug. He let up when he realized she was tapping out.

She made a noise that told him he was squeezing her too tight, but he couldn't help himself. He'd missed her so badly. "Is it really you? Like *really, really?* Nine Hells, it *has* to be. I missed you so much." He put effort into balancing as much squeeze as he could get and not break her. He couldn't stop the tears, though.

After a while—it could have been a minute, or an hour, didn't matter—he put her down on her feet. "How?"

She cupped his cheek and smiled up at him tenderly, making him feel accepted and complete again. "You come up with the weirdest friends." She turned back to the bathroom. "Come on out."

Leah poked her head around the doorframe slowly. "Is that you, Daddy Dexx?"

His heart squeezed itself with happiness. If this was an illusion, it was the best one ever. And if it was, he'd give whoever whatever they wanted. They had him cold. "Me in the flesh. Most of it anyway."

"Dad." Leah rushed forward, and a fresh set of tears and hugs took place. "Dad, you're squeezing too hard." Leah croaked out.

"Sorry, Little Leah, I've been missing you."

Dexx wanted to hold onto her as long as he could. But a new voice came out of the bathroom, one he didn't recognize. "Dad?"

That wasn't Leah. Dexx frowned and pulled his head back from her. "Huh? You channeling someone?"

"Dad?"

Dexx turned back to the bathroom. A boy about Tyler's age tentatively looked out from the bathroom with -blond hair and blue eyes and a face that looked so familiar.

"Babe," Paige said, her tone insinuating she had a big story to tell him.

Dexx put Leah down and looked at Paige. "There something I should know?"

She winced. "Um, yeah. First, let me introduce you to your kids." She walked over and set her hand on the boy's head. "Bobby."

Dexx's eyes bulged. "What? You're shittin' me. I'm dreaming, or holodecking or something."

Paige raised an eyebrow and reached into the bathroom to pull out two more kids. "This is Rai, and this is Ember."

"Heaven or Hell? All you gotta do is tell me which one, and I'll act appropriately." Dexx didn't know what he was saying. He was buying time to figure out how to react to this. His *babies* were grown up now. No helping them with their firsts. A shoot of anger coursed through him. "How?"

Paige raised her hand. "Let me explain."

Dexx didn't know what the story was going to be, but he sat down for it.

Paige ran both her hands over her head as she paced between the bed and the dresser. "We're pretty sure their accelerated growth is due to the fact that their spirit ancients are so powerful."

That actually wasn't the strangest thing he'd ever heard. "So, they just sprang up overnight?"

"Almost." She stopped and let her hands drop.

"Well," Leah said helpfully, sitting beside him. "After the president tried to kill them."

"What?" Outrage filled Dexx as he turned his full attention to Paige again.

She held up her hands and glared at her daughter. "We went to D.C."

He vaguely remembered being *very* pissed about that. "Uh-huh."

"And the president put us all in collars."

Collars. "You mean like the ones in Alaska?"

Paige blinked rapidly and looked away with a wince as if knowing where he was going with this.

"The same collars that made those shifters lose contro—"

"Yes!" She clawed her hands in frustration. "They're *fine,* by the way."

But were they? "Do you think maybe *that's* the reason they grew so fast?"

"How the hell am I supposed to know?" Paige slapped her thighs as her hands fell. "What I know is that Cawli was just as surprised as I was."

"Because this *never happened* before."

"Bitten? Sure. Adult? Yes. Babies coming out with these

spirits?" She shook her head and grabbed Rai by the neck, bringing her in for a hug.

Rai grumbled and struggled but finally settled.

It felt like a knife twisting in Dexx's chest. "And Bobby?"

He looked up from where he and Ember were messing around with the air conditioning unit.

Paige smiled at him and waved him off. "When they grew, they made Bobby and Kamden grow, too."

"What?" He'd been gone for a couple of *months*. What the hell?

"I know." She pressed a kiss to the top of Rai's head and pushed the girl to the bed.

She sat perched beside Leah.

"It hurt Kammy. I had to take the twins to the Vaada Bhoomi to protect him and Bobby both."

"Hurt?" Because he'd mated with a witch? Was this Dexx's fault? "How?"

"Doesn't matter. Bobby was able to heal him."

"Heal him?" Dexx was feeling lost.

Paige sank down on the bed beside him and took his hand. "The kids are okay. All the kids are okay. They're just... bigger than we'd expected." The sag of her shoulders and the lost look in her eyes told him just how hard this was hitting her even if she wasn't letting on.

He wrapped her in his arms. What a pair they were. He was losing himself, and so was she.

They worked better when they were together.

Leah piped up first. "We don't know, really, but the good news is that we're saving a bundle on diapers. No formula either." She grinned like a miniature Paige.

Damn, he missed that smile. "Silver linings. I like it" He released Paige and dropped to his knee, his arms wide.

Leah fell into his arms, hugging him so hard, it was like

she was trying to physically merge with him. She reached over and dragged Rai to them.

Rai tucked herself into him, resting her head on his shoulder and just staying there.

Until the two boys rammed into Dexx from behind with youthful enthusiasm. The sound of head butting—literal head butting—hit Dexx's ear pretty hard, but aside from a grunt from Rai and an "oops" from one of the boys, everything seemed fine.

Dexx didn't want to let them go. He didn't know when he'd become the dad guy, but he couldn't ignore the fact that he felt complete with them there. All of them. "I'm sorry."

Paige reached through the throng and cupped his cheek. "Me, too," she mouthed, her brown eyes shining with tears.

The temperature in the room dropped.

Oh, crap. Not now. Not yet.

Paige pulled away. "Are we safe?"

The Blue Lady appeared in between the two beds. "The Dexx can have them for a time only. The Dexx people must go from this place, and the Dexx must go from this place."

More riddles. Great. But also… no. Dexx needed this.

Paige frowned at him. "Who is that?"

Why was she looking at him like he was a horn-dog? "She's the 'currents' Rainbow's always talking to." But, seriously, she'd have to wait. "Okay. Message received. How long do we have?"

The Blue Lady turned to Paige. "We can tie back the strings of fate for a short time. The Dexx has his to meet and cannot be helped by the Paige. The Paige must dance to the unseen a while yet before reunion. But we made this place for the Dexx and the Dexx people. It is small, but there will be no danger."

Did any of that make sense? But Paige was starting to get a little pissed, and she raised her hands as if to call on her magick. "Pea, this is Blue Lady." And hitting her with magick was probably a bad idea.

The Blue Lady tipped her head to the side again, an octopus inching down her arm. "The Dexx has our favor. We have granted a boon unto him. This was The Dexx second choice."

Why did she have to say that?

Paige raised an eyebrow. "*Second* choice?"

Oh, come on. "Pah. Yes, because my first choice would have made this possible on my own but in the real, real world." Also, she wasn't the *only* person on the face of the planet.

Paige chuckled and turned her attention back to the Blue Lady. "Thank you. We'll try to use our time wisely."

The Blue Lady shook her head. "We doubt that."

Wow. What a— Dexx raised his brows at Paige. "The kids can go out and play?"

"No harm shall befall the Dexx people in this protected place." The Blue Lady's eyes glowed silver, and the curtains behind Paige billowed.

Okay. Creepy vibes aside, he bet his kids were strong enough to take care of themselves for... an hour. Maybe two. "Excellent. Because I'd like to give Pea a proper hello."

Paige narrowed her eyes, giving him the start of a good glare, but then tipped her head to the side and nodded.

"Ew, gross." Leah looked at Paige incredulously, her blue eyes filled with a little hurt. "Are *all* boys like this?"

Paige clamped her lips shut and nodded.

Seriously? Rude.

"It won't be long, Bean."

"Hey," Dexx said, a little hurt.

Dexx watched the door shut.

When it clicked, Paige slammed into him, taking them both to the larger bed.

Clothing flew, and things magickally hit the floor. Paige had about eight arms, but Dexx had like sixteen. She never stood a chance.

Sometime later, Paige stroked Dexx's jaw.

The blankets were messed up, but they hadn't been pulled to sleep under.

Paige raised up on her elbow and looked down at him. "You owe me some explanations, man kitty."

He wanted to tell her everything because maybe she could help him make sense of everything, or at the very least tell him how to fix Frey. "You got it. You see, Mario came to see me—"

Paige held up her free hand. "Five words or less, babe. You've got kids who want to spend time with you and twins you need to bond with."

"Babe, I get that, but this…" How could he explain every that'd happened to him when he had a hard time remembering everything? "It isn't that easy." So, he told her as much as he could about how Mario had laid the trap for him, how he'd fallen into it. She'd been interested in the wards and how they'd reacted, which didn't hurt *at all*.

"I still don't understand. Why *you?*"

"Why *not* me? I'm a pretty cool shifter." Okay. Now for the big stuff.

"Not *that* dummy." She slapped his chest with the back of her hand. "I mean, why you when they could have gone for *me* or Chuck or one of the other big players?"

Wow. "Turns out, I *do* have some worth that you've never heard of."

Her eagle-eyed glare said that wasn't what she'd meant.

But it had been what she'd said. Time to lay it on the line for her. "I'm an immortal."

"No, you're not."

"Yeah, I am." It was a little nice, making her feel like the idiot for once. "Not like you think, but with a *kadu,* I'm as good as. I keep coming back. Same person, different body, same bond with Hattie."

She raised her head, a puzzled frown on her face.

At least she was listening. "And I have a nemesis, too. Cardinal Bussemi. He's my brother from our first life. And he's inhabited by something called a bahlrok."

Alarm crashed over her face. "They're powerful."

"You're not kidding." But now it was time for him to make it perfectly clear to her why he couldn't go home. "He's after me, Pea."

"Your brother. This cardinal guy."

Dexx knew full well she'd remember Bussemi's name. She had a knack for forgetting easy stuff, but the difficult things, the names of the important people? Yeah. She'd remember that. "He got to me while I was inside your protections."

Paige didn't say anything.

Judging by how flat her facial expression went, that meant she was listening and thinking.

Good. "He's behind DoDO. I *think* he expanded DoDO to the U.S. to flush me out."

"You think this whole thing—the collars, the Registration Action, the *war* the president is launching on all paranormals is because of you?"

Well, when she said it *that way*... "Yeah." Which super sucked. "I do."

She raked her top lip with her teeth and sat up, facing him gloriously naked.

He reveled in it but stayed focused as he sat up, touching his knees to hers, trailing his fingertips along her leg. "Babe, he chases me in every lifetime. He's trying to get to the power I have, something I found with Hattie. I've been dodging him lifetime after lifetime, keeping him away from it."

"From what?"

"Shifter spirits. I think…" Dexx actually didn't know what he thought. "I think I helped them make the Vaada Bonky or whatever."

"Vaada Bhoomi."

"Yeah, that."

"But that would mean you have magick."

He nodded. Now, she was catching on.

"But you lose your clothes when you shift."

Yeah. There was that. "I think…" He listened to the distant references of memories he didn't fully have. "I think I had to hide because I think he got really close the last time."

"How close?"

"Close enough that he discovered *how* I reincarnate."

She shook her head.

"With the *kadu.*"

She shook her head again, but this time it signaled that she didn't want more information on that topic because it would just confuse her more.

She had to understand, though. "He scoured the world and collected all the *kadu* we'd had hidden. Each one belongs to another soul."

Her eyes warmed with worry.

He had the sense that he'd lost a lifetime lover, but… he had Paige now, and that's all he cared about. "A team, I think. But…" He shrugged.

"When are you coming home?"

It wouldn't be that easy. "When I can deal with Bussemi."

Paige closed her eyes and rested her hand on his knee.

"I can't bring this home to you."

Releasing a pent-up breath, she looked up at the ceiling.

"No. You can't. I—" She turned her gaze to him. "I can't deal with this too. I wish I could."

But her plate was... it was really full. With politics and the president trying to pull a Nazi movement and... "I'm sorry. This is my fault."

She gave him a frank and shut-up look. "Yeah, it is."

He chuckled and hugged her to the bed.

They cuddled like that for a bit, not really making out or doing anything. He just felt her closeness and kept feeling it for as long as he could.

"They're close. We're in trouble, but Roxxie and Furiel are helping."

"Roxxie? She doesn't have hardly any angel juice left."

"That's true, but... Furiel helps."

Paige groaned. "Do I want to know?"

"Demon. Probably not."

"And you never passed a phone?" She pushed away from him. "Couldn't pick one up and send a message, at least?"

"Babe." He tucked a strand of her hair behind her ear. "I knew this conversation had to be had in person."

She rested her head against his. "I miss you."

She had no idea. "I know."

"I hate you."

She hated his *Star Wars* reference.

But he loved this incredible woman. And their kids. And their family. And their town.

And he'd find a way back to her one way another.

9

W hen Dexx greeted the kids again, he had his clothes on, but his hair might have been a little messed up.

Leah gave him a pained ew-gross look, but that was it.

Playtime started.

Paige sat at the small table while Dexx and the kids rough-housed. Even Rai got into it after a while.

Puffs of fire or stabs of lightning erupted from tickled bodies along with squeals of laughter. His kids were *strong*.

But in the end, Bobby, Ember, and Rai piled on the smaller bed, sleeping.

Dexx sat with Paige at the table while Leah propped her head on her hands and crossed her ankles in the air on the big bed.

Dexx kicked back against the wall, almost sideways in his chair. "There's a lot to tell you."

Paige didn't react.

Leah nodded her head awkwardly, pressing her elbows into the mattress. "Yeah, well, Mom might have some stuff to tell you too."

Paige held up a hand to stop her. That didn't make Dexx feel any better. "You need to know just how much trouble this guy is and why you need to stay out of this fight. He's older than civilization."

"That means you are too, though." Paige sat up. "That makes you magick, but you're not. You have magickal items and ink. I was there when you became a shifter."

She was good at putting puzzles together. He'd give her that. "I've *always* been a shifter—every lifetime."

"Okay. So, what's this *kadu?*" Paige asked.

Leah frowned hard.

Well, he'd told her about Bussemi and just how bad he was, how she and the kids needed to stay off Bussemi's radar. He didn't know what else he could. Maybe it was time to listen. "What's going on with you?"

Paige shook her head, pinching her nose with her fingers.

"Well, for one," Leah said, bouncing to a seated position on the bed, "the president is trying to declare war on us."

Dexx had gotten that memo. "She didn't remember it didn't work for the Nazi's?"

Paige made a guttural noise, letting her hand fall. "We're in truce right now, but we're... Fuck. We're going to impeach her."

"Great." That would be the *least* she deserved.

"Not great."

Dexx didn't understand.

"She's on our side now."

"What? How'd that happen?"

"She's a human being. That's how. She saw what she was doing. Decided to make a change. I don't know. Lots of things."

"Okay." Obviously, there was a lot she wasn't telling him.

"Mom's part of the government now."

"What?" Like that. That was a big deal. Dexx didn't like

the government and didn't believe in big government at all. They shouldn't have the level of influence over their daily life like it currently did.

"It all *just* happened. I don't know. I literally just got done talking with her—"

"The president." Because he needed to get caught up.

"Yeah. And I got sworn in. For real this time."

"This time?"

She held up her hand to stall him. But then she shook her head, her expression filled with... slack-jawed dumb. "I think we might actually go to war if I can't find a way to fix this."

Real war? Sure, he'd talked about it. He'd spouted off at the mouth about it more than a few times. He wanted to create a country closer to what the founding fathers had wanted, something with more limited government and more freedoms. But... it was a little hard for him to picture war. It'd be in their cities—like the war with Sven in Troutdale?

Okay. Maybe it wasn't so hard for him to fathom. "Is that what you want?"

She nodded but didn't say anything.

He knew that she had this... love of government. Not the actual thing. She loved the programs they created to support people who needed it. He got that. He did. But he believed that programs like that should be run by the churches like they used to be.

But then... people like Paige who didn't follow the doctrines of any church would be excluded.

So, maybe there was a flaw in his system, too. "What are you doing?"

She released a puff of breath. "I'm a Secretary."

So, she was in the Cabinet, advising the president. She was in a position to become the corrupted politician he loathed.

She rolled her eyes as if seeing that thought on his face.

Okay. Right. This was Paige. *His* Paige.

"It's so big, Dexx. Just... so much bigger than me."

"But it's not." It super really was. "If anyone can do this, it's you." But only if she could use her magick to make it happen. "You can make peace." They were *so* going to war. "I love you."

"I know," she whispered. "What aren't you telling me about him? Bussemi." Paige leaned forward across the table and took Dexx's hands in hers.

They were warm for once and felt strangely comforting—more than they should have. The shift in conversation made him uncomfortable, though. He really wanted to turn the conversation back to politics. He could rant against the system all day.

"Every time you say his name, you wince a little."

"I do not." Dexx tried to pull his hands back but couldn't. She had them in a vice grip.

"You do."

Sometimes, he really hated her.

"I've been a cop for a long time, and I've seen a lot of battered wife symptoms."

Battered *wife*? "Name *one*."

"Fear of your abuser."

"You think I'm scared?" He wasn't. He was fucking *terrified* of the guy.

"So you deserved what you got?"

No. Maybe. "Pretty sure he has a good case. I mean, to hear him say it, I kinda left him in a lurch... like a million years ago." What a baby.

Paige smiled. Maybe less of a smile than showing off her pearly whites. "Pretty nice guy in the beginning, wasn't he? Charmed you a bit and wanted you around frequently?"

Wait. "How did you..."

"Cop. It doesn't go away just because I'm playing politics."

"Fuck." Dexx shot Leah a glance, wishing she was asleep. He didn't want her to see him like this. "Sorry, kid. Forgot you were there."

She waved him off, studying them both with intent.

That wasn't creepy at all. He went back to Paige's smiling face. "What in the nine Hells am I supposed to do now?"

"You have to stand up to your abuser. Realize it wasn't your fault, and he holds the blame."

Okay. Sure. Well, he was to blame. Yeah. But that didn't change a damned thing. "He broke me, Pea. You have no idea what it was like."

The look in her eyes said she had a slight clue. "Worse than losing your husband, then losing your daughter? Or giving birth to twins, fighting with your lover, having him walk out on you, and then nearly killing your twins with your magick flowing through their veins?"

Well, she understood pain. But like this? "No, babe. I mean, I appreciate what you went through, but..." He shook his head. "No. *Not* like that."

"Babe, you're strong, and you have to realize you need to face him."

Just the thought of it left him cold. "I can't. He's always three steps ahead. I can't beat him. All of us together couldn't beat that guy."

"You're fighting one guy. I'm fighting the government."

One-upping. He hated that.

"I'm just saying, if you're trying to tell me I can take on the entire fucking government, then you can take on one guy."

"With what? What can I do that I haven't tried in all these lifetimes? What's different now?"

"I don't know. But something. Something's *got* to be

different."

"I'm dumber. I have no magick this time."

"You're with us. You have a pack. You have a team. A coven. Three covens at your back?"

"How do you know I didn't have that before?" He didn't because he still didn't have those memories.

"I don't know!" She let her head hang down before she looked up again. "You have knowledge. What's that thing you always say? Knowing in most of the way there, or something."

"Knowing is half the battle. But this feels bigger than that. It's not enough. He's had time to prepare. Time to get where he wants, and now he's there. World domination. He's made DoDO legitimate in Britain, and who knows what he's done in other places? He's big time, and I don't know what to do."

Leah got off the bed and climbed into Dexx's lap, hugging him. She didn't say anything.

Paige rubbed his hand with a finger.

"And this spell or ward or whatever he put on me is going to kill me if I don't break it or remove it." He had to tell them just how royally fucked he was. "I can't shift. I can't even talk to Hattie, and there's so much he's done that I can't... I just can't."

"I knew I'd get to meet the real Dexx sometime." Paige's voice held all the love he'd ever heard from her. "Dexx, *I* know you're powerful. Even without your shift or magick. You *know* what to do. Maybe you created this lifetime to *be* without magick or your shift so you *could* devise a plan that didn't need either. Get back to... what you do best. You're a hunter, Dexx Colt. Work from there."

"It's like what I keep hearing about cell phones," Leah said against his arm wrapped around her. "How did anyone survive before those things?"

What a turd. "Heh. That's a little funny."

"See?" Paige narrowed her eyes at Leah. "Regain your confidence. But not too far. You can't afford to be cocky or arrogant—"

"I've *never* been cocky —"

Then come home. Please."

He could feel the desperation pouring off her. "I don't even know where to start looking to break a spell like the one the cardinal put on me."

"You don't?" Paige raised an eyebrow in challenge.

"Google it?"

"You might try that. I don't think you'll get very far, but you can try. Then come up with something better."

Leah sat back on the bed. "Sorry, Dad. When I was first learning to deal with my power and I had to hide it from Grandma, I had to figure stuff out, too. It wasn't fun, but if I can do it, I know you can. You're kind of smart and stuff."

Dexx dropped his head a little to hide the eye roll. Leah laid it on pretty thick, but he would have too. "Really, what I want to do is come home. But I can't. I don't know what's going to happen, but I have to finish this. What I mean is lift the curse. I have to lift the curse first. Then I can come home."

Paige gripped his hands a little tighter for a second. "You find him and beat him or find a way to escape him. Those are your options."

How could he without her? "I'm... tired. I've been chased and chased and chased, and I haven't had a break in, I don't know, a long time." Literally.

Her shrug said, "so what?"

That hurt a little.

"That's your life now. We have enemies everywhere. Even back home." Paige stood, pulling Dexx up into a hug.

Leah wrapped her arms around them both.

Dexx relaxed for the first time in a long time. Really relaxed. The emotions he'd been holding flooded out.

There might have been a tear. Maybe two. Certainly no more than that.

Abstract dreams chased Dexx through troubled sleep once they all settled down to sleep. Images that made no sense flashed and were gone. Hattie took up a large portion of the images he *did* recognize, but she was always injured, dead, or dying.

Dexx woke up sweating.

Paige had pressed herself to him, soaking up all his body heat, and at the same time, making it way too hot under the covers.

Leah shared the other bed with the kids, but they looked like they were sleeping well.

Dexx turned his head to Paige. Out cold. He pulled his hand from under her and sat up, pushing the covers around her. She hated drafts.

The Blue Lady stood motionless at the small table. He would have jumped if he hadn't been so sluggish.

Maybe his sleep had been better than the dreams felt.

He nodded and made a half-sleep grunt to her.

She cocked her head to the side. "The Dexx has been harried?"

He snapped a finger to his lips. "Shh. She wakes up angry." He tried his best to whisper, but it came out croakish.

"The Dexx people will not awake. We have them held in slumber."

"This was all an illusion?" His voice evened out, but it still sounded thick with sleep.

"The Dexx people are true. The Dexx people will slumber until we say. No harm shall come to the Dexx people."

"So, what is it you want from me? Swear undying allegiance to you or something?" Sleep tones rapidly fell away from his voice. "Because if you think you're going to bully me by using them... well, you'd be right. But... just please don't."

"The Dexx people shall not be harmed. We have given the Dexx a boon. We request the Dexx to an action."

"What, like you want me to repay you for something I didn't ask for?" The nerve of some people.

The Blue Lady tipped her head to the side and a crab-walked up the side of her head. "We can see much, do much. We have limits in places not ours. The Dexx is requested to an action. Will the Dexx take action or decline?" She didn't move, didn't smile or anything, but something about her words felt dangerous.

Which meant this was big and it was bad. And he'd probably feel like an ass if he declined. "Can you tell me something about it first?"

"The Dexx will not know."

Great. "Fuck me." But saying no would likely get him in some karmic trouble he couldn't afford with entities who were a lot stronger than him. "Can I at least say goodbye to my people?"

"The Dexx may offer salutations to the Dexx people." She pointed to Paige, still sleeping.

"Just Pea, huh?" Part of him was glad. If he had to say goodbye to the kids too? He might not be able to. "Well, I guess that's better than nothing. Fine."

Paige groaned and rolled over, her hand reaching behind her to touch Dexx. She sat up all bleary-eyed and mussed up. Her lip snarled when she saw Dexx was awake and talking to the Blue Lady.

"Hurry, coffee." Dexx motioned to the kitchenette.

The Blue Lady made no moves.

"I hope you don't think you're taking him away again.

He's coming home with me." She sounded like she'd been awake for hours. How did she do that?

"The Dexx will take an action. We have granted a boon."

"I don't care if you gave him an elephant. He's coming home with us."

Was she thinking like a baboon? "She didn't mean an animal, Pea. She meant—"

"I know what she meant. And I know what *I* meant. You're coming home with us." She slipped from under the covers, bringing out her witch hands.

Dexx *saw* those inky black hands. She'd told him about them, but he'd never seen them. Not actually. Whoa. "Pea, put those away. I think I have to do this. Besides, what about facing or fleeing Bussemi?"

Paige frowned at him, glancing at her magickal hands. "I changed my mind. I finally had a warm bed, and I forgot I liked it." Her hands held steady, but they didn't go away, either.

"Coffee?" Dexx felt the pleading come through in his tone.

"The Dexx will take the action." The Blue Lady shook her head and clasped her hands in front of her, a sea eel swirling around them. "The Dexx people will return to away. No harm shall come to them."

That sea eel was more than a little creepy. "Pea, I know you don't like this." But he had to go. This *was* the right thing to do. It was the *only* thing to do, but before he left, he needed her to protect something for him. "I need something from you. I need you to hide the *kadu*. I can't know where they are, so you have to hide them. Could you do that for me?"

"The what?" She gestured to the backpack in question.

"The Dexx will champion our child."

Dexx was listening. Really he wasn't. But he nodded at

Paige, letting her know that, yes, that was what he needed her to take.

"Our child will act with the Dexx."

Paige threw a frown at the Blue Lady as if also not really listening, but rolled her eyes and nodded with a shrug of "fine!"

"The people of the Dexx will return away."

Paige opened her mouth to say something pre-caffeinated.

Dexx stepped in front of her with his hands raised. "Okay. Listen. This could have been a lot of things. But the Blue Lady chose to do the right thing here and actually let us have some time together. I say we trust her. Hide the *kadu*. I'll come back when I can. Then all this can be put behind us. Yes?"

The currents turned to the bathroom. "Our child will be with the Dexx."

"Knock, knock?" Rainbow's voice was soft like she thought she might be interrupting.

Paige's brown eyes lit up. "Is that you?"

The two rushed together in a hug. Their voices overlapped too much to tell what either said. But pretty much, they just greeted each other.

"I see you met the currents. They're so nice, don't you think?"

"Um." Paige seemed stuck.

That's kinda where Dexx was, too. "Pea, I'm thinking the Blue Lady could be running low on patience. I love you, and I'll have Rainbow to protect me."

She shook her head, reaching toward him.

"The Dexx has agreed," the Blue Lady said. "Our child has agreed."

The room flashed white, and the scenery changed to one Dexx knew well, but never in the flesh.

"Aw, double fuck me."

10

Dexx stood stunned. "Really?" He didn't know *why* they were... *here* exactly, but he at least hoped that by being in the Time Before—or the Vaada Bhoomi because he *did* know the "real" name for it. He just thought it was dumb like someone had just been sitting around with Google and a translator and too much wine one night—meant that he wouldn't be attacked. Immediately.

"Oh, wow." Rainbow covered her mouth with both her hands, her eyes round in wonder.

They stood on a bluff overlooking a wide plain, with scattered animals grazing peacefully.

Why the fuck would the currents send him here? Though! Maybe he could find Hattie and re-establish their connection.

"This place is so beautiful." Rainbow still had her hands covering her mouth.

"Yeah." But the real question was, "Where was the trap?" There had to be one.

Cub. How are you here like this?

Dexx and Rainbow turned around.

Hattie stood in front of them, massive as always but thinner.

Rainbow's hands twitched over her mouth with a sharp intake of breath. "Hattie can talk? I mean, I think it's you. I heard something in my head, so I thought it was you, it *is* you, right? Wow, *this* is where you live? This is so awesome. I just can't believe I'm here seeing you. It's all just so cool. Right, Dexx?"

Sometimes just letting Rainbow run out of steam was the best thing to do, though his mind was running through more than a few rabbit holes, too. "Yes, it's Hattie. Wait, you can hear her?"

"Sure. Can't you? Oh, I'm so sorry." Rainbow bit her bottom lip for a micro-second and then bounced at the knees. "You didn't know she could talk? That's okay. Lots of people get weirded out by spirits talking, but I have a lot of experience with that, so I can interpret for you. She wants to know how you're here."

Sometimes... Rainbow left him confused. Like, how did she think *that* was the direction this conversation was headed, that he couldn't hear his own spirit animal. Then again, they'd had a really crappy few weeks, and he *hadn't* been able to hear her that entire time.

Rainbow raised a finger, her expression filled with intrigued excitement. "That's a good question. How *are* we here? I mean, I know the currents can do a lot, but I never imagined they could send us to another plane of existence. Did you?"

"Bow, if you talked less, you could listen more." Because he'd *asked* Hattie a question, his cat hadn't had a chance to answer.

"Sure, but then I wouldn't get answers to burning questions I have. Like where are we and how does Hattie talk? And what is this place? And why is Hattie so thin? And what's that?" Rainbow pointed in the distance to a sheer cliff with a hint of a red glow at the base.

Those were quite a few good questions. "And if you held your tongue, some explanations might be able to make it through the jibber-jabber." Dexx rested a hand on Hattie and looked to the cliff in the distance. "Yeah. What *is* that?"

The human you called lizard wizard left an opening in this place, Hattie's voice purred inside his head. *You moved him out, but the way was left open.*

A twig snapped to their right. Rainbow spun around, gasping with her hands splayed out.

Mah'se ran toward them. Not full force running, but not waiting around either. *You cannot be here.* He roared, his massive rack lowered as he charged his stag body toward them. *This is not your place.*

Rainbow nearly danced in place on her tiptoes. A squeal of delight keened from under her hands. "Omigosh! *You* are the absolute most beautifullest thing I've *ever* seen! Oh, can I pet you? You look marvelous. Dexx, how come you never said there was anyone like this here? How come you never *even mentioned* here? Oh, this is so great. I just wanna *eat* you up. You're so magnificent."

Mah'se skidded to a halt, his head high, his stag-eyes big and round. He'd actually *almost* been eaten by a human.

She held her hand out palm down like she would have for a strange dog. "It's okay. I don't bite."

Mah'se tipped his head to the side, his massive rack nearly touching the ground. *Did you not just claim you would eat me?*

"I would *never,*" Rainbow said aghast. "I would hold you and love you and tell you stories. We'd be besties." She shuffled her feet forward, inching closer to the spirit.

This had to end. "Rainbow, stop. Mah'se isn't a pet. He's the protector of this... uh, area." Who, oddly, seemed to be taken by a rusalka. Dexx took a step toward Mah'se. "She's mostly harmless. She really likes animals, and you must be on the top of her list of creatures to really like."

She has the taint of an elemental on her, the ancient and massive stag said. *An ancient. But different than others.*

"Yeah." She was. "I don't get it either, but here *she* is, and here *I* am. There were favors exchanged and angry feelings, and it's a long story, but no danger to you. So, I'd like to get past the whole 'you don't belong here' spiel. I didn't bring us here."

The spirit elk snorted, shaking his head, swinging the eight-foot antlers dangerously close to them. *You should not...*

Hattie rose to her full should-height, but slow as though she strained with the effort. *The two are here. And this is* my *bond.* She nuzzled Dexx and almost purred. She couldn't, but the feeling came through emotionally.

Rainbow closed in on Mah'se.

He stood his ground, but his head lowered, and his ears flicked back.

"Who's the most beautiful elk?"

Memories from hundreds and thousands of years past whipped through Dexx's head as he thought about just how old Mah'se was. Other animals just like Mah'se grazed throughout the ages, keeping a vigil over the lands, doing as he'd directed.

"Who are you?"

"He's kind of the lead protector around here," Dexx said, shaking it off. "You remember McCree?"

Rainbow nodded with a pained frown. She'd been captured with the Red Star team and held captives.

"Mah'se's the spirit he used to steal shifter abilities. So, you may not want to tell him all about eating him up. He's taking you literally."

Her petite lips rounded with alarm and understanding.

"I'm sorry we hit a cultural barrier here." She gave the elk a big smile and bent at the knee in an almost-curtsy-pee-pee-dance gesture. "When I say I want to eat you all up, it means I can't get enough of you. In a good way because you're so cool. I mean, who could? You're so big and strong and so sleek and rugged, and those horns? Let me be the first to say I like big hair." She shook her head, and her afro wobbled alternately to her shakes.

Mah'se raised a foot but dropped it again.

"And as far as big hair goes, I don't think you have *any* competition. Can I pet you? I'm *dying* to pet you. Are you as soft as you look? I mean, how would I know? I just got here. Can I pet you? Please? Please?"

Mah'se turned his head to Dexx as if in question.

"She may never stop begging." And she wouldn't. "She really is sweet, and I don't think she'd hurt you."

The elk stood his ground. That was likely the *only* invitation Rainbow was going to get.

Yeah. Except Rainbow wasn't great at taking hints. "Things would move faster if you just accept that she's a friend. She wants to pet you. Just let her because she'll start using more words faster."

"That's not true." Rainbow wrinkled her brow. "I'm usually quiet as a mouse." She turned to Mah'se. "I wouldn't hurt those either, but Dexx hunts those without any regards to their feelings. Me? I *love* animals, and I just adore anything to do with critters. Big ones, small ones, winged ones, water ones, just so many. Except the spider. Oo, that one wasn't nice. It was scary, and all those pointy legs and the way it moved— not natural. Not natural at all. But all the others, you couldn't *get* me to say anything bad about them, let alone be a meany. And another thing, I—"

Mah'se looked from Dexx to Rainbow and back to Dexx.

"I warned you." He shrugged at the spirit.

Mah'se dipped his head and took a hesitant step forward.

Rainbow stopped the flow of words and made reassuring clucking noises at him.

He sniffed her fingers, and after a moment, Rainbow positively mauled him. Politely.

She hugged. She petted. She put her head to his side. She scratched. She pulled his head to her lips. She cooed and giggled and carried on.

Dexx leaned closer to Hattie. "Kinda cute in a completely sheltered, overactive, special needs sort of way."

Hattie's reply was amusement through the bond.

When Rainbow settled to minor mauling, Dexx went back to the study of the red glow in the distance. "Do you know anything about that?"

Hattie followed his look. *None can get near it. I might have been able to at one point, but I am weak. Mah'se will not leave this place to venture near.*

"Why not?" Rainbow frowned at the stag.

My place is here. I am the protector of the spirits of this plane.

And going near the door McCree had used to trap the elk was a bad place to go. Dexx got it. He did. "You don't think *that*—" Dexx pointed to the faraway cliff, "— could be a problem?"

You do not know the pain of what I went through.

Oh, but Dexx did. He really, really did. "I remember clearly enough. I carried some of that pain. True, I didn't get the full monty, but I remember." A memory teased him but was unable to break through the wall in his head. "Doesn't matter what you felt. If those other spirits are in danger, shouldn't *that* be the place you go? If you want to protect them, then you go protect?" Face the enemy.

"Dexx." Rainbow turned a glower his way. "Be nice. He's doing the job he thinks he should be doing. Why don't you go? We'll be fine right here. Won't we, Mister Snuggle-bottoms?"

Dear gods. She'd just regressed to a small girl. "Right. Mah'se, have a nice day. Hattie, you with me?"

Hattie took a step. It might have been closer to a shuffle. They walked along the edge of the bluff, keeping the cliff on their left. He guessed they might be going wettish-ly?

Rainbow didn't move. She stuck right by Mah'se, a hand buried in his fur.

The elk's head swiveled as Dexx and Hattie shuffled by.

Time and space worked differently in the Time Before. Sometimes, it took forever to cross large distances. Sometimes, it didn't.

If there is a danger to the spirits here, Mah'se said quietly. *I should go as well.* He took a few steps, a little more actively than Hattie or Dexx, and caught up to them quickly.

Rainbow gave a little smirk and then hurried to his side.

Had that been an act? That little mink.

"I'm coming too," she said. "You'll probably need me to keep a sharp eye on things. Or important work. Yeah, important stuff."

Oh, that woman, but Hattie had him worried. "That thing still bothering you?" Dexx walked with Hattie at her pace. Much slower than it should have been. He didn't know *how* the spell was affecting her, but shouldn't it be better with him there?

You always watch the hunt, then ask if the hunt is hunting.

Dexx had no idea *what* that even meant.

The power is still being taken from me. From the bond.

That was what he was asking. "Is it still on my side? Or is it here now?" Because he was there and putting her in danger.

My strength is not here. You must stop the ebb.

Sure. As soon as he figured out what *that* even meant.

"Heh. That's kind of cool, you using boating terms." Dexx's mouth ran in front of his head, but he had to do anything to steer the conversation away from... him and his brother.

Do you wish to get to the source today? Mah'se had picked up the pace.

Rainbow had no trouble matching him.

"I'm going as fast as my cat can." And Dexx wasn't going to push it. "You want to go faster, you'll have to let her ride."

"Oo. Can *I* ride?" Rainbow bounced on her toes. "I've always wanted to ride a magnificent animal like you. You're the best one in the whole world. I mean this one and mine, you know. Can I? Dexx, a little help here? I'm going to ride, but I don't know if I can climb up all by myself."

Was she poking fun at him somehow? There was so much to this woman Dexx didn't get.

Mah'se shook his head, his antlers almost brushing the trees. *The little one will* not *ride on my back.*

"Never say never, dude." Dexx wouldn't put it past her to force the issue later.

Rainbow's expression was a little smug, her eyes calm and mature, but she kept walking.

What was she playing at? "That brings up an interesting question, though. *Why* can't we just teleport? We did last time."

"We can do that," Rainbow said with excitement. "I wanna do that. I've read all about it, and I think it would be such a lovely thing. Not as good as Mossy, but so cool."

Mah'se

"Mahhh say. Right-right?" Rainbow winked.

"Yeah. Mah'se, is there something I should know about? Every time I come here, something else is messed up."

That. Is. Why. You. Do. Not. Belong. Here. The tone in Mah'se's tone was crystal clear. At least to Dexx.

"I see." Rainbow rubbed her nose, her detective mask in

place. "Whenever Dexx comes here, he screws something up. I know what that's like. Dexx always comes right before something blows up. Like when he went missing, then he came back and knocked me and Frey and Tarik out and kidnapped us and took us all to London and then we all... well things blew up." For the first time, Rainbow lost some bubble from her voice as her gaze lost a bit of light as if pieces to a puzzle were snapping into place.

That is much the same way it is for this place. He brings change that none of us need. Mah'se's words were biting, but he rolled an eye back to Rainbow and softened the tone. He slowed down.

Rainbow rested her hand on his shoulder with a smile.

I am forced to walk, Hattie said, her tone surely. *Mah'se won't leave me. There are dangers here you have not seen. This place is not as easy as yours.*

Not as easy as Earth? Were they thinking of a different Earth? "Yeah, sure, I get that. There are many more dangerous things than demons and angels and witch shamans and deity mythos that can kill us or send us away at a whim. Sure. This place is *way* scarier."

That opening is many days away. Mah'se plodded along, his steps somehow impatient. He tipped his nose in the air in rapid succession—kind of like nodding backwards.

Dexx scratched Hattie behind her ear. He *knew* how good that felt. It was something. Not much, but since he might be the source of her weakness, it was the least he could do for his friend.

A fierce knot of affection came back through the bond.

After a long time of monotonous trudging, the bluff met the plain, and they turned left and headed toward the glowing cliff face. From the plains floor, the glow disappeared. It didn't matter. They knew where they were headed.

But Dexx had things to do, a family to save, and sometimes days here were hours there, but sometimes hours here were days there, and he'd already lost nearly a year. "Seriously, how long do you think it'll take to get there?"

As long as it takes. Hattie's tone was more resigned.

There would be none of that. *You aren't giving up on me, are you, girl?*

I am a shadow of myself.

We can get that back, can't we? Rainbow can't hear us, can she?

No, she will not. They will not hear us if we do not want them to. She swung her dump-truck-sized head toward him. *But as for the other thing, only time will tell.*

Rainbow was talking with Mah'se, though for once, she wasn't the one doing most of the talking. She'd actually managed to get him to share some.

Maybe she did have some magick.

Hattie didn't look good from the start, but soon Dexx felt her weariness through their bond.

The cliffs looked closer, though. Maybe?

"Let's stop here for the night." Dexx turned in a slow circle, only then finding them on top of a small rise.

Mah'se snorted. *This is too exposed. Something with cover on all sides is best.*

What was going to hunt them here? "Sure. Why not? Then, anything could take us by surprise."

Would you not like a fire, cub? Hattie asked. *I remember you liked to do that when we went out hunting.*

A fire didn't sound bad. "You know someplace like that like right around here?" Dexx scanned the area, but nothing really jumped out at him, which was kinda the point.

Just a bit farther. Mah'se continued walking and also continued with the story he was telling the rusalka.

They wound up in a thicket of trees Dexx hadn't seen from the top of the rise. He could just barely see the top of the cliffs in the distance. Hattie was beyond tired. He didn't know how much longer she'd be able to go. "This place should do nicely." Shouldn't it?

"I agree. Don't you, Maaa say?" Rainbow enunciated his name to comic levels.

The elk inclined his head. *This place will satisfy.*

"Good." Dexx was exhausted. His cat was exhausted. The quiet—the sheer fact that they hadn't been attacked for *hours* on end was allowing his adrenaline to lower to normal levels and, with that, his ability to remain awake. "Who has food?"

Rainbow stared at him with an empty expression.

Dammit all to the nine Hells.

11

Dexx needed food and sleep but wasn't sure what order he needed it in. "Let me guess. Nobody can kill a spirit here. If we do, the spirit dies forever." So, what were they going to eat?

Hattie raised her head from the ground.

Mah'se looked away from the humans. *Not every spirit here will die. And not every creature here is a spirit.*

So, food was possible. "Gotta ask. Can we kill one?"

"*Dexx.* That's so *very insensitive.*" Rainbow flicked her head toward Mah'se but tried to be sly about it. "We would never kill, Mah'se. But could we *harvest* a beautiful, deserving creature to sustain us?"

Must you kill to survive? Mah'se pranced a few steps away. *The animals here did you no harm, and you wish to snuff a life that only wants to live out its days in peace.*

"Shit's getting' deep now. A couple of things wrong with what you just said." Dexx squared off with Mah'se. "You kill to live too. Just nobody thinks plants have feelings or the desire to live." Having a dryad on his team had opened his eyes to a lot of things. "Second, just living is violent. If you *are* a protector, violence is your duty. That is the only way violence is countered. Well, and fear of something bigger, but hey, sometimes you'll actually have to *be* violent. Maybe even kill."

The cub speaks the way of life, as you well know. He has not spoken such wisdom in this life.

"Shut it, fat cat." At least she had enough energy for humor. "Oh, speaking of, could you put on a few pounds? You're making me nervous."

A good meal and having you near should help.

He had to hope so. "But we still need to break the curse."

That will be your hunt. It is not here.

Food first. "Rainbow, you coming?"

Rainbow glanced to the spirit elk with an uncharacteristic frown. "I'm going to stay here and make sure things stay peaceful. I don't want to disturb the balance here."

Dexx got the impression she was talking about something deeper than their conversation. What had Mah'se been talking to her about? "*Now* you're full of peace and love? Okay, I can live with that. Fat cat, can you come out with me?" He already knew the answer.

The time has come for you to hunt alone.

"That's a crock of shit. Big boiling number two pewter pot of bubotuber pus." He was pretty sure he'd caught the *Kung Fu* reference correct. But he understood she was tired. He was just trying to see if *goading* her would work.

It didn't.

His *ma'a'shed* would work for hunting, very nicely *if* he could hold on to it.

He circled the campsite and found stones that would work for a fire ring. He tossed several large rocks toward the group without really looking. "Make a ring with those. If anyone has fire, please make some." Rainbow was already gone from the site.

Okay, so *Dexx* made a really great circle and piled dry sticks in the center.

Rainbow made her way back and squatted with her arms around her knees while he put the last few twigs in place.

He looked up, and she stared back, intently watching.

"You can't make fire."

She shrugged. "Sorry? Water spirit. I'd totally love to learn, though."

Dexx sighed and picked through the rocks that didn't make it to the ring yet. He'd seen plenty of the right stones as they walked, so finding some should be a simple... Excellent. Flintstones with just the right shape and sharpness.

"Okay. So, the secret to fire is three things; fuel, air—mostly in the form of oxygen—and spark. Lose any of those, you got nothing. Heat is another big one, but usually spark covers the heat part."

"How did you learn how to do this?" Rainbow spoke on her chin, watching Dexx sort through the stones.

He picked up a dry stick from the ground.

He ignored Rainbow. "So you gotta make a little fire to get to a big one. So we make a nest. The sharp flint cut a neat slice into the old stick, and he stripped the bark off. Then he scraped the inside of the bark and soon had a fist-sized tangle of shredded inner bark.

Hattie circled and laid down on the ground and watched, but she wasn't interested in the fire, she watched *him*.

"What the three have to do together is make the right conditions for the three to work together. Oxygen is arguably the most important thing here. And the ratio of fuel to oxygen. That's why it needs to be shredded. Super dense wood won't light well, but if you throw that into the fire, it'll burn forever."

"Really?" Rainbow sounded impressed, but her smile said otherwise.

"No." Dexx shook his head, chuckling.

He cupped the wad of stripped bark in one hand and pressed a bit to the flint with his thumb.

"Now, the hard part here is finding another stone with the right properties. Carbon in an iron matrix. Steel, for anyone who knows their rocks. And gently strike." He reached in his shirt and pulled the *ma'a'shed*. "Or if you already have the right tools, use them."

Dexx scraped the rock and the knife together, and at first, all he produced was a scrape of the two. A few more tries, and he remembered the technique. Then sparks sprayed the ground and the dried bark.

A few gentle puffs of air and smoke wafted from the mess. The puffs grew in intensity, and a small flame flicked to life. With a few more concentrated puffs, the fire grew.

The burning bark went into the stack of twigs and caught fire. In a minute, the fire popped and danced happily.

Rainbow warmed her hands with a tired smile. "*That* was *so cool*. I wish I had a dad to teach me how to do that."

His heart hurt for her. *Every* kid deserved to be taught by a knowledgeable parent. "Well, you got me. Did you learn anything?" He held his hands out in a shrug.

"Yes, but there were about two hundred things you *didn't* teach. Like finding the rocks, and how did you know the stick had the right bark? And all the little things."

"Keep the fire going, and I'll show you more. Not too much of the leaves all at once. That makes a lot of smoke, and we want to be… unnoticed. Can you handle that?"

"Sure thing, boss. You know, if I had to be out in the middle of a magickal plane with only one person, I *sure* am glad I got stuck with you." She tossed a small stack of sticks to the fire.

"Thanks, I think. If you have things covered here, I'll go look for something to eat."

Rainbow stood close to Dexx's ear. "Hurry." She whispered with a quick glance to Mah'se. "I'm hungry."

She must really want to impress Mah'se. Why? He didn't seem her type. But then she was a bit more complex than he figured. Maybe. "Sure. Get right on that for you."

Rainbow turned around to make Mah'se comfortable. Or at least she yanked handfuls of tall grass to give to the guardian. Why was she trying so hard?

Time to head off into the grey overcast of the Time Before.

Every time Dexx had visited the place and had sat with Hattie on the bluff over the plain, where animals dotted the landscape. Not one had stuck around to be hunted.

Damn it.

He went back to the rise over their campsite. He still smelled traces of the fire, but that should help him hide. Mostly.

Gently, he poked his head above the rise to see... empty grassland.

He lowered himself back to the ground. "Come on. Really?"

He wasn't going to see anything from this level. The sound of animals pulling up grass and chewing loudly caught his ear. He lifted his head again to see a herd of... animals of some sort tore at the short grass.

What the... Nope.

He wasn't looking a gift horse in the mouth, no matter if it didn't follow the rules.

Twenty or so of the things—he actually didn't know what they were. They looked like a cross between a zebra, gazelle, and some kind of horse—grazed on the grass. None of them seemed particularly concerned

Hey, fat cat. Can you hear me?

All these animals had virtually the same markings of brown splotches on a grey hide with a striped rump. The males had antlers that gently curved up to end at a knob. He'd never seen these before, not even on prehistory documentaries.

Yes. Are you lost already?

The creatures looked strong and healthy, and none looked exactly like another. It was a strong herd. He needed to pick a big one, but not the biggest, and not a baby.

I need to know what these are and if they're okay to hunt. Dexx didn't think that these were the bond-human type animals, but he wanted to make sure. He found a likely target near the edge of the herd and stalked slowly toward it. He wouldn't be a threat until the very end.

I am cut off from what you see. We can still talk. If it is a herd animal, you should be safe.

It was a herd animal. So, at least there was that.

Do you need help on your hunt?

His target ate peacefully. *No, I just thought you'd like to see. I miss our hunts together. Kinda thought we could have one where we weren't jammed together in the same body.*

She grunted but didn't say anything.

Dexx kept his movements smooth and silent.

Do you remember when we did this together?

I do. You were less of a hunter and more of a playing cub.

Ouch. That hurt. *Was not.*

The buck of whatever animal that was kept eating, never looking up. A few more steps and he could throw his demon knife. With a little luck, he could get closer. The shorter the throw, the more likely he could bring the animal down. Another step. Another.

His heart beat in his chest, and his hearing sharpened and fuzzed at the same time. He heard his blood flowing, the soft rip of the grass, and the crunch of the blades being chewed.

The animal lifted a foot to step forward, swinging its head

in Dexx's direction. Thick animal lips gathered greens and short teeth nipped.

Gather, nip. Gather, nip.

Dexx let himself flow into the rhythm of the buck. He took one step forward when it looked away. He stopped when it swung back. Two more steps, and he closed the distance. He could reach out and hit the buck on the back. He *could*.

He slipped the *ma'a'shed* away. He didn't actually need it. Not for this one. He lunged at the buck.

It startled, just realizing the danger.

Dexx flew just over its back and grabbed its jaw with a hand, and kept on going over. The beast's head came around with Dexx's grip and kept coming over. The sudden resistance rolled him underneath and to the point where the body had to follow its head and flopped on its back, with its head bound up in Dexx's grasp.

The rest of the herd thundered away as the buck kicked the air, looking for purchase. It tried to scream, but Dexx had its nose covered and closed, his other hand on its windpipe and carotid arteries.

What the hell? Those were Hattie's instincts and hunting method. Did this place fuzz their spirit to the point where he wouldn't be able to recognize where she ended, and he began? Would it matter if he could keep her?

The buck's kicks weakened and slowed.

"Thank you, brother." Dexx didn't enjoy taking a life and needed to show his respect. "Your life will sustain mine and my friends. I hope you can come back and live in the peace you deserved. I will carry you with me always."

Wild eyes flashed once more with the last desperate kick of life, and the buck relaxed into death.

A sudden stench crashed into Dexx's nose. The thing crapped all over the ground.

"Yup. The glories of *harvesting*." Dexx stood and looked

around. The herd had settled not too far off on another rise. "The circle continues."

He hefted his kill and slung it over his neck. It wasn't the biggest animal, but he should still feel the weight more than he did. *Did you feel the kill?*

Yes. Hattie sounded pleased. She *was* a predator, after all, and this was how she survived. Well, maybe not now, but she had at some point, and hunting was her way of life.

In a shorter time than seemed possible, Dexx poked back through the thicket into the protection of the fire and the trees, and a boulder that felt familiar.

"Hey, boss." Rainbow stood from Mah'se, now lying next to Hattie.

Those two seemed to actually be making friends. Mah'se looked relaxed, and so did Rainbow. Nice.

"You bring back— aw." Rainbow's face twisted in remorse, but her tone didn't change. "This one was so cute. Did you *have* to?"

Dexx wasn't sure what she was giving the aw-face about. "What? You expected me to bring back slabs of meat on a Styrofoam plate wrapped in plastic?"

Her look of regret changed a little as she pushed her lips out and up toward her nose as if she was thinking the whole harvesting thing out. "Not Styrofoam necessarily..."

Oh, that poor sweet kid was going to get an experience of her life. "Well, this is what it looks like before it *didn't* die at the store. I guess I have to butcher it out?"

Rainbow pressed her lips together and set her shoulders. "No. I *know* how. Just didn't want to." She held her hand up, and she changed almost completely. Her eyes went black, and her hands turned to needle-sharp knives. Her teeth grew to sharp points, and her skin went to a dead grey.

Dexx backed up a little startled himself. So, this was what

a rusalka looked like. "I see. Do what you gotta do." Would there be anything left for the rest of them?

Rainbow worked with brutal efficiency away from the camp and was done a lot sooner than Dexx would have been. By the time she made it back, he'd been able to stoke the fire and check on his sleeping Hattie.

Rainbow pulled in a branch-made sled with meat, looking like a sadder, grimmer version of her normal self.

"Someday, you're going to tell me about your family reunions."

"Maybe not." Gone was the normal, chipper tone. "I don't like that side of myself." She looked down at the ground. "I'm a monster. A real monster."

A sentiment he understood all too well. "No more than me. Maybe less. You only chopped it up. I felt its life leave its body. Who's the bigger monster?"

Rainbow sniffed and wrapped Dexx in a bloody hug.

He hugged back. Monsters needed to stick together.

After the moment was over, Dexx threw Hattie some of the raw meat and tossed some chunks to the fire to cook.

Mah'se stripped leaves from low bushes and cropped the grass even shorter.

This was the first time Dexx had actually seen either of them act normally. "So, as a spirit, do you need to eat?"

Mah'se pulled viciously at a twig. *Only if we want. Food provides sustenance, but it is not to live. It instead gives life meaning.*

Dexx wasn't super sure what that meant. "Sweet. Sounds cool."

Rainbow had fallen silent for the most part after her transformation and sat with her knees pulled to her chest.

Mah'se went to his front knees, then plopped on the ground, curling around her. With a sigh, she turned and hugged his neck.

Rainbow hid a lot of pain deep, something Dexx could

relate to. He hid his pain with snarky and humorous commentary. She hid hers with happiness and optimism.

Dexx snuggled into Hattie's fur that felt tons better after she had eaten. She'd eaten quite a bit, too. So, he was hopeful she was on the road to healing.

Dexx kept one of the long leg bones, long and knobby on both ends. He cleaned it and dried it over the fire. It would work as another weapon if he dropped the knife again and as a reminder of the kill.

The four went to sleep. Oddly fast.

Dexx woke up, refreshed but without having any dreams at all. This might have been the first time he'd actually *slept* in days. Dexx wasn't sure what had awakened him, but there was a near-constant deep rumble that practically vibrated the ground. When he opened his eyes, the cliffs loomed above them. "How in the—"

Hattie raised her head. She looked almost normal. Her eyes were brilliant green, her fur soft and flowing.

Rainbow had managed to somehow burrow deep under Mah'se. She looked... really uncomfortable, but she breathed slow and deep, so maybe not.

Mah'se raised his head, looking around, and then made a move to rise.

Rainbow stirred and then stood, stretching. "That was nice. You make a great pillow."

The spirit looked at Dexx with worry in his brown eyes.

Dexx shrugged. "Not my rodeo, not my clown." Shit. She *was* his clown. And part of his rodeo. "She's a great kid. Big heart. Loves people."

Mah'se lowered his head to look Rainbow directly in her eyes. *You may ride with me.*

Her hands shot up to her mouth. "You mean it? Like I can ride?"

Dexx spoke up fast. "Don't be too out of control. Be cool,

okay?" Could she *really* have made a friend in Mah'se? She was an impressive woman, with hidden talents, for sure.

"I am the *picture* of cool, boss."

"Sure. Want help up?" He moved to give her a perch to stand on.

Mah'se took care of that by kneeling down while Rainbow clambered up. She was oddly graceful. Whatever.

The walk to the cliff was short. Too short. They found the source of the red glow and a thin haze of smoke that rose from it and disappeared.

Dexx and Hattie left Rainbow and Mah'se on the far side of the small rise so they could sneak up to the source of the glow, which turned out to be a massive cave lit from the inside with heat. Lava-like heat.

A mildly steep slope led to a hidden entrance of the cave.

Great.

Stepping to the slope to go deeper inside, Dexx was a little in awe of the cave paintings. But that wasn't what surprised him the most.

Merry fucking Eastwood and Mario Kester of fucking DoDO stood with their backs to the cave opening.

They were sacrificing a demon.

What the fucking hell?

12

Dexx backed up a step and ducked behind a rock. He waved Hattie back, and she crouched down in a stalking position.

What is this place? Hattie inched forward. How did she look clumsy and graceful all at once?

Sounds echoed from the cave. Voices.

Dexx peaked around the rock and looked into the mouth of the cave.

There they were, Merry Eastwood and Mario Kester working in a makeshift *hi-tech lab* in a *cave*. How did they get monitors and gurneys and *electricity* into the Time Before? And what the hell did they think they were doing?

Absolutely none of it could have been sanctioned by the AMA.

Mario held a knife over the demon, who was chained to a rock, ready to stab.

Merry held a cup half full of liquid in one hand and made swirling motions over the demon with the other.

The magickal vibration in the cave hurt Dexx's senses. He saw the magickal weave of their intent. Death and blood made powerful spells, but sometimes the result was just too hard to handle.

Mario spoke in words Dexx didn't recognize. Merry repeated his words and continued making the motions with her hand. She stopped at the end of her last chant and lowered the cup.

Mario stabbed the knife into the demon's arm.

The demon roared in pain, then brought his head up as high as his chains would allow. "You insignificant *mortals*. Do you seek to harm me? I'll pull you limb from limb and make you *watch* me *eat* the pieces."

Mario paused his chanting and bent to the demon. "I suppose you could," he said in his easy English accent. "Easily. If you could break these chains. But since you *haven't*, I'm guessing you *can't*. So, certainly, please try."

Merry raised the cup from below the altar, now full to the brim. She twirled a finger at the lip, and the liquid rose to meet it.

Damn it all, that was *blood* reaching out to Merry. *Demon blood.*

Okay. Obviously. She was a blood witch. That was kinda what she did. It was still gross.

She chuckled, low and throaty. "How much did you need? I'm thinking I need a bit of a recharge."

"When I'm done with this," Mario said with a put-out sigh, "you can have the rest. I won't need either of them."

Either of them? Dexx scanned the room again.

Holy crap, he'd missed a second person in the cave strapped to a table, covered in monitoring leads stuck to him with medical tape. Dexx was too far away to tell if it was demon or human.

On a small stainless hospital table on wheels stood a stone figurine.

A *kadu.*

Dexx's stomach fell. "What in the *Hells* are they doing with *that?*"

The actions are like I remember in our past awakenings. Hattie met Dexx's gaze.

What the hell does that mean?

You once did something similar, though I do not fully understand the purpose. You and I were not... Her eye narrowed slightly...*this close.*

Full of good news, aren't you? Dexx tensed to scoot back, but he heard Rainbow softly crunching up the rise to join them. He waved at her furiously to get back.

She frowned at him and shook her head, hiding behind the same stone he did. "What's going on?" She whispered as she pulled her head over the top. Her eyes grew wide as she ducked back into hiding and then frowned in thought. "There was a stone statue. Is that one of those papoo or doodoo rocks you have? Wait. Where *are* they?"

"Gave 'em to Paige. And, *yes*, that's a *kadu*. Wonder where in the Hells they found one." Though, he probably didn't really have to wonder. Bussemi'd had a lot of them, and Dexx didn't know if he'd been able to collect them all on his way out.

Merry and Mario turned from the still-swearing demon and went to the bound man.

"Will you stop playing with that?" Mario grumbled at her with a tip of his head.

Merry flicked her finger, and the blood danced. "I didn't know you were squeamish."

"I'm not. But if you ruin this, I'm going to strap *you* to the table to finish this."

She shrugged slightly but didn't drop her hand. She turned to Mario with hate in her eyes. "I think not. You wouldn't *be* here without my help. And you wouldn't get any further than *this*, either."

That was a good point. How *were* they here?

Mario rolled his chin in agitation. "Just do what we came here for."

What *were* they here for? Dexx made sure he was still hidden by vegetation, so he didn't have to continue ducking down behind the rock.

Rainbow didn't pop back up again. Her eyes were unfocused as she concentrated on listening.

"Just do it." Mario nodded to the man on the table.

"Yes, *master*." Merry's voice dripped with sarcasm. She placed her free palm on the man's chest and chanted something in a different language Dexx didn't recognize again.

The man heaved on the cart like he'd been jolted with a defibrillator. In the red glow of the cavern, the man turned darker.

One of the monitors with a graph on the screen went from yellow to green with a beep.

"What do you know, he was right." Mario turned to the monitor.

Who was right? Dexx had a suspicion it was Bussemi and that Mario was reaping the information Bussemi'd gleaned from his time tormenting and experimenting on Dexx.

"Get on with it." Mario turned to Merry. "We don't have a lot of time to summon and bind."

"Remember, it belongs to *both* of us." Merry lowered her head with a threat.

"Of course. Just get on with it." Mario didn't sound like he was in a very generous mood.

Dexx turned his head back to whisper to Rainbow, but she was gone.

Shit.

He scanned the short hill for her but couldn't find her anywhere. He backed down the slope and stood. "Where in the hell—" He found her making her way around an outcropping heading for a lower cave entrance.

Double *shit*.

He raced down the slope as quickly, skidding on the stones to cut Rainbow off. He didn't know if they could beat Mario *or* Merry in a straight fight here.

His fingers brushed along her arm.

She slipped away from him and barreled headlong into the torture chamber. She grabbed the first thing she could lift and threw it. A monitor. Plugged into the wall.

The cords snapped taut and whipped it to the ground. The crash brought Merry and Mario to attention.

Dexx rushed in behind Rainbow, not sure what they were supposed to do.

Merry finished her incantation, and a large upright stone ring floating above a stone well flashed a bright blue, then settled to a shimmery darkness filling the center.

Dexx leapt at Merry like a football tackle and smashed her to the floor.

The cup went flying, flinging blood everywhere.

Dexx freed his inner feminist and punched Merry in the face. He rose, destroying everything he could reach, following Rainbow's lead. Whatever her plan had been, she'd gone in half-cocked, but he had to back her play.

Though, it felt a little like karma. How many times had he rushed in without a plan?

Rainbow went full berserker and trashed everything within her reach.

He spared her a snap-glance and almost ran. She had turned into the creature that waited in nightmares and in dark stairwells. Her face had gone pale and sharp, her hair hung in lank clumps where her afro didn't resemble sticks twisted among it. Razor claws had replaced her hands and fingers.

She went after the monitors and yanked cords, spilled tables with equipment, stabbed and slashed, but stayed away from the demon.

"Human—" The demon roared either at Dexx or at Rainbow. "—release me, and I will reward you."

No fucking chance *that* was gonna happen.

Dexx spun on Mario, letting his leg bone slip in his hand to the end to use as a club. He swung as Mario danced back.

Rainbow kept up her destruction, destroying everything. When she got to the human prisoner, she began tugging at the leather straps.

Hattie and Mah'se ran to the cave entrance and stopped. *Cub, we cannot come in. The way is barred.*

Shit. Those two could have *really* helped.

Dexx swung his club at Mario's head.

The mage dodged.

Dexx swung the bone at Mario's side and connected, but in a flash of light, it stopped bounced harmlessly away.

This wasn't working.

Mario smirked and began weaving magick for a counterattack.

Dexx swiped at Mario's feet.

Mario jumped easily over the swing.

While Mario was preoccupied with flight, Dexx moved forward and grabbed Mario to full-on body slam him to the floor, just on the other side of Rainbow and the struggling man.

The weave of magick dissipated but left the room charged with unused energy.

Dexx cocked his arm back for another head hit, but Mario caught his fist with both his hands. He brought his legs up and wrapped Dexx, flexing hard, throwing Dexx to the floor. Mario sat on top of Dexx, but now Mario was locked up as they both strained to break free first and land a solid hit.

Rainbow worked the last strap on the man's leg.

His head swiped back and forth, spouting gibberish, and his hands and body shook with palsy as he reached for Rainbow.

The man's eyes locked on her. "Please." His voice came out as a croak.

Merry stood up, Mario's knife in hand, but she held it by the blade and said something Dexx didn't understand.

Mario let go and hopped off Dexx, turning to Merry. "No, Don't—"

Merry's last word hit the cave with concussive force. She took half a step back.

She flipped the knife by Rainbow's head, that buried right up to the hilt in the man's heart.

He convulsed once and stopped moving.

Dexx stood and grabbed Mario's shoulders, throwing him back to the ground. He got two more hits in before Mario caught his hands again and flipped Dexx over.

He didn't learn from the first time.

Dexx rolled on the floor with Mario, both trying to get a good hand-hold on the other, but they really only succeeded in working dirt into their clothes. Dexx finally managed to get the upper hand by rolling on top of Mario and scooping up the legbone club in his hands, and going slowly pressing toward his throat. "Going to choke you out, buddy. Then I'm going to feed you to my cat."

"You talk too much." Mario... twitched his fingers.

Dexx went flying through the air toward the stone ring, now gathering motes of light in the center. He hit the ground hard and slid hard into the stonework base.

A gentle breeze wafted across his skin for the briefest second. In the next second, the gentle breeze picked up to a goodly wind.

Dexx pressed a hand to the floor, trying to stand. The pain

rushed in from all sides, and the wind picked up to a good blow.

"I hate you." Rainbow rushed toward Merry, her rusalka hands clawed.

"Not today, little girl." Merry brought one hand up, hard and flat, her palm out, then twisted it inward.

Rainbow jerked to a halt, confusion replacing anger and fear replacing confusion in her eyes.

Mario lay on the ground, catching his breath. Whatever that spell was had to have taken a lot out of him.

Dexx stood and stalked forward against the wind.

Mario needed to die first. That bastard had months of torture to answer for.

Rainbow looked scared but confident. She had her battle under control.

"...I've been around a long time. I know things, even *your* people forgot." Merry slipped a slim-bladed knife from her sleeve. "I know how to bleed you and your power." Merry drew the knife back to throw but didn't.

The wind rose to a gale, focused on the stone ring and the glowing center. The ground heaved and gonged, echoing out to the flat land beyond.

Dexx slammed his hands over his ears.

The wind went beyond a gale, straight past hurricane, pushing anything not nailed to the floor, which was everything.

The cave boomed again.

Dexx held on to a rock outcropping.

Rainbow and Merry leaned into the wind, trying to stay upright, but they were done moving toward each other.

The cave boomed, the ground heaved. No, not the cave, the stone altar. It glowed with an inner heat from stone to deep orange. It smoked, gaining temperature fast.

Dexx felt the earth fall from his feet before it came rushing back again with force.

Before he had a chance to recover, the earth moved again, hitting him. Hard. The impact took his breath away.

No biggie, he'd fight without the air the rest of them had access to.

This was such a bad fight. He needed to get him and Rainbow out of there.

The wind ended abruptly with a dry sort of slurp and a thump.

The stone ring was as cold as the rest of the cave, feeling colder from the sudden absence of heat.

Rainbow stood frozen in place. She looked from Merry to Mario and Dexx. Rusalkas weren't cute, but a confused rusalka looked comical.

Mario hunched over, holding his stomach, and lurched away from the altar-well. He raised a hand, and a doorway opened. He stumbled through, and Merry followed, holding her face where Dexx had punched her.

Dexx twisted his head up to the stone ring.

The thing might as well be dead. It was now just a stone ring.

The demon was just as dead. No twitch, no signs of life. And no demon-holes to collect the body. That couldn't be good

He sucked air into his lungs, his ribs giving him pain.

Rainbow eyed the now-closed door the enemies had disappeared through and headed over to him. "You okay?" She glanced at the demon, chained to the rock.

A tear glistened at the corner of his eye from the pressure in his head. *Yeah, sure. I'm just fine. Why would you ask? I only had an entire planet body-punch me. It got a critical hit with a flanking bonus. What could be wrong?*

That was not your usual response. Hattie sounded confused.

"What did he say?" Rainbow could hear Hattie obviously, just not Dexx.

He said the world attacked him.

"It did? I mean, it shook some, but attack?"

That cannot happen. Mah'se sounded confused. More than a little. *The ground is just there. An attack is made by a living foe.*

The super-cramp in his middle relaxed a little, and Dexx pulled in a lung full of air. "I hate you all." Dexx managed after a couple of breaths. "Foe? Really? Did you learn to speak by old comics or something?"

His chest relaxed, and the pain faded.

The ancient elk glared from the cave mouth. *I speak how I speak.*

"Yeah, just, whatever. What the hell was all that?"

Hattie shook her head. The human move looked odd on her, but also well-practiced. *We don't know. That has never been done here.*

Dexx struggled to his feet. Things spun, and he needed the stone base to keep him upright. But he stood, damn it all.

Rainbow was uncommonly serious. "That was Mario and Merry. What were they doing here?" She helped steady Dexx.

"Thanks." He didn't want to admit he needed help. But Hattie would probably just tell everyone anyway. So, there was no point in hiding it. Once the spinning slowed to just under frantic, he took a step. He almost rolled an ankle but almost didn't count. "I don't know *what* they were doing. But if they were here, it wasn't good."

Rainbow turned over destroyed equipment, looking under the rubble and poking her nose everywhere.

"What are you doing?" Dexx leaned against the stonework altar.

"We're detectives. I'm detecting. We know they were here doing something bad. We know they brought a demon, a man, and a *kadu*."

She'd said the word right the first time. Were all the other times she got it wrong just play?

The demon body stayed where it had died. No blood, no trip home. Dexx almost felt sorry for him.

"Yeah." So, what *had* they been up to? And what had Mario said had been right?

Rainbow found the dead body. He was one restraint away from being free, Merry's blade still stuck in his chest.

Rainbow yanked the knife out and wiped the blood on the victim's pants. "I'm going to give this back to her. In her face."

"Wow, Bow." This was certainly a different side of her. "That's kind of dark for you, isn't it?"

"He was almost free. If there's one thing I can't stand, it's…" Rainbow glanced toward him. "Private."

"Um. Okay."

She bent over the dead man and closed his eyes.

Rainbow was chock full of contradictions.

Dexx tipped a table up and stopped.

A kadu.

Dexx reached down and picked it up, wondering why they'd have left this here.

But then he realized why. It was dead. No trace of magic flickered inside.

Fuck.

They'd killed the man and his kadu.

Who had he been? What was Merry and Mario up to?

Mario had looked more hurt than Dexx could take credit for, so what the hell was going on?

"Bow, could you—" Pain seared his head.

Dexx fell over into blackness.

Dexx woke with a splitting headache, the kind that light only made worse. And he was cold.

He cracked an eye open. He didn't see anyone right away, but that didn't mean much. Actual speech seemed like too much work. *You around, fat cat?*

He felt a brush against his mind, but no response.

The headache ratcheted down a fraction. Maybe a little less than a fraction.

Sorry. Hattie. Are you there? He stretched out his senses a little more.

He almost opened his mouth to try to use actual words. Then he felt a stronger touch.

Sorry, girl. Just this headache is—

Thank you very much for showing me the way in, a slithery voice Dexx loathed said inside his head where Hattie should have been.

Dexx jerked upright as fear jolted through him.

The headache was forgotten in the surge of fear.

Bussemi's voice was in his *head*.

I haven't heard from the beast for some time, Bussemi said almost jovially. *Seems it's either dead or scampering away like a scared rabbit. Or you.*

Dexx froze. How was Bussemi here?

Run rabbit, run.

Dexx did. He scrambled to his feet and took a step pushing hard for a sprint as far as he could get.

He bounced off a furry wall and landed hard on his ass.

Mah'se stood above him. *You are not well.*

No shit. "No, I'm not. I have to get out of here. He found me." Dexx'd been dragged out of the cave, but the red that had been there before was gone. Scorch marks trailed up the face of the cliff a hundred feet or so. The pile of equipment looked cold and clinical.

Let it rot.

Cub? Hattie sounded more than a little concerned. *Who has found you? The beast trying to enter the Time Before?*

"Yeah. Mister congeniality himself. Can I go now?"

"Where would you go?" Rainbow squatted next to him.

"Fuck." She was right. Where *could* he go?"

Yes. Where could you run I could not follow? Bussemi asked snidely. *Run and I will follow. I will end you.*

Dexx shivered. Not all of it was from Bussemi's taunt. "Why am I cold? Why didn't you build a fire?"

"I'm water and seem to be anti-fire." Rainbow shrugged with her palms up.

"Didn't I show you how like yesterday?"

"You did, and I followed your instructions to the letter. But..." She gave him a frank look of I-don't-know-how-to-be-optimistic-about-this.

"You're not just playing?" Or being ditzy?

She tipped her head to tell him that she *wasn't* ditzy.

She kinda could be. "How did you stay warm?"

Rainbow's grin quivered. "I used Mossy."

So, they were on knick-name level now.

"Just fine." Dexx sighed.

"What has you in such a mood?" She got up and rubbed her hands together.

Bussemi. That's what. But he couldn't take this out on her. "I'm just tired, and my head still hurts."

Does it hurt? Hattie picked her head up from where she laid. Dexx hadn't seen her curled up. She looked tired, and her fur looked ratty like mats had begun to take over.

"Hey, girl. Didn't see you there. Why didn't you answer?"

You did not call.

"I—" *Can you hear me now?*

Yes. Her head nodded in a very human gesture.

Dammit all to nine Hells. What was Bussemi doing in his head?

"Bow, go gather some wood. I'll start a fire. I suppose I'll have to collect food, too?"

Rainbow raised a finger. "I'm not completely useless. I already built a fire just like you taught me. But... you're gonna have to light it."

Dexx didn't quite believe that Rainbow was unable to light a fire. She really had built it correctly, so all she'd needed to do was spark. Instead of lighting it, he watched her try.

She really was an anti-fire.

He held his hand out for the flint and his knife. Dexx held her eyes while striking the steel and flint without looking at his work. Sparks sprayed the tinder and smoked immediately.

Rainbow stared right back and held her hand over the flickering flames, and they sputtered out.

Fuck.

With the fire properly lit, Dexx turned to Hattie. "Want to go?"

Hunt. She rose up, a little slow and creaky, like an old dog. *How are you being affected like this?*

The connection, our bond, is what is being attacked. I cannot help. This is on your side.

Yeah, I know. And now Dexx understood why, but not how. *Let's go get something to eat.*

They headed out. The cave might be a good place to stay for a few days.

Will you leave your friends all alone in this place? Bussemi asked. *What will you do when I find them? Or if I find you first?*

"You aren't here." At least, Dexx hoped not. Maybe this was like Scorpius and John Crichton in *Farscape*. A little mind nugget was infecting his brain but otherwise harmless. "You're a figment." Dexx swallowed hard. He *had* to be.

I assure you that I am as real as you— Bussemi cut off like someone shut a door in his face.

Where did he go?

Hattie had a smug look on her face.

Maybe someone *had* shut a door in his face.

I have some skill with perception. Hattie thumped against Dexx's back with her shoulder. *As long as we are together, I will keep you safe.*

"Thanks, my loving fat cat. I uh… he terrifies me." He'd never really admitted that out loud before.

You have stuck your nose against a prickleback. And you do not want to touch one again. You must learn how to face it without fear. Your Bussemi can be hunted.

"Porcupines aren't really in the same league as that guy." Though Dexx did appreciate the fact that he understood what a prickleback was and the analogy in the first place. It was pretty apt. "He… did things to me. I'd rather cross the continent than be in the same time zone. I'm just— I'm just broken, I guess."

You are not so broken that you cannot heal. And you will hunt him.

"I'm glad you have confidence." He did not. "Is there any game around here?"

There is always something to hunt if you know where to look.

"I hope so. I could eat a horse." But she could too, judging by the look of her.

Hattie agreed silently.

The two walked silently for a while as they looked for signs.

Does it look a little bare to you?

Things will come back. The mountain has been a bad place for a long time.

Time worked differently in the Time Before. *Like how long? Because I don't remember it here before.*

Much time has passed since the last time you were here.

If you say so. Let's get a rhino and go back.

Are you certain you would like one of those? Uncertainty filled her voice.

No. Not really. He was mostly hiding his feeling behind jokes. *I just want enough that we all can eat. Is there something like that we can get?*

A little patient stalking will get us food.

A little patient stalking. What that wound up being were several small antelope type grazers. Dexx lugged four of them, and Hattie carried two in her mouth.

Rainbow barely contained her glee when they came back. Her eyes lit up, and she bounced on her toes.

She didn't even put up much resistance when Dexx asked if she would harvest them. She *did* pull them behind the bushes to dress them.

How long could Hattie keep his mind safe? How long could *anything* keep Bussemi away? The currents had blocked him, and now he was back. Hattie blocked him, and how long before she couldn't? Bussemi seemed to grow in power. How?

Dexx sharpened sticks with the *ma'a'shed*. Roasting sticks had never been easier. He speared meat and propped it above the flames to get the juices flowing.

Rainbow tore in, taking huge chunks out with teeth sharper than normal, and Hattie did too, but she went after guts first, then gorged herself with the meat Dexx didn't cook.

"Damn, there's a lot of gross in this camp."

Rainbow raised an eyebrow as she chewed. "Yeah—" She swallowed a bite and ripped more meat off. "I'm not sure what I did in the cave, but I'm starving."

It seemed to be the case with everyone except Mah'se. Dexx blew on a strip of cooked meat. "Wish we had some salt. Some steak seasoning would taste good too."

"Mm." Rainbow nodded.

"How long was I out?"

She held up her finger as she chewed and swallowed. "It's hard to tell, but I'd say a few hours? It took me a long time to finally give up on that fire."

"Oh." The tingle of a headache tickled the inside of his head. "Well, I'm done. I'm going for a walk. Hattie, you want to go?"

Hattie rose to her paws and shook. Her fur looked much better now.

"Please don't burn the camp down. I'd hate to come back to smoking cinders." Not that Dexx thought that was likely with as anti-fire she was.

"Sure thing, boss, I'm just gonna eat." She waved him away with the back of her hand. "Shoo."

Dexx led Hattie away.

They didn't go very far before Dexx sat down on a low hill facing a horizon in the distance. "I've been doing some thinking. Like in between trying to die and not *actually* dying. When I leave here, you aren't coming with me, are you?"

Not like we are now.

There was more she wasn't saying. So, he gave her time.

If you found a way out now, we would no longer be bonded.

"We could just bond again, right?" That might actually be their answer.

That is possible. But you are magick borne, and your essence is bound to the stones.

But he'd been bonded to her through a bite before. "My *kadu.*" Which hadn't been around when he'd been bitten on the blood moon in Colorado only a handful of years ago. But that wasn't his biggest problem. "I have to break the ward Bussemi has on me before I can go back."

Yes.

"That's all, no pressure." Lots of pressure, but he'd already known that. He wasn't sitting here asking her to repeat how bad a situation they were in. His mind was working through possible solutions, and coming up blank. "Let me just dig my ward-breaker out of my other pants. Oops. Forgot those in the real world."

She growled, low and quiet.

He figured if anyone got him, it would be her. "I'm not mad at you. Really I'm not. It's just my frustration at myself mostly. I keep thinking that if I did things differently that maybe I wouldn't be here like this. Wedged—" He speared his hand out and twisted it. "—between a rock and Bussemi." He pulled his *ma'a'shed* out and flipped it into the dirt.

Hattie sighed.

He reached forward and pulled it out, palming the handle.

Hattie laid down, her paws out front. She nudged her head against his shoulder, nearly pushing him over.

"Fat cat. Go on a diet."

Cub. Learn to hunt.

He had proven he could *hunt*. But what would it take to take down prey like Bussemi? Someone he'd been running from for lifetimes. The sheer magnitude of that thought hit him in the face. Fuck. "How come I haven't spent more time here? No, don't answer that. If I— we get out of this, I'm going to spend more time here."

Hattie rubbed her head on him again. This time, he scratched her behind her ear in the thick fur.

The tingles of the headache increased.

Dexx imagined he could hear Bussemi's whispers coming through the bond.

Fuck him.

"So I gotta ask, I'm sure I did before, but why doesn't the sun pop out, or set or anything?"

This world moves like the water or the sky.

"Duh, water and sky move the way they move in the real world, too. What I'm asking is why is it different here?"

Why does it have to work the way you are accustomed to? Who is to say that is the only real world?

"Dammit. Why do you have to inject logic into my perfectly lined-up way of thinking? All those riddles got you philosophical, now?" He nudged the cat, joking around with her taking a bit of the edge off his growing anxiety. "I'm only kidding. You might have a bit more wisdom than I want to admit."

I know.

"Kind of my line."

I know.

"Dammit." But he didn't really mean it. He wasn't really feeling the push to antagonize her. He just wanted to talk.

To keep his mind off the growing low throb in Dexx's head as he absently rubbed his hand over Hattie's fur.

She was soft and warm, but a bit coarser hair than a housecat would have. When he reached the end of her paw, he dug a claw out. "Shit, those are big."

You have seen them many times.

"Yeah, when I'm slaying bad guys, but not in sit down and say 'Hey, I have claws I wonder what they look like not all bloody.'"

Hattie chuckled in his head.

They sat for a while overlooking the plains where the sun never set in companionable silence.

Rainbow ruined the moment just as his headache reached painful. "Hey, are you guys coming back? We were worried about you."

"No, Bow. I just wanted some alone time with my favorite cat." He rubbed his temple, trying to break through the pain.

"What's wrong? I thought the currents were taking care of that." She squatted down and took Dexx's face in her hands. They were cool and gentle, and for a moment, the pain let off a little.

Not enough to bring back the moment with Hattie, though. "Guess it's not working so well anymore." Dexx pushed her hands away gently and stood. "We should be getting back. Maybe I can sleep the pain away."

"Won't those get worse unless you… uh, break the spell?"

"Yeah." Dexx didn't know that, but he was getting that feeling. He led the way back, rolling his head to loosen his muscles and help put his head on right.

Mah'se waited for them back at the camp, laying down by the fire staring into the coals.

"Fun pastime, isn't it?" Dexx sat on the ground across from the giant stag.

It is more enjoyable than I would have put to it. I do not like fire.

"Yeah, I bet most animals don't. I can't control it. Shit, you generally can't light it." He stared into the coals, grateful the light of the fire wasn't setting off his head. He pulled the *ma'a'shed* out and scratched in the dirt.

As he let his mind go, the headache shuffled someplace distant as the coals took more and more of his thoughts.

Rainbow shook him. "...starting to worry me. Please be okay."

"Huh? What?" Dexx looked around for the danger. But there was none—still just the four of them out in the middle of nowhere in the Time Before.

"You were talking. And you were drawing."

"No, I wasn't."

"You *were*. See that?" She pointed to the scratching in the dirt.

It wasn't just scratches with the demon knife. It was clean, precise. And it looked a helluva lot like a map.

"What the Hells? That doesn't look like any place I've ever seen before." He stared at the lines and symbols.

"Oh, my." Rainbow took a step back and met his gaze. "I've seen this before. I know what this is."

"Care to share with the rest of us?"

"I dreamed this."

Great. "So, we're dream sharing now?" What could that mean, though?

She bit her lip, her expression worried. "And I know how to get there."

14

"**Y**ou've got to be shitting me." Dexx stood up, trying to make sense of the map, looking for something to hope for.

"I wouldn't do that, boss. You're my favorite turd."

Damn it. She made him laugh. "Okay, you get points for that. Now, about the map. Why do *you* know it, *I* do not, and somehow *I* draw it?" And was this something he could use, or was this Bussemi?

"Who knows how these things work?" She shrugged. "They just do. And if it helps, why ask why? If we can get here—" Rainbow pointed to the edge of the drawing. "—I can get us here." She pointed to a spot on the map that looked like a can of worms plopped in the desert.

Dexx made a noise halfway between a word and strangled frustration. *Can we get to the edge of the map?*

That is a place I do not know. Mah'se and I will travel with you, but you will have to lead us.

Could he *trust* the information? Damn. Damn, damn, *damn it*. Dammit all to hell. "Do you have *any idea at all* how to get to this place?" Asking Rainbow to take them to a place nobody knew was a long shot. A real Hail Mary kind of thing.

Rainbow scrunched up her face and set her chin on her finger. "I'm feeling the pull that way." She pointed to the direction Dexx always thought of as west. The trees grew taller in the distance, and as far as he could see. That forest could be immense.

If this was Bussemi's doing, he'd proven he had influence on Dexx. Certainly. On *her,* though? "That's as good a direction as any. Start now or later?"

She looked around their camp. "I dunno. When would *you* say the best time is?"

Hattie was looking good at the moment. Mah'se was fine. The sun never really set. They'd all eaten and had eaten well. And waiting around wasn't going to buy them anything. "I guess now's fine."

"Okay."

It didn't take them long to break camp, to put out their fire, gather the remaining meat, and head out toward the tall trees.

Dexx left first, not wanting to waste any more time.

Mah'se and Hattie ambled along behind him.

A minute later, Rainbow caught up with them, puffing air. "I found this when you were out with Hattie." She held out the fire-hardened bone Dexx had made from the deer thing he harvested the first night in the Time Before. One end had broken off to jagged, sharp points.

He wasn't sure why he needed it. "Thanks. I think. Do I even need to keep this around?"

"Sure, why not? You worked on it a while, so…"

He shook his head but grabbed the knobby bone and pressed the points into the ground. "I hope this trip doesn't take long." He wasn't sure why they were there, but he was *more* than glad to get a short respite. He needed one. That was for sure.

"Hey, boss, can I ask you something?" She turned her head to him as they walked.

"Is there anything I can say to stop you?"

"No, probably not." Her normally peppy smile was damped a little as her expression turned somber. "So anyway, why tonight? Why did you pick to start tonight instead of after we sleep?"

"What kind of question is that?"

Confusion rolled off Hattie, too.

"I'm trying to get a feel for leadership. You never know. Someday I may lead Red Star. That'd be cool, wouldn't it?"

He'd *actually* prayed that she never had to lead herself out of a paper sack, let alone a whole police department. And although she was much better recently, that probably wouldn't happen. Though he *was* discovering there was more to this woman than he'd at first thought. Did she have it in her? "Sure."

"So, why did you?"

"Decide to leave now?"

"Yeah."

"We wouldn't have gained anything by staying. We were rested, fed, watered, and still no closer to finding a solution to our problem."

"What do you think our biggest problem is?"

There were a few. "Bussemi."

"Haven't you been chasing him for lifetimes?"

Dexx nodded, not having a real answer to give her. "Or he's been chasing me? I don't know. I have to figure out what's different this time."

"Okay. So, let's run down the list."

That was an idea. He hadn't tried that yet. "Well, for one

—" He skirted the first big tree of the forest. "—Hattie says our bond is different."

"How so?"

He was not born with me this time. He had to be turned.

"Why's that?"

We decided we needed our bond to be stronger when he died the last time.

Dexx had to find a path around a rather large rock, but either way was steep. "So, we decided to have me come back powerless was the right way to go?"

I did not decide this, and I do not know why you chose this path. Hattie leapt onto the boulder and disappeared on the other side. *Before this lifetime, you never needed my opinion for anything.*

Rainbow made a *yikes* face and edged on the down-hill side of the massive rock.

Yeah. It didn't sound as if they'd always had the best bond in their other lifetimes. *Sorry, fat cat.*

Hattie didn't respond.

"So, without powers—without magick—I needed to be bitten."

It appears so.

There had to be a reason. If only there was a way to regain those memories. But what if he discovered the secret to this life and the Bussemi-version in his head discovered it?

Well, maybe that Bussemi-bot wasn't connected to the real Bussemi. Maybe it really was like Scorpius in *Farscape,* an implant made to slowly invade Dexx's mind until it was able to start taking control. Did that make him feel any safer? Not really, and yes. "What did I gain in this lifetime that I didn't have in the others?"

Hattie snorted as he finally joined her on the other side of the boulder. *Besides a clan to join you?*

A "clan" of people he couldn't afford to bring into this fight? "Yeah. Besides that."

She puffed out a breath. *Nothing*.

"But what if *that's* what you were supposed to find this time?" Rainbow threw out there as she stumbled on a root and caught herself.

Dexx shook his head. There was no way he was volunteering *any* of his people to be slaughtered by Bussemi because that was *exactly* what would happen.

"Think about it," she continued, massaging her palm.

"You okay?"

She waved him off. "What if with your magick you were just too much of a jerk?"

Hattie snorted.

Rainbow widened her arms and gave Dexx a wide-eyed look of "see?" as she continued down the widening path.

The trees fell away, and soon they were in the middle of a sprawling plains. Maybe the forest hadn't been that big. Or could the walk have been shortened?

"What if your magick was the issue."

Well, he'd entertain following the train of thought. "Continue."

She bounced on her toes as she walked. "You and Bussemi were constantly fighting."

"Right." Did they *always* fight? Did Bussemi always find him?

"He's chasing you through lifetimes."

"Maybe poking around and stumbling on my incarnation."

"Sure. You team up with a spirit animal to get away from him."

And it'd worked. But *why* had he done that originally?

"But that wasn't quite *enough*. You then invested lifetimes trying to gain more power, just like him. He's trying to gain more power. *You're* trying to gain more power. You chose a sabertoothed cat. He chose a rock demon." The look on her face said Bussemi had chosen better, but she wasn't going to say that with the sabertoothed cat so close to her.

She was working toward a good and valid point. "So, what did I get this time?"

"Well, a new wardrobe every time you shift for one."

She seriously wasn't funny.

She smiled anyway and scrunched up her shoulders as she stepped into the tall grass. "And... us. You're still kind of an ass. Okay? You are. This thing with Frey—which, by the way, there's something wrong with her. She's not this... *this*. Ever."

"I'd been thinking the same thing." But what?

Rainbow nodded, tipping her head to the side and doing this weird eyebrow wave thing where one went up and then down as the other one rose and then fell. "But that's gotta be it."

That couldn't be it.

"You've got Paige, the Whiskeys. With them, you got almost a whole town, two covens. You've got us—and that's not something to laugh at."

"Bussemi brought you all in, though."

"Through you and only you, and then we all broke out, so... did he? Really?"

She had a point.

"And you have a pack. And you're part of a bigger pack—which is growing, by the way. I don't know what's going on there, but there are more shifters *flooding* in. The currents are all excited about it."

Dexx didn't need to know why. "So, you think the thing I should do is to bring all of you all with me to fight him?"

The look on her face said no as her dark eyes went darker as she remembered being in Bussemi's custody being tortured, but her tone was chipper. "Yup."

Her face told him what her words didn't. He was on the

right path to keep Bussemi as far away from his team as he could. As Paige would say: the end, have a lovely day. "It's something to think about." Over his corpse.

But he also had something else to think about. He had Bussemi in his head. *Can he just get in here?*

Only you can break that bond. Hattie strode next to him, her shoulders working back and forth. *You, cub, are the hardest of all the lives we have shared. I believe your water woman is onto something. Coming back without magick has given you something you never had before.*

So, something beyond people who could die if they stand beside me.

Perhaps.

They walked on in relative quiet. Rainbow wasn't great with silence, and, frankly, neither was Dexx. He didn't feel comfortable inside his own head for so long without at least a small commercial break and, without an audiobook or music to break the silence, it was Rainbow, Mah'se—who wasn't a talker—and Hattie.

Bussemi tried to join in a few times, each time pushing forward with a headache, but Dexx reached over, touched Hattie, and politely invited his mind-virus to leave him the crap alone. They arrived at a vast lake. Or an ocean. The beach stretched on in both directions.

That was fast.

The land wishes us to arrive, Hattie said, a little surprised.

Well, if that was the case, then maybe this wasn't a trap. "So, now what?" Dexx scanned the ocean beach but saw only sand and surf and cliffs in the distance.

Rainbow gave him a scared face, pulling her head into her raised shoulders. "So now we go under."

"Under *where*?" It'd better not be the ocean. But what were they there for? Why had the currents sent him to this place?

"Under the *water*." Rainbow snapped her fingers and winced. "*This* is the edge of the map."

He had to hope that the laws of physics didn't work here. "Fuck me if I'm going for a swim. You don't know what's out there. Not me, I'm not going." What kind of idiot made a map *under* the water?

Rainbow snorted and stepped close to the water's edge. The surf didn't pull away when the rest of the wave did.

That is for your own good. Hattie very carefully did not step close to the water.

"You really think so?" Because he wasn't. The information he'd received came from... dreams? Dreams from who? What was their intent? *Why* send dreams and not a note or a messenger?

Like the Blue Lady?

I do.

Why? How do you know this is right?

The same way I know when to run or to fight. Hattie raised her nose to the air, her nostrils working. *You must go.*

The next wave came in and wrapped around Rainbow's ankle. She looked like someone had thrown a warm blanket over her.

Mah'se turned around to look over the water.

Rainbow wasn't Rainbow anymore. Her afro fell in lank mats over her head, and she went pale. Her teeth grew sharp and elongated. Her eyes went from a warm brown to a filmy, dead brown. Then they lit with a blue glow that made them less inviting than merely dead.

Okay. So, maybe whoever *had* sent a messenger.

She beckoned to him with razor-sharp claws. "Come here." The rasping voice had none of Rainbow's warmth or tone. "Come to me."

The fuck he would.

His foot slid forward.

"Hey, Bow. We can talk about this."

His other foot passed by the first.

"Come to me." The claws urged him forward.

He took another halting step.

He needed answers, sure. But he needed the person he could trust, and this version of her wasn't it. "Bow. Don't do this. We'll figure something out. Just stop. Bow, you're starting to scare me."

His foot touched the surf. Cold water invaded his shoe.

She retreated to deeper water, up to her waist, now.

Water invaded his other shoe, and he stepped up to his shin. He was already not warm, and the cold made him shiver.

"A few more steps, Dexx." A smile pulled back the corners of her mouth, and the teeth showed clearly.

Dexx didn't like this. She'd stripped away his will, and that wasn't cool. He swung his harvested leg bone at her.

Her upraised hand shattered the bone. The pieces fell into the water and sank.

Dexx looked to the shore and Hattie. She was gone.

Mah'se was headed inland too, with a thin trail of dust rising behind him.

Rainbow lost a little of the paleness and added the cold of blue to the dead skin. "That's it. Keep coming."

The cold water hit his man-parts. They went for warmer parts unknown, and his breath was sucked out. He couldn't breathe.

He went past shivering into just under convulsions, but his feet moved forward.

Rainbow disappeared beneath the waves.

Dexx took one last gulp of air before the water closed over his head.

Rainbow glowed a soft blue, beckoning, always beckoning. His feet came off the floor of the ocean, and the water drew him forward.

Rainbow smiled with malice and death at her fingertips and struck.

15

Dexx only had time to belch out his air in a scream before Rainbow was on him.

She wrapped him up in a strange hug and covered his mouth with hers.

He struggled, but her strength overpowered him easily.

Her mouth was over his, but she hadn't made any move other than to wrap him up.

He stopped struggling.

Clean, cool air flowed into his lungs.

Gross. So unbelievably gross, but he had air.

Rainbow pulled away from him. He held his breath, of course. But he had a good lung full now. He could hold his breath for a while. A minute anyway.

He almost let his air go again. The surface of the ocean had receded to the point that it was only a faint glow *hundreds* of feet above them.

Rainbow breathed for him again.

They flew through the water like it was air. His fear didn't release him, though, because he couldn't release the fact that he'd been led into the water by a rusalka. Drowning men were kinda what they did.

The only thing he could do was recall that *his* Rainbow Blu would never kill him, even in rusalka form. The water turned black, and still Rainbow dragged him further. They had to be thousands of feet down. That couldn't be right. Ocean depths like that could— no, *would* crush anyone. Submarines, too.

She went deeper, and as Dexx concentrated on the black water ahead, he felt the water slip past like a gentle breath of wind. Then the darkness lifted, and a blue aura took its place.

The light continued to bloom until it became the exact color as the Blue Lady. Rainbow's hand went from just a thing gripping him to the pale blue of death, connected to the tatters of a shroud covering a dead thing dragging him deeper than anyone had survived unaided before.

A... *warp* in the blue light began to form in Rainbow's path. The water just looked *funny* ahead. A dome appeared in the blossoming light. A massive dome as big as a city. Maybe bigger.

He couldn't see anything beyond the warp of the dome.

Rainbow dragged him down to the ocean floor and landed softly on the bottom sediment puffing upward and swirling around them, bouncing off the dome wall.

Rainbow stepped forward into it, tugging Dexx with her.

The strangest sensation spread over him as he walked through. If a blanket could pull tension over a body then dissolve as it pulled tighter, that might be close to what he experienced. That and a faint tingle.

This was a ward, then. What kind of ward was anybody's guess. He didn't recognize the weave of magick that kept it alive.

But there was air.

Dexx pulled in a breath with hands on his knees as he

gasped. "You... could have—" He pulled in air. "—warned me. I thought..." Water fell from him in waves, soaking the dry sand and rubble.

Rainbow was dry as if she'd never been in the water. She still had her rusalka body on and whipped around to him. Her dead black eyes turned warm brown and alive. Her hair went from lank to a full afro, and the death shroud dissolved to clothing he recognized.

"Killed you? Is that what you thought?" She rolled her eyes and sighed at him. "You *actually thought* that I was going to—"

"Stop." He didn't want to have this conversation, but she'd... "You stripped me of my will, so, yeah."

"You weren't listening. When you dig your heels in, that's it. I knew it was my way or none at all."

Words from Sheriff Tuck, his chief of police, came back to him. *"I trust my guys. I give them the discipline I need in them and trust that they'll do the right thing."*

That stung.

Dexx hadn't given his guys, his team the discipline he should have.

Rainbow had learned the lesson.

"I'm nervous."

"Truth." Rainbow shook her head and looked away. "I realize how terrifying I look as a rusalka."

Dexx coughed. "I have big teeth when I shift." He needed her to not hate herself in the same way he was. "What *is* this place?"

"Couldn't tell ya—" She frowned as she looked around. "—It's *your* house. I only knew how to get here."

Okay. That was certainly curious.

They were in an underground city. Well, the outskirts of one, anyway. They were on a rise that looked over a once-grand city. Even ruined like it was, it was beautiful.

Everything had the same monotonous blue tint to it, but strangely that fit the mood of the place.

"What are we supposed to *do* here?" If they had to just be here, then something would happen, right? If they had to *find* something, something would glow or ding or rattle. That's how the video games he'd played worked.

Rainbow furrowed her brow. "Well, your map had us going inside the city somewhere."

"*This* was on the map?" All he recognized was what looked like a can of worms. Just squiggly lines in the dirt.

"Sort of. Now that I'm here, it's starting to make a little more sense to me? I don't know how. But I think we have to find the north gate and then kinda go straight from... there?"

"If only we had a compass."

"Well, we could just follow the wall. The north gate should be marked. Then we go in and find whatever you have hidden down here."

Yeah. If he'd managed to magickally hide an entire city under the ocean, that'd be exactly what he'd do. Right? "How do you know this? I have no idea what *any* of this is, and you're all, 'Hey this is here, and this is there, and gosh, all we have to do is read the signs.'" Dexx picked up a rock and threw it at the dome wall.

It hit the water and immediately sank to the ocean floor.

Dexx was... frustrated and fed up and was tired of being led around. "How did you know this place was here?"

"What if..." Rainbow licked her lips and looked around, shaking her head.

"What if what?"

"I don't know. Like, We're connected somehow."

"The Blue Lady—"

"The currents. That's who they are."

"Sure. Whatever. She asked me to do something for her.

But she never said what." Could the Blue Lady have sent him to the undersea city? Was that his action?

"The currents teach, but they rarely spell everything out. Sometimes we have to learn it on our own. They will give a direction, and you go forward. The lesson sets deeper that way."

Dexx didn't know if that made him feel better. "What if there's nothing here?" There had to be, but what if…

"We should probably move." Rainbow pointed with both her thumbs in a direction. "And stop crying about what ifs."

She was right. He took in a deep breath and studied the city. What if she was right? "You're the only person you can count on, you know."

"I know."

"I could get you killed."

"I know that, too," she said quietly. "Dexx, I'm not a naïve little girl. But I also know I have to trust. I trust the currents, and I trust you, equally as much. That's why you are now and always will be alpha. Deep down, you *are*."

Dexx dropped his head down. He couldn't let her see the tears forming in his eyes because she'd daggered him hard in the feels. "Fine. Let's find this north gate."

They picked their way down the rubble-strewn path to the city. They passed statues and structures that didn't belong to the city proper but was more like a city on the edge of the city.

The destruction was impressive. But equally impressive was the remaining structures.

They hit the ground level of the city and began to walk around the ancient ruins. The rubble led to tall walls that hid taller structures beyond them.

Further in, the buildings looked better, but still mostly a loss.

The structures were mostly of stone, though other things

resembled something more *organic*. Could the builders have *grown* their buildings?

The diffuse blue light had an odd feel to it and made a proper assessment difficult. Colors were mostly different shades of blue. Yeah. A little hard to really study.

"Hey, boss?" Rainbow narrowed her eyes at the partial walls.

"Yeah?" Dexx tapped chunks of broken rubble away with his foot. If he'd put this city here for a reason, what could it have been? And if he'd been that powerful once, how hadn't he managed to kill Bussemi?

"You think this place is in our world, too?" Rainbow pulled on a shaft poking from the ground.

It took him a moment to see the resemblance to a decorative tree in the real world. A culture had lived in this place.

Just how hard *was* Bussemi to kill? "Hard to say. It could be." No, it couldn't! What was he saying? The physics on that was... brain-crampingly complicated.

"Is this... *Atlantis*?" Rainbow's eyes widened as she turned to him. "You don't think, do you?"

A past version of him—Dexx Colt—had hidden the city of Atlantis? He swallowed his snort. "Hard to say. It could be."

"I bet if we found it in our world, we'd be millionaires. Billionaires. Maybe even—"

"Hush. There could be things in here we don't want to find. Or to find us." What if this hidden city wasn't to give him answers but to bury something that should be forgotten?

"Do *you* see signs of movement?" She motioned like she was throwing the idea away.

He just didn't want either of them to make it this far to get dead. "Shouldn't be too sure of anything."

"Okay, but if anyone was here, they would have sent out armed guards, and the trail behind us is about two inches thick with dust. Don't get that if there's someone around to move it."

She had a point.

Hattie? You still around on land? He was, too, technically. But it should be soaked by miles of water above.

I am here, cub. Are you with the water creature?

Yeah. Noticed a complete lack of help by you or Mah'se, the not protector. You left me to die. But at this point, you just left me.

Some things you will have to take care of on your own. She sent a thread of amusement.

Had they set this up?

"How long do you want to walk before we set some sort of camp?" Dexx could sit down for a good long time. Dry out. Dry was good. Things were chafing—sensitive bits.

"That's *your* call, boss. I'm dry."

"Okay. Well, I'm not. I need a fire and some dry clothes."

"Grumpypants." Rainbow gestured to the right. "How about there?"

Through the toppled and broken walls was a gap too straight to be rubble. And on the side, a symbol like the letter A, except that its third leg was drawn from the bottom point to the middle. So, an awkward A.

"Race you." Rainbow took off at a sprint.

He sprinted after her. Even eked out a win by a step or two. He actually should have been faster.

He was weakening. Was that Bussemi's spell? Was the spell the reason he was in Dexx's head? Was that how he'd gotten in?

They collected their breath and stopped at the open fifty-foot-tall gate that hung twisted on one of the hinges. The other side didn't have the gate at all, but a suspicious step looked like it could be lying on the ground under debris.

"Impressive trees." Dexx nodded at the timbers held together by iron straps five feet wide.

"This place is amazing." Rainbow touched the gate. She jerked her hand back, a bolt of static electricity lengthening a foot before snapping out of existence. "Ouch."

"Defense system?" Dexx reached a hand to the gate. He knew he shouldn't, but if this was *for* him, then it wouldn't be rigged against him.

"What are you—" Rainbow stared at him like he was stupid.

Dexx touched the wood, but a warm tingle ran through his arm. So, maybe this *was* set up for him. "Defense system. How can a ward last that long?" He touched the wood and the warm sensation faded. A tingle started in his head, as the headache that was Bussemi threatened to show himself. And here Dexx was without Hattie. "We're going to have to find a spot and camp. I've got a mean one on the way."

"Mean what?" Rainbow looked confused.

"Ward sickness. The Bussemi spell that's slowly killing me? The headaches that you know, I have to pass out for." Dexx peered through the gate into the city inside. The street had a long curve. They could camp there and have plenty of time to react to an ambush or raiders. Or camp in a not-as-ruined building and hide with a fire in a hearth. He was going for Option B. "Let's get into one of the more stable houses and make a fire. Is there even anything to burn here?"

"Don't know. But only one way to find out." Rainbow walked with a cavalier step into the first place with a door and walls.

"Wait." Dexx pulled at her shoulder. "Let me go in first. I can smell better and see better."

She gave him a dark look. "I'm a rusalka, not some dumb blonde."

He ignored her and pulled air through his nose. Testing it. Nothing. The air was stale. Or was it?

He stretched his senses out, mostly for the enhanced vision. Nothing there either.

His ears heard Rainbow breathing, and her heartbeat just fine. Falling dust could have made noise, but not a speck floated in the air. So, no movement.

Could this place be as dead as it looked?

"I don't see or hear anything. I guess we go in and see what's what."

Rainbow gave him a look that said she could have told him that, then fell in step behind Dexx.

The first building they went into didn't have a ceiling. They didn't have most of the walls either, but they had to start somewhere. An ancient fluted column had fallen through the building at some point, but it was hard to say if it was recent or old. The dust seemed to have an even coating everywhere.

Dexx and Rainbow split up. Complete destruction dominated the next room he walked into. There were dd shapes under the dust that could be cloth or thicker dust.

"Boss," Rainbow called from across the small building.

He poked his head back around the corner.

She held up a draped square of cloth, the same blue of everything else they had seen so far. A fine powder floated gently to the floor as it slowly disintegrated. "Think we can burn it?" Her expression said no and that it might be a lost cause.

"We have to do something fast." He needed to dry off, maybe change clothes. He was starting to get cold as the temperature seemed to drop. Maybe it was just that he was wet and now standing instead of moving. "Keep looking, but maybe focus on wood."

"I've got cloth." She dropped the fabric to the floor and disappeared again.

Well, if that was all they had, then it was what he'd work

with. He was... wet. Dexx dug out his flint and *ma'a'shed* and struck sparks, which flared larger than they should have. At least it worked. But they might have to be careful with what they burned.

He then emptied a space of dust on the stone floor and gathered enough stone rubble to make a ring for the fire. Rainbow brought more blue cloth.

"Is that all of it?" He arranged the last of the fire ring and struck a lingering spark with his flint.

She set some of the cloth in the ring.

The fire set immediately.

"That shouldn't do that." He stood and gestured to the growing flame. "It's like it's *happy* to burn."

"Do we put it out?" Rainbow raised a hand as if ready to use her anti-fire magic to put it out.

Dexx watched the flame for a minute. It had definitely caught fast and was eagerly burning, but the flames stayed at a comfortable height. It didn't seem to want to spread beyond the rocks, so...

"No." He could *feel* magick of some sort coming from it, but not anything bad. "It *wants* to burn, but it doesn't seem to want to be out of control." Which was weird. Right? "We leave it for now."

"Hey, I want to show you something." Rainbow motioned to the other room.

Dexx's headache ratcheted up. "We gotta make this quick. I've got a headache coming on." And Hattie wasn't there to help.

"Won't take a minute." She led him to the next room where the fire cloth had come from. "Look at that."

There was more of the cloth. Not like a fabric store or anything but a small pile, and it wasn't blue.

"It's..." Red. A vibrant, not-age-dulled red.

"Yeah. Crazy. And it's thicker than the other stuff." She

reached down and tugged at the cloth. It looked rich and velvety soft and wasn't disintegrating.

Dexx reached out to touch it. The cloth was soft and warm to the touch. "How much is here?"

"I don't know. Bunch, I guess."

"Let's pull this out and see what's here."

They wound up with two extremely large bolts of the cloth, enough to make two blankets.

That was exactly what he needed because this headache wasn't leaving, and he didn't want to be unconscious and cold.

But he did want to be unconscious. This headache thing needed a cure. And quick.

16

Dexx was unconscious. He'd been that way since he'd laid down next to the fire he'd built. He'd known it since he'd put his head to the ground with a pounding splitter.

He had a warm blanket over him. He had a fire to keep the night out—if this place ever had night. He even had a bodyguard, if Rainbow could be called that.

What he *didn't* have was peace. Bussemi invaded his thoughts as soon as he closed his eyes.

Do you like Kupul? His voice was irritating inside Dexx's mind. *I destroyed the city because you thought you were above yourself. There is no escape from me.*

Just like every time Bussemi had access to his mind, Dexx ran. Or tried to. The visceral feeling made him ill, but there wasn't another choice. He *had* to run. Run from the monster that had killed him so many times before.

The darkness he ran through formed into an unlit night of a tree-lined street. Trees blurred by, and his footsteps sounded loud against the pavement. The monster was behind him, chasing, always chasing.

Until the monster flared up in front of him.

Expansive leathery wings spread out, meeting at the body of an overlarge demon. Red skin stretched across its body, with forward curving horns and fire in its eyes and mouth.

Demons were one thing. A thing he could handle. Pedestrian, even.

Bussemi? He was something on a different plane altogether. Dexx didn't have his memories, but he *felt* the overriding fear. Was it from being tortured for so long or from the past lifetimes? He couldn't remember.

The nightmare shifted. The tree-lined street became a vast ancient city with white columns and colorful banners hanging over broad avenues.

The sky had angry clouds, and the wind whipped torrents of gales through the streets.

A dark speck against the sky grew larger, and a shape appeared. Leathery wings and the demon body. A bahlrok.

Lightning flashed outside the city, crackling along the protective dome. The earth bucked and toppled buildings and columns. Screams filled the air.

The bahlrok motioned, and the waters of the bay swelled to hundreds of feet. They crashed against the dome, once, twice, and then cascaded through the streets.

People ran, but not nearly fast enough. The waves caught them and caused destruction on a massive scale.

The bahlrok laughed, obviously pleased.

Dexx ran before the tsunami. Lightning cracked against the buildings on either side of him, splintering them to rubble. Wind blew the dust into a sandstorm, blasting at his flesh, stripping his bones clean—

"*Gah—*" Dexx bolted straight up from his blanket.

Rainbow squatted next to the fire, idly poking a stick in the flames. "Hey, sleepyhead. Wow, that didn't last long. How are you feeling?"

He raised a hand to his head. The splitting had stopped, reduced to a low-level ache that would definitely dampen his temper threshold. "I need him gone."

"Your brother or whatever?" She pulled the stick out and rolled the tip in the dirt.

"Yeah."

"I agree, but I don't know how you're gonna do that." She stood. "Well, I think you've slept long enough so we can get moving anytime now. Come on. Roll out of your bed." She flashed him a smile—a bright cheery one.

"Why are *you* so happy?"

She shrugged and looked around. "Because we're here together. Two peas in a pod. Paige would make *three* peas in a pod, but two will do."

"We're in a ruined city that could collapse on us at any second, and you're just happy because we're here together?" He was a little bit, too. "You got problems. Serious ones. How long was I out this time?"

"Like eight hours."

Dang it. Okay. He needed to figure out why he was here and what he needed to learn. Bussemi was going down. One way or another. And... hopefully, there was some clue here.

Like the fact that he'd destroyed this city.

Why? He'd *said* because Dexx had been too full of himself, but what if it was because he'd gotten too close to finding a real Bussemi solution? What if that's the reason the past Dexx had saved this city? To protect that secret?

Great. Now, all he had to do was find it.

"The fire is *still going*. And it looks like it hasn't even burned a little bit. This place sure is strange. I wonder what it was like when it was new. Or how about its last day above the—"

"Bow, let's get moving." He understood now that when she went off on a verbal vomit, it was because she was bored.

Or at least, that was his best guess. "We'll roll these up and use them again. Hopefully, we won't have to."

She pulled up her blanket. "Sure is nice to have something a different color than all this blue. I mean, it's a great color, but there sure is a *lot* of it."

Dexx took care of his blanket, wondering where he should start.

"Why do you think there'd be all this blue? Is it a symptom or something else? What does it mean, I mean..."

She carried on, and Dexx shut off his ears. She'd run on like that for hours more, but over the course of time, he'd become used to it. He was comforted by it.

They didn't have anything to tie the rolls with. He set his knee on the blanket, keeping it tight. "You didn't find any rope with the other stuff, did you?"

Rainbow stopped the litany. "I don't know? I was more interested in the other stuff. Hold on." She left, her bag uneven and loose.

Rainbow came back, a stunned look on her face and a golden woven rope in her hands. "How did you know?"

"Know what?"

"How did you know there was something to tie the blankets with?"

"I didn't. I just wanted to know if there was."

"But you rolled that like you *expected* it. Not just curious. Like you already *knew*."

"I didn't, I—" But he *had* rolled the blanket and asked her to get the ties right where everything else had been. The first house they came to, the room he'd let Rainbow inspect. Not creepy. "I just... want the rope. Please?"

Rainbow handed it to him and he tied his blanket. Then, he did the same for Rainbow, reveling in the mundane steps, not sure what he was feeling about traversing the city.

He finished with her blanket and handed it to her. "Why

didn't your dad teach you any of this stuff?"

"No parents." She took it from him, her lips flat, her expression purposefully chipper. "They abandon me when I was really young."

"What? That's—" He suspected her parents had known what she was and hadn't been able to *actually* bring themselves to kill the baby monster "—horrible."

"That's the way my life has always been."

Maybe that was the reason she blindly trusted him more than a sane person would.

Well, he was going to do his best not to let her down, but that meant shrugging off whatever funk was blanketing his resolve and move forward. The answers he needed might be here, and they just had to find it. Hopefully, it'd be like the magick fire or the magick blankets or the magick rope, and it'd just magickally find them because this city was large, and he didn't know how much time they had. "Let's go. We got a thing to find, and X marks the spot."

"There really wasn't an X on the map."

"Whatever. The map brought us here. Were you able to interpret the spaghetti markings?"

She shook her head. "I thought maybe you did."

Not even a little.

He left the room and the shelter without another word. He heard Rainbow behind him, but the noise she made was muffled. His ears had less power than he was used to.

Bussemi's ward or spell was eating at him, slowly killing his bond.

That fucking… That guy he couldn't name.

Dexx trudged on up the wide avenue.

Blue was the color of the day again.

They walked for an hour, following the main drag through the city, occasionally peering down the side streets, but always coming back.

Rainbow started talking again to break the silence. He put her on ignore. Not because he was mad, but because things were looking... familiar. The shape of a partial column matched with a flicker of a memory. A doorway had the feel of a place he'd been before.

The broad roadway began to change into more of a memory than the ruins.

A domed roof came into view at the end of the gently curving main road.

Dexx saw both the memory and the present ruins overlaid. The ruins were the same blue as everything else, but the memory had the dome a gently swirling iridescent color, with wisps of the iridescence floating from the top of the dome to weave into the protective dome that flowed over the entire city.

Ghosts of people flickered in and out of the past. A smiling woman wearing a toga. A man walking with purpose, his legs tangling in his clothes. A demon laughing with a human.

A demon?

He and Rainbow closed in on the building. Sudden knowledge filtered in. The building was a temple. *His* temple. Dedicated to magick and cooperation between the magickal and mundane.

"I found it."

"... but *she* didn't even consider what *I* thought about it. What?"

Dexx stopped. He set his blanket down, studying the temple. "What we've been looking for. I found it." He pointed to the structure. "*That* was important when this place was alive."

"I agree, since all the roads seem to meet here, but are you *sure*? I mean, we *are* looking for that needle in the pile of needles."

"Yeah. That too."

Rainbow opened her mouth and closed it. "I— it feels weird to me. Like it's... I don't know. It's weird. I knew this girl once..."

Rainbow picked up her story, Dexx let the words roll over him.

The approach to the temple was far more intricate than he'd figured at first glance. More than one main road lead to the temple—like Rainbow had said—and even though it seemed to be the center of the city, the largest remaining structures were still beyond the temple.

Statues littered the plaza the roadways formed. They had been placed at each intersection and point.

Dexx's memory overlaid the ruins. Most of the statues were rubble now, but they had been grand once—images of people, animals, and other creatures that felt like a story.

There had been wolves and great cats, and things that no longer existed. One had clearly been a bird very similar to an ostrich, but instead of a cute flat beak, it had a proportionate head of an eagle.

Rainbow fell silent. She studied the remains intently.

Another had been a griffin in a fight with a manticore. Natural enemies.

A huge base with only clawed feet in ruins had once been a dragon, its wings open and standing regal.

Paige would have loved that.

A pair of statues stood on either side of another road, but both were snapped off at delicate legs. They'd once been a pegasus and a unicorn.

Damn, those were cool, but they must have been the imaginary statue lane. Unicorns didn't exist.

Or did they? He didn't feel like they'd had statues of pretend things made for this temple city.

As soon as they passed those two statues, Dexx felt the power shift.

Like a ward reactivating.

Like coming home.

"What was that?" Rainbow asked, breaking a silence he hadn't realized had formed.

"Something woke up." Dexx put a finger to his lips. *Be quiet.*

Rainbow nodded and looked around with eyes that gave off a silver sheen.

They took a few more steps forward, but Dexx put his hand to Rainbow's arm. "Stop."

"Why?"

The power he felt before intensified. At first, it felt like a low buzz, like a wheel bearing going out, but then it changed pitch like a car shifting gears. A slight pressure pushed at him, not *against* him, but not *with* him. "Can you feel that?"

"No. I felt something earlier, but now, nothing. Should we go?"

She felt nothing. Could it be a trap? This place had the feel of the stones, his *kadu*, but only far more powerful. This was uniquely his. He'd *made* this. Or at least had had a major role in it.

Didn't mean it wasn't a trap. He didn't know why he'd been sent here, after all.

"Stay here." He let go of her arm and took another step. The power increased.

Water. It was like water. The deeper he went, the greater the pressure.

He took another step and the ground hummed. The fine particulates rose just above the ground in a haze.

Dust fell from statues and buildings, and a wall of force stopped him. It could have been glass, but infinitely clearer than anything manmade.

Rubble cleared from his feet. Gleaming silver script appeared. Not ornate, but definitely not plain. They were in words he could read: *Say your name.*

What the hell? He turned to Rainbow, but all she could do was shake her head.

The pressure increased. He felt the ebb and flow, imagined the swirls of magick wafting from the dome. Or could he *actually* see it?

Say your name.

The thought wasn't his. Not Hattie's, or... or the monster's.

He cleared his throat. "Dexx Colt."

The power sucked itself back into the dome so hard and so fast it created a gentle breeze enough to move the powder-fine dust.

Then, nothing. No magick.

Great. What the hell?

For a moment, nothing happened, then the power exploded out without noise, but he felt the wave like an explosion.

Sunlight and color bloomed in the destruct—

The city was whole, vibrant, and living.

People and creatures walked by without pausing to look at them. They were dressed in a hundred different fashions— togas, skins, leathers, and fabrics that looked almost modern. There were creatures who preferred no clothing, but didn't look obscene. Were they memories?

A man stood in front of Dexx, tall and radiating command. His hair was cut short. What hair he had left, most of it had balded in his younger days..A slight smile pulled at the corners of his mouth and set off crow's feet at his eyes. "Welcome." The man had an accent, a lilting, almost musical accent that complemented his deep voice. "I— we, have been waiting a long time for you."

17

Dexx opened his mouth, closed it. He didn't feel like he was being attacked, so there was at least that. He turned to Rainbow again, who was wide-eyed and slack-jawed.

The was *no trace* of the ruins. They weren't in the *ruined* city. So, was this in a past moment? Like a time trapped in amber?

The sudden living colors jarred into Dexx's eyes after the monotonous blue.

"I can guess this might be a little shocking to you," the new guy said.

Dexx raised an eyebrow. "You could say that."

The smile grew on the man's face. "I— we need your help." The man stood there completely at ease.

There was something familiar about the guy. What was it about him? "I'm kinda low on resources at the moment. Looks like you have a bunch, though." He gestured around to carts moving by animal and by magick.

"You have exactly what I— we need." He tipped his head

to Rainbow. "Daughter of the currents, be welcome. I extend my humble greetings."

"Oh." Rainbow's hands covered her mouth, and her eyes welled with tears. "Oh."

The man looked back to Dexx. "She's not very welcome in your world, is she?"

"Um, not really. I kinda picked her up, and then she followed me home. Strays, am I right?"

The man threw back his head and laughed. "I knew you would have humor. Come with me. I *know* you have questions. I would."

"Gotta ask. Are we dead?" Dexx lifted his hand to inspect it. Would he even know?

"No, but where you are, *I* am dead." The man gestured for them to follow as he took a step back. "This place will fade, so time is short."

The gesture and the eyes. Dexx realized why this man looked so familiar. They were *his*. Recognition must have shown on his face.

"Yes, I am you," the man said with a relieved smile. "A long time in your past. Do you have the stone?"

"Stone?"

"The *shamiyir*. Or a version of it. It was made in another of my—our lives, but I have been able to recover it when I need it. Do you have it?"

Dexx felt around in his pockets. It wasn't there. He dug in them, fingers searching.

"I have it." Rainbow raised her hand, the smooth stone with the strange markings in her fingers.

"Most excellent. Keep it safe, or at least don't drop it. If you two would follow me, this spell cannot last forever." He turned and led them toward the temple.

Okay. So, this was weird. "How did you—" Dexx caught up with the man.

"I am—and you are—a very powerful wi'tch. The magick of the world flows very strong in us."

They crossed under the brilliant white and ornate gabled roof. The work to carve the stone must have taken generations to finish.

With each step, he felt more at home, more like a memory settling in after being gone too long.

The floors were polished tiles four feet to a side, and the walls looked like plaster, but the process of manufacture was closer to layered chocolate. Just not as edible.

"Not this time," Dexx said with a chuckle. "I'm a shifter, but that's about it."

"You have found Hat'ai? That is something I would like to have done. This life is not one where we are one."

"Huh? I thought we were always together."

"No. We are bound now and forever, but we are not always together in my lifetimes."

Well, that was interesting, but... "How did you *do* this? I mean, you speak English, and, *fuck* I'm really here. I can touch stuff."

"Me too," Rainbow said, her eyes narrowed, her expression filled with wonder.

"The monster of your time." The man stopped and turned to them.

What? Who? "A little more specific, please. I deal with them daily."

"The one you fear."

Bussemi. "Oh. *He* brought me here?"

The man chuckled. "No, *I* brought you here with help, but *he* is the reason I did. I cannot defeat him. He's too powerful."

That wasn't the answer Dexx was looking for. "Then, we're fucked. I can't beat him either. 'Cause, like, you know,

I'm not uh, I can't do, uh, the thing—" He jabbed a hand forward like a spear.

"You have to find a way. You asked how and why this moment was possible. I studied your language to speak to you. I pulled the strings of time and reality to bring you here. I— *we* need your help."

"I'll do what I can, but Bus— *that guy...*" Fear ran through Dexx. "I can't. Sorry. Everyone that goes toe to toe with him becomes a grease stain. I'd like to help, but no."

"Perhaps I can help change your mind."

Probably not, but the man could try.

He turned and started deeper into the temple.

"You know my name. What's yours?" Dexx tried hard not to stare at all the wonders around him.

The man chuckled. "You won't believe me."

"Why? Is it Carl or Wayne or something?"

"In this life, they call me Dekskulta."

Yup. Dexx laughed. "What the fuck, man. Recycling names now? There's a sense of humor for you."

"It means great leader."

"It could mean death to whitey. That shit is funny." And now he knew where Kate got the name from. The elves must have long memories.

"As you say. There is humor, but no less true."

"Okay, Deks. So, why am I here? Why are *we* here?" He glanced at Rainbow and flared his eyes as if to ask if she was okay.

She frowned back as if to say, *of course.*

"I admit. I did not know the *sheneshae* would be with you, but all the better. I can alter my plans, and it will be like I always knew."

Why did that even matter?

The open inner temple doors were nothing short of amazing, just like the rest of the city. Polished wood with swirls in the grain that looked like the spots of a jungle cat. The slabs were each a single piece twenty feet high and ten feet wide. They had to be six inches thick. Huge hinges of a silver metal were bolted to each panel.

"This place is... wow." Dexx reached up and stroked the wood. Smooth.

"What is this place called?" Rainbow stopped at the doors too, but she turned back to the city, watching the bustle of the city in its full glory.

"Kupul. It means 'key.' And this is where it comes together. I've worked hard to make a place where our kind is welcome."

"Magick born?" Not a large leap of logic.

"Indeed. Here, we can be ourselves—shifter, elemental, magick. Even Rin'bau's people are welcome. The balance is here."

Rin'bau. Dexx laughed. "No, Deks. Her name is Rainbow."

"Ah. Yes. I have trouble sometimes with names. So strange. Come. Time shortens."

They walked by things that would have been treasures in the real world. Statues and carvings and paintings. All of it in the open.

What would he give to have this place in his world? Where Leah and Rai and Ember would be accepted. Bobby could live without fear from the angels or demons. Paige could practice openly, and Leslie—well, Leslie was a different story.

This place would be— he didn't have the words.

"I'm having trouble wrapping my head around this. Why me? Why now? Couldn't you just go find a version of us you could team up with and take him out yourselves?"

"I would have if it was possible. Things in your time are— what's that word?— turbulent. The lines have been disrupted

185

to the point where I could reach *you*. You have the chance, the opportunity to end the threat. I am doomed here. I will die protecting this city, this place I built for us all."

"That's the shittiest plan I've ever heard."

"Is this Atlantis?" Rainbow drew her finger along the wall.

"I am not familiar with that place." Dekskulta stopped, tapping his thumb to his chin.

Damn, he looked like everything Dexx fought against. Responsibility, humility… responsibility.

Rainbow tipped her head to the side. "The story goes Atlantis was destroyed in a day and a night, falling to the bottom of the sea."

"Is that so?" Dekskulta dropped his arm. "Well, all stories originate somewhere. Maybe it is. You could ask the *sheneshae* of your day. They might remember."

Rainbow rested her hand lightly on a marble pillar. "What's a *sheneshae?*"

Dekskulta smiled sadly. "What I worked hard to build will be washed away entirely. Your people are known to us as the *sheneshae*. They are artisans."

They walked further into the temple, under the dome, which still swirled with iridescent light, sending pure elemental magick above into the atmosphere.

Along the curved walls, sconces held glowing spheres casting the interior with warm light, and under the sconces were alcoves with carvings of wood and stone. Some were intricate, and others were crude to the point of accidental shapes.

Dexx felt a connection to the place. "What's this then?"

"Do you not feel it?" Dekskulta had a slight smile still.

"I feel *something*, but I can't say what it could be." But he could guess. "I would say a ward tree? But more like ward temple."

"Not completely accurate, but you have the idea. The magick here flows out to the city. It helps keep the peace. After all, peaceful creatures turn violent when they meet their natural enemy. I feel one connected to you."

"A natural enemy to me? Like Bu— like that guy."

"No, a peaceful creature of sorts. It has an enemy. The two cannot be on this plane together."

What? But then Dexx remembered that as the alpha—if he still was that—he had a connection to his pack. Hattie wasn't a danger. But Leslie might be? Rai's thunderbird might be. Ember's rajasi might be. It was hard to tell what Dekskulta was even referring to. "Ah. Yes. Yeah." But it could definitely be Leslie's griffin. His enemy was a manticore.

They walked from the dome room and turned down a corridor.

The hallway they stepped into was much smaller and less grandiose than the rest of the temple. It was utilitarian and sparse, much more like a reinforced stronghold than a temple built for wistful idealism.

A knot of concern grew in Dexx's belly. "Hey, look, this better not be a trap. I'll go down swinging."

"As will I," Dekskulta said with a slight smile. "This place was built to hold up to time. This is not trap. It will be needed, and so are you."

The walkway wound down in a spiral. But not a tight one. More like a parking garage than a staircase.

The floor leveled out and straightened to an antechamber filled with people. No, not just people.

An angel with wings out stood across from a demon.

The demon was tall and muscular, with wicked teeth and mottled skin of green and brown, with spots of sickly red. "He has come?"

Dekskulta bowed his head. "He has."

"This is who you have?" Dexx went on instant alert. His

hand went for the *ma'a'shed* in the sheath. "Angels and demons? That's most of your problem right there. Angels do what they do for their own reasons, and demons? Well, demons operate on the basest levels. Can't trust either one."

The angel and demon looked at each other.

"Here and now—" Dekskulta gestured to them both. "— they are not enemies. They are different sides to the same coin, and while their preferences differ, they have common ground to stand on."

The angel leaned forward. "Might I have your name?"

He didn't know it? "I'm not sure that's a good idea."

The angel pulled away again, not ruffled at all. "As you wish."

The demon tipped his head. "Call me Ba'aziel. I understand you will have need of us."

"Not me, pal. Demonology one-oh-one."

"Deeply troubling." The demon looked up to the angel.

"Come inside." Dekskulta stood in front of the doorway and motioned for Dexx and Rainbow to enter.

Dekskulta led them to a plinth in the center of the room. On the plinth sat an amethyst crystal as big as his palm. Silver and bronze runes covered the crystal. He clasped his hands in front of him. "One thing I did in my first life I regretted was sparing my brother. We were powerful on a scale you can't imagine. He still maintains much of his power, and every time I'm called back I have less."

"Dexx's eyebrows shot up. "You look plenty powerful from here, *old* me."

"I am quite gifted, yes. Perhaps as great as Genael, the protector of this part of the world, but my brother is greater in power than I. Only *one* of the reasons I built this city. My hope had been to create a place to balance him, negate his influence. It will fail."

Damn it.

"My life has been given to bring the magickal together, not to sunder it. I know you well enough to know, that you do not place the same value I do on life from any plane of existence."

Well, when *he* said it... "I do what I have to. I don't go out—"

"I think you misunderstand. You may not place the same value, but you may be *exactly* what we need. I cannot end him. Maybe *you* can."

Without magick? Probably not. "What, you won't even fight?" Maybe this guy wasn't him in a past life after all.

"I *will* fight. To the very end. But I cannot do what is needed. I have seen you, and I know you. You must fight. And I will help you."

Somebody knocked at the door.

Dekskulta looked to the new person.

Not a person, but a demon. One Dexx recognized. "Furiel? You? How are you here?"

The demon looked from Dekskulta to Dexx. "This is my home. I do not know you. I never forget a face."

"No, you *do* know me." In another... time?

Furiel held out a black leather scabbard and ignored him, turning to Dekskulta instead. "It is finished."

Dekskulta took it and pulled on the grip. A black blade with a scarlet edge appeared.

"A *ma'a'shed*. You made him a demon knife?" Dexx touched his own.

"Most likely the same blade." Dekskulta nodded. "Do you know how to wield it properly?

Dexx shrugged. "Yeah." Mostly. He didn't want to be seen as the biggest goob in the room.

"Thank you, Furiel. I'm glad you will not perish." He turned to Dexx. "This is why you are here." He pointed to the amethyst. "One day, you will need this. And one day, you will know what to do with it. This cannot be in the world of men until you are ready to hold it. So, it will stay here, safe until then."

Cryptic, but hope. "What's it supposed to do?"

"I cannot tell you."

"Fuck me." Frustration exploded in Dexx. "Nobody ever gives me a straight answer. Why the fuck should past me break the cycle?"

"I know you do not like knowing." Dekskulta spread out his arms. "I will say that when you know, you will agree that this should be kept as secret as it can be, especially with your... affliction."

So, this *was* instrumental in taking care of Dexx's mind-wart. Now, how to keep that information safe? "But you let all these assholes in on it? Looks like a pretty big hole in your theory."

"None here know what it does or is. They only know you need it, and that it is vital."

"They just trust you on your word?" Did Dexx? Hell, no. But at least now he had a little hope. "Wow."

"I trust *you*." Rainbow frowned at the stone as if trying to figure it out.

Did that mean that if he said it was bad news, she'd help him destroy it? "Look, I'm not in the business of trusting too much. Gets a lot of people killed. You can—"

"If you love and trust your family, Pahge—" Dekskulta put a funny breathy sound in her name that made her sound exotic. "—then you will. This is for you." He gestured toward the crystal with his head.

But how? It was hard to create a plan without information.

"And this is as well." Dekskulta lifted the *ma'a'shed* and handed it back to Furiel. "And this." He opened his hand to show Dexx the smooth stone with the runes. "Keep these safe. Since he knows you, you will survive. Safe travels, my friend." Dekskulta put his hand on Furiel's shoulder. It had the sound and look of a final parting.

Furiel bowed his head to Dekskulta, then to Dexx, and left the room in quick strides. The other angel and demon followed him down the corridor.

So, this was how Furiel had been assigned to Dexx. Did that make him trust the demon more? Or less? "What's going on here?"

Rainbow shuffled a foot. "He's dying. Am I right? Today is your last day, isn't it?"

"Yes," Dekskulta whispered.

"The fuck? No. Get your people out. Make another holy city or whatever this is. Don't be a martyr and go down with the ship. You can build this again."

Dekskulta gestured around him. "If only we could. What I intend to do is take as much away from my first brother as I can, to pull as much power away from him we are able. There is a possibility that I can permanently take a portion of his power before you enter into battle with him."

That... could be hugely beneficial.

"The creature within will never rest, and my former brother will be tormented forever, but it must be done."

That explained the pure hatred Buss— that guy had for Dexx.

"But you can't kill him?" Seems like you have all you need *right here*."

"Very nearly. But we don't have *you*."

Dexx patted his chest. "I feel like I'm here right now. Let's get this done with." With backup.

"You aren't here," Dekskulta explained gently. "The magick is strong. You are here in every way except the most important."

"Hattie?"

"Hat'ai is important. I wish is could have been with her. That would have been something to behold."

Dexx stretched his senses. *Fat cat, are you there?*

He waited for her to respond, and there might have been a tingle, or his imagination. If she was there, the bond wasn't active.

"The magick will fade soon," Dekskulta said. "I can answer questions until the end."

"Can I see the currents?" Rainbow asked.

"I am sorry *sheneshae* Rin'bau. Had I but known, I could have prepared, but I will make some arrangements. I can do that, at least.

"Sure. Whatever would be great. Thanks."

"Dexx Colt," he said, turning. "I am setting a guard for this place. They will know you if they survive."

"What do you mean *if*? Furiel survives. Why wouldn't someone else?" Everyone always talked in riddles. Even himself.

"I have sent him away. The things he holds are too valuable to fall into enemy hands."

"Fuck. Fine. Show me how to use this." He held out his *shamiyir* with all the runes. "I have to break this ward, or curse or whatever Busse—your brother has on me. If I can't —well, all this pretty bullshit is for nothing."

"You are warded?" Dekskulta frowned. "What sort?"

"You don't know? Buss— your brother put a curse on me. It was supposed to take my memory away, but now it's on slow burn to kill me. I'm dead if I can't break it. Hattie, too."

Dekskulta's look turned troubled. "I did not see this. You are sure it is his curse?"

"Yup. Pretty much told me all about it, except how to break it. Even had my— our *kadu* and threatened me with it."

"Do you not know how to work the stone?"

"I said I didn't. So no I don't."

Dekskulta tipped his head to the side. "You said—"

The temple bucked.

Everyone in the room hit the deck.

Dekskulta and the room faded. The angels, demons, and others faded along with it.

"It has started. Trace the lines for center and without—"

As Dekskulta faded, so did his voice.

"—alter the web to invert, then…" The voiced faded as the room bucked again, but this time it didn't affect Dexx and Rainbow.

They were in the same room, the amethyst softly glowing in the deep blue of everything, with the dead silence of thousands of years of solitude.

The room hadn't changed in layout. It was just… dead now.

Dexx saw things he hadn't before, though. The glow of the of the underlying magick. It had somehow been looped back on itself, slowly building. This place was like a fossil of pure magic.

Skeletons of demons sat against the walls. How had they not been called back to their own plane? Why were they even there?

The purple crystal sat on the plinth, exactly the same as it had been. Except it had a soft glow like the walls and the floor. The magick inside pressed against the runes, begging to be used.

Only one problem. He didn't know how.

"A few more seconds was all I needed. Fuck."

"You'll have plenty of time to think on it while you're dead." Mario said as he stepped into the room and smiled like the cat who ate the canary.

18

S hit.

Mario raised his hand, making the Jedi choke gesture.

Rainbow already faced him, one hand at her throat, the other reaching impotently for Dexx. Her mouth moved like a fish out of water.

Dexx closed his hand around the *shamiyir* and snatched the amethyst from the plinth.

Time stopped.

Mario's other hand froze in the act of coming up, a spell already forming. The weaves of the spell looked like lightning, bent and welded into a cage. If that went off, they wouldn't stand a chance.

Dexx's mind filled with spells. Reverse Mirror, Black Spear, Earth Rot, all sorts of them. If only he had a spell to get them out of there.

A spell was highlighted in his mind—a dimensional door.

He selected it in his mind and grabbed Rainbow's arm.

They slipped through space and appeared in the central

plaza of the ruined city, now a monotonous blue, where the silver script had asked for Dexx's name.

Rainbow gasped, breathing again. "Boss?" She looked more than a little terrified, but her eyes roamed the streets, searching for danger.

You must ignite the blue. There is still too much here that can be used against me. Dekskulta's voice echoed through his mind, almost a whisper of a whisper.

Tell me how to use the stone.

Be yourself. You will discover it.

Dexx clenched his fist in rage. Why did everyone always talk in riddles?

Ignite the blue. Like the city? If it hadn't burned the night before, it wasn't going to that day.

Burn. A list of spells popped into his head. Fire Minor. Fire Greater. Fire Signal. Fire Brand. The list seemed to go on and on. He had no time. However Mario had found them, he'd be back.

They couldn't leave this place for DoDO to search through.

He didn't waste time with the list of fires. He went to the very end, the last of the fire spells. Final Immolation.

He activated it, not quite knowing how.

The spell tore out of his mind like a shock of thunder.

Nothing happened. Dust and other fine debris fell from rubble piles and walls from the wind, but nothing else.

Why wouldn't things work the way it was—

Mario stepped through a gateway, silvery with motes of light that looked like shooting stars falling in. "I want that crystal."

Mario looked like Mario with the pale blond hair slicked back and the pale blue eyes. He sounded like Mario with the slight English accent to his nearly nasal tone. He was stupid-as-fuck like Mario. But was he really Mario?

Anyway, this wasn't Mario. His magick didn't *feel* right.

Dexx tried to see through the meat suit to the demon inside, but nothing revealed itself. The air around smelled just like everything else.

Dexx brought the amethyst closer to him. "I was told it was a secret, so, no."

"Hand it to me, and I will take you home. Get you out of this place." Mario held out his hand. "I can teach you how to use your magick."

Well, that was unexpected. Nobody had ever offered *that* before. "I don't need help. Got this covered."

"You don't even have the key to use it."

"The key?" Then a gong went off in his mind. He grabbed Rainbow's sleeve, and the list of spells faded to a corner of his mind. Dexx realized why his previous spell had failed. He hadn't given it a sacrifice, which... that's what the word immolation meant, even though Dexx had no idea how he knew that. "We're leaving." He wasn't sacrificing Rainbow or himself. But Dekskulta had said the blue needed to be eradicated, almost as if offering up his ruined city for the catalyst to the spell. "This place isn't what it used to be, and the neighbors kind of suck." The spell list came to him when he needed them, so what else did he need?

He wanted to get back to Hattie, *had* to get back to Hattie. A highlighted spell came to him.

Return.

Mario gathered energy and expelling it like a magnet. The bolt of lightning was as thick as Dexx's wrist and not the normal sort of cracklingly fun lightning. It wasn't laser straight, but it didn't waste time either.

Time didn't stop this time, but it slowed significantly. This couldn't be magick. This had to be Dexx's survival brain kicking in. He told his final destruction spell the thing he wished to sacrifice. "Kupul." And then immediately thought of the next spell. *Return!*

Time sped up, faster than time should flow.

Dexx's spell ignited, sucking the bolt of lightning past him, using it as the nucleus of the explosion. He and Rainbow turned into ghosts as the entire city jumped with the red-white of a nuclear blast.

He closed his eyes, and the vast boom in its infancy cut off as if interrupted.

The air felt different. Open. Less oppressive.

He opened his eyes and stared at the shoreline of the ocean.

Hattie and Mah'se sat beside each other, not far away.

It's Mario. We have to—

A doorway opened to a blast furnace pushed by cosmic winds, like an explosion in progress.

Mario stepped through, smoking and stumbling. He stopped when he saw the four together. "You." His lip curled in distaste.

How the hell was that guy still alive?

"Today, you die." Mario spread his arms wide, and doorways opened in the air. Not one or five, but *dozens.*

DoDO agents poured out as fast as the people behind them could push.

Rainbow glowed blue, her hands out in claws.

Hattie didn't wait. She tore into the hoard of DoDO agents as fast as they came out. Bodies piled up quickly.

Mah'se took a little longer. His head swiveled from Dexx to Mario and the invasion and back.

Fight. Dexx shoved his *shamiyir* and the amethyst into his pocket and grabbed the *ma'a'shed.* He shifted his energy into the blade, extending it to the *mavet.*

Rainbow gouged a slice out of the incoming waves and formed spears of ice, sending them into the masses.

Doors stopped forming and solidified. More came through every second, more than the four could take on together. They were going to be overwhelmed.

Mario turned his attention back to Dexx. "I warned you." The next instant, Mario moved like a dancer. His arms swayed, and his feet moved. But this was the deadliest dance Dexx had been invited to.

Elemental attacks hit Dexx from every angle at once. Under, over, behind, and in front.

Dexx needed to move quickly. The *mavet ma'a'shed* slashed through rock and lightning like they were butter, but there were too many attacks.

Sharp stone spears thrust upward through the ground, gouging his flesh. Frozen water smacked him in the head.

You must fight and win against him. Bussemi almost roared in his head. *He cannot be allowed to have such a weapon.*

Dexx flinched from the torrential pain ripping through his head. Bad timing. He missed the fireball coming, and it scored a decent hit in the middle of his chest.

Fuck, if he had to fight on *two* fronts, he was a goner for sure.

I will show you how to use the crystal," Bussemi-voice said. *"If you do not fight when I come to take it.*

Like that was even an option. Of course, he was going to flipping fight. Dexx slashed through a bolt of lightning that would have ended it all if it touched him. He spun to meet the ice he knew was coming.

Mario had a predictable pattern. Huge attack in front, flank attack to immediately follow.

Fuck both of you. Dexx jumped back as a spray of bullets stitched the ground alongside him.

Hattie, how you doing?

Hunt.

Okay, good enough.

Rainbow had a swath cut through the DoDO agents and was steadily making her way forward. If a shuffle could be said to be steady. She had her own attacks she had to deflect. The good part was that that water made an excellent shield, but a better weapon.

Mah'se went for a more direct attack, lowering his head and charging forward. That proved to be a pretty good shield all by itself, and magical attacks were abandoned as the antlers plowed up people eight feet on both sides.

Dexx fell to the ground from his dodging leap.

A DoDO agent drew a wand on him. She made the movement for a metal bind from earth and fire magick.

He needed to stop that!

No response came from the list of spells.

He held up his hand and flailed.

The air thickened, pushed outward from Dexx, turning into a gale, and then a wall of pure force.

The DoDO agent had been blown back. *All* of everything had been blown down. Even Mario hit the ground.

In the sudden quiet, Hattie and Mah'se struggled to pick themselves up. Water pooled around Rainbow.

On the horizon, a red glow appeared and rose above the water.

Why would the sun rise now?

The glow rose, and the light went from red to white, which shifted to a spearing light too bright to look at.

Dexx ducked his head. *Look away. Don't look at the light.*

Hattie and Mah'se struggled to get up, but Rainbow dropped her water shield and buried her head in her arms.

Light cascaded over the beach with heat. Kupul was gone. Dexx felt the fluttering, like a balloon out of air. He lost something he never knew he had.

Mah'se and Hattie grunted with pain, but at least they hadn't looked into the light. Hopefully, they hadn't.

Screams of humans— DoDO agents—said they had.

A second wave of wind tore across the water, vaporizing the surface into steam that looked like rampaging ghosts bent on vengeance.

Oh, fuck. There *had* to be something for this. A spell. *Something.*

A list began to spread itself in Dexx's head of shields, and he picked one at random. The spell locked into place just as the searing heat turned the beach to a glowing mass. It radiated around and over his magick, over Rainbow, Hattie, and Mah'se.

When it disappeared, all that was left was darkness.

Dexx let his head fall to the ground, letting go of the breath he hadn't known he held.

He'd saved them... somehow.

A minute passed. Maybe two. More? Dexx didn't know because he was just tired and ready to stop being chased. He didn't let go of his shield, though. He didn't have the energy to move, to find higher ground, somewhere away from where the DoDO agents had just had doors open to before. But he wasn't letting go of that shield until he had to.

The light grew into what looked like an overcast day. The shield he'd made was clear. Waves of steam wafted from every surface the heat had touched. The searing heat had turned the surface of the beach to glass.

How long would it last? Was there a word to dispel the shield, or... he wasn't a witch. He might have magick now, but he didn't know how it worked or what to do with it.

Cub. What did you—

Dexx shook himself. They needed to get moving. *Later. Is everyone else still... still here?*

I am trapped. I can see, but I cannot move either.

Dexx tried to move, but his exhausted bones didn't want to move. *That blast had to have been me. I don't really know what I did, so I don't know when this'll end.* "Rainbow?" Would there be another wave of magick? Heat? Water? "You got ears, kid?"

"Thank the currents," she called not far away. "I thought it was only me. I can see the water. It went way out. We gotta go, but I can't move, though."

Water leaving in a hurry wasn't good. But it could be because the water had evaporated and not because it was a tsunami. He had to hope. "Just hang on." Because his limbs weren't moving either. Why? "I have to think."

Give me the crystal, Bussemi-voice snarled. *If you don't, I will hunt you forever and, when I find you, I will kill you and break your* kadu *and take it anyway. If you give it to me, I will spare your* kadu.

Like that asshole was going to let him escape if he Dexx *gave* him the amethyst? He didn't think so. *I wouldn't give you the time of day.* He had to figure out a way to get them to move.

You are my puppet. You will *give in. You are—*

The shield popped. Cool air drifted across his face.

As soon as the shield lifted, he could move. "Okay, guys. I think it's safe now." Dexx stood, crunching against the thin glass. Had he been the thing that had held them all pinned?

An arc of lightning shot past him. Tiny slivers of the bolt flaked off and sizzled his shoulder.

Once, he'd been careless with his capacitive discharge system on Jackie and had been hit with fifty thousand volts. That didn't hold a candle to the flinted zap that barely grazed him.

Mario closed the distance, his fist raised.

How had that man survived?

Magick. Obviously, but fuck! Dexx dodged once and again, but the third bolt clipped him on the ear. His vision swam for a second. Dexx was tired of this shit. He powered forward, smashing into Mario, taking them both to the scorched ground. Glass splintered into pieces too small to use as a weapon. He might be picking slivers for years, though.

Mario rolled, landing on top.

Dexx felt the pull of earth shift beneath him punched Mario in the ribs. Damn, that hurt his hand. He pulled his hand back painfully useless. "You're different, Kester. You change your hair?"

Mario called another blast of Earth, hurling up from the depths.

Dexx diffused the blast, but and though he didn't understand how, he managed to convince Earth that Mario was his target.

The smack sent them both flying, but Dexx rolled with the landing and stood.

Mario wasn't fazed much, but he moved more cautiously.

How in the nine Hells was Mario impervious to damage?

"I'm sick of you interfering." Mario crouched, circling Dexx.

"Shouldn't have pulled that kidnapping shit. Should have backed off when I told you to back off when we first met. Don't blame me for your incompetence."

Mario put his hands together, forming an A with his first fingers, and the rest curled under and touching knuckles.

"That's a new one." It was, but he saw the pull felt the weave, and knew the intent. The spell took time to generate, but once it was finished, Dexx and the rest would be petrified. He pulled the *ma'a'shed* and fed it his energy. He charged Mario with a slash.

Mario danced back and raised a magick shield, dropping his other spell.

The *mavet* bounced off with a clang.

Rainbow rushed forward but stayed back far enough not

to be in the way. "How do we help?" Rainbow looked tired. She had a hand against Mah'se, holding herself up.

There was no way she could fight another battle. How could Dexx? "Stay back."

"You have two options, Colt. Give me the stone, and I let you free." His shield radiated iridescent light along its surface.

Not going to happen.

"Don't, and I kill you here. Maybe I kill your friends while you watch."

Mario'd offered to do that already. "Do you bad guys all read the same manual?" Dexx had to think of another option because... he was kind of striking out here. "No. I choose Option Three. I kill your sorry ass and pour it in concrete, so the worms don't have to suffer the indignity of having to recycle your shitty carcass."

Mario pulled his head back and narrowed his pale eyes. "Always crudely elegant, aren't you?"

"At least it isn't a riddle." Though he still didn't have a working *solution* worked out yet.

Mario wasn't attacking. His magick was stable, not forming anything offensive or defensive.

Was he as tired as Dexx? "Feeling your age? Thought you wanted a fight."

Mario sneered. "You have nothing that scares me. You might have, but you're too broken to be a real fight."

Broken but not down. And Mario was hiding behind that shield a long time. Maybe he *was* tired.

Mario drew himself up. "You aren't even a fly now." He gathered magick in a vortex.

"Well, you're half right." Dexx couldn't see Mario's magick intent yet. "More like a murder hornet." What could he do that would counter that? "Take your best shot." And miss.

Rainbow his shield with water from the beach of glass with a thick tendril of water.

Mario fought against the lack of air pounding against the barrier of his own spell.

"Do something, Dexx. I can't hold him."

How had Mario gotten so powerful? He had *some* power, maybe a lot, but the level of magick he'd thrown around?

He needed something to *kill* Mario.

The list was empty. No spells. Nothing came to mind.

He had his demon blade. He charged Mario for the second time, ready to cut him in two.

Rainbow's water prison broke apart and splashed at Mario's feet as he swung.

The smack of the *mavet ma'a'shed* against the shield exploded in fire and sparks.

Dexx flew back, landing hard.

Mario lay on the sheet of glass of the new beach. He groaned, throwing an arm over to rolling on his side.

That bastard wouldn't *die*.

We have to run, cub.

We have to— what? Stay and fight Mario? He'd already hit Mario with a nuclear blast, and that barely slowed him down. *Are we good to run?* And what could he lay down on Mario to keep him from following?

The horizon lifted. Not much at first, but soon it would be a big problem tsunami.

Mario groaned again.

The swell increased speed, and the pronounced bump on the horizon was unmistakable.

A tsunami was coming, and they were still on the beach.

"Run. We have to run now." Dexx gathered his feet under him and stowed his *ma'a'shed*.

Hattie caught up to him. *Get on my back. You won't get far enough from it.*

Mah'se had Rainbow already up, and they charged away. That stag could run *fast*.

Dexx climbed on Hattie's back just as the wind picked up.

The wave was coming on strong.

When Dexx looked back, Mario was gone.

19

Run fast, girl, run fast. They might still survive the rush of water at their heels.

Rainbow leaned low on Mah'se's back. She gripped for all she was worth as she bounced against him. Even with the grunts of pain, she still wore a maniacal smile.

The tsunami chased them. Water never touched their feet, but Dexx urged them to keep going.

We need to find cover. They needed rest, that was for sure. *Or do we need to stop?* Should they just keep going?

Hattie didn't answer.

Do you know any place nearby we can go?

Hattie faltered a step but kept moving.

Yeah. Stopping and resting, hiding? That was a great idea. *Damn it, you either tell me what's up or else.* What "or else" might be, was a bluff. He felt drained. He wouldn't hurt Hattie, ever, but he could threaten?

I am losing the strength the hunt gave to me.

Fan-fucking-tastic. *Do you know where we can hide? Let's rest. Let's eat.*

Mah'se interrupted. *There is a place. We do not like it, though.*

That was better than running till they were dead. *Our options are somewhat short. Let's go there and hope for the best.*

The party veered in a lazy turn to the left.

Dexx kept his senses peeled for anything that might be chasing them. He didn't know how much longer they ran for because time there didn't work the same. But they weren't followed. A pile of stones rose on the horizon. *That the place?*

It is.

Doesn't look so bad to me. And it wasn't. Until they got closer. The pile of stones manifested into a ruined city. Maybe. Or a ceremonial site. Or, well, anything but an unwelcome feeling settled over Dexx.

A wide outcrop of flat stones might have been a roadway. A haphazard collection of logs resembled the remains of a teepee.

The further they went, passing things that were *almost* pieces of a lost town or something civilized, the worse he felt about being there. Things felt... creepily familiar.

Point taken. You don't like it here.

A tingle began to buzz in Dexx's head. Crap. He really didn't need Bussemi. Not now.

Shit. The ward sickness is coming.

Another presence barged into his mind. Bussemi shouted, basically on a repeat of everything he said whenever he overcame the barriers in Dexx's mind. Take the *kadu to him or blah this, death that*

Wow. He just never got any new material. The single good thing that came from Bussemi-voice was that the overwhelming fear of the man created in Dexx was on a steadily increasing fade. Dexx was more pissed and annoyed at the man now. Yeah. He could invade with a powerful headache. He could threaten all kinds of stuff. But... that's all he was at this point. Dexx needed a Bussemi solution? Well, being able to practice thinking around him could be part of that.

You will— Bussemi fell silent for a moment, and his voice changed — *Where have you taken yourself? I feel it.*

Feel good? Feel bad?

Hattie slowed as she came around another pile of stones that really resembled a town square, like in old-time England, but the square was built around a huge boulder jutting toward the sky.

You cannot be there. You will leave that place. You will do it now.

Was that... Bussemi pleading? The voice seemed anxious. Whatever it—

Hattie walked past the pile of stones, and it was like a cold blanket had been draped over Dexx.

And Bussemi was... silent.

Well, if Bussemi didn't like it, Dexx was sure to stay awhile.

Dexx jumped off Hattie's back at a run and skidded to a halt. He stopped behind a large rock, watching the back trail for signs they were being followed.

Everything seemed as quiet as refugees could ask for.

Dexx didn't relax, not intentionally, but with nothing on the back trail, and with something creepy about the ruins keeping Busemmi silent, he just sort of *did*.

Rainbow was already gathering wood for a fire and moving rocks around.

Which was refreshing. They finished making camp and sat beside the small, sheltered fire.

Dexx watched Hattie rest, worrying about her. He wanted to go hunting but didn't know if they had the time. Mario probably wasn't dead, But if this place somehow kept Bussemi quiet, maybe it would hide them from Mario, too.

At least long enough for Hatti to rest. For them all to rest.

Dexx didn't realize he'd shut his eyes until Rainbow's light touch woke him. "I think they found us."

It was almost inevitable. Dexx had no idea how to even

get high ground here. He didn't know how Mario was here. He shouldn't be. DoDO shouldn't be either.

However, on the very edge of the horizon, the clouds lit and flickered, dimmed then lit again.

Hattie joined him, her shoulder almost touching his. She radiated heat.

"Dollars to doughnuts, *that's* Mario."

The lightning flickered into a strobe. It crested the horizon and rushed forward, gaining ground on their hideout.

He let his head drop. "Fucking hell."

Hattie pressed his warmth into him. *Maybe he will not find us.*

Dexx raised his head up, watching the lightning come closer. He pulled the *ma'a'shed* out and transformed the knife into a sword, knowing with their luck, Mario had found them. Somehow.

Dexx had never really been scared of Mario. Not even when he thought he was an agent. But this new and improved Mario, looking like *Doc Oc* moving in a *Spider-Man* comic, was terrifying his extra limbs braced themselves against the ground and sky.

The cloud of lightning and Mario closed on them *fast*. In seconds he was close enough to see, tatters of his clothes clinging wetly to his body. He dropped to the ground, landing with a small thud as his lightning limbs disappeared.

Let's find cov—

Hattie darted forward. She slammed into Mario, rocking him backward but not taking him off his feet.

Mario dodged forward, batting at the cat, but she moved, dancing back and around.

Dexx made to move forward but found himself frozen.

Mah'se charged from Mario's blind side, head down, looking like a bull. He clipped Mario and spun him around.

Mario threw lightning. At the same time, the ground heaved. It missed Mah'se, but only barely, but the sudden rising of the earth tripped the stag. The passing bolt left scorch marks in the elk's hide as he plowed into the ground.

Dexx tried to move again and couldn't. What the hell?

Hattie used the distraction to turn and head back to Mario. She reared up, both paws spread wide, her claws out. She was going for full rend and dismember.

Mario gave her an uppercut with crackling blue energy.

She flew away and hit the ground hard. She didn't move.

Hattie. Dexx would have gone for Mario's throat too, but he couldn't move. The *mavet* was frozen, just like the rest of him.

Mario straightened, ran his hand along his slicked-back, bright blond hair. "Give me the crystal."

Dexx struggled to move a foot. He needed a spell. Anything.

"I am simply done with you." Mario moved closer. "Give me the crystal, now."

Dexx was stuck. He couldn't *move*, yet both Mario and Bussemi had insisted Dexx *give it to them*. That gave him an idea. "Take it. Go ahead and take it from my warm, grasping fingers."

Rainbow floated into view, held by a spell of Mario's. A simple immobilizing snare, but it didn't do anything to hide her anger. If only looks could kill.

Mario held his hand out. "How about now?"

No. "You don't even know how to use it." Neither did Dexx.

"Maybe I could give it a whirl?" His mouth pulled into a grin.

Dexx was stuck. Hattie and Mah'se were down. Rainbow was on the power-fritz. And Mario wasn't taking them out at that second. Why? "You never said what you want it for. Maybe that'll change my mind."

Mario looked away dismissively. "And perhaps just killing you and taking it is the best way to move forward." Mario moved a half-step forward and then stopped.

Okay. Dexx *was* on to something. But... what? "Why haven't you?"

"Because I like to see you suffer." Mario grimaced as he tried to take another step forward. "Your pain is the sweetest tea. Like a balm to frayed nerves." Mario flicked a finger toward the captured rusalka.

Rainbow started screaming. She changed from human to full rusalka and slashed at the magick prison in reflexive anger.

He saw the magick touching her. A wave of Mario's magick cascaded over her.

The information came to Dexx on the spell's intent. *Wall of pain.*

Useful to know the spell. Maybe. But how was he supposed to fight it?

Spell slice.

The words were in Dexx's mind, but he couldn't make it work. Was the thing that stopped Mario stopping him, too?

Rainbow's anger and escape effort ratcheted higher.

He *had* to do *something.*

Mario kept his hand out and his eyes on Dexx. "Last chance. Give me the crystal."

Dexx calmed himself and focused. He needed a way out of this. He needed a spell he could invoke that would stop Mario, free them all, and get them to safety.

A list of spells exploded in his mind.

Okay. This was good. He was starting to figure out how this thing worked. Great. He looked through them as quickly as he could and chose one. Not randomly, but not as strategically as he could either. Or it chose itself. Power crawled its way from his core to his fingertips agonizingly slow, then it snapped back into his core and exploded out into the world. One instant, he was held immobile, and Rainbow was screaming, and the next, she was quiet and still on the ground.

Mario stumbled back a few steps like he'd been hit by something large.

Spells lined up and fed themselves through Dexx, one after the next as he moved forward.

Was he walking? Flying? It didn't matter. He attacked.

Mario recovered from the initial hit quickly and shot spells and wards at Dexx in a stream. Both slammed spells at the other, but every time Mario released one, Dexx had a response, and vice versa.

He needed something more. The spell duel had quickly become a stalemate.

Whatever the source of the spells came from, helped again. The spell popped out a technique for fighting while wardcasting. He could use his sword to cut through Mario's attacks and cast his own.

Mario only had his own magicks to defend and attack, and those were slowing down. Had he finally exhausted his magick reserve?

Dexx barely had control of his own body., Some part of his subconscious literally pushed him through the magick use. And the skill with the sword. He felt the reverberations of a long past lifetime bubbling up to fight Mario with him. Almost *as* him.

Cast. Slice, cast. Dexx fell into the rhythm of the fight, using the sword to cut offensive spells while casting his own. His new powers were hella cool.

Mario defended, spells ending as Dexx cut through them.

Mario was better than he ever had been, but Dexx had somehow gotten better.

Spell after spell fed through Dexx like bullets on a belt through a Gatling gun, and his sword became a blur, slicing every attack that came.

Mario took hit after hit, blast after blast. He was on the defensive, and any attack spell he managed to get out, Dexx sliced through easily and without thought.

Then, Mario fell, unable to cast more. A part of his aura dispersed a few magickal attacks, but not enough.

Dexx had Mario on the ground, cowering and beaten. A few more hits, and Mario would be toast.

His previous incarnation had *amazing* powers. Now all he had to do was learn it all.

The wards and spell lists wavered and then fled. The power that had just a moment before shot out in a frenzy dissipated like fog. The sword gained weight. A lot of weight. He wouldn't be able to swing it much more.

Mario hunched up in his crouch, beaten and a bit bloody. His skin steamed and smoked in places.

"What the...? Where the hell is the—"

He saw the fireball form, but it took him off guard. It hit with the force of a truck. Okay, so he'd never been hit by a truck to know, but it should be about the same as that blast. His *shamiyir* flew from his other hand, but he managed to maintain his hold on his sword, but it shrank to its knife form. He skidded through the dirt to a stop.

Mario raised his hands, glowing power in both of them. He advanced slowly, with a bit of a limp. "Give it to me now."

Dexx rose as slow as Mario moved forward. "First off, no." Dexx puffed, out of breath. Mario had to be tired, but he didn't look it very much at all. "And second, what the hell did you do? How are you like *Dr. Strange* all of the sudden?

Yesterday you barely had enough power to lift your spirits. And today? Fuck, me."

Mario leapt at Dexx, casting dozens of spells simultaneously.

Dexx saw the lines of magick clear as day. He knew what they were, what they were supposed to do. Killing spells. All of them. And all of them aimed at Dexx.

He swung his demon blade right into Mario's chest. It sank deep, but somehow the blade met resistance.

"Checkmate, motherfucker."

Double checkmate. Some spells hit, and others missed—sort of. Dexx became a conduit more that wound over and through him, then through the *ma'a'shed* and into Mario.

Mario convulsed but still not dead. The anger that had been there before turned into confusion and pain. For just a moment, Mario looked like he had the last time Dexx had seen him. A mediocre level leyline mage.

Mario disappeared in a flash of light. Then the magick backlash exploded at Dexx.

The last sound he heard was his own scream mixed with Bussemi's.

He'd won.

Please, oh please, could he die now?

D exx... didn't die.

His body hurt way too much to be dead.

Except for his head, which hurt but didn't have any trace of Bussemi or the ward sickness for once.

He felt Hattie in his head, so at least she hadn't been hurt too badly.

The smell of cooking meat pulled him out of his desire to sleep more. Rainbow talked softly as she moved around. Obviously, *some* time had passed, and *something* was being done while he was out. "How long?" His voice croaked and cracked.

Short soft grass under him was chilled and damp, but not uncomfortable. They were on another plane. It might have been the plain he sat with Hattie and watched the grazers nibble on. He'd have to open his eyes to find out.

Rainbow shuffled to his side. "Hey, boss. Just a day this time. I got some food cooking up. I haven't heard from Mario or anyone else. I think you got him good this time."

"Good." He could use a day without being chased. One eye opened.

Nope, they were still in the ruins, in the natural ring of boulders.

"Hey. We got a fire going. And food, too. You hungry?" The fire danced shadows against the tall stones.

Dexx cracked his other eye open. "How did *you* start a fire?"

"Well, actually, we kind of worked together on it. I can set it up, but making the fire *burn?* I'm still—" She shook her head. "Being a water elemental is one thing. Being unable to survive? That's dumb."

He chuckled and then wished he hadn't as his ribs creaked. "So how is everyone? Last I saw, Mario had all of you down."

"It wasn't that bad." The look in Rainbow's eyes said otherwise, but she kept her tone chipper. "It was just pain, mostly. A little bit of time, and we were all good."

Just pain. She'd said it like the pain was a small thing like a glass of water. Just water, just pain. What had she gone through that she had that kind of resilience?

Fat cat, you hanging in there?

As well as the hunter in prime hunting lands.

So that was strange. She said words, but the feeling was a different set of words. she was lying.

He braced his arm and sat up. Rusty hinges were easier to move. They complained less, too.

A pound of dust fell from him as he changed positions.

"You need a bath." Rainbow pinched her nose with her fingers.

"Thanks. Any other really important hygiene comments you'd like to throw my way?"

"Yes, but I think we should have hot water and a mirror first. I mean, I could go for a good soak, but I'm a water girl, so that could be just me. But you're a boy, and the first thing they do is stink. Not a bad stink, really, but I could probably ping you from a mile away. Hey, we could try that, you know. As soon as you get something to eat, I mean. Did you want to do that?"

Dexx held his hand out for Rainbow to grab. She pulled and levered him up.

Dammit. Dirt found had its way down in places that it never should be. "Point me to the tub. I need a week for some of this."

Hattie and Mah'se were curled up on the ground outside the range of the campfire light. All Dexx could see were paws and heads in the dark.

Wait. Darkness? "Is it night?"

This place works differently than other places, Hattie said. *When will it get light out?*

When we get to the light.

Of course. Just get to the light, and it'll be light. Of course.

He took a better look at his surroundings. Firelight played off the boulders set in a rough circle with large gaps in between them.

The place had a familiar feel to it like he'd seen it before. But when?

Rainbow moved to the meat speared on a stick and suspended it closer to the flame.

He *had* seen the place. In his dreams, in his memories. Dinner, however, looked good. "How—"

Rainbow grabbed the stick of meat and handed it to him. Her optimistic cheer pushed her to nearly vibrate. "Don't get me wrong. It wasn't as easy as you made it look, but we got it handled. And see here—"

Dexx held up his hand, sorry he'd asked. "Shh. I just woke up. Things hurt, and I haven't eaten in a day." He smiled.

She returned it with a locking motion on her lips.

"Thanks. Roast beast is my favorite."

Dexx took his food and crossed the campsite to a boulder low enough to sit on comfortably. He hadn't even seen it until he sat down. So maybe the place was a bit more comfortable and familiar than he knew.

Sitting on the rock, his memory went on playback.

Rainbow, Roxxie, and the rest of the gang in the abandoned warehouse office were watching his memories from the *shamiyir*. He tore a piece of meat with his teeth, revealing the pointy end of the stick. Rainbow didn't have a knife.

He slapped his empty sheath and looked at her expectantly.

Rainbow smiled again but batted her eyelashes as if to say she wasn't giving it up.

That wasn't acceptable.

Rolling her eyes, she reached over and pulled the *ma'a'shed* off the blanket behind her, holding it carefully by the blade.

He took it and put it away. He spoke past the chunk of meat. "You were careful with it. Nicely done, probie. There might be hope for you, after all."

The clearing was familiar to him, in an ancient memory way.

"I remember this place." He motioned around them.

"Me too." She shook herself. "It's kinda spooky, you having that rock memory and then bringing us here. It's like you knew what was going to happen. Too bad you couldn't leave yourself a note or something."

"What?" Holy crap, she had a point. What if he *did* know he'd be back here? This was the last place he'd seen his first brother. When he could have killed Bussemi and made this life a little less dangerous. This was the place he'd first seen his *shamiyir do* anything. It projected his memory on the walls of an office.

Rainbow narrowed her eyes and tipped her head to the side. "What are you thinking?"

"I... don't know yet." A note. Coincidence? Too much had already felt like it wasn't just randomness settling in on him. Deksculta seemed confused that Dexx didn't know how to use it. Dexx handed the stick back to Rainbow and stood up. He dug his small stone from his pocket and held it in his palm. "He said it like it was easy. Like any simpleton should be able to figure it out."

"Boy, he got *you* wrong. You aren't just any old simpleton." Rainbow gave him a wink.

He mock-glared at her in return, then studied the rock, spinning it on his palm. How to use it?

As it spun, he stared at the runes carved on it. They were nothing more than darker blurs on the violet surface.

They didn't slow. It spun, magick sparking against his palm. The building heat more than friction could account for, growing hotter, spinning faster instead of slowing.

Rainbow took a step back.

It flashed white-hot for an instant then hovered in place over his palm, glowing brightly.

He jerked his hand away.

Visions flashed in his head, then flashed out and displayed across the campsite like holograms. He faced off against the younger version of Bussemi in his early magick days.

Another flash and another scene.

Bussemi had been driven off or escaped, the vision wasn't clear. But Dexx was safe with Hattie. She had offered him a way out. To be *more* than he was. He had everything he wanted.

A small movement caught his eye. In the shadowy circle of the flames, a child cowered against the rocks.

A child.

A small girl huddled from the light and warmth.

His child.

He spoke in a language he didn't recognize. The memory replay had sound. Maybe it was a special memory. Sure felt like one.

The little girl didn't move immediately, but she looked less afraid. Slowly she crept forward, and then tears came.

Was she scared *for* him or *of* him?

He scooped her up in a hug and held her, speaking into her ear, still in a language he couldn't understand.

The memory version of Dexx held out the stone and put it into the small girl's hand.

Hattie—Hattai spoke into his mind. *The cub cannot stay with us. What we do will be too great for her to be a part of.*

Memory Dexx spoke silently. *But this is my child. I cannot leave her. What if our enemy comes back?*

He will *be back to kill this one if we don't leave. There are many enemies, and your cubmate is just one.*

Memory Dexx kissed the young girl's head. *What have I agreed to? You tricked me.*

That is not how this works. Cubs are good, but they cannot hunt with the hunters.

Memory Dexx buried his face into the girl's shoulder. The gruff sounds were obviously him sobbing at the last time he was going to see his child. And woman-mate.

How many lifetimes had Dexx created kids and then left them to fight *this* fight? The guilt him. Hard. Bobby, Ember, and Rai had all grown up. Fast. Without him. He *was* a terrible father.

"I'm an ass." Dexx turned away from the memory and faced his real-and-in-person cat. "Did we even *try* to see them again?"

Hattie rose from the shadows and sat next to him. This *is*

why we do not come here. The emotions of this place are too strong. Every version of you that enters relives the pain.

"That was a shitty thing to do to a little girl. Did we even try?" Like with the twins? Bobby and Leah? Was he fighting hard enough to return to them? Was he focusing enough on getting back to them?

Cub. She had sorrow in her sending. *This is not the place to relive it.*

He knew it wasn't the time, not with the way they were being *hounded*. But when would be the right time? He *missed* his family, his kids. Paige. And he wasn't... used to... He had feelings. He knew that. But he was just always better at pushing them down. "Why not? Because I'll *feel* better about leaving them?"

This place has too much power already. It hurts us to be here.

Did his emotions feed this place? And how did that hurt their bond? "Maybe it should hurt me too."

Rainbow put her hand on his arm. "You did what you had to. The kids'll understand. Paige'll make sure of that."

If she had time to. Maybe.

"You would do it again to keep your people safe, you know. Leaving to protect them? It's what you do, boss." She shrugged. "Protect when nobody else can."

He hated being sulky, but he was definitely feeling it. And he had no real experience to handle it. "Doesn't look like it from this angle." He turned to his spirit partner. "Do we do this *every* life?"

No. There were times when you were an only child, or you never took a mate or didn't have cubs of your own. There were others when you'd keep them. She sighed as if to say she wasn't completing that thought. *You had a few when you kept them safe.*

Did knowing this make the hurt in his heart—the hole in his soul feel better? "That little girl—" So like Rai. "—probably hated me forever after that."

"I don't think she did." Rainbow's voice was filled with sadness.

Oh, right. She'd been abandoned too.

"She kept that stone." Rainbow took a seat on a nearby rock and clasped her hands between her knees. "You see how she's holding it? She never hated her dad. She probably grew up knowing you kept her safe by distance."

Could he see that? "Sure looks like a failure in my book."

"I bet she lived to be strong because of you."

He had to hope so because he—Fuck. He was still *living* this life. He still had a chance to do something better. He still had time to kill Bussemi for *good* and protect his kids and watch them grow, and torment Paige with his terrible jokes she never understood.

Something about the place changed. The deep sorrow and regret lifted. Not completely, but noticeable.

Another layer of Rainbow surfaced. How had he missed her great qualities before? She helped because she wasn't a monster. She might be a rusalka, but she was never a monster. She hid because nobody ever saw past that part.

Paige had.

And now Dexx had.

"Fine. We aren't here to remember how shitty a father I've been. Did I leave myself a message?" Because *that* was the important part right now.

Rainbow shook her head and looked around. "It'd have to be hidden somewhere, right?"

Probably. Dexx blocked the still-blazing light from the stone with his hand and looked around the area. Rocks filled the area from the size of boulders bigger than a dump truck to the little seat he knew well.

At the base of one of the large boulders, a glint caught his eye. "There." He went to it and scooped dirt away from a metallic line until they uncovered … a sign.

Runes. Only bigger than the runes carved in the stone.

But they still meant nothing to him. Nothing at all.

The light faded from the *shamiyir,* and the rock dropped to the ground. Dexx picked it up, warmth flowing through his hand. "Damn." There had to be a way to read this.

"If you left it for you, then it *means* something."

That he understood. "I don't think I like any of my past lives." He had to find a solution to Bussemi in this lifetime. But… using a crystal and some runes he couldn't read? How was that supposed to help?

"Let's think like you."

Okay. How would that be? Charge in with half the information and get his ass handed to him? That's how he'd been thinking lately. So, no. Not that way.

"Your old you knew that you had to protect the people in your now you's life."

That seemed like a likely assertion.

"The only way you could was if you came back. Over and over. Learning new things each time. Maybe dropping off new information."

Again, super idea, but only if he spoke runes. He needed to take a picture or something. Because if there *was* information there or… memories stored in the amethyst that had to be unlocked by this rune? Geez. This was dumb.

But it'd had to survive over the course of entire lifetimes, so this couldn't be an *easy* puzzle. Just in case it fell in Bussemi's hands.

Right. He *was* going to take Bussemi out once and for all this time. He'd figure out how. Eventually. Hopefully soonishly.

"It's time to get back to our world." And hope he maintained his connection with Hattie, but there was nothing left for them here. Bussemi was out there. "Ah." Rainbow winced. "I don't… know how the currents brought us here."

Or how Mario had gotten there. "Hattie, Mah'se? Any ideas where the great egress is?"

Rainbow rubbed her face and frowned at him. "What's that? The great egress?"

"Just a story about the circus and how they kept the crowd moving from attraction to attraction by telling the exit was soon." While he was talking, his mind was working, twisting, plotting, trying to find a way out, a way to hide from Bussemi, to find his weakness, to use the amethyst. He needed to continue to ramble to make his brain work faster. "But at the time, nobody knew what the egress was. Books weren't a big—" Dexx stopped as something hit him. "Books."

"Sorry, I didn't pack any." Rainbow looked at him like he'd lost his mind. "Not that I had a choice or *knew* we'd need any. I like to read." She turned around, studying the area as she babbled. "It's just a little hard, and I don't read the smart stuff. Mostly romance. I think it's funny when the guy has *no* idea how to turn a girl on, you know—

"Bow." Dexx put a hand over her mouth, realizing at that moment that when she babbled, she was doing the same thing he did when he babbled; thinking. "I know a way out."

"But we haven't broken the ward on you yet. Don't we need to do that first?"

Probably. But he had the stones. They could find someone on the other side to help break Bssemi's ward. Maybe. Paige had the Whiskey books, and *those* could have the answer. Or the books in the library. But this place was out of answers.

Dexx knew exactly where to go. "Hattie, do you remember that one place? The library?"

21

Dexx waited for the cat to answer. She had too many bones showing to be called fat anymore. So he demoted her to just cat.

Hattie growled. *Yes. You will not go through that place.*

Yes, we are. It was the only way he knew. *I'm going home, and you can stay there until we figure out how to jam us back together again. You'll be safe.*

It will not work. If you leave, we will be separated, and there may not be a way back. You are still a cub that does not understand.

I might understand more than you think. He had to hope so. At some point, he was going to have to learn—the right things.

You always think of the impossible hunt.

And sometimes I get what I'm hunting.

Rainbow looked at them curiously. "Do you know how to leave this uh... this world?"

"I think I do." And it might not be super pleasant, but it shouldn't be... bad. The goddess was *gone*, as far as he knew. "It's in Bastet's territory, sort of. Maybe right next to it. So how about it? Want to go ruffle some feathers on a book?"

Rainbow's expression said she had no idea what he'd just

said. "I'm in. I mean, if we all are, then I am too. Mossy? Say you will."

This is not a good idea. The great elk stomped a foot. *If things were normal, we might have stepped right to it. But things are not normal, and we cannot move like we are used to.*

Dexx turned to look at him. "I don't understand. Travel here's always been weird."

Your condition changes everything. Mah'se took on the tone of a lecturing professor. *The magick from your world is affecting you and your spirit bond. You are trapped in this space just as if you were on your plane.*

Well, crap. "You seem to know a lot about my world since you've never taken a bond."

Just because I am not willing to go there does not mean I am ignorant. I passed from there a long time ago, and here is a better place.

"*Most* of the time, sure." Shit. Okay. Re-prioritize. They needed to get out of there, and he needed to think of a solution. He kept talking as his mind worked. "As long as you know, evil wizarding witches don't strap you to the plane and suck your energy out. I'd say this place is way safer."

Rainbow's hands went to her face in shock. "Is *that* what happened? That was Copper McCree, wasn't it?"

Talking about a history he actually knew was helping him work through his problem. "Yup, that guy." He had the amethyst. "And before then, we were mopping up demons." He'd unlocked his magick. Sort of. He still didn't know how to use it. "Protecting the plains from marauding demons."

That was before even you.

Dexx was barely even paying attention to the conversation. "Yeah." He was trying to *learn* how to use his magick. "Before me." He'd be able to fight and keep his clothes. "But the general feeling is the same." Right? That would happen?

Mah'se stared at Rainbow. He swung his head to Hattie. *You won't get to the desert without me.*

Desert. Was there a way to create a mental desert in his head as a protection against Bussemi?

Hattie didn't shrug, but somehow she managed. *Maybe. I am not at my full strength, but I believe we would get to the place without much trouble.*

Mah'se flung his head. It made him look playful, but the kind that could kill a person. *You would say that if you were almost dead. Your last lifeblood leaking out, and you would spit in the forever's eye.*

What could he do outside of this place? It didn't matter. He couldn't do anything else here. Any more time resting or learning or... whatever would be a waste of time his family couldn't afford. He wasn't abandoning his kids this time. He wasn't putting them in danger this time, either. But he would save them. Hattie nodded once. A very human gesture.

I accept. We have been... not enemies for a very long time. I have found that I like your company. Your companions are tolerable as well.

Was that a flick of the eyes to Rainbow? Had she rubbed off enough that *Mah'se* liked her being around?

Okay. That was interesting. But... also not worth Dexx's full attention.

But she did have that effect on people.

Rainbow clapped her hands once with a big grin. "Oh, *perfect*. This is going to be the best."

"We should rest first." It was going to be *something*, but what? Their luck hadn't been smooth so far. "I'll take watch while everyone else sleeps. Sound good?"

"Sure." Rainbow made a tsking noise. "Too bad we can't toast some marshmallows or tell stories. This is just like camping in the movies. Except the bad guy already tried to kill us and didn't get *any* of us."

With the deep emotional drain of the campsite gone, Dexx felt so much better. Lighter.

"He got us all pretty well. Get some sleep." Dexx had a

little problem to work out, so they'd have a fighting chance. "We leave when everyone wakes up."

"Sure, boss. Have a good night." She went to Mah'se, who had been turning in place, and wrapped her arms around his neck. After she let him go, he dropped to the ground, and she curled up next to him.

Dexx was happy to see their growing bond. Rainbow was a nice person, a genuinely good one. Mah'se wasn't so bad as far as know-it-all elks went either.

She will feel the loss when you leave. Hattie sat next to Dexx, her head inches away from his.

They seem to be getting along rather well.

They are. Hattie let herself down to the ground, looking like a sphinx. *She might make him decide to take a bond. Your child of the currents is not normal, even for one of us. We have been lucky for her to be with us.*

That was probably the first time anyone had *ever* said that about Rainbow. *Rest if you can. How much strength will you gain back if I bring back something to eat?*

Enough.

Enough for what? I want to get out of here, hug my kids, and have a fantastic life, but I won't leave you to rot.

Hattie turned her head up to him. *You must do what you feel is right, of course.*

That felt like a verbal slap. *Is it legal for you to quote movies? I'll have to check on that.*

Hattie didn't purr, but right then, he had the feeling she would be.

Rest. If you sleep, do that. I'm going to poke at my rock and keep watch. And try to see if he could find a way out of there. This wasn't their end. He'd get them out of there, find a way back to Paige and the kids. And keep Hattie alive.

Hattie didn't reply. She just laid her head on her paws and closed her eyes.

Dexx pulled his stone from his pocket and studied the marks.

Runes. They had to be. He traced the lines as he'd done before. The rock warmed at his touch, but nothing else happened. He hoped that after Dekskulta and the city of Kupul that maybe, just *maybe* he could prod more out of the thing.

What had Dekskulta tried to tell him?

He just had to concentrate. The one thing about his past selves, they'd all been pretty smart. They might have even known that Dexx—this version of him—wouldn't have the ability to just reach in and unlock the *shamiyir*, let alone the amethyst.

Unlock. He was still pretty sure that rune on the rock had somehow been a key.

He dropped his hands to his sides and took in a deep breath. He absently tapped the rock with his finger and dragged it across the top of the indent. A piece of stone slid away.

"Shit." He snapped his hand back up and looked at the stone.

Sure enough, a piece of the stone had slid back. It didn't do anything more, but he felt power leech from the stone. It infused his body. Stress and soreness he hadn't even known about drained away.

Hattie sighed and rolled to her side. She looked better, about as good as Dexx felt, which was a lot.

At least there was some relief. Just eating the creatures of the spirit plane wasn't going to keep her up forever.

He slid the rock closed and felt the power subside. Not fast, but like a slow leak on a tire, like there was plenty of air until the next gas station, but it needed to be dealt with.

Dexx sighed and turned around the campsite.

Mah'se had gathered plenty of wood, so Dexx banked the fire and left the campsite.

The ruins had been built right up to the rough circle of rocks, with the remains of a wall bare feet away.

Atlantis- Kupul had been much bigger and grander and more complete. There could be many reasons for that, but these ruins had more... personality in them.

They were smaller. Cozier.

The street looked more like a path, but it had no plants and few rocks in the way. It wound around like a snake, but he stayed close to the campsite. On his way back to the town square, one obvious pedestal on the outside could be a gravestone. Or just a podium.

He closed in on the stone marker and looked closer. Symbols had been carved on the stone and were close to faded away.

Dexx traced a few of the lines. They were simple, like stick figures, but after a minute, a story became clear.

There once was a man and a woman. They had two children, and those children had children—Dexx's story.

He had a family. Apparently, his brother had a family, too. But one day, the brother went dark. That must be Bussemi.

The stick figures didn't say why, but the brothers fought, but they could never win against the other.

Until one day, the dark brother made a deal and gained an edge. The other brother found his own help. That must have been Hattie. He and Bussemi had fought, and people had died. Dexx had run.

Had his been family killed? What had happened to Bussemi's family? In the end, the shadow had won the battle, but the war continued through time.

Dexx's children lived. They kept the memory of the two brothers alive for as long as possible, but in time, the memory faded. Until one day, when the two brothers would seek each other out to finish the fight.

"Forever." The symbols faded near the bottom of the stone, but the story filtered into his mind, much like Hattie did. And at that moment, Dexx knew why.

"My kids waited for me to come back. They didn't hate me." Somehow, his little girl had still loved him until the day she'd died. She'd always wanted to see her dad again, if only for a little while, and she had been denied.

Bussemi's war had taken her light away. But she'd somehow been strong to the end and had built a city for him to return to.

She had been smart and capable and loved her father as long as she lived.

How many people could he continue to let down?

He stood, and the world changed. No warning, no noise or explosions.

One instant, he stood in the dark of night in the ruins of a long-forgotten village, and the next, he stood on hard sand, a sprig of grass between his feet.

He'd found his way out.

Better still, the rest of his little band of merry-women-spirit-animal-men had been transported along with him. They were sleeping just like he'd left them. The fire was gone, the rocks too, but everything else was in its spot where they'd left them.

The horizon was lit with the deep blue before the pinks and oranges of dawn.

He saw the low hills in the distance. They had no vegetation.

In the pre-dawn, a vast desert expanded in front of them.

Bastet's desert. The library wouldn't be far.

Mah'se raised his head, grains of sand falling from his

antlers. *Well done. I'm happy I don't have to go through the black lands.*

Dexx cocked his head to the side. "Pretty bad place, I'm guessing?"

Dangerous. Even for one as strong as you.

"Stop. You're going to make me blush. Do you know where we are?"

Do you not? Mah'se didn't sound snarky.

"We're on the edge of Bastet's territory, her desert, but I couldn't say more than that."

We have a long walk. Her domain is vast, and the place you are looking for is beyond it.

"Okay." Damn it.

If we are here, there must be a reason for it.

Dexx was glad the elk thought so. "Why can't *somebody—anybody* just drop off a manual so I can study up on this stuff?" He probably wouldn't have cracked the book open if it landed in front of him. "It kind of looks like you're comfy there, and I want Hattie to sleep a bit longer." Dexx was *eager* to go, to get back to his family, but not at the sacrifice of Hattie. "I got a boost, but she still isn't up to her best. I'm going to sit here and look over our next new problem."

I will sit with you.

Well, that was a change. "You can admit to liking Bow. She's everything you could ask for in a fangirl. And she can kill hecklers too."

I do not need protection from those.

"Yeah, I can see that." But sometimes, Dexx did. He was glad in that moment it'd been Rainbow who'd been forced to come along with him. "You never stepped up to the plate. Never took a bond to see. Sometimes, you just gotta leap in, even though it's scary."

I chose another path.

"You did. You appointed yourself a protector but in the

wrong place. I'm thinking you'd be a good spirit bond, but I shouldn't bust your balls about it, though. On the other hand, thanks for coming along. You've been more than I deserved."

Mah'se didn't respond. He turned his head to look over the desert.

Behind them, the plains stretched out to beyond the horizon, the overcast skies covering all the way up to the border between realms.

"Have you been here before?"

I haven't ever felt the need to enter the realm of the desert queen.

"Really? Cat got you scared?" That struck Dexx as funny for a second. "You spend all your time with the hugest cat ever, and *she's* the one you don't like?"

There is a difference between Hat'tai and the queen.

"Yeah, but it's fun to watch you squirm. I don't like the queen of cats any more than you do. But if we have to cross her land, we have to cross. Besides. I got a buddy on the inside if you catch my meaning, and maybe he'll help us out."

Do you know a member of the court?

"Yeah. We go way back." Lynx had once been one of Bastet's cursed temple cats. He wasn't there anymore, but maybe if Dexx dropped his name, it'd help.

The two watched the desert and the slight breeze blowing the sand while Rainbow and Hattie slept.

Hattie picked her head up and looked around, but she didn't feel surprised. She stood and stretched and sat next to Dexx. He reached out and hugged her close with one arm.

As soon as Rainbow stood and stretched, and worked her muscles out, and ate and scraped her teeth, and complimented Mah'se on how comfortable he was, and puttered around, they were ready to go.

Dexx took a swig of water and swished some, and spit. "I don't know how long this is going to take." The respite had been nice, though, and he didn't feel so... guilty and torn. So, there was that. "So, let's not waste any time."

"Okay, boss. I'm ready to go."

Dexx and the rest set off into Bastet's territory. They walked into the blazing heat, and almost immediately, Dexx questioned if this was the only move.

Dunes grew, and the hills became small mountains of shifting sand.

They crested one sand hill and dipped to the bottom. As they climbed to the top, they found the desert had people. Seven of them in black robes stood on the next dune as they struggled to make the top of theirs.

Hattie growled and crouched, ready to fight. She sent one word to him. *Djinn.*

Fuck.

2 2

Dexx pulled out his *ma'a'shed*, pouring his will into the blade, making it a sword. He patted his pocket for the reassuring feel of the crystal and the *shamiyir*.

Rainbow stopped short. "Like the djinn who attacked Tarik?" She narrowed her eyes. "What do they want?"

"I don't know." What were they doing *here*?

"It's okay, isn't it?" Her tone was optimistic, but her gorgeous brown skin took on a sickly rusalka sheen as she prepared for what might be coming. "I mean, we can be here, can't we? Nobody owns the desert, do they?"

The djinn hadn't moved. Were they letting the four recover from the shock?

"Hush, Rainbow," Dexx said carefully. "Let me do the talking. Just look as intimidating as you can and *be quiet*."

Rainbow stood tall and slid into a semi-rusalka.

It looked like she was learning some stuff, too. Dexx shifted his stance. The hot sun pressed its searing light into his entire body. *What do we do? Attack?*

That would be unwise, cub. They could have hunted us before we knew of them. We wait.

Dexx stood up, releasing the *mavet*, but still kept the knife ready.

Mah'se dropped his head, his antlers came down in front of Rainbow, like he was protecting her.

The djinn in their black robes began walking single file toward their dune.

"Be ready, Bow." Dexx didn't know what else to say. Of course, she was getting ready. She wasn't dumb enough to just stand there after she'd helped Tarik with his djinn attack. In case they get frisky, I want you to rusalka as best you can."

"I have nothing here, boss. We're so far away from water. I can't even feel it."

"It's under the sand." At least he'd seen it on some movie some time, an Aborigine going into the desert with a hollow stick and finding water.

"Uh." A pained look filled her expression. "I *can* feel it, but I can't get any to come up. It... sleeps here?"

Well, he had to try. She *was* changing skin tone a little, so her rusalka was at least there.

The last of the djinn disappeared in the hollow just as the first's head began popping up on their dune.

Be steady. Hold steady. Dexx directed that at the cat, but the words were for him.

If only he had better control over his *shamiyir*. It could be super useful.

He slipped his hand in his pocket and gripped the amethyst. No help there, either. He didn't have an intent, though. No useful spells or advice came up.

The first djinn crested the dune and stopped a respectful thirty feet away. The rest stopped behind him. He looked a lot like Tarik. Middle Eastern, but he had tattoos dotting his face, swirls along his cheekbones and around his eyes. Many more hid beneath the black robe. "Greetings to the first of the greatest and to the great leader." His voice was smooth and practiced, though traces of a demon accent came through. "Hat'tai and Shedim Patesh. Greetings to Mah'se, the protector of the great Time Before. And greetings to the child of the currents. Be welcome here, and may you find water and shade today."

"Uh, sure. I hope you do, too." Dexx stayed on guard. They could be trying to fake nice, and demonology rule number one applied. "We're crossing to Bastet's temple. We don't want any trouble." He could handle one, and together they could probably take two or three with them, but seven? They were goners for sure if the demons came for a fight.

"We have been watching you for some time. If you continue on this way, you will indeed reach the temple of Bastet. Instead, may we entice you to come with us? Water and shade will be found for you. And rest for weary travelers."

That sounded nice. From a demon. Maybe they were different here. Yeah? Or maybe not. "Who are you? And why've you been watching us?"

"There have been many aware of the destruction under the great ocean." The djinn narrowed his eyes a fraction. "You did not think only *you* would notice?"

He had a point. An explosion that took out thousands of miles of coastline couldn't *possibly* be hidden. Not that they were trying to hide that anyway. "None of your kind were affected, I hope."

"No." The djinn licked his lips with a pale tongue. "Those events did not concern us. But when you came here, we asked for permission to collect you. Bastet agreed. You are to be our guests."

"Guests?" Dexx knew full well that the djinn hadn't put any inflection on the word, but Dexx had *felt* one anyway. "Why does it feel more like a prison walk?"

"My apologies." He bowed his head slightly with a smile, the kind a strong adversary gives a lesser opponent. "My name is Ifrir. If you come with us, we can find you refreshment."

Dexx turned to Hattie. *What do you think? Are they lying?"*

They waited for us. In the open and did not attack. This is poor hunting, and they could have already done us harm if they had intended to.

She had a point. The djinn didn't have to wait, and an elaborate trap like this had flaws big enough to drive a bus through.

"You game, kid?"

Rainbow furrowed her brows. "Doesn't rule number one apply here?"

Nice one. Yes. Demons always lie.

Ifrir looked to Dexx, the question clear on his face.

"Yes." But did they have options? Not likely.

She shook out her hands, and her skin tone went back to a nice supple brown. "Okay then."

Maybe she didn't get the message? They were still in danger. Rule number one *clearly* still applied. He gave her a wide-eyed frown, tipped head look asking if she was with him.

She shrugged and told him to shut up and keep talking.

Okay. Maybe she was getting wiser. He turned back to Ifrir. "Tell me we're talking indoors? Like cool air, colder beer?"

"Refreshment will be provided, yes." He gestured to the pyramid, his clawed finger barely poking out from the sleeve of the robe. "But I cannot stress enough the request you have been offered. You *must* come with us."

Well fuck. They *were* prisoners. But the djinn had a reason for being polite, which was interesting. There just wasn't any other explanation. Double hell, all to hell.

That didn't alleviate the fact that Dexx had to get back to the real world, though. He had to figure out a way to use the crystal, power up, defeat his centuries-old brother, and protect Paige and the kids from an immortal bad guy. How long was he going to be *incarcerated* for?

Stay sharp, fat cat.

Always, was her calm reply.

"If you will follow us, the walk shall be short." The seven shambled away, the robes swaying, just brushing the sand as they walked.

Dexx grumbled and put the *ma'a'shed* away. "I'm parched." He really was, but he was really just looking for the exit door.

Ifrir took the lead, and the rest fell in behind.

Dexx walked with Hattie. *Can they be trusted at all?*

They can be trusted as far as they have stated. I do not like the demon kind. You and I are the same in that way.

We are. But until they give us a reason to go down fighting, I'd rather have a beer. Or six. And then go home. Sober.

Mah'se walked behind Dexx and Hattie, his shoulder almost touching Rainbow's.

They all crested the dune where the other djinn had waited. A pyramid loomed a few hundred feet away. *Those* hadn't been there before.

Damn. Ifrir had said the walk would be short. The big question was if they hadn't gone with the djinn, would the pyramid have still been there? "So you keep these out here for weary travelers, eh?"

Ifrir smiled. "It is where it is. You will find it is to your liking."

"I'll bet." Dexx tried his best to sound positive, taking a page out of Rainbow's book. It may not have worked, though. He might need a bit more practice. Rainbow made it look easy.

The dune ended abruptly with a cobblestone path that led to a shaded courtyard. Long strips of wide colorful cloth hung between the pillars, providing shade and about twenty degrees of cooler air. It wasn't real air conditioning, but after the heat of the sun, it sure had the same effect.

The courtyard itself was large and squared off with perfectly rounded pillars forty feet apart and squared stonework running above them.

The perfect open air Egyptian courtyard. Glyphs depicted other symbols of Pharaoh's Egypt: the scarab, Anubis, Osiris, and others. Honestly, Dexx couldn't tell one from a Yugo, but since he'd heard them mentioned enough times in the past year, odds were good they were in there.

The courtyard led to another in the same style, all leading to the base of the pyramid with a large doorway set in the side. Ifrir led them into the darkened interior of the pyramid, the temperature dropping even further.

Six of the djinn disappeared down a corridor, leaving only Ifrir to escort them.

Dexx smiled in spite of himself. Now *that* was cool air. So, the pyramids were big because of a temperature difference, not egos. Good to know.

The hallway led to another set of doors that swung silently open as soon as Ifrir was three strides away. That was cool.

But when Dexx stepped inside, he stopped. "Holy shit."

The room was lit from dozens of hidden wall sconces and was about as rich-looking as Bill Gates, or Steve Jobs could have ever asked for. Gold and silver lined absolutely *everything*. Carpets, furniture, wall hangings, pillars, even the highly polished *floor tiles* were lined with it.

But that wasn't all. Even the people had gold and silver highlights, and they were barely dressed at all, with filmy bits

—if they bothered with bits at all. Men were perfectly sculpted, and the women were a bit more so. *All. Of. Them.*

"Wow." Rainbow pushed in. "Dexx, have you ever *seen* anything like this before? They're *gorgeous.*"

Leave it to Rainbow to blurt it out.

Ifrir turned to them. "Your rooms are this way. We are curious about your timing. Why have you come to us now?"

Timing? There hadn't been any timing at all. They'd blown shit up, and they'd landed here. "We're just lucky, I guess." But the question sounded... deeper. "Why are you planning a party?"

"There is a... ceremony of sorts happening right now. You were not sent here?"

"Wouldn't *you* know that better than I would?" Something was going on here, and Dexx needed to figure out what that was.

"Oh, wow," Rainbow exclaimed. "I wonder if this is what ancient Egypt *really* looked like, you know when it was ancient. Do you think so, Dexx?"

Well, if she couldn't keep her mouth shut, hopefully, she'd baffle 'em with bullshit. *Nobody* pegged Rainbow without a thorough study.

Wait. *No one* pegged Rainbow—even him. Was this a cover? Like her being cheerful in the face of danger? He had to hope so. "I couldn't say. This is my first time here too." But he kept his eyes open for anything that could be useful. Paige and the kids. Paige and the kids. Killing Bussemi. Paige and the kids.

I see nothing, cub.

Ifrir led them down halls big enough to accommodate even Mah'se's impressive rack. Egyptian style paintings and hieroglyphs covered every wall and the entire floor. The ceiling was rough but flat and even.

Ifrir finally stopped at a door. "These shall be your apartments while you stay with us. Should you need anything, you have only to pull the rope. Someone will be here to see to your needs right away. I am needed elsewhere." He dipped his head and walked away without opening the door.

"Okay." For a prison, this was a weird one. Dexx tried the door. It slid open silently, just like the front doors did. With Ifrir gone, the hallway was clear, but that didn't mean it wasn't watched. The motioned for the others to go in.

Inside was more of the same, but without people or demons or anyone. The open room had lavish couches that looked about as comfortable as anything as he'd ever slept in, and more doors suggested more rooms further in.

Rainbow squealed in delight. "Eeee! Oh, my goodness, I've never been to a hotel so fancy." Her happy face faded. "Once I stayed in a motel, but it had two beds and no bugs, but this? This is *way* better." She tossed her head at a doorway. "Come on, Mossy. Let's go check it out." She crossed the room and wonder of wonders, Mah'se followed close behind.

They only had a few seconds of panic when they had to figure out how to get his antlers through the door.

Dexx stood in the middle of the room, trying to puzzle out what the heck was going on. "What odds do we get?"

For survival? Hattie prowled to one of the piles of pillows on the floor and flopped over on them. *They would not have invited us in only to kill us.*

"You've never seen *From Dusk to Dawn*, have you? They let you in, then feed on you all night." But hopefully, that wasn't happening here. "So. What are the odds?"

I do not think we are their first concern. Hattie's yawn was nearly as wide as her teeth were long. *"We are here at a bad time, and they need to see us at any time they choose.*

That didn't make him feel any better. "I have a bad feeling about this." Dexx looked around the room. The bright-colored cloth draped on the walls was a nice touch. It gave them texture and color and made their cell look happier.

"Hey, boss," Rainbow called from the next room. "Come take a look at this."

Dexx hurried until he saw what Rainbow found.

Large doors led to a courtyard all their own. The sun beat down from a cloudless sky, with perfect blue outlining the pyramid.

The courtyard even had a large wading pool. Now *that* looked inviting.

Dexx didn't understand the physics of their prison at all. "Damn. This is the perfect resort. Leave it to demons to have paradise perfected."

"What do you think they want with us?" Rainbow sobered as if dropping her mask of cheer.

"Don't know. Whatever it is, we got here just in time." Good or bad, though?

"They didn't attack. We're still alive. Why didn't they just... grk?" She mimed, slicing her throat.

He chuckled. "Could be because of Hattie and Mah'se. They have a certain place in everyone's hearts here. With djinn, though, it's not warm and fuzzy. We've sent more than a few backs, and some of those haven't returned yet. Maybe Bastet forbade them to do anything to us. If she did, why wouldn't she just come to collect us herself?"

Because she was a goddess?

Dexx drew in a deep breath and sighed. Too many questions to answer without more info. "Get on the rope. See if you can get anything in here that looks like a beer. Oh! And a bath. We can discuss how to get to the library after we eat and cool down."

"Sure, boss." With a grimace, Rainbow rose, putting her cheerful mask back on. "Coming right up."

Dexx stayed outside in the courtyard until there was a

knock at the door.

He left Hattie and Mah'se outside, basking in the sun by the pool.

A servant who looked human stepped in. She was the very picture of Egyptian perfection, her face and body. She was dressed like everyone else, which meant there was almost nothing covering her.

Rainbow smiled at the woman. A great big smile.

Dexx wasn't the only one who could appreciate the woman's lack of outfit. "Bow. Keep it in your pants."

Her smile faded... a bit. But she watched the servant girl with obvious appreciation.

"You wish something?" the woman asked.

Okay. *This* was nice. "Yeah. I'd like a tall beer and a bath. Got any of that around here?"

Her face drew in as she thought.

"If you don't, that's fine. I'll take cold water if you have any."

"And I'll have water and fruit," Rainbow said, tipping her head to the side and appraising the servant like a meal. "And a big steak. You got that stuff, right? And your number. I'll take that first."

"Bow, stow it." Dexx folded his arms as she shooed him away with a hand.

"I will attempt to accommodate you," the woman said with a small smile and a bow of her head. "Will your masters be joining us?"

"Masters?" Dexx looked at her from the corner of his eye.

"Of course. Surely you have masters coming. Or are you on a summons from them?"

"I think you have us confused with another time. My master is me. And we came here because the invitation couldn't be turned down if you catch my meaning."

"As you say." The young woman did a courtesy-bow with

things doing things that... well, only Paige should be doing.

She straightened and turned to leave but gave Rainbow a smile over her shoulder.

The door shut behind her.

"Got her number, now what?" Dexx pressed his lips together at Rainbow.

"I don't know yet, but the night is looking up." Her smile lit the room up a little more. "I'm looking for the bathroom."

A bath really did sound good. He still had sand from the tsunami and the dip in the ocean and the—it'd been a long few days. Maybe the pool would work. "You kids and your hormones."

Rainbow looked at him like he was dumb and then looked into the courtyard with *feeling*.

"What?" They didn't know each other well enough to be able to play Pictionary.

She strode out to Mah'se and Hattie.

Dexx followed, blowing out a breath.

Rainbow stood in front of Mah'se for a moment, then relaxed.

Mah'se turned to Hattie, and she relayed the message. *The little cub reminds you that she is pretending. She quotes your demon rules to me.*

"Oh. Damn." Rule number one.

Rainbow was right. Assume everything they said was a lie, even if it wasn't an in-your-face kind. But she was going overboard flirting with the help.

They'd stepped into something sensitive. Dexx didn't know of a situation like this where his pecker actually *solved* a problem instead of making it bigger.

He patted his sheath with the *ma'a'shed*. He'd have to keep it close.

Damn it all to *hell*, how did they get mixed up with a pyramid *full* of djinn?

23

Their drinks arrived soon after. The servant girl knocked politely on the door, and before they had a chance to call her in, the door swung open.

She held a tray of the most amazing things Dexx had ever seen.

A roast that looked cooked to perfection, glasses of water and, goddess bless, tall bottles of amber beer, still with condensation dribbling down.

"Oh, you angel." Dexx took the tray and set it on a table tucked against the wall.

He snatched one of the bottles and pulled a long draw. It tasted great and felt amazing. "Damn, I needed that. Thanks... uh... what's your name again?" Pretend. Right. Pretend to be friendly.

"You may call me Sekhet," she said softly.

Another servant came in, carrying a tray with meat and other fruits. He took it directly to the courtyard.

Dexx opened his mouth to try and be friendly. He took another drink of his ale instead.

The male servant left without saying a word.

Sekhet tipped her head to the side. "I have been asked if your masters will be joining us soon?"

"You're beating a dead horse. Got no masters around here. Or anywhere." Technically he could call Chuck or Sheriff Tuck his bosses, but master? Best leave that in the past where it belonged. "You're kind of on this master thing, aren't you?"

"As you say." She clasped her hands in front of her, squishing her boobs together. "If there is no further need of me?"

That was a loaded question.

Rainbow still had that look in her eye. That *wasn't* pretend.

"Yeah, sure. Pull the rope—" Dexx made a flourish, hand to chest, "—and ye shall arrive, posthaste." He let his hand drop. "Got it."

Rainbow put her fist to her ear, thumb and pinky out like it was a phone, and mouthed, "call me."

The door shut on a smiling Sekhet.

Dexx and Rainbow dropped their smiles and dug in. Right about the time, they felt like they might pop, Dexx put a juicy piece of meat back to the tray. "You don't think they drugged us, do you?

Rainbow kept chewing. "Too late now. Besides, why would djinn need to drug us? They could just blast us, right?"

"Maybe." But the numbers still weren't adding up, and he still had to get back to Paige and the kids. "They seem very happy to keep us entertained. But that slip about our masters? What was that?"

Rainbow shrugged and disappeared through the other door.

Oh, fat cat, Dexx sing-songed in his head. *Would you come here, please? I need a word.*

Hattie entered. Mah'se followed right after only fighting the doorway for an instant before making it through.

Do you think it's safe to take a bath and then a nap in here?

As safe as it is to eat their food.

"Does that mean we shouldn't have eaten?"

It means you ate their catch. It may be nothing. Do they not always look for a better deal? Right now, they seem happy to keep us content.

Her words were ringing as "familiar" to him, but without any real context. As if he'd heard a story with those terms once a long, long time ago. *They sure do. But I have to ask if we're just jumping at shadows. They could totally be on the up and up.*

Hattie didn't respond. She just laid her scrawny body down on a carpet.

"Yeah, you said it." Dexx went through the other door and found the bathing room, where Rainbow was already soaking. After an awkward exchange, they shared the rather large and perfectly warm bath. Then, they both headed back, laid down next to their animal companions, and fell asleep.

What seemed like moments later, Dexx's eyes popped open, and dug in his pocket for his little *shamiyir* with the rune markings. Somehow while he slept, his subconscious mind had been working on the puzzle.

"Slip and slide," Dexx murmured low. He didn't actually want to wake anyone up.

Hattie raised her head.

"Sorry, fattish cattish. Go back to sleep."

Hattie stood and stretched. She showed ribs, and her hips were bony even after eating.

Something had to be done soon. He'd be dead from the ward sickness, and so would Hattie. He was breaking this damned ward curse.

His answer was in his hand—sort of. *Come with me.* He motioned to Hattie and went out to the small courtyard. The sun lightened the horizon of the coming sunrise. "This place is stranger all the time. Why is there a sunrise and sunset here, and never back on your cliff? I know I've asked, but this place is just... strange." But he loved it as long as Hattie was here.

Why do prey eat greens? Why do the greens not walk?

Dexx shook his head. "Things are the way they are. That's what you mean, right?"

Hattie just stared at him.

"I'm catching on to your little tricks and sayings. I should ask you questions in riddle form so you start answering straight."

Hattie just looked at him.

"But as it stands, I think I have one riddle figured out. Sort of." He bounced the stone in his palm. "Watch this."

Dexx positioned the *shamiyir* with a rune out. He'd slipped that little piece out before. This time, he turned it and slid another piece out along the runed edges. That much was easy. He slid more pieces out like flower petals. He flipped petals over until the runes lined up.

The petals locked together. "That's new." With a flash of light, the runes flowed with liquid metal. More runes appeared on the rock flower.

What you are doing feels familiar. Hattie watched intently, her hot breath oddly soothing.

He folded the new runes open into larger flower petals.

Now he had the *shamiyir* open quite a ways, and the runes made a familiar symbol. He'd seen it on the pavers in Kupul.

"He asked why I didn't know. Why would he ask that?" That meant something, but he didn't have enough information at the moment.

I don't know. Hattie felt like she *wanted* to help but couldn't.

"Now for the tricky part." He closed his eyes and felt the

shamiyir. Really felt it. He let his senses flow around and in it. "Dexx Colt."

The *shamiyir* didn't do anything visible, but heat spread through him like the first time he'd held it. No, *not* like the first time.

The heat flared in his chest and took his breath away. He tried to drop the *shamiyir*, but his hand didn't obey.

Heat burned his insides and his brain.

His skin should have charred. His clothes should have caught fire, but at the point when he should have been a fireball with only ashes to mark his last stand, the world stopped.

The courtyard in front of him wavered in gold light as though from behind a fire.

A cold mind-touch alerted Dexx.

You showed yourself to me. The shamiyir you hold is mine. Bussemi-voice purred like a cat kneading claws into an arm. *I can reach you now.*

Another voice spoke, but he didn't feel it like he did Bussemi. *He will not have you. Not this day.* That wasn't Hattie. That sounded like Dexx's former life. Dekskulta.

Finally.

My work lives on in you, Dexx Colt, Dekskulta said. *You will grow into the wi'tch you were meant to be.*

But would it be enough to take out Bussemi for good?

Give me what is mine.

How about no?

I will make sure your sacrifice is remembered. Bussemi sounded calmer, but not by much.

How could Dexx use Bussemi-voice to win against the actual Bussemi? Like, could they use Bussemi-voice to create a mind-vaccine? Or something?

He can't hurt you, Dekskulta said. *He can sense me, but he cannot harm you.*

"I—" Dexx froze as the ward sickness split his head. Couldn't hurt him? Kind of like saying the sun couldn't blind.

If you had given what I wanted, you would not be here.

Dexx was seriously over this guy. "You got a way to shut him up and to stop my head from splitting open?"

Dekskulta's voice thinning as the headache strengthened. *You are my future self, and you have enough strength. He may not think you do, but he is blinded by hatred. You must shed your ties to the bond and take your destiny. You can defeat him. I have seen it.*

Enough of the shit. He'd had enough of everyone using his head to play games in. He closed his eyes and squeezed. The ward sickness headache came on strong, blasting at his head, pushing at him to lose consciousness.

Vertigo and pain silenced everyone.

Hattie's the only one who gets a parking space in here. Little by little, he pushed the pain back.

"Get the hell out of my head. You two want to fight, do it on your own time and in someone else's head."

Pain flared and then receded. The heat from the *shamiyir* came back, and the golden glow in front of him faded.

Bussemi screamed at him. *You can't do this.*

Well, *that* seemed to have hit a nerve.

"Can't what? Undo whatever it is you did to me?" The glow evaporated, but the pleasant warmth stayed.

You cannot use the shamiyir. You do not know how to stop the power from growing beyond your control.

Nice. So, Dexx'd just found his weapon.

Time caught up again, and he took a breath. A real one. "I don't believe you."

I will teach you how to use the power, Bussemi-voice said calmly. *Just do not use it. Not yet. I will rule this world, and more. If you agree to come to me, you shall be the ruler of your world. You can save the paras from extinction. You would be their god, and you would be my vassal.*

What did that word mean again? "I'm not a boat. Not for anyone."

Bussemi paused for a moment. *You would be my instrument in this world. Together, we could challenge any plane of existence.*

"That sounds like a lot of work. No."

I will rule—

Dexx cut off the voice with a force of will.

He did a double-take, listening for the voice, feeling for the pain in his head. "No way. Really? Did I just turn him off?"

He knew the answer, but it wasn't his thought. Dekskulta had left whispers in his head. He had the power of the *shamiyir.* But to keep it, he'd have to sacrifice something. Someone he wasn't going to let go. He'd save Hattie and himself, and everyone else. He would.

Cub. Hattie sounded surprised. *You have found your magick.*

"I did? I guess I did." He flexed his hands. It coursed under his skin, just like when he and Hattie had first bonded.

His heart tore. Hattie looked weak. She *felt* weak. How was he going to help her?

You have found your magick. She sounded sad this time.

There was magickal power there, but not much. He *could* feel the level increasing, though. No wonder Mario had beaten him. He barely had any. More swirled into him, but not quickly. It rose like a power bar in a video game, but more like fuel in a gas tank, though.

He held his hand out, and it sparked. One tiny, insignificant spark. It would do for now. "I did. Now I have to figure out how to use it." And help her and kill Bussemi and protect Paige and the kids. At least his list was getting shorter. He bounced the rock in his hand, the magick flow halting each time he lost contact with it.

The demons in this place might feel your power. How will you hide it?

"I need to hide it? Why?"

We have sent many of them away in our past. This is a den for the demons.

He honestly had no idea how to handle the djinn. "They almost blasted us with an invitation. Are we supposed to fight?"

They do not want to fight. They have many things to think about before they do that.

"Like what? What am I missing here?"

You are here. Outside the bond. The water creature. Mah'se. We are safe as long as they fear us.

Okay. That was good information. "They can't tell three of us aren't up to snuff?"

Dexx and Hattie split apart was bad enough. Rainbow shouldn't be *anywhere* close to a desert. Mah'se was the only one of the three that might be considered a threat to the demons.

You have your magick. That should keep them from openly hunting of us. You are now dangerous to them.

"That's... cool." Just the thought of having power like Paige was a bit off-center. *She* was the witch. He was a demon-hunter-turned-shifter.

The contact with the stone was... well, was amazing. Just like it felt like it was his, the magick felt familiar, like a bed or his butt print in Jackie's seat.

But he also didn't feel the... drain of the spell Bussemi had put on him. "Is the ward broken? Do we just mind meld and... I don't know."

Is the prey dead just because you cannot kill it? I do not feel any different than before.

Damn it. "Great. So, I feel better, and he can't get me, but *you* are still boned. How the hell do we get out of this?"

He remembered Dekskulta saying something about leaving the bond behind.

No. He and Hattie were a unit. Two sides of a coin or some shit. She could be a pain, but she was *his* pain, and she hadn't ever steered him wrong even when she was wrong.

Time to make his choice.

He needed to win against Bussemi and return to Paige and the kids. But he wasn't doing that without Hattie. "We're here until we break this thing. The currents sent us— me here to *do* that." They had, hadn't they? He loved Paige more than his next breath, but he would never forgive himself if he sacrificed a part of him to be with her. And the kids. Hopefully, they would forgive him for staying a while longer.

Hattie walked over to him and nudged him.

"Fuck. Girl, we'll find the cure. And this was a *big* piece. Probably time to get out of here, though. Let's get the Rainbow and Horns. We'll go to the library and send Rainbow home, but Mah'se can go back to his cliff. You and me? We stay until we merge." And hopefully, that would happen real soon.

Thank you, cub.

With a mental push, the stone twisted and folded back into the small rock it had always been. Dexx stuffed it in his pocket and stepped through the doorway into the great room.

Rainbow's eyes were barely open, and her mouth looked a bit slack.

That was exactly the way Paige looked in the morning before coffee.

Did Rainbow drink coffee? If she did, he knew how to take care of things, sort of. The coffee maker might be a plane away, but they had a rope.

"Sleep well?" Dexx kept his voice positive without perky. Paige hated perky this early, but Rainbow did positive. Damn all the fine lines to walk around women.

Rainbow nodded, a yawn opening her mouth to insane proportions. Her teeth looked sharper than normal. "I did. I think."

"Are you okay?" Her teeth stayed sharp.

"I'm great. I think this place is good for me. I hardly had any nightmares."

"Um. That's *normal?*"

Rainbow nodded, but before she said any more, there was a knock on the door, and it swung silently open. Their serving girl stood there with a covered tray. "We hope your evening was enjoyable."

Dexx kept his eyes in his head. She had possibly *less* on than she'd worn the day before. "Sekhet, right?" He gave her finger guns and a bright smile. "We're good, thanks."

Rainbow's eyes lit at once, and she stepped forward with a bright grin. "Oh, yes. Everything was great. Is that for us? Are you a djinni?" She walked to the center of the great room, standing next to Dexx.

Whatever her night had been, she smelled a little more feral.

"We know a djinni," Rainbow said with a slow, sultry blink. "Well, we work with one. He's one of the good ones. But I haven't met any others to compare him to."

Sekhet's inviting smile slipped a fraction. "You have? He is your companion?"

Dexx went on high alert. He *did* work with a djinn, and her smell went to insta-scared. "Well, companion might not be the complete right word, but yeah. We do."

Rainbow seemed oblivious to the undercurrent. "His name is Tarik. But he might have another name. We wouldn't know because he never said he had others."

Sekhet placed the tray on a small table with a slight stumble. "I have brought your meal. If there is *anything* more, please do not hesitate." She turned with her smile still on

Rainbow, but her hand trembled, and she still smelled scared.

Dexx waited for the door to close. "What the hell just happened?"

Rainbow lost her smile, too. "I think we just snagged a tripwire."

"Why did you have to blurt out his name?"

"A hunch. We had nothing, Dexx. We were just waiting for them to tell us what they're up to, and that's stupid. Sometimes you just gotta take a shot." She mimed shooting at the door.

Dammit. She had a point. That sounded familiar, too. Didn't *he* say something like that to her? Nah, couldn't have.

Dexx barely touched the lid on the tray before another knock sounded and the door opened for Ifrir. He bowed his head. "Many pardons, but I have heard you know Tarik?"

So, they were getting somewhere. "I know *a* Tarik. If it's the one *you* know, I couldn't say. Is this a continental breakfast? I'm more of a steak and omelet kind of guy."

"I must insist you come with me. A matter of great importance has come up, and I believe your party can shed some light on things."

Dexx looked over his shoulder at Hattie and Mah'se. *Trap?* The djinn had treated them just fine until now but admitting they knew Tarik had made an immediate impact.

Mah'se turned his head to Rainbow, who'd just lifted the lid on the tray. Grapes were piled high on sprigs of wheat. *There can be no doubt. Because they did not harm us before says they needed to be sure of who we are.*

They crouched low in the grass and let their prey forget the danger. Hattie stirred herself.

Damn. It. Do we have a choice? Can we get out of this before they get claws in us?

They already have their claws in us. Hattie walked slowly forward.

Dexx fell in beside her.

Mah'se followed them with Rainbow at his side, eating the handful of grapes she'd pulled from the tray.

They followed Ifrir through the gilded halls and another open courtyard into a smaller building, a lower squat one that looked more prison than decorative like the pyramid.

It might have been smaller, but it was still impressive. This had long corridors with intersections everywhere. They took so many turns in the first minute that Dexx had no idea where he was or how to get out again.

They finally spilled into an amphitheater. Djinn lined the rows of seats, some cheering, others jeering like they were at a football game. The noise crested at just below deafening as they walked in.

Down at the center of the amphitheater was a group of five people.

A djinni sat at a raised desk like a judge's bench, and two other djinn faced each other at opposite sides of the desk.

Dexx's eyes went wide as his brain caught up with his eyes.

The rest of Red Star was down there.

And they were on trial.

24

The general noise in the place cut off sharper than a *ma'a'shed* could slice. Every head turned to the newcomers.

Ethel threw her hands to her mouth exactly the same time as Rainbow did hers, the grapes hitting the floor with a wet splat.

"You're here! I worried so much." Rainbow rushed forward.

Dexx caught her before she could get too far. "Ifrir, what's going on?" He stepped back from the demon, his hand going to his knife.

He gestured to the Red Star team. "You know them? The maimed djinn in particular? He is the compatriot you spoke of?" He didn't smile. He didn't frown. He seemed like a cop just doing his job as well as he could.

Tarik stood there, motionless, without emotion.

Dexx narrowed his eyes, not completely sure how to answer. "Yeah, he's mine. What's he doing here? What are *all* of them doing here?"

The djinn behind the bench spoke up. He wore silky black

robes, just like any judge in the real world did. The sleeve fell to reveal his demon arm as he pointed at Dexx and Rainbow. He had good solid middle eastern looks, though. "Ifrir, what is the meaning of this? Who are these humans and—" He cut off, and his eyes grew wide. "Shedim Patesh. Why are *you* here? You were not summoned, and this is none of your concern if you were."

"My pardons *qady*." Ifrir bowed from the waist at the judge. "We found them wandering the desert toward us, and they admit to knowing the accused. We brought them as soon as we knew."

"You know the accused?" The judge—the *qady* shifted his eyes to each of them.

Dammit. Why was his team doing here? *All* of them here? "Sure, I know Tarik. What's he accused of?"

"Then you must join the other accused."

Hattie growled low, but the sound carried across the courtroom amphitheater.

More than a few demons scooted a fraction away.

"Shedim Patesh and the guardian are not called to witness." He tipped his head ever so slightly to the ancient spirits.

Did the judge look slightly worried, or was that his resting demon face?

"Not until you tell me what's going on." Dexx looked around the stadium to the different djinn, all seated, but with an air of readiness.

The djinn judge stood. "You will come and stand with the defense. Ifrir, take the humans into custody."

Dexx drew the *ma'a'shed* and converted it.

Rainbow's eyes flared and went a little dead, her skin losing its luster.

Hattie and Mah'se went tense, ready to fight.

The rest of the demons in the amphitheater stood. Violence was about to descend on them in waves.

The judge stood, smashing a palm-sized stone to the desk. His robe glowed with demon magick. "There will be order in here!"

The djinn stopped, some looking toward the *qady*, others looking at Dexx.

"The court will sit or be removed. The defendants will take their place or be destroyed. Honored guests will take their positions, or they may depart." He passed narrowed and angry eyes across the amphitheater. "Let me be clear." He leaned forward and rested his fingertips together. " Anyone here disrupting the proceedings from here on out will be destroyed."

Dexx didn't drop his sword or relax. "Demonology one-oh-one." Nobody but the humans would be killed. And maybe *one* djinni, but the judge made a good show.

"Dexx." Tarik stood and called out. "Come down. You will be fine until this ends."

Tarik didn't say anything about what would come after.

Dexx let the sword drop and checked the status of his magickal fuel-up. He might be able to light a bonfire or kick a house-sized boulder from a cliff, but he wouldn't be able to defend against a room of demons. He didn't know *how much* he would have when he gained full strength. So, it wasn't something he could count on.

"He may keep the *ma'a'shed*. It is his by rights." The *qady* waved his hand lazily to the knife. When Dexx didn't move, he pressed his lips together. "You have until my count of three before I kill you. Stand with the others."

"Come on, kid. Let's be convicted together." The sword shrank, and he put it away in the sheath. "It's not all bad news, though." Dexx leaned to Rainbow and whispered in her ear. "I got a secret." He got his magick. He might only need time now. Hopefully, they had enough.

She scrunched her eyes and studied Dexx while two demons circled around to collect them.

He scratched behind Hattie's ear. *Keep your eyes open. I can't see them being too friendly to us.*

I am not asleep here.

Sweet. Feels like a nightmare to me.

Dexx and Rainbow were escorted down a central stairway to the courtroom floor.

Ethel lit up, quivering as she restrained herself and waited until Rainbow got to arm's length and the two hugged.

Frey's face pretty much said everything. Dexx was the problem, and if anything bad went down, it would be his fault.

Okay. Something *had* to be wrong with her. She still wasn't letting go of this? She reminded him of a horse with a burr under her saddle. So, what was the burr? "Hey, guys. Miss us?"

"No." Frey turned back to the judge.

Michelle passed a look of question to Dexx.

He wrinkled his nose and shook his head slightly. Answers later.

Alwyn smiled big. "Hey, partner." The word sounded weird coming out in a British accent. "Just about took you for dead."

"How long you been here?" Time passed strangely in the Time Before, but Dexx had a rough feel for it.

"Got here two days ago. Damndest thing we ever—"

"The defendants will remain quiet until called to testify."

You will need to carry the pup with gentle teeth. Hattie sent an image of a momma cat carrying kittens.

Yeah. Any insight into our current situation would help.

The judge continued to speak like things had never interrupted. "...has long been the right of djinn to carry forth the right to punish any transgression against our kind."

Apparently, that didn't cover sending them back to Hell because Dexx was guilty, guilty, guilty. When Tarik had been attacked, Dexx'd sent a *lot* of djinn to Hell on that day alone.

"The defendant is charged with knowingly allowing himself to be captured and to allow obscene rights to be performed on him. How do you plead?"

Tarik stood, tall and straight, looking as fresh and calm as he ever did in the station. "I plead not guilty."

Hold the bus. Tarik was on trial for being attacked?

The stands erupted with noise. Screeches and booms echoed off the walls. Spells lit but were never released, hovering over many of the demons.

The judge raised his hand, and a black globe of crackling energy formed. "The court will cease."

Whatever that black ball was, it had an immediate effect. The djinn went silent, and the magick dissipated.

"Let the record show the defendant has plead not guilty for the second day. We will now proceed with the evidence against the defendant Tarik of Djinn.

A small, wiry djinn stood up from the front row of t seats. He bowed low to the judge. "Most honored *qady*, I was there. I witnessed and was part of a team of necessary benevolents to keep Tarik pure. He broke our attempts to help and gave the humans the way to perform the ceremony."

Dexx leaned to Frey. "What's he talking about?"

"When we cleansed Tarik of the demons possessing him." Her lip curled up in a snarl. "Apparently, a lawsuit was opened and a warrant issued. We walked right into an ambush."

"They're suing Tarik for being possessed?"

Frey turned her head to Dexx. "Are you deaf? Yes, they

are. Now be quiet and let me handle this. Just hang out with the kids." She pointed at Alwyn with her jaw.

Oh, this little attitude problem wasn't going to last much longer. "No. Aren't you a bit—" Dexx stared around them, looking for the right words. "—crazy when it comes to demons close to you? Except for Tarik, of course."

"I said to let me handle this." Frey pressed her lips together, spearing Dexx with her blue eyes.

Dexx didn't need an inner-team fight in the middle of this trial. "Sure. Do something neat." But he wasn't going to do anything while he waited for her to fuck this up either. He pulled Rainbow to Alwyn and leaned in close. "How are things, really?"

Alwyn spread his hands apart. "I can't say. I've never seen a trial like this before. But if I had to guess? I'd say not good. She talks, and the judge—the guy they keep calling *qady*—shouts her down. She's going to get us killed. Or worse."

"Do you think it's because she's a Valkyrie?" A natural enemy of the demon?

"… nothing benevolent about possessing him at all." Frey's eyes were narrowed, her anger bubbling just below the surface.

"Honored *qady*," the wiry djinn said as he stepped in front of Frey, blocking her from the judge, "there isn't any proof of such a thing. If there was *any* wrongdoing, it was the defendant and his followers. And *Shedim*, of course. The proof we need is right before us, altered."

Tarik wasn't a demon anymore. At least not a full demon. And they seemed to think it was impossible that Tarik might be following the humans and not the other way around.

Spoken like a real lawyer. The entire trial was a show. But why?

"The guilty parties stand before us. Most, anyway. We cannot bring the angel involved to us, as you well know."

Several djinn in the stands chuckled, the sound malevolent.

Angels and any sort of demon didn't get along well. And Frey was an angel... of sorts.

"Do you mind?" Frey's glare lingered on the demon.

"You interrupted me, defendant. This is our day. You may, if you wish, try to explain away your transgression on yours."

Frey reached to her neck to pull her sword.

Dexx stepped forward and grabbed her wrist. "Hey, this is a *whole room* full of demons."

Frey's lip curled up. "*You* are *not* leading here."

"You're done." Dexx turned to the judge. "Honored *qady*, my associate isn't... feeling well. May I take her place and argue for us?"

Rainbow raised up to her tiptoes to whisper in Dexx's ear. "I didn't know you knew about demon trials."

Dexx leaned back and said out of the side of his mouth, "Demon one-oh-one pretty much works in any courtroom." Hopefully, he could lie and bluff as well as a demon.

The small djinni passed a look to the judge, then to Dexx and Frey struggling with her hand at her neck. "It is agreeable to me. If the injured party is agreeable."

The wiry djinn showed teeth at the team. "Honored *qady*, we do not care who speaks for them."

"You may proceed." The judge turned his head to Hattie and Mah'se and scrutinized them for a few moments. He nodded his head to the prosecuting djinni.

"As I was saying, they maimed Tarik, quite possibly at his own pleading. I personally know many of us are... different. Their personal views are not normal."

The djinni sounded like any one of the millions of lawyers out in the real world. Full of shit right to the top.

"The desecration of one of our kind cannot be overlooked here."

Dexx had to agree.

"If this court were to let this go, there might be others who would just decide they can do whatever they please to us. This must not go unpunished."

Dexx agreed, but he didn't agree with making the *victim* responsible. "Honored *qady*. If I may interrupt?"

The judge turned to him with a sigh that said he wasn't pleased.

Dexx was treading on shaky ground here, but he charged forward. "I know it's the honored prosecutor's day, but I feel like we should make this a little more... consensual— er, contextual." That slip of the tongue might have been accidental, but it fit the situation. He bowed slightly at the waist but never took his eyes from the judge.

The judge pondered the request.

Dexx stood and flicked his eyes to Mah'se and Hattie. *Be cool, guys.*

Mah'se looked at the judge's bench as though there might be some good grazing beneath.

The *qady* and the prosecutor stared at Dexx, then each other.

"Your day is tomorrow." The judge said sternly.

"Clearly, today is your day. But there are things that might be forgotten or overlooked if they cannot be addressed as they come up."

The prosecutor put on a show of frustration. "Honored qady, they are like children. No concept of propriety."

"Only one of the things I need to address, honored qady." Dexx smiled for all he was worth. He had to put them at ease first. Dexx waited patiently. Or outwardly patient.

The demon threw his arms up. "If they have no tricks, Honored *qady*, I will listen."

"Then, you may speak." The judge tapped the ebony against the stone base.

"This trial, while perhaps necessary, is not complete. I'm *sure* you'd like to have *all* involved receive their just punishment. There are witnesses and other participants unable to attend. You mentioned an angel, who I'm sure you meant Genael. He *should* be here. At least *one* representative from the organization of the Department of Delicate Operations, Mario Kester, should *also* be here. As well as the thousand or so demons and other djinn who invaded Earth and were banished."

He could have heard a mouse fart in the upper bleachers. They weren't prepared to hear that.

Dexx turned to address the stands. "Wouldn't *you* like all responsible parties to face justice? Can justice ever be served if you have a few but not the lot?"

Wiry Prosecutor djinni rose from his bench. "I said no tricks."

Dexx painted on a look of innocence. "I would never. Councilor, I'm absolutely sure you have a rock-solid case, but shouldn't you bring in all guilty parties?" Dexx looked up to the stands again, but not for support. He needed to judge the impact of his words on the court.

Amazingly, they seemed to be having an effect. More than one demon stroked a chin or tapped at its lips.

Dexx covered a smile by scrubbing his face. They couldn't win in a straight-up court battle. Not in their house, but frankly, he needed time.

"I claim trickery." The prosecutor held his arms wide. "Honored *qady*, they seek to muddy the waters." The smile he shared with the court could have greased a zillion cars.

Dexx put better than even odds that prosecutor slime was part of the invasion.

For the first time, the judge looked genuinely thoughtful. "Are all guilty parties here?" He leaned forward at the bench.

Wiry Prosecutor lazily gestured at Red Star. "These are all

who presented themselves. We all know it isn't easy to venture outside this realm now."

"Is it true that there are more? Who is this Genael? Is this the angel you mentioned?"

"Honored qady—" The wiry djinn backpedaled, but he took a breath, ready to continue.

"Honored qady," Dexx spoke in the brief silence, "the fact is you *can't* have a full legal trial without the rest of us."

The courtroom buzzed with low murmuring.

Dang, that sure stirred 'em up. Dexx felt the shift in the room. *What do you think, fat cat? I bet we could wrap this up right here.*

Cub, I don't think—

"The thing is, *your* guys attacked *us*."

The courtroom exploded.

The judge banged his gavel on the pedestal base, the booms deafening.

The demons lining the court didn't even pause.

The judge smashed the rock several more times, calling for order, and when the noise ratcheted up a little higher, he called "Guilty, guilty, guilty," slamming the rock each time.

On the third slam, the court vanished.

25

The sudden quiet seemed almost as loud as the noise.

Dexx reached out to the bars of the large cell, confused as to *why* they were there. "Huh. I guess they didn't like the truth."

Frey rounded on him. "You stupid son of a bitch. I had things under control until you stepped in. What the hell were you even doing?"

Winning. At first. Only one thing made sense. "We were headed here one way or another. That was a kangaroo court."

"I had them listening. They were softening,"

"No they weren't." Dexx tugged on the bars of the cell. They looked pretty close to the cell back in Red Star, but this was a large holding cell built for mass incarceration. "They were playing you for a fool. Rule one of demonology. If their lips are moving, they're lying." With a couple of exceptions.

"Now we'll never know, will we?" Frey turned on her heel and went to the furthest corner from Dexx. She lasted almost two seconds, then began to pace.

Hattie? Can you still hear me?

Yes, cub. Did that go the way you wanted?

Okay, that had riled them up badly, but now what? His magick tank still hadn't reached the quarter mark—he hoped —and the demons would be coming before then. They would blather and monologue.

Alwin fell against the bars of the cell. "Can someone explain what happened? I still don't know why we were there. Here."

"It was a show trial. We weren't going to be walking free. They wanted a reason to drag us down. That's why they kept asking me and Bow where our masters were. I thought we were going to upset the trial. I bet everyone had a hand in how they were going to do this. After you guys came into the Time Before— "

Dexx cocked his head at Frey. "Wait. How *did* you get here?"

Frey held up her hand. "Don't. Just don't go there. This is *your* fault."

"How in the hell did they get you?"

Frey glared with her freezing blue eyes and refused to speak.

Michelle looked like she'd eaten a cat and like she might puke at any moment.

Alwyn shook his head and shrugged.

He looked at Ethel.

Her sapphire blue eyes rounded. "We— well, certainly *I* don't really know. We left you and Bow in Monaco. Sorry, by the way." She shrugged and smiled sheepishly. "And when we got to the middle of the ocean... poof. We wound up here."

That sounded... about par for the course. "That's crazy." But only because of Atlantis. Had what he done affected them?

"No, it's true. We were headed—I don't actually know

where we were headed. That thumb drive was a *complete* bust, by the way. No new information."

Frey made a guttural sound as if to shut Ethel up.

Dexx was over that, though, so he pointedly ignored her.

"Frey and Tarik probably knew," Ethel continued, also ignoring the Valkyrie. "Maybe Michelle, but not me."

Dexx noticed she hadn't mentioned Alwyn. He turned a wrinkled brow to Frey. "You didn't even tell *them* where you were going?" Yeah. There was *something* seriously off with her.

"What would you know? I couldn't risk my team on your —" She waved a hand at Dexx. "—incompetence. Good riddance. But you *still* manage to fuck it all up. Got us down here in a fucking cell."

Okay. So, if this *was* an outside spell... Pieces of the Frey puzzle were starting to click into place. It would be so like Bussemi to curse a member of his team to poison it. And that's what Frey was doing. She was getting her team into danger by being too stupid to live through her aggravated ego. But how could he figure out what that spell was and release her from it? They needed Frey. *His* Frey. "No matter what I said, you were on your way here."

But he also understood that *reason* was going to get them *nowhere*, especially if she'd been cursed. Crap. "So, the big question is, now that we're here, how do we leave?"

"*I* could have talked us out." Frey pointed at herself, stepping right up to Dexx's face. "Our day was next. Tarik would have shown them what really happened."

If this was Bussemi, then his curse could be pushing Frey to this confrontation. If he followed along, would it *ease the pressure* on her? He recalled his headaches from Bussemi-voice. When he finally allowed the cursed voice in, the headaches retreated—with a good nap. What if this was like that? Well, no time like the current to test-drive the theory.

"Really? Would you have got him off for what I did, or what *you two* did together?" What was he even saying? It didn't matter. He was picking a fight. On purpose. "DoDO had a hand in testing on him too."

Tarik *had been* experimented on since the time he lost his demon status. In ways only *he* knew. Huh.

Frey closed her mouth. She turned around sharp but still aggressive.

Okay. Maybe that *had* worked. Just enough aggression to dull the edges. Good. Good-good-good. Now, if Dexx could just magickally find a cure? He reached into his pocket to grab the stone to see if he could get a list of save-her spells.

The highly ornate door with gold and silver swirls leading to the cell area opened for the wiry djinn prosecutor, who was followed by Mah'se and Hattie.

What the hell? *Are you two in jail too, or what?*

Mah'se answered over Hattie. *We have been given permission to see you.*

Hattie looked sick again. Too scrawny. Maybe he could help her more when his magick topped out. *When can we get out of here?*

Mah'se dipped his head like he might charge Dexx. *You are to be held.*

The door opened again to admit the *qady*.

Crap. What next?

Frey spun Dexx around. "*I* will talk. *You* will watch. I might be able to talk us out of this mudhole you stuck us in."

"Not this time." And he wasn't sure how to push the off button without getting into *another* fight with her. In front of the judge. "We take him on together, or you won't take him on at all." Dexx stared into her eyes. He didn't have his alpha back, but maybe something showed through with his growing magick.

Frey refused to look at him. "You can be my number

two." She held up a finger. "For *this* only. You're still top on the shit list."

What else was Bussemi working on with this curse? Trying to make him feel inferior? Dick move. "Well, if you insist." There wasn't a chance that she'd keep her calm long enough to talk them out of the hole they were in.

The *qady* stopped in front of Dexx and Frey. "Never in all my days have I seen impertinence such as that."

Dexx might as well start things off right. "I know, right? The nerve of you holding a trial without all the evidence in was—" He rolled his eyes so hard his head followed. "—*way* out of line." He smiled and tapped the bars on the cell. "So, if you'd like to just... that'd be great. Yeah." If he could knock the demon off-center to get a glimpse of what was *really* going on here, they might have a chance.

The wiry djinn's eyes matched Frey's for pure anger. "Our laws were followed—"

"By two blind demons followed by two deaf ones? Yeah, I know how that goes. This one time—"

"Silence." The *qady* spoke low but with force. He had a spell strengthening his words.

Dexx saw the circles with runes that lit as he spoke. Cool. When he and Hattie got out, they would be *unstoppable.*

Hey girl, you want to be the most powerful shifter that ever was? Well, I got my magick back, and we're going to get welded back together and show some punk demons who rules the roost now.

The bond is all I have ever wanted. Your magick is not of me, but since it is from you, it will be as you say.

Dexx groaned inside. *You gotta make it sappy?*

The *qady* raised his chin, and his eyes swirled with blue. "You have been found guilty."

"No." Dexx crossed his arms and leaned back on a leg, "We were *pronounced* guilty. There's a difference. Why doesn't the fact that Tarik was *attacked* by your djinn make a differ-

INTERNATIONAL TEAM OF MYSTERY

ence in your court of law? What rule are we not seeing here?"

The qady narrowed his eyes, glancing at the wiry djinn. "You were found guilty. Sentencing will be as follows. The humans—" He pointed at Alwyn, Rainbow, and Ethel. "—will be set free. Under close supervision, of course. Should *any* of them attempt to attack another djinn or other demon again, they will be executed on the spot. No trials, no appeals."

Ethel and Alwyn might live just fine under those conditions. Rainbow was a daughter of the currents. It might be interesting to see how the currents and demons dealt with each other. Probably get along famously since both were pretty much killers.

"The offspring of the ascended will be banished forever."

So, Frey. Okay. That didn't sound so bad since Frey couldn't come to the Time Before on her own.

"In the desert of Bastet's realm. There, she will roam forever."

Oh. *That* wasn't very nice.

Frey opened her mouth to speak.

Dexx put a hand on her arm because something *was* going on there. Another person who *reason* would not affect. "That's kind of harsh, don't you think?"

"You have no right." Frey's growl grew. "You will let me out of this cage *right now.*"

The demon studied her with impassive eyes. "No." He pointed to Michelle. "The dryad will be given to me personally. She may live a long time, but she will be my slave and a source of sustenance. It has been too long since I have dined on an ash of your magnitude."

Michelle turned a very unpleasant shade of green.

Dexx should have remembered. She and Tarik had started out on rocky ground because he was a djinni. He'd completely forgot they fed on dryads. Seriously? None of this was going to happen. But how could he rationalize with these djinn? "That's bullshit." His fire had been lit. Anger furrowed his brow. "Let me out of here. Let's talk about this like men." That got no response. "Or are you a coward?"

The *qady* turned a cold look to Dexx. "You will be kept in the dungeons forever."

Well, that had certainly gained a response. "We know you and your bond. You will not be allowed to kill any more demonkind."

Ha-ha. Right. "Fuck I will." But how to turn this around? He had no ideas. And none of his old tricks were going to *work* this time. Well, he *did* have a *few* new tricks. He still wasn't at full strength in the magickal realm of spell-ness, but maybe there was something there he could use. Something to cut their way out.

His list of spells came up, some highlighted with glowing runes, but most were dark. He couldn't use those. Because he didn't have the energy or the ability?

Didn't matter. He had options.

One of the spells on his list looked interesting enough, though. Translated in his mind, it came out to be laser slash.

Dexx swiped his hand out and down, trailing a bright red flash of light that sizzled through the bars and the *qady* in an instant.

The djinni never had a chance to move. His body and head fell in two different directions.

"Eek!" The small djinni prosecutor screamed like a child frightened by a spider and vanished.

Bars fell from the cage. Not enough to squeeze through and leave yet, though.

Dexx had used most of his available magick in that spell. He'd have enough for another slash soon, and now they knew he wasn't helpless. More demons would be coming fast.

"Come on. Help me push." Dexx grabbed the cut bars and pushed hard. They were still solid enough, even cut.

Alwyn and Rainbow slammed against the bars next to Dexx, pushing as hard as they could.

At least they appeared to be putting effort into escaping.

Whips of wood wrapped around the bars. "Move." Michelle sounded in no mood to argue.

Dexx didn't have to be told twice. He scurried out of the way.

The bars bent inward with the screech of tortured metal.

"How did you—" Frey stared at Dexx with wide eyes.

"Got a few secrets left in me, sweetheart." He pushed at her to get her moving.

She did.

Hattie and Mah'se didn't move from where they stood.

"You gonna help or just sit there and look good?"

You are the embodiment of reckless. Mah'se stepped in front of Hattie. *Hat'tai is in no condition to help in this foolish attempt. You have no concept of...* anything.

"Then stay out of the way." Hattie really didn't look good. If she let Mah'se keep her from the action, then she might be worse off than she let on.

Dexx pushed his team through the bars, leaving himself last. His magick was flowing back into him, but slower than before. Why him?

"What the fuck?" Dexx stared at his hands. Why would he refill slower, *now?*

"What's up, boss?" Rainbow turned around to help him out of the cage, but he didn't need any.

"It's me— never mind. Let's just get out of here." The door from the other room looked inviting, sort of. *What's on the other side of that door?*

A waiting room. Mah'se still felt the need to answer for Hattie.

Okay, would you let my *bond speak to me, please?*

Hattie walked forward to Dexx. She looked him right in the eye, her deep green eyes filling him.

You got this, girl? We get out and get to the library. We fix us, and then we fix the world.

Hattie blew out a breath from her nose. *Yes. Fix us.*

The rest of the team took positions on opposite sides of the room. Frey and Tarik went to the door the *qady* had entered from, and the rest went to the only other door. A completely grey door with silverwork scrolled over most of the space. There didn't seem to be a lock on it, but there wasn't a knob to turn or twist, either.

You bet. Can you help with the djinn?

Mah'se backed up a step. *We cannot take up arms against the djinn. That was the deal to leave. We will not be welcomed back in their realm, but we never ventured here before. The deal was a sound one.*

Then break it. We need your help to leave. Unless you're too big a chicken?

Rainbow hugged the spirit elk. "You're right, but you've to come with us and get out. We can't trust them very far."

You can't know the position you placed us in. You want us to perish for the likes of you?

Rainbow backed up a step and frowned at the elk. "He did what he could, Mossy. He's right. I think. We weren't going to make it out of this. They don't leave room for talking your way out. We *have* to fight this time."

Mah'se actually rubbed his massive head against Rainbow's shoulder. *This is how it has to be.* He took a step back, away from Rainbow.

It was the elk's choice. "Fuck 'im. Let's get out. Then we regroup and reassess." *Ready?*

Yes.

276

Michelle yanked hard on the door. The empty hall on the other side was as welcome as a cold beer.

The hall wasn't decorated like any of the others they'd seen before. The slate grey was more worked, like steel.

She ran down the hall to the next door and pulled. It didn't give, not even with her strength.

Frey pulled her sword and charged after.

Ethel, Rainbow, and Alwyn followed.

Tarik had no expression he walked down the corridor.

What the hell did that mean?

Dexx pulled his *ma'a'shed* and transformed the blade. *Demon doors were no match for a mavet ma'a'shed.*

He almost stepped on Tarik's heels as they left.

And stepped into the arena filled with screaming demons.

26

What the hell is going on? Hattie had been right behind Dexx, but she was gone, as was the hallway, the cell … everything before was *gone*.

But the outdoor arena with thousands of spectator demons was alive and in living color.

The entire Red Star team stood in the relative places they'd been in the hall. Just now, they stood on an open field of packed dirt with three tall columns in random places.

Dexx turned slowly, taking in the thousands upon thousands of demons. Some looked as human as Tarik, and others were as grotesque as week dead bodies. "What the hell, Tarik? Did you know about this?" He let the *mavet* tip touch the ground. This didn't feel Egyptian. More like Roman Gladiator days.

The sound of cheering reverberated through the open air, the sun high, raining down oppressive heat.

"I only knew it was a possibility. They must have been preparing this since we arrived."

Now *that* made sense. "Rule one. They lied the whole time." Dexx had good reasons to make that his first rule.

Somewhere in the stands, a rhythmic thumping started. The sound spread to the entire stadium. They stomped and pumped their fists and chanted in time.

Tarik had to speak up to be heard. "At least partially, yes. I *do* believe the *qady* intended to consume Michelle over a long period of time. Dryads are prized."

Michelle looked three shades of sick.

"Comforting." He pulled Michelle close to him. Of them all, she had the most reason to fear.

Tarik stood on her other side. Yeah, he was one of the good ones.

Frey walked forward aggressively, brandishing her sword. It caught the light and reflected it in all directions. "Come and fight me, cowards."

The laughter stopped the chanting, at least.

Dexx's sword hummed with anticipation.

The court had had hundreds of demons. So only the most interested or powerful or influential had been able to watch the courtroom drama, but *thousands* were able to watch the executions.

Damned demons.

"Okay, Tarik, so what's the play?"

"We will not know." He twisted around, apparently unruffled, but his fingers twitched as though working on spells.

Michelle stopped moving. Her expression bordered on frozen panic.

Frey stopped her march forward, and when she saw Michelle, she retreated to the dryad. She cupped her hand to the back of Michelle's neck and pulled her forward, her eyes glaring. "Knock it off. Get your ass in gear. Got it?"

Michelle shook like an aspen in a slight breeze.

Dexx pushed Frey back. "First off, I think *I'll* be in charge again." He knew that would be a challenge, but... hopefully, Bussemi had included some contingencies to keep Dexx alive long enough to take what he needed. And if that allowed Dexx to live, he'd figure out a way to buy time for his team, too. "Second, leave her alone. This is *any* dryad's worst fear." He had a worse fear now—Bussemi— and he could very well freeze when the time came. That *couldn't* happen. "So cut her some slack. Now, nobody knows what they'll be using to execute us, so we need a defense."

"*I* am the best defense," Frey growled as she prowled away. "Just stay out of my way."

Not a bad idea, but... "How about Ethel and Rainbow? Both are just regular humans here. Help me protect them." He pushed Frey toward Ethel. He didn't do that with the intent to stop the curse or push the curse. He did that because he honestly knew Frey—*his* Frey—would be the best defense for his human teammates.

Alwyn already had his hands up and glowing, trying to watch everywhere at once and looking mildly comical.

Dexx turned to Michelle. Outside of Frey, she was the strongest one on their team. "Hey. You gotta help out here. I know it's tough but stay with us. Let's win. Okay?"

Michelle sent roots into the dirt and pulled them back out. "The stink. It's *everywhere.*"

"Yeah, it is. So, keep your cool, and do what you can. Watch Frey and Tarik. If things look weak, just do what you can. We'll *all* leave together. You got that?"

Michelle's roots touched the ground again and pulled back into her feet. "I think so. Oh, gods, I never should have..."

Nope! "Stay close. We'll help each other. Teamwork makes the dream work. You *know* that."

Michelle actually scrunched her eyes at Dexx.

"That's my girl." He led her back to Alwyn and Rainbow, realizing he'd never had to call Michelle his girl before.

That… was weird. "Tarik, what's the plan? Why haven't they sent anything out yet?"

"The possibilities are many. I do not know why."

Fuck. "This waiting can only help us, right?"

"Not if the wait drives us to panic. Then our adversaries do not have to be so powerful."

The djinni had a point.

Who would they send out?

Cub.

Where are you?

We are here. We must watch you die.

So, Mah'se's with you?

Yes.

Just sit tight. We'll deal with this and get you out of here. If he could get his team out first.

My duty is to protect those of the Time Before. That is what I will do every time. Mah'se sounded like he was hiding behind his job, but with conflicted emotions.

At least there was that. *Next time I see you, we're gonna have words.*

The closest of the three columns shook and rose, the ground vibrating as stone ground together. A hole in the base took shape, like an elevator without a door.

A dark shape waited inside until the column stopped. Dexx stepped between the thing and Red Star.

Frey stood at his shoulder. She never looked away from the creature inside, but her words were all for Dexx. "We win this. Then we're going to have a talk. And I intend on winning."

He did, too. With a powerful spell? Or… some magick pixie dust? "Great, can't wait." Chances were pretty high that they'd start easy and go rough.

Not that demons couldn't afford to start with death. They just seemed to want to watch a show—ancient Roman style.

The shadows in the elevator moved. A lion stepped out. No, not a lion. This thing was bigger. A sabertoothed cat. It charged.

Dexx dropped his blade down. A cat. It looked a lot like Hattie. "No."

Before Dexx had a chance, a fireball screamed through the air blasting the cat to bits.

"No!" He screamed, but it was drowned out by the sudden collective cheer of the demons.

He spun on Alwyn. "What the fuck, dude?" *Hattie?*

I am here. They are playing with your emotions. Making the kill taste sweeter.

Alwyn's eyes were wide as he looked from one column to the next. "We're not supposed to kill the things coming through?"

"Maybe." Yes! "Don't kill any more sabers. Blast all the old-time elks, though. Do it twice." Dexx raised his sword and shifted his grip. *Bastards. Bastards, all.* Demons didn't play fair, so he had no doubt they'd at least *think* about putting Hattie in the arena against them. That thought chilled Dexx to the bone.

"Sure thing." Alwyn's voice quivered.

The column sank back to the earth, possibly resetting for another creature to come out. This time, two columns rose.

Dexx charged the closest exposing hole. There wouldn't be enough room to run in, so he slid in like he was stealing home and slashed with the sword.

He barely registered Frey screaming at him to stop.

The crowd of demons roared as he slid in the gap and swung the sword. He barely felt a tug as the creature inside fell into two pieces.

The column continued to rise and light the inside. A pure white pegasus twitched on the ground. Blood and gore splattered the walls and Dexx.

He heard Frey's frantic screams, then.

Well, shit.

Dexx *understood* her anger and grief. He did. But if he'd allowed that pegasus to survive, it would have tried to kill them, or Frey would have endangered the lives of the team to keep that winged horse alive. Which was probably what the demons were betting on.

So, yeah. If things continued to escalate, they'd probably throw Hattie in there against them.

Would he make the same call? Hell no. But Frey hadn't *bonded* to that horse.

The column stopped the rising, and he walked back into the sun.

Frey's face was one of complete horror, with two rivulets of tears.

Maybe this would be enough to… reset the curse?

If it even was a curse. It *could be* just Frey being a Valkyrie.

No. Dexx *needed* her irrational behavior to be a curse. He *needed* that. One he could fix. Her being too dumb by anger to live? That wasn't.

"Dexx!" Rainbow pointed at the other column.

It'd stopped, too, and another winged creature stepped out on strong legs, with a sting on the tail.

Manticore.

"Oh, shit." Dexx ran back to the team.

Frey was on her knees, her sword at her side on the ground. She sobbed like a little girl.

She was a woman of extremes. If this *wasn't* a curse, she was more broken than Dexx. "Alwyn, Tarik, Michelle. Hit this with everything you have." He tapped Frey with his foot. "Hey."

Frey fell to her side.

Okay. So, maybe the demons had known *exactly* how to disable Frey. Either have her turn on her team to defend the winged horse, or she'd just fall over weeping when he died. Great. "Bow, Ethel, get her up. We need her."

Ethel knelt next to Frey, speaking but he couldn't hear what she said over the excitement of the demon crowd.

The manticore slowly stepped forward and roared as it spread its wings.

The crowd renewed the cheering.

"Michelle, I need you to grab that sting and keep it away from us." Was there a way *out* of this arena? "Tarik, can you keep its attention?"

"I can. I will try." Tarik drew symbols in the air. The first was a protection sigil, and the next was a confinement rune.

"What are you doing? I said, keep it busy, not cage it."

"Those are the first. I will— Dexx." Tarik's horizontal pupils constricted. "You can see my magick?"

"Yeah." No time for that. "Now, eyes on the prize. We don't get a second shot here." If they got out of this, he might have a whole lot of explaining to do.

While they worked on the manticore, Dexx scouted the arena for weakness using his newfound magick-seeing ability. "I wish Roxxie or Furiel were here." Dexx couldn't hear himself over the roars of the crowd.

The manticore rushed ahead, spreading its wings and springing into the air.

Michelle whipped her arms forward, her lithe limbs snaring the tail as it flew over. She jerked hard as her vines drew tight. She might have been taken for a ride, but she'd rooted to the ground. Instead of her taking flight, the manticore lost height and slammed down. Hard.

It spun around on its lion paws, snarling and slashing at the vines holding his stinging tail.

Alwyn released a firebolt that bounced away into the stands.

Tarik released his magick, and the manticore moved in slow motion. The clawed foot came closer to Michelle.

Dexx sprinted for the manticore with a roar.

It turned its head just long enough.

Dexx's first slash bit deep into its side, but not enough to kill it. He pulled the sword free and swung at the tail, low.

The *mavet ma'a'shed* slipped through the armor-like scales and severed the tail, spewing a yellow fluid over the beast.

Michelle sprung back, still holding the twitching tail.

The *mavet* vibrated with need. The need to soak in the creature's blood. It pushed Dexx to violence.

The manticore roared in pain and pawed the ground, turning back to the team.

Dexx was more than happy to let it drink. He swung on the backstroke, hitting the manticore solidly in the neck. The head rolled away, a snarling roar still opening the mouth wide.

Blood soaked into the blade and the earth. The *mavet* calmed.

This time the crowd settled. Jeering and boo's cascaded to the arena floor.

Dexx slowly scanned the stadium. *Where are you? Can you get free? There won't be any better cover for you than this spectacle right here.*

We can leave. Mah'se answered instead of Hattie. *But they may invade.*

So? You'll just have to kill them there. Not a big deal. Better an invasion later than Hattie in the arena now.

But maybe it *was* a big deal. Mah'se and Hattie had power, but so did the demons. How many could they take on before they were killed?

Mah'se agreed as if sensing Dexx's thoughts.

So, you watch us fight. That might even be worse than dying *in* the fights.

Yes. Hattie felt full of rage. *She* wanted to be there to fight with Dexx. To kill the monsters the demons brought out.

Don't worry, girl. We'll get out of here and get to the library. Paige said there's a lot of information in there, and if there is help, that's the place we'll find it.

Hattie didn't respond but to ratchet up the hatred for the monsters. *Yeah.*

They needed a way out.

A small door at the walls opened.

Dexx moved to wipe the sword on the manticore's pelt but remembered there wasn't any blood because his blade had claimed it. Gross, but it gave him power and strength. "You'll take manticore blood but not the pegasus?"

He received the impression that the *mavet ma'a'shed* wanted a certain type of blood.

Great. A picky eater.

A woman walked out, carrying a golden tray with a silver domed lid. As she got closer, Sekhet walked calmly toward the team.

This wasn't the time to serve beer. Maybe it was between rounds or some—

Or maybe they'd put her in there, forcing them to kill her. No. He needed to get her—

A spear flashed from the stands and skewered Sekhet to the ground, the covered tray of goblets spilling everywhere.

She spasmed, trying to catch her breath, blood coating the spear and her lips. She looked up to Dexx for a moment, betrayal clear in her eyes.

Sekhet fell limp against the spear. The tip had been driven deep and kept her from falling over.

"Bastards!" Dexx yelled at the stadium, turning to include all of the demons.

Sekhet's hands twitched in death.

The crowd resumed the overwhelming noise.

Dexx walked back to the team, his mind racing. They needed a solution. A way *out* of there before things got even more way out of hand.

Ethel and Rainbow still hadn't made progress with Frey.

The djinn were cleaning up pretty easily. Frey was down. Dexx doubted... everything. Who was next?

Dexx checked his magick. He was still gaining, but slow. How long would he have to wait before he could do some *real*?

Somewhere in the stands, a chant began. Within seconds the sound drowned out everything else. The demons were again stomping with the chant he couldn't make out.

"Aw, Hells. What now?" What spell could he ready? Where would this threat come from?

The last of the columns began to shake and rise.

"Get ready, guys. The Stay Puft Marshmallow Man is coming."

Michelle stood up, clutching the tail of the manticore. "You're shitting me."

Dexx looked at her in surprise. "You get that one?"

"*Everybody* gets that one."

"I don't." Rainbow stood, but her expression said she didn't really care. A smile tried to come out, but she was terrified.

Hell, *Dexx* was terrified. "*Ghostbusters*. The first one."

The *mavet* hummed in his grip. It didn't do that unless it felt something it wanted. Crap, oh crap.

"We have a bad thing coming. They sacrificed Sekhet for it."

"Oh." Rainbow's voice was washed away by the stomping and the chant.

The column rose twenty feet and stopped, but the shaking increased until dust fell in soft trails. The tower cracked, then cracked again, and again until the column fell.

The stands exploded in another cheer as the rubble rose and shook the arena floor.

A screech cut through the noise.

That didn't sound small. That sounded huge.

Frey picked her head up and stared death at Dexx. She rose to her feet and charged the pile of rubble as a green snout pushed up.

What was she *doing?* Dying *quickly?*

Frey jumped over the snout and disappeared behind the rising head.

The biggest head Dexx had ever seen rose from the earth followed by the biggest neck, body, wings, legs, and tail. "Dragon."

It stood fifty feet high on its four legs. Its wings almost spanned the width of the arena.

In one movement, the dragon snapped its jaws on the dead serving girl, and she disappeared. It roared, it's head high in the air.

The crowd erupted in excited screams.

"We're fucked." He didn't have any spells that dealt with dragons. At the very least, he didn't have enough juice to light a spell up that would deal with one.

The dragon found the team huddled together and paused. It inhaled deeply in what looked like preparation for a fire blast.

This wouldn't even be a tussle. They'd be fried weenies.

The thing hadn't exhaled yet, but Dexx felt the heat in the arena rising. Where could they hide from that? Behind the manticore body? Inside the columns? "Really fucked."

It stopped pulling in air, flexed, and paused before blowing fire across the arena floor in a swath coming toward them.

He grabbed Ethel's arm, shouted something hero-worthy at Tarik, Rainbow, and Michelle, and made for the manticore body. They flew over, rolled, and tumbled behind it.

The fire stopped.

The crowd and the arena went dead silent, except for the terrified breathing from him and the team and spots of crackling fire.

Dexx poked his head up. The bright green dragon's eyes lost their color, and smoke rolled from its mouth as it fell to the ground.

Hot air expelled from its mouth, but no hotter than a space heater would have. Hot, but not deadly. A massive burp followed, putrefying what was once good breathable stuff.

The crowd stood in stunned silence. Not a word. Not a dropped cup. Not a fart.

Frey stood at the base of the creature's neck, her sword embedded in its spine, still cutting. She walked along its neck until she came to its head and hacked until it fell from the body. She kicked the nose and walked back to Dexx and the rest, her eyes darker with each step. "You killed my Roda. *You killed my Roda.*"

Oh, crap. Had she been bonded to the pegasus? "Whoa, what? I didn't... what are you talking about?"

Frey raised her sword and advanced.

"You've *never* told me about a bonded horse!" Dexx quickly parried the strike. He barely managed to counter *any* strike. Frey came at him wild, her skill with the sword only just a pinch better than his.

He fought on the defensive, keeping Frey from turning him into bloody ribbons.

This was the demon's plan. If they couldn't kill the team, one of them would.

Plan B. Knock her out.

She smashed at him, and he swung, mainly to stop the barrage of hits.

What the hell was this mess? His parry caught her blade in between the split of the *mavet ma'a'shed*. He twisted, pinning her blade and locking them together.

"Stop this."

"You killed my horse."

But had he? A little fire began in his belly. "You mean, the djinn locked him in a cage and made us fight him."

"*You—*"

Dexx punched her in the gut.

Frey doubled over.

"Maybe. You saw that sabertoothed cat we killed first thing? Looked a lot like Hattie, huh?"

Frey glared at him.

"It wasn't."

She breathed as the words seemed to settle over her.

"So, maybe this wasn't your horse" Dexx knelt on her sword arm and dropped the *ma'a'shed*. He drove his fist to the side of her head. She still wasn't something he could count on.

Her head bounced off the ground, but she wasn't out.

She brought her knee up and jammed it to his side.

He fell off, trying to bring air in.

Frey stood and released a barrage of punches and kicks Dexx only saw after she hit him.

He fell to the ground, waiting for the air to fill his lungs again. He rolled out of the path of a foot as it came smashing down.

Air finally invaded his lungs in time for him to see she had her sword again.

"You've had enough time." She stepped forward, right into a black hole, and disappeared.

Leah poked her head out of the hole. "Come with me if you want to live."

Shit! Was that really her?

She could get the team out.

Dexx scrambled to his feet and grabbed the *ma'a'shed*. How would he know for sure? He couldn't leave yet, not without a cure for Hattie. He turned to find his cat. "Hattie!"

Arms grabbed him from behind and carried him toward the portal. He fought. No. he *had to* get his spirit animal.

They fought harder.

The stands erupted with screams of hate and destruction. As one, the demons poured down, like maple syrup overflowing a plate.

Dexx twisted to get free. *Hattie! Hattie!*

Cub. Her voice was deep and rich and full of everything he loved about her. His love *for* her.

As soon as he broke the plane of the doorway, his soul *ripped*. Something that had been a part of him forever was just severed.

Dexx fell to the other side of the doorway. He stared at the living room of the Whiskey house in a daze, everything different. His smell was gone. Things were fuzzy. His hearing was muffled.

Leah, Mandy, Kate, and Rai stood there.

"He's home," Leah breathed.

Oh, those beautiful kids. But... *Hattie?*

Nothing.

Darkness claimed him and, this time, it went on forever.

Hattie was gone.

27

Dexx knew how to talk to Hattie. Whenever he wanted to, all he had to do was imagine a black space. Fill that space with a tree, grass, light. Fog would keep the space close... cozy. Then, she'd meet him there, and they'd both walk into the fog... and poof— the Time Before.

The bluff should have been there. The plains and the creatures should have been there. Mah'se with all him pompous, *You shouldn't be here* should have been there. Hattie should have been there.

So why in the nine Hells was the world still dark? Where was his ancient spirit shifter animal?

He felt a slowly growing pool of energy that marked his returned magick. But no Hattie.

Where the fuck—

Dexx opened his eyes.

He was in bed. The warm covers over him told him that. The ceiling wasn't decorated in gold, and the quiet was... *quiet.*

No, there *were* sounds. A rhythmic banging outside. It stopped. Picked up again, then stopped. Was that a hammer?

A list of spells opened in front of his eyes. Enhanced Hearing, Enhanced Voice, Bubble of Silence, Dispersed Wall of Sound. The list went on and on with the varying amounts of magick associated with the use of each. None of them or all of them combined would scratch what he had now.

If he had a gauge reading, he'd be about three-eights full. That wasn't a lot.

He felt the breath in his ear more than he heard it. *Hattie?* Silence.

He twitched as another breath tickled his ear.

Paige. He was... home? Oh, no, no, nononono. He had to go back and save Hattie. He had to—

Sore muscles didn't let him get more than an arm raised.

The ceiling looked *familiar* in a good way.

Paige was asleep, her breath warm and... just like he remembered. How long ago had that been?

He'd come home, the one place he fought to be. With the one person he wanted to be with more than any other. And here he was, his dream fulfilled, and all he wanted was to go *back*.

He'd accomplished this by sacrificing his longest relationship.

Words echoed back to him. *All you have to is sacrifice her.*

He hated his past life. *Fuck you, Dekskulta. I see you again. We're gonna throw down.* But he wouldn't. That incarnation was dead.

Sure, threatening to kick his own ass, not to mention a past life would be the biggest empty threat next to—

I told you not to use the shamiyir. Bussemi's voice in his head almost sent him to the floor in a massive twitch, but he hurt. A lot. *You did not listen. You never listened to me.*

Instead, Dexx rolled on his side away from Paige. The

least he could do was spare her from Bussemi, at least in little ways.

If Bussemi could see through his eyes, he didn't want him seeing anything important. He wasn't going to share Paige, not now, not ever. *Get out of my head, or so help me I'm gonna stomp a mudhole in your ass up to mine.*

Threats are only good threats if you can back them up. I can.

Goodbye, asshole. Dexx turned him off once before, using his power, using the stone.

This is the real world. You can't get rid of me like they *did.*

Right. Now, just *how* had he done that before? *How about my mind, my space. Just go away.*

If you remember, I told you to resist using the shamiyir. *You had no idea how to use it, and now here you are. We could have been great. You and me. Our… internal counterparts and us. The world would have been ours to change as we saw fit. You could have been the face of the changing world, and I— I would be the power of forever. You, born to die to live again. You could have been the messiah the world has been waiting for. Two thousand years. You could have been the son of God.*

Dexx snorted but let Bussemi-voice ramble while his mind scrambled to recall how to shut the voice up.

Paige let out a small sound as her hand twitched. What had she gone through? She'd never believe his story, but maybe she would. She'd been to the Time Before—the *Vadda Bhoomi*. He'd never call that place such an obvious play on… his snark left him.

Bussemi had to be dealt with first. He wasn't bringing this level of bad to Paige's doorstep. *And you'd be God, right?* Dexx reached for his magick, reaching for what had worked the last time. *That's so played out. What the hell do you want to rule over this planet for? It's moments away from destroying itself anyway.* The only problem was the last time, Dexx'd done it on instinct. *Just… go make your own world. It easy. Make a universe, fill it with all the jack-off ideas you want, then animate some clay with ideas of their own. Just don't make an apple tree, and you're all set.*

You oversimplify. Creation is more than—

Paige squeezed Dexx's hand.

Time was over. Dexx's instincts kicked in, his magick surged out, and... Bussemi's voice disappeared.

Dexx closed his eyes. His love, the mother of his kids. His... shifter witch. His instincts would always be to protect her.

"Hey, babe." He forced himself to turn and looked at her, even though his soul ached as though a part of him had been cut out. It had been.

She levered herself on the bed beside him, feeling amazing.

She stared at him for a moment, then crawled over him to sit on the edge of the bed.

"Hey. So, uh, everyone tried to fill me in, but... yeah. I'm just really confused. Where were you?"

He didn't feel like telling her much. He was just so soul-achingly tired. "Just... a lot of places. I know I should have texted or called. I just—" But what? What could he say?

She frowned at him, but her brown eyes weren't angry. "Do I need to care about any of the stuff you did? Like, is this a mess I need to clean up? Does this affect you being arrested —well, I mean, soonly arrested for what you did in England?"

England. That'd been so long ago. "Not this latest thing, no. The demon trial? I don't think they'll ask politely if they can *arrest* me. It's just one more amazing thing I've had to deal with."

Her shoulders drooped, but she forced an interested smile on her face. "What was the gladiator ring thing? I assume that's why you're..." She gestured to his bruised body.

Really? That was her response? After all, he'd gone

through, and she was going to give him a should sag and a pasted smile? "That was our sentence."

"Do I need to know?"

He was starting to get a little upset with her. "Nah."

She frowned in confusion. "And the girls saved you."

Had they? Fuck. They probably thought they'd been big damned... His breath hitched in his chest. Hattie was... gone.

"And you're safe?"

"I am." His voice was thick. "We are now. I promise."

Paige shook her head and took in a deep breath and then launched into what had gone on with her. She... was pissed. Sure. Yeah. She was. And he'd probably understand that better in a day or two.

But for now? All he could do was give her empty answers and responses to what she said. He didn't *care* about the political shit she was going through. He didn't *care* that her life was so complicated.

He... hurt. And he just wanted...

He wanted the woman he loved with the remainders of his heart to hold him and tell him he'd be okay. She pulled away and rested her elbows on her knees, and reached out a hand to him. "What's going on with you?"

The pain grew. *So many* things went straight to the shitter since DoDO used him for their lab rat. "Too much to list. Be specific."

"I—," Paige said, she flicked her fingers from her head.

Danger. That meant frustration.

"I've got a very delicate situation, and you're not listening. So, what's going on that broke your ears? Because...."

He ground his teeth, his green eyes flashing. Fine. She pushed. Pushed him right over the edge. "I lost Hattie."

She stopped mid- breath. Now she understood. "How?"

"I fucked up," he whispered. "I had help. It might even

have worked. I'll never know. In the end, I charged ahead, and I thought I could wiggle through. She was hanging by a thread, and I swung the sword anyway."

"I'm so sorry."

He realized he wasn't making any sense. He didn't care. "We were separated as soon as I crossed the barrier to the Time Before. That's where the currents sent Rainbow and me. Mah'se tried to kick us out, but Hattie wouldn't let him. We uh, me and Rainbow, and... Hattie—" He swallowed hard, not even sure why he was babbling *this part*. It wasn't the most important. "—we decided to go. Mah'se couldn't be left out or whatever. We found my past life. A huge city down there under the ocean. Big as Denver. Maybe, I don't know. But they had the right idea. He almost made it work."

"Who?" Paige's expression said she was left with more questions than answers. "You saw people there?"

He didn't care what she understood. His heart needed to understand. He hadn't *felt* anything like this in... so long. "My past life. He almost had a place where all the paras could live. Free from the fears of mundanes. Then Bussemi came—"

"How did *he* get there?" Paige's eyes were wide.

"Do you remember *Farscape?*"

She nodded.

"When Scorpius implanted himself into Crichton's brain?"

Her eyes widened with understanding.

Thank goodness. "He invaded every thought. He— my past life—was kind of a douche, actually. But his vision was so close. Just think how different our world would be if we had a place all our own. Where we could let the rest of the world burn and be safe behind our walls."

Her expression said that'd be nice. "That wouldn't work. A place like that would draw the wrong sorts of attention."

She hadn't seen the city in its prime. "It would if it just popped into being right now, but if the world grew up knowing? Babe, you *know* we'd be on the first plane out."

"No. We would stay. We would help the mundanes from—"

"They have always been afraid of change. Afraid of something different. Easily swayed into violence, prejudice."

Paige inhaled and took his hand again. "Let's table that argument. So then what? Scorpius-Bussemi was there? I got lost after that."

Right. "The past me gave me a crystal, and... Bussemi wants it. Badly. And Mario attacked, and the memory blew up."

"How did Mario get there?" Paige shook her head again, this time in disbelief.

"I don't freaking know." It'd all been so out of control. "He just was. We escaped and found the desert. We were going to the library, and some djinn got in the way. They were pretty cool at first. Then we found out Red Star was on trial, and... we lost by telling the truth. Got put into the magickal gladiator fights. Pretty sure Frey wants to kill me. I killed her horse, I think. Then pow, Leah pops through a door, goes all John Connor, and I blacked out." And lost Hattie. "That was my day. How was yours?"

She waved him off. "How did you get a crystal from a memory?"

"Magick. It's way over my paygrade. I'm just a shifter—with no shift." That hit him. Hard. "I'm not even that anymore. I guess I have magick now. I'm still filling up, but it's super slow in filling the tanks."

"Wait." She closed her eyes for a long moment and then opened them again. "You have magick?"

"Sure. I guess." Did that make up for losing Hattie? No.

She nodded, her gaze glazed.

Silence gathered between them.

"She's really gone?" Paige asked quietly.

"I don't know," he whispered back, his heart twisting. "Hopefully not."

She raked her top lip with her teeth. "Look. Daw—the president is going to work to get DoDO out of the country."

Dexx met her gaze. He doubted *anyone* could get rid of them. Not with Bussemi pulling the strings.

"She's setting up negotiations to discuss your team's extradition. Meaning, we're talking about sending you guys back to England to stand trial. And if you go, I can't protect you."

Great. Another trial. Would they lose by telling the truth on this one too? Probably. "For what again?"

"What you did in Parliament."

"That was—oh. Right." Without Hattie, he didn't even know if he *cared* anymore. The hole in his soul was just so... big. "I'm just so tired."

She grabbed the lower half of his face, digging her fingertips into his under-jaw as she let her head fall.

Great. She didn't know what to do with him either. He knew he'd get up and fight. Eventually. Of course he would. But not that day. Not that second. He needed to take a beat.

Bending, she cupped his face and pecked a kiss on his cheek. "I've gotta go, but I love you."

He... needed her to stay. "I love you, too." But the world needed her too.

She straightened and bit her lips. "Tell the kids I love them?"

He nodded and stood. "Always."

She paused at the door. "Don't break the world, 'kay?"

He wasn't going to make any promises.

But first, he was climbing back into that bed until he was ready to get up.

28

Dexx sat back down on the bed. Keep the world together. Keep the house together. Keep himself together. Baby steps, right?

You were never good with family, Bussemi-voice said. *Isn't that why you left your first one to fend for themselves, and me to die wounded in the wilderness?*

"Go away." At least Hattie's riddles had made him better and weren't designed for torment. Well, maybe a little torment.

You will have to come to me. You can't comprehend the new power you have, and I'm the only person alive who can teach you.

Dexx was barely able to dredge up the will to care. "Paige can teach me. Leslie can teach me. Hell, *Alwyn* could teach me. You're firmly in the rearview, pal." If he could stay clear of *anything* having to do with Bussemi, that's exactly what would happen.

Dexx firmly put Bussemi in the back of his mind, using his magick to do it.

Dexx dressed in his clothes. It felt good to wear *his* things. He hooked a finger in Paige's *second* favorite pair of silkies. He ran a thumb over the fabric, remembering an easier time—one where rules and consequences were far away.

He just needed to feel one thing. "Damn." He tossed the silkies to the pile and pulled a shirt on.

His head poked through the hole, and he stopped. On his dresser sat the stones, his crystal, and the *ma'a'shed.*

The *shamiyir* looked like any other rock with runic inscriptions. It sat in the broken bowl *shamiyir.*

Knowledge rippled through him, but too much was academic and not practical. He knew the names of spells, but not the best one to use in a given situation or how to activate them. Dekskulta had all that knowledge. He... just wouldn't.

The *ma's'shed* went into his waistband at his back. He tucked the crystal and both *shamiyir* in pockets. He left his car keys.

Jackie could hang out for a while longer. He wasn't feeling it right now.

He opened the bedroom door and stepped into the hall. Ember and Rai sat across from each other at Tyler's door.

"Hey, guys." Dexx pushed his sorrow aside and put on a smile. "What are you doing here?"

The twins scrambled to their feet and slammed Dexx with hugs.

He hugged them back, grateful to be able to do so. "I missed you too. Sorry I missed... so much." Maybe he didn't need to get to work today.

The twins didn't say anything. They just held on to him for a while. Okay. He needed a good hug.

Rai wriggled out of his arm first.

"What's on your agenda today?" Holding their hand might be too young for them now, so he draped an arm over a shoulder on each side of him. It hit him at that moment that he didn't know who they were. What their likes where. What they hated.

"Why?" Rai looked up at him with serious eyes.

That stabbed his heart. So many things would change if he could change time.

I sure miss you, girl.

Bussemi tried to invade again, but Dexx's attention went back to the kids.

"I guess you guys are to thank for pulling me out?" He wished they'd just left him there. He would have dealt with things on his own. But he wasn't going to lay that on them. They'd done what he'd taught Leah: think on their own and to do what they thought was best. He couldn't argue with that.

"No." Rai looked down at the floor with a slight frown and then looked away. "Leah was really the one who did the most. And Kate. She knows a lot more than we thought she did."

Leah. Where was she?

He put on the happy face he didn't feel. The kids had done something the adults hadn't been able to, so there was no reason to fault them for it. "Where is everyone? I say we go and thank them."

Ember smiled up at him. "Yeah, that's a great idea. Let's do that."

"Lead the way." Dexx waved him forward.

Ember raced down the hall and down the steps, calling for them to gather.

Rai hung back and slipped her hand in Dexx's. The small palm and fingers felt perfect, though much too big.

He closed his eyes before a tear could escape. Damn, his feels were *raw*. He waited until he could talk. "Come on, kid. We'll be late." They walked downstairs hand in hand.

Leah's reaction just about mirrored the twins. He let Rai go in time to brace himself and catch her. How did she seem so much bigger in just a couple of months? "Little Leah. I missed you."

She mumbled something into his shoulder. She could have been reading the phonebook for all he could tell.

Downside number three to losing Hattie. No enhanced... anything.

He put her down to see the rest of the kids gathered. Tyler, Mandy, Toby, and Kate. "Hey, guys."

They dog-piled on the ex-cat.

There may have been tears.

Finally, they broke apart, and Dexx moved them to the couch. He fingered the long tear in the fabric where Ember had tried to catch himself from rolling off. "Where to start? How in all the universe did you find us?"

Kate pointed at Leah.

Leah pointed at Kate.

Too funny. But that was good. Just being with them, interacting with them was helping him put his emotions back in order. "Mandy, you got another point of view?"

She sat in the armchair kitty-corner from the couch, her legs crossed, her arms locked with a bright-eyed stare. "They're both right. Leah didn't think you were in the real world, and Kate was more than happy to guide us through the Underhill portals. Ember and Rai did the heavy lifting. The rest of us helped in small ways."

Amazement blossomed in him like a flame refusing to die. "You found a way *into* the Time Before? Without using the library access portal?" Dexx's list of amazing magick didn't include a magick doorway to Hattie's realm. And then another thought followed. If the kids could do it again, he could go look for Hattie.

"It was just that one time." Mandy scrunched her brows.

As in, it couldn't be replicated, or they'd only done it the one time? "Not what I meant. Do you think you could...

open a door so a person could *enter*?" Hope dared to spark in his chest.

"Why would you want to, Dad?" Leah sat up straight. She looked *exactly* like Paige at that moment, but blonde and blue-eyed. Piercing detective eyes, and way too much determination to let it go.

Dexx wasn't ready to share that yet. "I forgot something back there." Hattie needed him. Thinking of her as dead... no. She was alive and hurt and needed him.

Tyler jumped up from the floor. "Come on. I've waited for shifter tag for a long time. Can we, Uncle Dexx?"

That slammed his thoughts down. "I, um— gotta give you a rain check, buddy. Work is calling me. They're probably burning desks without me right now." He stood and gave them all hugs before he gathered... shit, he didn't need anything more to head to work.

Leah hung on for an extra-long time, and Dexx was happy to oblige. "Thanks, kiddo. Seriously," he whispered in her hair. "You guys did an amazing thing. I don't think any fifty witches together could have done what you did. I love you."

"I love you more," Leah whispered back.

They broke apart, and Dexx turned away from the kids quickly. He couldn't let them see what his eyes were doing. "See you tonight."

"Okay, you bet." Tyler's excitement wouldn't be held back. "I wanna go blow some stuff up." Shuffling sounds meant Toby had stood, and the two boys were headed to the backyard.

Dexx opened the door to the garage and stopped.

Leslie waited for him, leaning on Jackie, her arms crossed.

He closed the door carefully. "Hi, Les." The glow in her eyes meant he was in deep shit. Spells ran through his head. *No. That isn't needed.*

It's exactly *what you need.* Bussemi-voice sounded like he could be in the garage with them. *She is the enemy. If you aren't careful, she will snap. These creatures are dangerous. They need to be tamed.*

Shut your hole. Dexx shoved him to the back of his mind again, wondering how in the world he'd manage to actually purge this mind-virus.

"Where's Hattie?" Leslie didn't normally pull punches, and this was the knockout hit first.

"She—"

Leslie advanced on Dexx so fast she might have magicked her way over. "What happened to my alpha?" she growled at him. "You know the consequences of Robin on his own. Now, what did you do?"

"I made a series of bad decisions." Sure, he'd had no way of stopping the kidnapping, but he'd been overconfident. He'd let his guard down.

"And now Pea is out there, working her ass off, and the one person she needs most is here having a pity party." Leslie shook her head and left it tipped to the side for a moment. "And fuck all if I know what I'm going to do. I *need* an alpha." She pointed a very straight, very dangerous finger at him. "That's the bottom line. *Find her.*" Fire burned in Leslie's eyes. Then she brushed by him with a shoulder check. She almost twisted him sideways.

Damn, when had she gotten so strong? Probably the same time he ki— lost Hattie.

He had to find a way to get her back.

Jackie sat unfinished, ready for a few hours of work to make her run. She was just a car. Dexx took Paige's car to town.

Maybe work could keep him occupied. The paperwork didn't seem so… arduous anymore. But could they just get back to where they'd been after everything they'd been through?

He took his time, observing the speed limit and counting to three before pulling away from stop signs. Too many bad things had happened because of him.

Bussemi gradually turned the volume up the longer Dexx drove. *We made things that nobody alive today could imagine. Not even your most powerful incarnation had what we each had.*

"Why don't you just shut the hell up?"

You need someone to instruct you. I am that person.

"You gonna tell me about your friend? The big red one?"

You are unable to comprehend him.

"So, go find a shaft and mine it."

Bussemi didn't answer.

Red Star came into view around the trees. The building was home and a completely new place at the same time. He'd been gone for a long time. In this world, it had been only a matter of a month... maybe two? Not long.

It felt a hell of a lot longer to him.

At least his code still worked at the gate. He parked Paige's car, touching the lock button twice to hear the chirp of the siren to confirm.

The doors opened smooth but clanky as they always had before. The rear cells were empty per normal.

He didn't hear the noise until he opened the door to the bullpen.

Frey was bent forward aggressively in the face of another woman. "Fall in line, or you *will* be fired. This is *my command,* and you're insubordinate. Move. Now."

The other woman actually pushed Frey back, raising her pixy face in defiance. "Not sure who you are, sister, but you best be steppin'. This is *my* house." Her features went sharp, looking less human by degrees.

His entire team stood behind Frey, looking confused more than anything else.

Behind the other blonde stood another team, including

Barn and a short ugly man that reminded Dexx of a *Garbage Pale Kid*.

What were they— oh yes, Paige had said she'd had to hire a few people. Anger flared for an instant. *He* was the lead dog here, not... *Hattie?*

He wanted the lead, the alpha spot. Had he been a leader because of her? Or had that been because of him? Time to remind himself who he was and had been before Hattie. "Both of you stand down." Dexx let the door swing shut.

Frey turned her blazing eyes on Dexx, then back to the woman. "You stay here. I'll deal with you after I'm done with him."

He was going to fix Frey. Now.

A third blonde woman stepped out of his office, looking just as confused as everyone else, but confused and *in charge*. There was something in her amber eyes that held authority like a weapon

Frey took a threatening step toward him, her expression telling him how she was going to *handle* him.

Oh, crap. "Don't do it. Stand down!" Dexx pulled his *ma'a'shed*, ready to convert it, but realized he couldn't *use* it. *If* this was a curse like he hoped, he needed a spell to break it.

Frey didn't stop. She reached behind her neck and pulled her sword out. "I'm going to kill you."

His list of spells fumbled. "I said stand down. Do it now." When they finally showed themselves, they ranged from death to detention. That wasn't what he was looking for.

"I told you to stop." She stalked slow and deliberate toward him. "Begged. You didn't listen then. You never *listen*."

Did she think he still had Hattie? "Stop now, and I will." But she was still mourning the loss of her horse. Had she even really lost him?

"Why don't you go ahead and do it *for me?*" She took another step. Threatening.

Bussemi laughed. Not the evil genius laugh, but pure amusement. The old man guffaw was... creepy in Dexx's head.

Dexx found a good spell, many spells actually before she crossed the bullpen. He waited to use them. Last resort kind of thing. They would have to be released in the right order to work right. "Last chance. Stop now." Dexx's heart thundered in his chest. This could backfire.

Bussemi was right about not having a teacher. All the magick and none of the finesse was a volatile mixture.

Just before she came within striking distance, he released the first spell.

It relaxed her nervous system enough to drop her blood pressure. Enough to give her a head rush.

He rolled his shoulder and released the next. A wall of force designed to make more pressure the further into it she walked.

The third spell worked in the lower brain functions. A subliminal spell that simulated fear.

Frey stopped walking, unable to press forward through the force and the simple shock he put her in.

It was the best his magick could do to fake an alpha push.

"You—" Frey licked her lips. "You're you again?" Her eyes narrowed, and searched for the cat in his own.

"Stand down," Dexx repeated. "I don't have enough patience to ask again." He stowed the knife in its sheath, watching her. Had this all been about his alpha? About Hattie? Or was this something more? Was she rational again?

Bussemi stopped his old man cackle. *You faked their trick. That is— well, I am impressed, young pupil. You did well.*

Suck a bag of dicks, you old fart. Dexx pushed him away again.

The second woman at Dexx's office door spoke. "You made it. I didn't expect to see you for—"

"Why wouldn't I come in? Fit as a fiddle." Dexx might fool them, but...

"Scout," the woman in his office said, "meet Dexx Colt. He's the *old* boss." She looked in his eyes, but he couldn't read her. "Let's talk in private, shall we?"

It was time to see what changes Paige'd made. "Yes, let's." Dexx walked past Frey, their eyes locked.

That's right, pupil, do not let her see you weak. She's a true hunter, that one.

Why wouldn't that asshole stay gone? *Can you come up with something not so stupid to say? Any idiot can see she's a fighter. Are you seeing through my eyes or what?*

Not like you do. But I get impressions. Enough to know. Would you like to know how intruding a mind meld is? The process isn't that hard with the right technique. You might actually be good at it. I don't remember that clearly.

No. Now fuck off! Dexx followed the woman into his office and watched her sit in *his* seat.

"Um..."

She looked at him as he motioned with fingers for her to rise out.

"Mine." He wasn't giving it up. He'd fought too damned hard for that position. "Thanks."

She paused for a second and smiled tightly at the desk, obviously running a dialogue through her head, then looked at him with amber eyes. "Of course." She smiled and stuck out her hand. "Stef Lovejoy— call me Stef. Formerly FBI Director of the Portland office. More recently, acting Director of Paranormal Law Enforcement. Paige told me you might be stopping by."

Dexx took her hand. She had a firm grip, oddly surprising. Most women tended to limp fish, but she charged right in.

"Director?" That was a new one. "Of Paranormal Law Enforcement? Neat. Do you have a badge or something?"

"No. The assignment is rather new. Your wife offered me the position. I decided to take it."

Anger flared in his chest. He wanted to hit something. Very hard.

Dexx walked around her to his chair and sat. He leaned back and steepled his fingers. That's what the guy in charge did, right? "I see. Walk me through this. What am I looking at here?"

"Mind if I sit?" Stef gestured to a chair.

"Please." Rage built, and he welcomed it. Another level of bureaucracy? Would he have to ask to have bathroom breaks now?

Do you see? Come to me. You will be the man on top. You would answer to no one.

Shut... up! Dexx shoved him away harder with a greater force of magick.

"Now that we are out, as it were," Stef said lightly, "there's a need for a federal force."

Sounded like a load of crap. "We worked just fine in the dark. There's no more of us now than there was before. Seems we did just fine without another level to make people's lives miserable."

"I understand how you feel. Believe me. I was a director of the *FBI*." She used soft tones.

To seem less threatening? "I was a director in *DoDO*. Had an office and everything." For a few weeks. And he'd been an assistant. But she didn't need to know that.

"Paige said you lost your shifter." She said softer. Definitely not less threatening.

The caged rage boiled over.

Dexx shot to his feet. The lightning spell leaked out, arcing from his body, touching the desk, and the walls, leaving jagged trails of arc burns behind them. The rest of the room darkened as Dexx glowed bluish-white with electricity. "The very next words you say should be chosen carefully. That is none of your business."

"I understand," she said so calmly he'd have thought he was fuzzy. "But what *is* my business is making sure that as paranormals, you and I and all of us are granted the same protections as everyone else. I don't want you to do anything different than you have been."

It unnerved him that she didn't seem to *care* she was surrounded by *lightning*. "I'm not a stool pigeon. And I'm not going to sit by and watch as paras are treated like shit. You stand in my way, and you won't stand very long."

She met his gaze and raised her chin. "I think you have the point of it. We *won't* be treated like second class citizens. My job is to stand in front of the bigger guns so you can do what you do. I have a request, though."

The bolt *wanted* to be released. The energy building in him brought pain.

Kill her, Bussemi-voice said. *She will betray you. You* don't *have to answer to the lesser creatures. She is weak. You can burn her so thoroughly that not even ash will remain. Remove your obstacles.* Bussemi made sense. Sort of.

An image came to him. Rainbow. As she turned into a different form. Clawed and inhuman. And the sweet chocolate-skinned girl ashamed of what she was.

Go. Away.

He remembered a battle between him and Hattie. They'd fought for control. Dexx'd won barely.

He raised his hand, balled it into a fist. Starting at his feet, he pulled the energy up, gathering it into a pinpoint.

The blue-white light arced away from the walls and collided with him. It crawled through his body. With the agonizing slowness of Christmas, it pooled. Gradually it went from his body, leeching until it crawled through his arm to his clenched fist.

Once there, he crushed it, made it smaller until it wouldn't collapse any further. He pushed it, squeezed until the particles stopped moving.

The light in the office came from the overhead lamps again.

"You aren't a run of the mill paranormal. I didn't know you were also a..." Stef pressed her lips together.

"I don't know what I am." His anger seemed to recede with the lightning. His tank of energy was significantly less after the near-miss.

"But you're done now, right?"

He nodded. He was.

"Good. *You* are the boss. Chief Tuck is *your* boss. *I* am Chief Tuck's new boss. You do what you do here. I'm here to help."

"Glad to hear it." If only he had his sense of smell, he could tell if she was lying. "Please send Frey and the other one is here."

Stef left, closing the door softly behind her.

Dexx opened his hand. A crystal the size of a quarter sat in his palm, glowing a soft blue.

29

Dexx sat back in his seat. Well, *that* could have gone better. He just hoped he hadn't pissed off Tuck's new boss too bad, Ms. Ex-FBI Director. Paige knew some pretty powerful people. He preferred it when they weren't thrust into his life, though.

To say that the next meeting went badly was, to put it mildly. Scout was the woman Paige'd put in charge when they were away. Frey took exception to that. Because she was being an emotional and irrational asshole in her grief-stricken state? Or because of a curse? He didn't know. He did know he was grief-stricken, and he wasn't acting ou—

He'd created a crystal with his brain. Maybe he *was* acting out.

Stef took the seat across from him after Frey and the new girl stormed out of the office.

They didn't want to share the lead. They each wanted it to *themselves*.

"A piece of advice?" Stef sat on the edge of the seat, straight-backed with her hands on her clipboard covering her lap.

Dexx looked up, trying to figure out where he stood with this woman. "Please. Let's hear it." He didn't want to.

"Put them on a rotating schedule. You have one rooster in the henhouse until they get to know each other. Then switch it up. You have two strong wills out there and a fragile department. We don't need too much excitement too soon."

"That's—" He paused his reflexive shoot-down reaction. "—not bad." He leaned forward, tapping his new crystal on the desk. "Only here to help?"

"My job is not yet... solidified. But yes. I take the federal side of things, and you take care of the criminal side of things."

"Some could argue those are the same thing." Dexx rested a fist on his knee. What was the crystal? Bottled up magick. Could he use it like a savings account?

"Some do." Stef sighed and looked pointedly away. "I've seen that fine line more than once—another piece of advice. Stay within the boundary of the law. Be very respectful of what and how you do things. There are phones everywhere, and I doubt all the people on this side of the fence are on our side."

Even this felt... good after being out of it for so long. "Yeah. I get a monthly ass-chewing whether I need it or not from Tuck." He looked up at the wall behind Stef's head. "I remember where I was taken from, right here in this town." He'd have to have to make sure there were always two people when they went on a call so that never happened again.

Stef's expression turned somber—not that it'd been overly pleasant before.

Dexx stood up. "Are you based here, or someplace more important?"

"Someplace more important?" She shook her head, clearly not understanding.

"Is this your office space or what?" he growled. "I guess what I'm asking is if you want me to take a desk out there."

"Oh, Hells, no. You will share this one with me. I have an office in the staff headquarters, but here is where I've spent most of my time so far. There's some crazy stuff going on right now. But don't go back out there and lead from the ranks. You lead from here."

Hadn't Chief Tuck said something almost the same?

"I'll bring a little table in here if I need something." She turned her chair away from his desk and toward one of the shelves, using it as a desk. "You're here. Be the leader they need."

Leader. Did he have that in him without Hattie?

Yes. Yes, he did. "If you insist. We could share the desk, too." Dexx took a deep breath. He let it go slow. "Okay. So uh, thanks."

"You aren't the first guy to have... issues with where you are." Stef turned back around to use a corner of his desk. "Being the person in charge can be tough after being a field agent for so long."

Dexx could only agree. But he didn't say anything. He spun the little crystal in his fingers, feeling the solidified elemental spell. It pulsed with a regular beat, trying to escape, to do what it was called to do. If he could find a way to plug it in, it might light a house, a big one, for a month or so. Maybe. He didn't know.

"Believe it or not," she said, "we're on the same team. I'm in the same boat you are, so it's in my best interest to help you as much as I can."

"Okay, you made your point." And he didn't need to hear any more. Seriously. "I can't do this all on my own, and I have a support team above me. That includes you and Tuck and Paige. Where do we go from here?"

Stef leaned back in her chair and folded her hands over

her abdomen. "That's on you. What did you do before... everything went to hell?"

"I took naps. Lots of naps." He hadn't.

"That's probably not a good idea in the current climate." Stef scrunched her nose and shook her head playfully.

"Yeah. Probably not." The day wasn't getting any younger, and Dexx had a police precinct to run if Stef wasn't taking his position. "So, I guess we play the name game. Let's go out and break the good news to our teams."

"They're *your team*. I'm just your shield." She smiled and stood. "After you."

They walked out to the bullpen, green with the life Paige had put into it. The curtains of leaves and features made for individual cubicles in the open space.

Quinn's desk still had a soothing waterfall plant that made bubbling noises, almost like the ocean. Would she return after this was done? After DoDO was taken down?

Ethel sat at Rainbow's desk as they whispered to each other.

Dexx could have heard if Hattie—

A couple of new guys stood by themselves, looking at the old Red Star team. They looked out of place and a little awed, like seeing legends in real life or trying to place the stories they'd heard to faces. Probably that.

Dexx stopped close to Frey's desk and looked at his team. Tarik didn't quite hover over Rainbow and Ethel, but he stood uncomfortably close to them.

Alwyn tried to look confident, but he looked more lost than anything, not being part of either group.

They were missing a person. Always someone.

"Hey. Where's Michelle?"

Rainbow frowned and drew her eyebrows down. "Nobody told you?"

"If I'm asking, then, no." Rainbow. Have to love her or strangle her. She was too valuable to strangle, sooo…

"Oh. I guess that makes sense. So she went home for a bit."

"Home?" Was she expecting to get paid for that? "How long are we talking?" This could be a problem. They needed everyone on deck.

But for what? What cases did they have? And how was Paige going to "free" them of the crimes against them? Could they even enforce the law here? But Stef hadn't said anything about that…

Ethel picked up where Rainbow stopped. "To the grove. She didn't look so good, you know, with all those djinn around. I think she went home to recharge."

Well, that made sense. "Great. She's a battery."

Rainbow snickered.

Ethel laughed.

Time to do what he came to do. "Okay. Red Star. Meet Red Star. Red Star, meet your big boss… future big boss."

His team shuffled their feet. The new team obviously knew who Stef was.

Dexx pointed at the short one. The Garbage Pail Kid. "What's your name? What's your power?

Barn laughed, and Rainbow giggled, but absolutely nobody else moved. Meh.

"Joel." The short man stood as tall as he could go, which put the bar pretty low. His upper lip sat on one tooth. "Goblin."

"Run that by me again?" Why would Paige hire the *goblin*? Just how desperate had she been?

"You said *goblin*?"

"I am. Underground intelligence."

"*What*?"

Barn hid behind his laptop screen, but his bulk jiggled, hiding a laugh attack.

"I have friends in low places," Joel said as if that explained everything. "Plus, I'm pretty good in a scrape." He smiled, his lip lifting off his tooth.

That was... not adorable. Special? A special kind of special, sure.

Dexx turned to the taller, wider looking man. He wore a suit buttoned up over a vest and a high collared violet shirt. He held a bowler hat in one hand. He looked like he'd dropped right out of the turn of the century. The *last* century.

"My name is Rocco," the man said, putting his hand to his chest. "You can call me Roc, or Mr. Rocco, or Mr. Roc. I'm a gargoyle, most recently of Denver, looking to make a difference in this little corner of the world. I have density manipulation and flight. I also can blend in with the scenery, which makes me perfect for reconnoitering."

Reconnoit—Dexx tried not to laugh.

"I also am most skilled at endurance and enduring."

"Okay. That's..." Dear God. "...good. That's good. My team— the team, here before is..."

The introductions took a while. They might have taken a minute in total, but it was way too long.

Barn he knew, but he let the others introduce themselves.

Alwyn was one he listened to.

"Alwyn ab-Rhys, from Southwest Wales. I *was* an operative of the organization Department of Delicate Operations, which I am sure you all know of. I have since rescinded my ways, and now I'm here to support you in any way I can."

Joel and Roc went from mild to aggressive in a heartbeat.

Dexx folded his arms, and they stopped moving. "Alwyn has proven himself more than once. We got off on the wrong foot, but anyone can make a mistake, right? He's our resident spellcaster and has significant elemental control. We lost

Paige to other commitments, but we picked up an Alwyn. He's a good guy."

Stef didn't move, but she seemed to relax.

"Who stomped out of here with Frey?"

Stef stepped forward. "That would be Scout. And I doubt they're together. Anyway, she's a harpy and Paige's first choice to fill in as leader while you were... occupied."

So now the introductions were over.

"This is a police precinct. We answer to Sheriff Tuck." All stuff they should have already known, but Dexx needed the internal psych-out to do what he needed to do.

"Get the calls that come in. For now, just get along. We'll work out the pecking order later." Dexx turned to his office then turned back around. "So, what the Hells are we working on, anyway?"

"Ghost attacks, but we solved that one and handed it off to Paige, who handed it off to the President of the United States. Yeah. That's how that one went." Stef tapped her folders. "You more than a few from Sheriff Tuck. Got something for everyone."

"Oh." Dexx let his good-thinking face show. "Hand 'em out. Alwyn, buddy up with... Joel." That couldn't go wrong. "See if you can learn the ropes."

He'd have to ask Alwyn about the little man later.

"Get to work." The office called his name. He left the door open but couldn't see anyone.

They didn't scatter immediately, but he heard Stef talking to them. The mood seemed to be much more subdued.

He pulled the *shamiyir* from his pockets and sat down.

Time to solve a mystery or two. Or take a nap, whichever came first. He still hurt when he moved.

He set the stone and the bowl together on the desk. His tank filled up, maybe faster than it had, or not, it wasn't important at the moment.

Pieces of a puzzle. The crystals were solid magick. Pretty easy. The stones helped feed and channel that magick. Also, pretty easy. How did they fit and work together to make amazing magick? *That* was the million-dollar question.

He should know the runes along the side. They felt familiar, like his handwriting. They should if he'd made it in a past life, but what was he supposed to do with it? If only he could read the runes. They had to be runes, didn't they?

The bullpen outside became quiet, or at the very least, he couldn't hear any voices.

Maybe he had a spell to translate this.

He sat back and scrubbed his face.

You cannot know until you come to me for help.

Oh, for fuck's sake. "Oh, no. You can go suck on some pig feet." Bussemi always seemed to intrude right at the worst time. Well, actually, *any* time was the worst time.

You will come to me. We must rule together. I have... been rude. You cannot know the depths of my anger—

"Rude?" Dexx jumped up from his desk again, almost yelling at Bussemi. "I have a couple of suggestions concerning *rudeness*."

Rainbow darted in the room, a stapler in her fist raised comically high. "What's going on?" She asked a little breathlessly, her eyes wide with concern.

Crap. "I'm having a conversation with myself. I didn't like what *myself* said. It was rude. Go back to working. Or go home. We've had a hard... um... time away."

"What about our new boss?" Rainbow dropped her hand to her side, finally concluding there wasn't an enemy to staple.

"You got *this*, boss." He jabbed both thumbs at his chest. "Go home. Rest. Call up your girlfriend and have a romantic night. Or whatever. Go reconnect. You deserve it."

"You mean—"

"Please. Go now, and just pretend you're doing exactly what I told you to do." Dexx smiled and nodded.

Rainbow mimicked him. "Yeah. Recon stuff." She tapped her lip with a finger. "Thanks, boss. I owe you one." She turned and disappeared like she had magick... of the disappearing kind.

Dexx sat back down. He spoke lower, so he wouldn't accidentally call in anyone else. "Listen here, you wrinkled, over-stuffed, bastard from a previous life, rude doesn't cut it. You tried to kill me, and I don't like that."

Let me... apologize. Bussemi for all the world sounded like a wizened kindly grandfather. *I indeed fell into a rage. These many years, I have been... angry. I sought revenge and never had the chance to properly dissolve that anger.*

What was going on right now? "Never properly worked out your anger? Well, now I'm glad you got over your hostile intent. Go away." Dexx concentrated on Bussemi and imagined himself shoving the little old man out of a door.

The silence in his head could have drowned the Titanic. A couple of times.

"How in the nine Hells do I do that? Gotta remember that one."

The crystals. What were they supposed to *do?*

He put the blue crystal down and held the larger. Runes carved all over. Gold and silver. Why would there be two types of precious metal?

Gold had properties that worked well with ley magick, and silver had properties that aligned with elemental and spirit magick better.

He dropped the crystal to the desk. How did he know that?

"Dekskulta? You here? Listening to me?" He stopped talking, letting spirits talk through him. Was that a thing, now?

Nothing. *Damn it*. Now he was going crazy on top of everything else.

So gold worked with ley magick. Silver was an elemental thing. Could that be useful?

He picked up the crystal again and traced lines. Gold flowed into the silver and vice versa seamlessly. That wasn't normal. The two metals had different melting points.

Power jolted him. Brief contact and then nothing. His meter went to full in the space of a heartbeat.

The amethyst filled his magick all the way up and hadn't lost anything. Except, it felt more unstable than it had before.

He put it down. "Maybe I don't need to play with that a lot."

"Finally, something we can both agree on." The silky tone of derision preceded Merry Eastwood into his office.

30

D exx sat back in his chair. "Merry Eastwood." What was she doing there? "I'm glad you came by. Saves me the trouble of tracking you down. Your face looks better."

Merry stood at the door, her arms crossed and leaning on the jamb. "There are things we need to... discuss."

"Damn straight there is. You're under arrest. I saw you where you didn't belong, raising some sort of monster, killed more than *one* being, and tried to kill me. Your list is growing longer by the minute." But was any of that *illegal?* Or even in his jurisdiction.

Fuck.

"Come now." She smirked in a cool, calm sort of way that was meant to be relatable. It said something like, *We're fellow rule breakers. This is what we do.*

He wasn't buying it.

"We both know you can't do that."

Okay. So, she wasn't buying his schtick either. "Sure I can. It comes with being a police officer. And not just *any* officer, but the captain of an entire precinct." Dexx rose from his chair, digging through his drawers, looking for a pair of cuffs. Good spelled cuffs.

"Besides—" Merry pushed from the door, shrugging with her hands raised. "—I come bearing gifts." Like she didn't even hear him.

"The kind with knives right behind them?" Where were his damned handcuffs? Did he *have* a pair? "'Cause those are my favorite." When was the last time he'd used them? "You're under arrest. Please be patient while I dig up the cuffs."

"My gifts are the type you want to hear. And if I'm under arrest, I won't be talking to anyone but my lawyer. Seems as though now you have a choice." She pressed her long-nailed fingertips on his desk. "Lock me up where I'll be out in a matter of hours. Or listen to what I say, but I walk free."

Dexx stopped rummaging through the desk to look at her. As far as bad ideas went, this wasn't the *worst*. There was a reason Paige... didn't... hate her horribly. He weighed the pros and cons. Merry Eastwood was a killer. Convicted, and set free... by Paige, but still convicted.

He could throw her in a cell and let her rot for her past crimes alone until she wanted to talk. Everyone needed to eat, and Merry had a big appetite. She was killing to stay young.

But she wasn't wrong. Her lawyers *were* really good, and they *would* have her out in record time.

Stef's words came back to him. He had to stay inside the law. Paige had managed to get her released—probably legally because... Paige. Which meant he'd need new evidence, which he didn't have—no skirting the edge.

But this was Merry freaking Eastwood.

He let out an aggravated sigh. "Let's hear it."

"I'm so glad you have the good sense to cooperate." Her smug smile looked attractive on her as she sat.

So would his boot in her— "It's my first day back, and my patience is kinda thin. Get on with it."

"My conscience is bothering me." Merry leaned back and almost sneered.

"Should be searing hot by now. Surprised it's only *bothering* you."

"Quaint." She raised an eyebrow and steepled her fingers. "No, my participation in that place. The one with Mario Kester?"

Yeah, that got his attention. He could arrest her after she confessed. Maybe?

"I was under the impression we were there for something... different."

"I can't imagine *how* he hoodwinked you. Did he offer you candy from his van? Maybe seventy-two virgins to be sacrificed for a long life?"

"I take it back. You are not quaint. You are crass."

"And you're about to be arrested." He wasn't sure what for yet, though. "I'm going to need something a bit more action-oriented, or you're going to get reacquainted with grey again."

Merry pulled in a deep breath and raised her chin, defiant and accusatory at the same time. "Mario misled me. Instead of tapping a new magick source, he raised a demon. I think. It has power. When you and... that other woman attacked, it escaped the containment ward we had set up. It took his body, and now he's more than dangerous."

Dexx blinked several times as the big answer to his burning question was revealed. "You... what? Run that by me again."

She sighed and rolled her eyes slightly. "Instead of a magickal source of power we could use so I wouldn't be forced to use my... personal brand of magick, he raised some sort of creature that took control of his body. Possessed him."

"Yeah, I know how possession works. And you're claiming you had *no* idea what he had planned?" If Dexx could work it right, he'd have two birds with one confession. And that explained how Mario had taken that beating and had kept on moving. Whatever it was had way more juice than a simple demon. They couldn't survive the way Mario had.

What if it was another bahlrok?

No. They couldn't survive two bad guys with the same demon-type. That was... fuck.

"I was prepared to stop him." Merry pressed two fingertips to her temple as if easing stress. "I would have once I recognized what he was, but I was too busy trying to defend myself against your detective woman. *You* did not let me help."

"Well, I guess the man you killed—" Which was an arrestable crime if he had evidence. "—was just an accident." That he could still arrest her for if it'd been in his jurisdiction. "Or did I see that wrong, too?" He needed to talk to Stef about expanding that.

"That was... unfortunate." Merry pressed her lips together like she had to think hard.

She did. He remembered the man asking *to be* killed.

"I attempted to free him. The woman caused me to miss. The fault doesn't lie with me, but your incomprehension of what you saw."

He remembered quite a bit. Even fighting with Mario. He'd had a pretty good view.

"Besides, there is no proof, and anything that happens off this country's soil cannot be prosecuted by law enforcement of this country. Something Paige is discovering already."

Dexx wasn't sure what she was talking about there, but he was sure when they had a few more moments together, he'd get the skinny. "Got it all figured out, don't you? Still

haven't heard anything worth keeping you out of a cell."
Even if he couldn't put her in one… legally.

"You'll need my help to keep *you* out of jail."

What? "What sort of bullshit you dropping on me now?
I'm not headed for jail. Of *any* sort."

Her expression said otherwise. "Mario is stronger, and
he's growing more powerful. The creature inhabiting him is
fighting for control. Just as Mario is. You will need my help to
rid the creature and send it back."

Interesting bargain. The whole reason she was out of jail
in the first place was because Paige had needed her help to
take Sven down. "Pass. I'll take him by myself." Not likely.
"Moving on, tell me more about *me* heading to jail. Why?"

"Because. You *are* an international fugitive."

Paige *had* mentioned that. Briefly.

"Once they know where you are, you *will* be extradited. I
can stop that. I can provide legal counsel, too. *If* I'm free. You
see? There are *many* reasons to leave me be. I have far more
value as an ally."

He hated that she was right. "Then we just have to
disagree." Dexx gathered the papers strewn around as he
searched for handcuffs. "What is his weakness, according to
you. Just so we're clear."

"I'll give that to you when you need to know." Her eyes
sharpened as she looked down at his desk. "Where did you
get that?" She pointed to the large purple crystal.

Ringa-ding-ding. She'd thought they were down there for
a power cell. This power cell? "Down at the corner of Nunya
and Bidness." He scooped it up and opened a drawer to
throw it in.

Merry's hand lanced out and took it. Her eyes grew wide
with lust. "How much do you want for it?"

"Bring back the man you killed." Because she couldn't.
"You can have it then." He gripped her wrist and squeezed.

Even without Hattie backing up his strength, he still had plenty enough to hurt. His other hand swept over the top and pried it from her hand. He twisted, and the crystal came free. He dropped it in the drawer with a clatter and nearly slammed it closed.

Her eyes widened and then narrowed as she jerked her hand away. "You can't be serious."

"Sure. You go back and recover his body and put his life back in it. I'll give you the crystal. If not, you can go back to the hole you slithered from, or I can put you up here." He smiled pleasantly.

She crossed her arms and feigned disgust, but her attention remained on the drawer.

"Never took you for a rockhound."

"There are many things about me you wouldn't be able to speculate about, Mr. Colt."

"Well, here's something. I *guess* our little talk is over, and I *guess* you're leaving. Or I can *guess* they'll be sweeping your ashes to throw in the trash." Several lists of spells ran in front of his eyes, from heating the room to immolation so hot the pavement would melt. He didn't think he could actually get away with using any of those, but they were there anyway.

"You couldn't conjure enough fire to spark an imagination." The small lines around her eyes said she was re-thinking that.

"Finally hit a nerve. Either you're useful, or you're in jail. Which one is it?" Damn. He wanted to keep his little magick secret a while longer. His magickal side was quickly becoming second nature. No wonder Paige was... the way she was.

"I may have come at a bad time." She narrowed her eyes and took a step back. "I understand your position, and I came to offer assistance. Mario will be more of a threat than you realize. Even with…" She glanced at the drawer and then blinked her dark gaze up to his. "…that."

She hadn't seen Mario come after them in the Time Before. There was exactly zero chance that he'd be underestimated.

"Yeah. It may be a bad time to come knocking on my door. I saw you kill that guy, and I think there's a better than even chance you knew exactly what you were doing, and things got fucked up before you could take the advantage for yourself."

Her eyebrow raise said he wasn't far from the truth. "There is one more thing that may interest you." Merry lost a bit of the snooty high lady speak and leaned in. "You have a price on your head. There's a bounty on your life."

"You couldn't lead with that?" Fuck. He forgot about that. He'd been in the Time Before so long that it had dissolved to a non-issue.

"You are easily led astray."

"Tell me about *this bounty*." Like who was behind it, though he had a pretty good idea.

"I cannot tell you much. What I know is someone very powerful is behind it. It's… high. I also know it originated right here in Troutdale. You have a powerful enemy in your back yard."

What? Okay. That was news. "Why can't we all just get along?" Dexx slammed back into his chair. "Is that all? You're doing less good than you think."

"My offer stands. But I'm afraid it has a time limit. I'll keep the offer open for a day. You have twenty-four hours to decide. Then, I'm going to leave it all up to you."

"Good to know. Don't let the door hit your ass on the way out. We're not set up with the sharks you got." Dexx grinned at her. That shit was funny right there.

Merry huffed and turned on her heel, her heels clicking on the floor tiles on her way out.

How had he not heard those when she'd come in?

He pulled the crystal out from the drawer. This thing had nearly Thanos-level magick, but how to use it without being fried?

Bussemi wanted it. Merry had dropped all pretense just to hold it. Could he use it to get Hattie back? All he would need was a gate to the Time Before. How to accomplish it? The kids opened a door big enough for the entire team.

Hold on a sec. Merry freaking Eastwood had walked in and out of the precinct, and not a soul had stopped her or warned him.

He stood and dropped the crystal in his desk drawer on his way to the door. He poked his head out to an empty bullpen. "Bow? Anyone?" The place could have been empty a week for all the noise now.

That was weird. Okay, so he'd told Rainbow to go home and to find a girl, but where would everyone else go? Stef wasn't even there.

He left to go down the stairs to Ethel's hidey-hole. His shoes made a soft padding sound as he took the steps carefully.

Dexx rested a hand on the *ma'a'shed* as the floor of the dungeon widened out to reveal... Ethel quietly working, with her earbuds in, drowning out outside noise.

He touched her shoulder.

Ethel jumped with a squeal. "Good lord, Dexx, you nearly stopped my heart."

"Yeah. That was kinda funny." Was it, though? Yeah. Yeah, it was. "Where did everyone go?"

"They left when you gave them stuff to do. My bet is they're solving cases. It's kind of what we do here." She gave him a confused look and pulled her head back. "You know?"

"Thanks. I've been here a while. Stef left, too?"

Ethel nodded. "She said she had to get to the office."

"I thought this was her office." Hadn't she said something about... He actually wasn't sure what she'd been referring to.

"I guess there's more than one, now." Ethel sat on her high stool and swung back and forth.

"You glad to be back home?" Dexx pulled another office chair out and sat in it, putting his feet on the table.

"So glad."

Yeah. So was he.

"At least here I know what the bad guys look like. And it's harder for them to get to me through you."

"I guess you have a point. What do you hear from Andy?" Her kinda boyfriend.

Ethel looked away. "I left him a message. He probably thinks I moved on. We've been... busy, you know."

"He'll understand. Can't see him being a dick when we're international heroes."

"You don't watch the news much." Ethel spun the chair to her computer. Her fingers flew so fast over the keys they sounded like a rainstorm. She sat back to let Dexx take a look.

The screen showed a picture of Dexx, obviously taken at DoDO. He didn't look too bright with wide eyes and his mouth slightly agape. It was his DoDO employee badge from Britain.

"That's a stupid picture."

Ethel didn't respond other than to tap another search. It showed them fighting DoDO outside Parliament. Out of all the action, only he was in focus.

Even Rainbow had obscuring features, like the dead look she sported so well.

"You're wanted. We *all* are, but they have you on the top

of the list." She winced. " Except Alwyn. There isn't even a missing person's report on him."

"They probably assume he's dead." Damn and double damn it all to hell. Merry Eastwood *knew*. Extortion alive and well.

"Good point. He wasn't with us until we ran away from that demon thing." Ethel nodded. "Anyhoo, I have some samples to retest. Got some evidence off the victims of the ghost attack. Or at least Joel thinks we do."

The ghost attack they'd *solved* already? "Yeah. Thanks, you super-brain, you."

"Sure thing."

Dexx plodded back up the steps to the bullpen. How could they be— it didn't matter. *You did this, didn't you?* Dexx let his mind pick up the intrusion of the cardinal.

I did nothing.

You made sure we were fugitives. Fuck all, you little twat.

This can be changed. Join me, and you will never need to worry about the squabbles of the lesser people.

"*They're just lesser now? What happened to 'only you will rule the entire galaxy'?*

My enthusiasm overtook my nature.

Dexx was in a box. He couldn't leave. He couldn't work without showing his face. Damn. "You dirty old man. I'm going to—" What? What could he do to Bussemi? Talking in his head was one thing, like trolling on social media.

Everyone talked a big game, but when it came to throwing down, they ran away like the cowards they were.

Dexx could take on anything. Except Bussemi. That time being broken over and over had done something to his head.

He stepped into the bullpen, ready to rip into Bussemi with empty words.

"There." The new girl, Scout, pointed at him with a claw for a finger. "Just like I said."

"Scout? Yeah, I'm here. Where else would I be?"

Sheriff Tuck walked out of the office. "Sorry, Dexx. I'll work this out, but right now, it has to be this way."

Dexx stopped. "Tuck? What way? What the Hells are you talking about? I haven't broken the city. I haven't skirted the law. I haven't even issued a ticket. What *way* are you talking about?"

Tuck dropped one end of a pair of cuffs from his finger, his lips hiding behind his silver mustache, but the rest of his expression made it clear he wasn't pleased. "Dexx, you're under arrest."

31

D exx stared at Scout. If she was trying to make friends, she wasn't doing a great job of it. "What the hell, chief?" Why would Tuck be on the wrong side?

"I don't have a choice. This came down from the feds and their new toys."

Dexx looked over at Scout, his question clear, but he didn't need to say anything.

She set her jaw with resolve, her hazel eyes flickering doubt.

Dexx leaned against Rainbow's desk. Her monitor still showed a dozen roses on the screen. Somebody was getting a little somethin'-somethin'. Good for her. "Stef was just here. She never said anything about it." Toys? It had to be DoDO behind it.

"She isn't actually in a position to do anything, one way or another." Tuck looked over his shoulder at two people in very nice suits with him.

He knew one of them. His *boss* from England, Sayyid

Maxwell, the number two or three guy in the England chapter house.

"Mr. Colt," Sir Sayyid said calmly. "I'm sure you can appreciate the sensitive nature of the situation you have placed both our countries in."

He wasn't going to take the bait. "Sir Sayyid. Come to torture me again?"

A frown flickered across Scout's forehead.

"Don't worry, Sayyid. I have the list of the others in on it. Your day is coming, and you're on *my* turf this time." Dexx swiveled back to Tuck. "*This* is your guy you're taking orders from? Someone has their wires crossed."

Scout's eyes shifted greener as she glanced from the DoDO agents to Dexx with growing uncertainty. "What's—" Scout's jaw loosened and dropped a touch.

"These are DoDO's finest. Yeah." Hopefully, she'd start filling in the blanks a bit. He pulled a list of possible spells he could use against Sir Sayyid and the other guy. He tabled them when he felt their offensive *and* defensive magicks building.

Dexx could survive that, even win in a spell battle with these two DoDO directors.

Sir Sayyid's strength went far beyond most of any of the witches in DoDO, and the other guy had a few spells ready that might take a few seconds to get around.

Tuck and Scout would likely die in the exchange, though. So maybe that wasn't the best course to take.

Tuck fiddled with the cuffs in his hand. "Will you cooperate?"

Scout stepped back. "Somethin's not right here."

"Sorry, kid." Tuck shook his head sadly. "You should have waited when we were alone."

Dexx had his fair share of royal pooch screwing sessions in the past. "This is what happens when you get shitty about

335

who gets to be in charge, Scout. We'll work on that when I get back." He held his hands in front of him, ready for the cuffs.

Tuck gave Dexx a long studious look, then put the cuffs away. "You've done some growing up, son."

Dexx kept his hands in front of him. "Had to. I had people like this breathing down my neck constantly for the last year at least." He nodded to Sir Sayyid. "Ain't that right, Sir Douchebag?"

Sir Sayyid stepped forward, almost around Tuck. "You are under arrest. You do not have to say anything, but it may harm your defense if you do not mention when questioned something which you later rely on in court. Anything you do say may be given in evidence."

"Wow, even *acting* like you're the real police." Dexx'd had to learn the British form of arrest while he'd been part of DoDO when he'd thought they might have been legit.

"I assure you, we *are* members of law enforcement." Sir Sayyid shook his head sadly as if he bought his own bullshit. "I will now search you for items, which may be used against you in a court."

Dexx stepped back. "Uh-uh. You lay one finger on me, and I'll fry you and your buddy. Now, if my boss wants to, he can. You SOB's can kiss a frog."

Sir Sayyid froze in place as soon as Dexx warned him.

That was new. Had Bussemi warned them?

"You have no choice," Sir Sayyid said, though his expression held a fair amount of caution. "Come with as a duly arrested criminal for extradition."

Scout narrowed her eyes and shifted her weight toward Dexx.

That was potentially a good sign, but Dexx didn't know this woman, so he didn't know if he could believe her body language. "Chief, do this by the book. You have to take me to jail until this gets untangled." There really wasn't any laws that Dexx could think of like that, but did Sir Sayyid know? Probably not.

"Okay, son" Tuck's blue eyes snapped with attention, and his crow's feet became more pronounced as if he was smiling. "Come with me. I'll drive you to the station."

"As long as the trash don't ride with us, I'm okay with that."

"Should I go too?" Scout raised her chin and eyed the two DoDO agents.

"No," Dexx said, keeping his tone peaceful and non-yelly. "You stay. Tell Paige. Let her know. She'll make sure the right things happen."

Scout blinked a few times, then tipped her head to the side in a nod.

He started to the door where more black geared people waited. More DoDO.

"Sorry," she whispered on his way by.

Yeah, they'd be having a talk after this.

"The mayor. I'll call her."

"Sure," Dexx said over his shoulder. "Call the news, too. Make it go wide."

Scout nodded.

Stupid kid. Worked up because she thought she should have more responsibility. Or maybe that wasn't it all. Maybe he was just assuming because it looked like two cats trying to scratch the same post. He didn't know.

In the truck, Dexx relaxed. "What's it look like?"

Tuck ignored his question. "Took a lot of guts to come quietly. If I didn't know any better, I'd say your time away has mellowed you out some." He looked at Dexx out of the corner of his eye. "A year?"

Dexx nodded. "Time demon." He sighed heavily. "Well, I *wanted* to flambé the place, but I remembered you'd make me do the paperwork for that."

Tuck snorted and backed out of the parking place. He paused, his hand on the gear shift. "How would you—"

Damn. It. "I don't want to go too deep into it, but I have some magick."

"But you always said you didn't."

"Times change." Dexx twisted to look behind them as Tuck put the car into gear. "We going through with this? I mean, are you going to let them take me?"

Tuck knocked his sheriff's hat to the backseat and scratched his head. "I'm going to stall as long as I can and hope that Paige can work some political magick. But right now, yes."

It was the right call. "Bastards. *They* kidnapped *me*, and now I'm the bad guy? Aren't there laws about that sort of thing?" Dexx turned around and slammed back in the seat.

"All they have to say is that you went willingly. Your presence in their country and on film is all they need. You boarded a flight there?"

"Yeah, why?" Dexx had a sinking feeling that the whole plane ride had been a setup. They had door magick that could take them across the world in an eyeblink.

"You could have, at any time approached an officer or customs agent and told them you were being held against your will. You obviously were not. Got passports and everything stamped, I'm sure."

"Dammit. The ass hats kidnapped me, rewrote my memories, and *then* shipped me out of here." But this was a new day. Magick was allowed in the courts now. He could explain all that.

"The footage of you attacking their seat of government is false, then?"

"I never attacked Parliament. I was *defending* them against

DoDO and Cardinal Bussemi." He should have just let them get boned up the ass.

"The footage shows a completely different story. We'll fight for you, though. Whatever it takes." Tuck stopped at the four-way and turned right onto the main street.

"Seems like they got this all buttoned up. Don't know what you're going to do to stop them."

They sat in silence as Tuck turned left off the main street up the steep hill to his police station. Four news crews were already set up, cameras rolling on reporters speaking into the lenses.

Tuck took his traditional spot in the back of the station. "Don't say a word to the reporters or anyone else. They'll come at you and blast questions." Tuck reached around to retrieve his hat and put it on. "*Don't* take the bait. The court of public opinion is more skewed than the real one."

Dexx opened his door as the rush of the on-location reporters reached them.

How had they managed to shoot off two thousand questions in eight seconds went far beyond any spell he had in his arsenal.

"How come you aren't in hiding—"

"Did you mean to start a world war—"

"Is it true you killed the Prime—"

"Are you a government assassin—"

"Was this a covert action—"

Dexx tried to push through the press of reporters, but they locked ranks and refused to give him a chance to move.

The questions kept flooding him. Most of them were way off base and kind of amusing. Government assassin was a good one, but an incompetent government assassin boiled his blood.

Tuck tried to pry them away, but the cameramen ignored

his attempts to pull them back. "Move along. You're impeding a police officer—"

The reporters were brazen, all trying to out-compete one another, trying to get a rise from Dexx.

"Did you kill—"

"Is it true—"

"Are there others—"

"Did you mastermind—"

"Were you contracted—"

"Are you a shifter thing—"

"What went wrong—"

"Are you the only surviving—"

How the hell did these mental midgets keep their jobs? Why couldn't they just ask if it was a setup or why an international terrorist ring made him the fall guy? Anger built in him.

Spells that would freeze or fry them came instantly to his mind. He could blow them over with a blast of wind or call a bolt of lightning strong enough to fry equipment. That one should work.

Don't let them live, Bussemi-voice sneered. *They won't love you or understand you. Roll fire through them. Turn their blood to acid. You have the power.* Bussemi's tone had no fire in it. The reporters weren't even people to him. They might rate lower than mouth scum, just to be brushed away.

Get out of my head. They might be reporters, and they might just be worse than fuzzy teeth, but they were still people. Just people.

Why would you champion those who want to see you publicly executed? They live for the ratings, not you, not the story. They serve a different master, but that master could be you. Us.

Dexx kept fighting to push through the throng, gaining inches. *You mean you.* Reporters had a job. Some or most of them might not even like what they do, but times were hard, and the more resources they had access to made life a little easier.

I mean us. *They mean to use you for their own ends. Not for the truth, but to gain an advantage over their competitors.*

Like you wanted to use me for your *ends?* Dexx pushed the cardinal from his head. The trick worked, but only for a while and only if he kept his cool.

"How many did you kill—"

"Is it true you used human shields—"

"Can you show us a trick—"

Tuck wasn't having any luck. He made eye contact with Dexx. Helpless. Not if they wanted to keep a pretense of Dexx being a good guy.

"They say you're dangerous—"

"Can you reveal —"

"Were you contracted—"

"Why are the paras trying to kill world leaders—"

Damn it. Now they hit a nerve. *He wasn't.* World leaders were trying to kill *him*.

He prepared his spell.

He looked out above the trees and pointed. "Holy shit! Is that Homelander?"

As one, the reporters turned. As they relaxed their stance, he pounced with his freeze spell.

Every single reporter froze in place, quiet, all looking at nothing over the trees.

"Huh, I guess it's not." Dexx wound through them, being careful not to knock any of them over. "Come on." He flicked his head to Tuck.

"What—"

Dexx tapped his lips with a finger. "Shh. Let them look."

When they entered the building, Tuck stopped him. "What did you do to them? If you hurt them, I can't—"

"Nah. Nothing so terrible." Dexx walked a half-step in

front of Tuck, going to his office. He turned to talk and walk at the same time. "I let them believe there was something to see. They wanted an answer to something, *anything*, that when I gave them one, I just kept them looking. It'll wear off in a minute. Now you said we could get out of this?"

Tuck narrowed his eyes. "I said we'd fight. Got a few calls to make, but you aren't out of the country yet."

Dexx sat heavily in the seat across from Tuck's.

Tuck sat in his seat, not quite obscured by stacks of folders. He took one down and began to look over the paper with a pen. "Tell me what happened."

"Out there? I'm not sure I know what you want." He wasn't going to pull any punches if Tuck asked.

"Start at the beginning. How about how you got tangled up with DoDO. Then go from there." Tuck didn't look up from his work, but he'd been in his job long enough. He probably didn't need to.

Dexx snorted. "Well, I was all alone at work. I got a call, so I went to investigate..."

Tuck listened while he worked for almost ten minutes. His pen moved slower and slower, and finally, the paperwork sat.

"Roxxie, the angel? Paige told me she couldn't do what she used to." Tuck laced his fingers on the desk.

"Somebody is misinformed, or someone is lying. All I know is Roxxie sent us in there. She couldn't get us out, though. Well, we smashed a bunch of shit— privately owned, of course, and likely to do us harm, so I didn't think you'd mind. Anyway, we go in and tear the place up, and Quinn stops me and tells me that she won't help me—"

"Hold on. Back up. You said Quinn. Would this be the Quinn Winters you spent all that time trying to find? What and why is she doing with DoDO?"

"Dipped in tar if I know. She said she was doing good on

the inside. She helped. More than I could. She risked her life to get me the info I gave to Paige. She broke me out once and then helped when Red Star came in. I'd give up a lung to have her back on the team. Way back when, I didn't know how far I could trust her, but now I know. She'd be valuable."

"Where is she now?"

"Couldn't say. Left her there in the house. I hope she wasn't there when we attacked Bussemi." Hopefully, they didn't find out she'd been helping Dexx.

Tuck sat back and listened to the rest of the story, his fingers laced but resting away from any sort of police work. He didn't stop Dexx but to ask a few questions, but mostly left Dexx to talk.

"— and then she was running at me full tilt, ready to lop my head off, and the doorway opened, and we came home. I don't know how the kids did it, but I need to go back. For Hattie. The sooner, the better."

"I'm not sure I understand how you got or regained magick. Is it because you're a shifter?"

Dexx's heart twisted. Hattie, all alone, and maybe dying. He couldn't bear to think she had already died. "No."

"Then, how?"

"It's so complicated I don't know where to start unraveling it. The life I'm living right now, it's just the *next* one in a list of them. So, in the first one, the one where Bussemi and I were brothers, I made a stone that recycled my soul into a new body. My memory of who I used to be gets washed, but my power stays. I'm almost always a shifter, something that happened in my first life, too, I guess. Anyway, another of the first ones made a city where paranormals could live in peace, but Bussemi attacked. The old me made a way for the magick to come back, but he knew there'd be a sacrifice. And when I find him again, I'm going to beat the ever-lovin' shit out of him. He's a douche."

Tuck leaned forward, "That sounds like any number of complaints I've had about *you.*"

"Me? Why?" That couldn't be. "I'm a nice guy. Don't go out of my way to cause trouble. I'm accommodating. I'm—"

A knock on the door interrupted him. They both looked at the opening door.

A uniformed officer poked his head in. Officer Shirley nodded at Dexx, then to Tuck. "Got Merry Eastwood here to talk with you. *Both* of you."

Tuck sat up straight and sucked in a breath, his bushy brows high. "By all means, show our most notorious witch in."

The door swung wider at Merry's approach, her phone up to her ear. Classic rich bitch syndrome. "Of course I will," she said into her phone. Hand still up to her ear. She greeted them both with a smile. She pulled her phone away and held it to Dexx. "The phone is for you."

Dexx wrinkled his nose at the phone. "Who is it? I'm not going to get an STD, am I?"

"That depends on you," she said as if she'd eaten grapefruit. "I'm sure your discretion has a fairly low bar." Merry held the phone steady, but her patience seemed stretched.

Her phone looked fancy. Super fancy. Slim and wide and probably the best screen resolution that could be had.

He took the phone and put it to his ear. "This is Dexx, captain of Red Star Division. How may I help you?" See? Professional as fuck.

"Mr. Colt," a semi-familiar woman said. "I believe we have a few acquaintances."

Where had he heard that voice from? "I'm not sure you're talking to the right person. Who are you?"

"This is President Flynn."

Dexx almost dropped the phone. Merry Freaking Eastwood was playing a new and stupid prank. "President? I don't think I voted for you." What was he supposed to say to her?

"Almost half of the country didn't. Don't feel bad. The reason I'm talking to you now is because you have some powerful friends. I put the extradition on hold and diverted it into peace talks between the global paranormal community and foreign nations. A detente, if you will."

That sounded... great.

"I'm asking you to be our representative for the paranormal world. A position like this could potentially keep you safe from prosecution. Both here and abroad."

Dexx sat numb for a few seconds. Did she say what it sounded like she said? "Shouldn't you be talking to Paige about this?"

"Her butt isn't currently isn't in the frying pan."

Fair. "You want me to sit down with those ass clowns and talk peace? Did I come back to the world I left? They kidnapped me, tortured me, brainwashed me, and rewrote my memories, and then made me attack my own team. What's your angle here?"

"Look. Your wife has... changed my outlook on the paranormal community, but I'm not completely sold. I still think you're a danger to our world."

Dexx scratched his free ear, not sure what to say to that.

"And no, you won't have to deal with them on their territory as they'd tried. You'll be on neutral ground."

Something didn't sound right. He didn't need Hattie to tell him there was a rat somewhere. "What's really going on here? Come clean with me, and I'll consider it."

She paused.

Merry gave him an exasperated look.

Tuck looked like he was having a coronary.

"I was not told you were savvy," the president said with a sigh. "Okay, here it is in plain English. My administration is on shaky ground. You hammer a peace deal for your people and the rest of the world, and I can guarantee safety for you and your family. *If* you can cut through the layers of crap. It works out this way: you help me, and I can help you. Plain and simple."

Wow. The lady just told him in no uncertain terms that she needed a win to stay in power. Did he want that? "This really sounds like Paige's area. I'm shit at negotiations. Like I could sell you a carb, but you really want some injectors."

"What?"

Great. He confused the most powerful person in the free world.

"My best feature is killing demons. This deal ain't that. You follow me?"

"I understand you don't want to, but if your wife is any indication, I think you'll do just fine."

"You know we aren't married, right?" He *needed* to pop the question. Like before the world got swallowed by the biggest fireball since the sun went main sequence.

"I was not aware. Back to the subject at hand. Can I trust you to be with the delegation I send?"

Damn it. DoDO *needed* to be burned to the ground, and the people turned to salt licks for wildlife. But... if he could deal with governments directly, he had a chance to derail DoDO everywhere.

He looked up at Merry.

Her dark eyes told him to take the offer. She *knew* what he was being told— asked to do.

What would Paige do? She was the strongest woman he knew except for maybe Leslie. They would charge in and take control, and soon the poor saps would be eating from their hands. Whiskey women had a way with things.

But for him? This wasn't his type of op. "Fuck. Oops, I mean, you better keep *me* safe if I have to talk with these aaa —people."

"You will be in good company. I suggest you pick your people well to go with you."

This was going sideways fast. "Run that by me again? Pick *my* people?"

"I wouldn't expect you to go alone. Peace talks, talks about peace with a brunch with foreign dignitaries? That's never handled by one person alone. Can I count on you?"

"Uuuugh. I guess." Could he tell the President of the United States no? "How many do I get to take? And where is this supposed to be? I really don't want to go to D.C."

"For something like this, we'll move it someplace all parties can agree to. Don't worry. We'll handle it on this side."

"Okay, fine." He'd always wanted to say this. "Have your people call mine. We'll do lunch."

"I *was* told you had a certain way with words. Have a nice day, Mr. Colt."

"Yeah, you too." He handed the phone back to Merry. "Merry Eastwood is going out on a limb. What's in it for you?"

"I have just as much to lose as you do." She stowed her phone in a pocket he hadn't seen on her business class type dress with a smile.

This woman was like a walking trap. "No, you have a plan. Or you don't go with me."

She raised an eyebrow, the opposite corner of her mouth rising, pleased. "I don't think you have a solid grasp of the situation." She sat in another of the chairs in the room and leaned back with her legs crossed daintily, like a queen passing judgment. "You pick the people going with you. That doesn't mean you pick everyone going. I will be there as a representative of... a very powerful group of people."

Probably the same people who owned most of the country. "Son of a bitch. Of course, you have an angle. Twist the one percent for the one percent."

"That's a very near-sighted way to view things. How on earth would a poor person pay another poor person a wage? My interests are far more ranging than you can imagine."

Tuck watched with his eyes moving from one speaker to the next like it was a tennis match.

"Well, I imagine whatever you come out of there with, it's going to benefit Merry Eastwood."

She narrowed her eyes and shrugged.

He hit close to the mark. "Chief, can I count on you to run my security detail?"

"Nope. I run the entire county, pup. Not just a tiny town. You got the better people for that, and I have a piling tower of work right here." He snapped his fingers and pointed to Dexx on his way to his chair behind his desk. "But I do wish you luck, son. Congratulations."

He had two women clawing each other's eyes out to see who was going to run the place. "Chief, where did Sir Sayyid get to? I thought they were right behind us."

"They were." Chief Tuck nodded. "I believe they were stopped on a traffic violation."

Merry sat forward. "You—" Her eyes pierced the air, but a corner of her mouth pulled up.

Tuck tapped his desk with a finger. "I believe you need to get back to work. Make this town safe for Ripley."

His adopted daughter, who was also a part of his pack. "She's part of my crew, so yeah. I need to go think about things." Fuck. He wouldn't be going to the Time Before unless he could get the girls into sending him as soon as he could pin them all down.

Merry stood. "Remember to bring you're A-Game, Dexx. We're all going to need it." She strode out without another word.

Dexx watched her leave. "You think she's really on our side?"

Tuck sat there for a minute just staring out the door, his mustache hiding his expression. "I've known Merry and her entire clan for a long time now, and I can't say. They do the things they do for their own reasons."

"They got few good eggs in there, and Pea believes in them. It's just Merry is their big problem."

Tuck pulled another file off the pile, making the stack below it higher. "Go get your things and team ready. Do us proud, son."

Proud. Maybe he could learn a new trick. He'd certainly used up all his old ones. "Sure. See you on the news."

Dexx made it as far as the bullpen before shouts stopped him.

Sir Sayyid and his minion caught up to him.

If the president had called him, inviting him to this meeting, that meant he was off the hook, right? "You rang?" Dexx gave them an innocent, wide-eyed look.

"You're under arrest by the power vested in me in the name of Parliament and England."

"Catch up with the times, bud. You're actually two seconds away from me arresting *you* for stalking and harassment. Make your decision now."

Sir Sayyid and his minion looked at each other. Sir Sayyid's phone beeped, and he jammed his hand in his pocket, staring at the screen.

"We gonna throw down? We can do it here or in the parking lot."

Officer Shirley walked up behind the DoDO agents, his hand resting on his pistol. "These men bothering you, Officer Colt?"

Holy crap. Shirley coming to his rescue? That man was getting an invite out to the house *tonight*. "Are you?"

Sir Sayyid put his phone away. "We were obviously mistaken. We're going to leave this fine city to its inhabitants. Good day to you both."

The minion's eyes just about fell out of his head. "You can't be serious." The man had no accent at all—homegrown radical.

"I am. We leave right now." Sir Sayyid gave Shirley plenty of room as he walked by.

It was nice watching those two walk out of there empty-handed. "Thanks, man. I owe you one." Dexx remembered to relax around the man and found he already had. "You know, you still haven't brought the family out. You're coming tonight."

Shirley looked into space for a moment. "Sure. What do I bring?"

"An appetite. More than that is up to you. We're experienced at the whole more-for-dinner thing."

"What time?"

Dexx didn't know how much time he had left. "Soon as you get out of here. I'll make sure people are on their best behavior."

"No worries. And, uh, you can call me Jake."

"Sure thing." Things were finally looking up. "See you when you get there."

Shirley nodded and went back to work, weaving his way between desks that looked the same as at Red Star—without the plants. There were just more of them.

Outside, he realized he didn't have a ride. Going back in wasn't going to happen. That was like claiming a victory, then looking stupid.

The town wasn't *that* big. Dexx began to walk back to Red Star. A small, green car pulled up next to him. "What are you doing out here?" Rainbow sat in the passenger seat, next to Molly, her girlfriend.

"Walking back to Red Star."

"*Back*? What happened?" The door opened, and Rainbow got out.

"Misunderstanding. Got it ironed out. Mostly."

"Get in." Molly leaned close to the wheel so she could look out at Dexx.

He could claim his victory and save face too. "Sure."

Dexx had to hand it to Molly Hammond. Her car was meticulously clean, and smelled good. The trip back to the Red Star precinct was a blur.

Scout waited for them with the mayor. Her eyes popped when Dexx walked back in with Rainbow.

"Just a misunderstanding. Fixed it with the president." But he crooked his finger at Scout. "We have to discuss something."

The mayor wasn't letting him get off that easy. "I was worried. I wasn't for sure what I was going to tell Paige."

Dexx wasn't practiced at dealing with her. He knew who she was, of course. Kinda—not really. "Sorry. We're good. Thank you so much for coming out."

She narrowed her small eyes on her round face. "You're really okay."

He gave her a firm nod. "I really am." Not.

"My job here is done, then." She turned on her heel, her head high, and walked out, her heels sounding loud.

Dexx let Scout lead the way to his office with dignity. He was going to fire her or bust her to beat cop. She defended herself the best way she could, and Paige *had* given her the post.

It was *possible* he might have stepped on her toes a little, but dealing with emotional trauma had a tendency to shorten people's viewpoint.

She left his office knowing she was on probation and to never do that again.

He outlined work for everyone and went home.

Time to get the kids to send him back to Hattie for a while.

He walked in the door to find Leslie and Tru standing in front of the TV, watching a news channel with headlines scrolling across the bottom. They were *glued* to the screen.

"Hey, guys. What on the tube?" When was the last time he sat down for a comedy? Or something with explosions and action?

Leslie gave Dexx a vacant stare. "The Pope is coming to America."

"So? Doesn't he do that all the time?" The Pope seemed to be a nice guy. Super shitty with his leadership picks and probably less than stellar with brain activity, but generally a nice guy.

"He's scheduled to mediate peace talks between paranormals and mundanes."

"He is?" Hold the phone. Was *this* the mediator the president wanted him to sit down with? Merry had no chance of engaging in business talks with the guy. All religion, no business. Popes were famous for having no business acumen. "When?"

Tru didn't turn away from the set. "A week."

Leslie half turned to Tru. "Wonder who they got to do that? Probably Pea. She seems to be the only one really pulling for our people out there."

"Actually, I think *I'm* the guy going to the summit— talks, whatever."

Leslie whirled on Dexx. "No. You have people here to take care of. You *will not* leave us here to take care of the things you should be doing."

She had a point. He couldn't just take off. But then, it was a payment of sorts. Extradition or delegate. Not much of a choice, really. "I have to. The President of the United States called me." Or Merry.

The look on Leslie's face said she was dumbfounded. "What's to say it's not a *trap*. You ever *think* before you do these things?" Leslie wasn't pleased. She had a hard time controlling Robin if she didn't have an alpha to help keep him in check.

"Trust me. I know. This isn't the best circumstances, but we do what we have to."

Leslie lit her eyes into an orange glow. "You *know* what happens if I don't have the alpha around, right?"

Her spirit animals ate all the poodles. "Yeah. You learn to keep him under control until you have a new one." Time to get on that plan to get Hattie back. Dexx left before she could really get on a roll. Officer Shirley was going to have fun if he came over, and Leslie was in a snit.

He opened the garage door. Jackie sat there, ignored. His heart fell. Did he want the car anymore? He opened the door, and the smell of familiarity wafted over him. Old times, less complicated and happy.

Before he knew it, he'd twisted his butt into the seat. He closed the door and sat there.

Paige.

Hattie.

Leslie.

Jackie.

Leah.

Did he always have to let the women in his life down? Would the talks with the Pope even change anything? Anything at all?

But if he was going to make the peace talks, he couldn't jeopardize that by going to the Time Before. After he got back? Hattie was the first person he was getting back.

He closed his eyes and felt for Hattie. He went to the

meeting place. He went as far as he could. Nothing. Hattie was gone.

Damn. It. Could he make a difference in the talks without her?

A few days would tell.

Bussemi had waited in Hattie's spot, invisible but not silent. *In a few days, you will come to me, and we can discuss your allegiance and how you will be raised above the servants of this world.*

How did Bussemi get in after he'd been pushed out? *Now, why would I even entertain the idea? I'm going into the talk with your boss, not you.*

You're talking with me. Then Bussemi laughed as he left on his own.

33

Dexx held on to the idea that Bussemi-voice had lied to him. Demon rule number one applied to Bussemi more than anyone. If he truly was like the Scorpius-implant, then he couldn't know. But if this was really Bussemi? Then he had way too much information on Dexx, and things might be about to get real bad.

The talks were full steam ahead with solid news coverage about the unprecedented delegation between paras and normies.

Jackie became his hideaway. He could sit in her seat for hours, trying to break through to the Time Before.

Dinner with officer Shirley had gone as good as could be expected. Better than, even. He'd brought his daughter out, and she'd played with the kids. Well, they'd entertained her at least.

He'd had the biggest showboating kids of all time. Rai and Ember had taken turns shifting into animals and tossing magick back and forth. They'd made rising heat currents and had figured out how to use bed sheets as parasails. The

Troutdale kids never had any better friends than the Whiskey kids.

Leah had refused to try to open a door to the Time Before. Refused and wouldn't even talk to Dexx after he'd tried to demand she open a door just for a second so he could retrieve Hattie. He wasn't facing Bussemi on his own.

When he'd seen the tears in her blue eyes, he stopped. He pulled her into a hug and had whispered how sorry he was to be such a douche.

He mourned Hattie and promised to find her just as soon as this was over. Whenever he wasn't working, he mourned her. He *knew* she was gone, and the hope of getting her back was just… a smokescreen. His oldest companion was truly dead.

Jake Shirley met him at Red Star the morning before they headed to the talks.

"Morning, Jake. What can I do ya for?" Dexx put his hand out.

The news still reported the Pope's visit every half hour, but Dexx couldn't shake Bussemi's assertion that *he* would be there. Also, since that night, he hadn't been back.

Jake playfully slapped it away. "Put that away. Never know when it'll go off." He smiled for a moment, then looked at the ground a little more serious. "Did you mean what you said the other night? You really want me to tag along on your summit whatever?"

Dexx blinked several times. He never thought Shirley would accept. "Yeah, sure. Hell, yes. You have leave or whatever?"

"Turns out, I get paid for this. Special assignment. I asked the sheriff about it, and he approved it on the spot. So yeah, I'm in."

Great. Except… if Shirley went, wouldn't he just be a body at Bussemi's feet?

No! Dexx had to stop thinking like that. "Yeah, okay. So, it's you and Alwyn on personal detail. Rainbow's going to as a key witness. Glad to have you on the team." Shirley was a good guy to have around. He had the perfect police aura of competent but not-in-your-face.

He smiled and then backed away, heading out.

Dexx walked in the front doors with a better feeling about the talks. One more on his side couldn't hurt.

He'd be the first in the office. Might even get a few extra zz's before the mad rush. Or a couple of extra Rainbow reports finished.

The feeling turned to a sinking sensation as soon as he walked through the doors.

Frey was in Scout's face again. She had the other woman by inches, but Scout looked to have some muscle and wide shoulders. They squared up in between Frey's and Michelle's desk, who had taken more personal leave, so Scout had been using the desk.

Why couldn't they get along?

The yelling on both sides prevented him from deciphering this latest clash. "Hey, knock it the hell off." Dexx raised his voice to catch their attention.

No good. Scout's features changed enough to see her inner harpy. Frey had her arms splayed out, ready to attack or defend.

"I said—"

Frey and Scout both moved at the same time. Claws went for Frey's throat, and a fist went for Scout's solar plexus as a sword came out.

Frey was hit once, twice three times by harpy claws as her own sword came up and caught a fourth swipe.

Frey's boot came up and slammed into Scout's center.

She folded, and Frey went for a finishing move.

Dexx caught them both in a suspension spell he never saw come up. Scout in mid-flight, Frey in kill mode.

"What the hell is wrong with you both?" Dexx came around to Frey's front.

Holy shit.

Frey would be dead in minutes. Blood seeped from shredded vitals, slowed by the stasis. Her throat was nearly slashed through.

Scout had ripped her open with complete devastation. But where Frey would be dead in a minute, Scout was about to die in less than a second if he let them go.

The suspension spell held them in time. Sort of. They still felt the *flow* of it, and if released, they would continue as they had been, in the process of killing each other, but luckily their bodies were held a moment in time.

It was time to figure out what was wrong with Frey. "What the fuck is wrong with you?"

Frey was in a bad way. Healing castings came up, power pooling. He didn't know how to release it.

"My two best in here killing, *actively killing* each other?"

Damn. It. Always before, he'd worked big spells instinctively. Now he was trying to actively use his magick, and it wasn't easy.

"And you wanted to show me how grown up and ready you are for the lead? Or is it kill and be killed? Think I should let you both continue? Both of you are dead. Right now."

Dexx pushed at the release command. It was stuck. Kind of like grabbing a fishtail. It kept slipping away.

Frey's blood hadn't yet had a chance to completely bleed out, and there was an impressive puddle sprayed before he'd wrapped them up.

Maybe he needed to do less at once. He had active control over the stasis.

He let Scout go, her flight into the desk uninterrupted like the spell hadn't happened. "That's your punishment. Now get up and *act* like a *woman* in charge."

Scout picked herself up, her harpy features still prominent.

"You still want to be in charge out here?"

Scout nodded.

"Good. Now, wait in the office. I'll talk to you next." Oh, fuck. The heal command still wouldn't go through.

Scout turned to the office and slammed the door.

Wait. Something trickled through—just a smidge. The blood stopped leaving and hung at the open wounds.

"As for you—" Dexx paused as he looked at Frey and her injuries. Something wasn't right about her. He couldn't see what exactly, but he felt it, hidden in her fear and anger. Aggression. Hate. Selfishness. Like a little time-release capsule. And wrapped around that was the fine twine of power, constantly stabbing into the aggression, feeding it.

Was it preventing the healing?

There it was, a ward so small and so beautifully crafted it looked almost like her own personality. But it wasn't. This was the work of a master, someone who had the time and luxury to make little items like this to torment.

"Hold still." Dexx was relieved this was something fixable. He smiled since she had no choice *but* to remain still. The stasis generally kept her and all of her fluids right where they belonged.

He dropped the major healing to go for a lesser.

He selected one to knit flesh and tissues back together. That was an easy one to select but harder to employ. He had to see the injury. Had to see the tissues.

Frey didn't move, not even her eyes, but she would feel the flow of time and hear Dexx. The magickal comprehension went way beyond his understanding, but all he needed was for it to work.

The flayed skin sucked up her blood. Severed vessels and torn pieces of flesh stood out, reaching for their counterparts.

Frey's neck began to knit at the deepest part of the cut. Skin repaired and closed one gash at a time. Soon, Frey was whole again. But he couldn't let her go. That tiny ward curse had to be cut out.

Dexx tugged on the magick, testing it. It moved, tightening its grip, surging more aggression into her.

Well, shit. If he poked at it, it defended itself. Dexx tried the elements. Singly and in combinations. Every time he touched it, it surged a little more. Frey struggled against the spell, now. She quivered, her lip twitching in the beginnings of a snarl.

"Easy, sister. I got you. Hold on. I'll pull you out." The ward became visible to him, glowing a deep red.

Muscles along her arm wiggled beneath her skin.

"Fight it, Frey. You got a leftover in there. Bussemi has you wired for bear. I think he made you his ace in the hole. Give me a minute. This isn't you." Thank goodness. "You're hard as any man I've ever known, stronger. But you were never an asshole. You fight for me, fight for you."

Frey moved against containment in slow motion, just fractions of an inch, but she was breaking her cage, flaking away at the stasis holding her.

Her natural Valkyrie resisted the binding.

He hadn't chosen a strong enough spell.

But if he could talk her down...

"I need you here. You can help yourself, make it yours, expel it, kid. You got this." Dexx spoke in a calm, tone even and soft. He had to alter her thinking enough to grab the ward.

The glow passed orange into yellow, pushing Frey past

her limits, dumping aggression and hate into her blood, driving her forward.

Her sword came up over her head. Slow, but moving, gaining height.

Dexx could push more power into the spell, but that had a real possibility of breaking her forever. "You Frey, I need you. Whole and strong. We wouldn't be the same without you. Help me break this curse. Fight."

Her head moved up and twisted to Dexx, the effort shaking her skin. The sword moved further up.

"Fight it, Frey. Help make you again."

Dexx dug at Bussemi's handiwork, pushing at it with the elements and ley energy. The ward tightened faster, changing into a blue-white heat, charging Frey.

There. A loose thread of magick frayed in the ward. Tiny, insignificant, but important. He pulled on the thread, pushing at the knot, digging hard.

"Stay with me." He had to give her the soul-strength to fight this. "You were there when we helped Tarik. You were there when we fought Genael. You were there when we took on Cooper and Sven. You. Come on, help me take this curse out."

Frey's head looked right at him, now eyes full of the hate Busssemi carried for Dexx. "Dks— the word just short of a growl. The sword raised to the top of its arc and came down, creeping forward, killing his spell little by little. "H...ep... me."

"I'm here. I got you. Fight. Fight." The knotted curse went white, the lines of energy glowing past color and burning Frey from the inside. Anger, hate, and fear pulsed through her.

What was he supposed to do?

What any good cat did with a dangling piece of string. He grabbed the thread and yanked.

Frey broke through, her sword crashing to the ground, splitting a desk almost in two. She collapsed in his arms, sweat slicking her skin.

"Damn." He gently let her down to the floor, casting a delving, searching for the Bussemi's curse. "Stay here, Frey. Can you talk?"

Frey didn't move, didn't breathe. Her eyes were half-lidded and unmoving. He had something for this, he did. Somewhere. Where was it? Where?

There. He spun the casting into her chest, massaging her heart, pumping blood. The place where the ward had been was clean, with no visible trace. But it hadn't been visible before, either.

"Breathe." Desks crashed as someone rushed him.

Rainbow slid in, shouldering Dexx out of the way. "I breathe. You make her live."

Could she— the ocean trip came back to him. She could give Frey cool, clean air if he could make her heart run again.

He needed more than massaging. He needed electricity—a shock. Frey was losing time. She needed more.

"Bow, move. Don't touch her."

Rainbow scooted away from Frey's body.

He lit his hands with lightning and touched her chest, letting the bolt pass from one side to the other.

Frey convulsed, her back leaving the floor.

"Breathe." Dexx gestured Rainbow ahead.

Two breaths, and Dexx was at the electricity again. He used more zapped, as hard as he dared.

Frey lifted from the floor on a cushion of anti-gravity created by the shock. She dropped back to the floor. She convulsed once and drew in a breath.

And shattered a window in the office with her scream.

For once, Dexx was glad he didn't have Hattie's hearing. He dispelled his lightning and collapsed against a desk.

Frey relaxed, unconscious.

Rainbow lurched forward, reaching for Frey.

Dexx held her back. "Wait. She's frail. Give her a second." With his magick, he watched her heartbeat, weak and thready. Then, one beat. Two. The beats became steady, stronger.

Dexx relaxed and let Rainbow go.

She touched Frey's face gently, fixing loose strands of hair into place. Then she pulled her up into a hug. She let Frey down gently. "Will she be okay?"

"I don't know." He had to hope so. "Be careful with her." Her heart picked up the pace, becoming regular.

She wasn't awake, though.

Dexx probed at her with magick. He wouldn't be able to see what was injured unless she woke up.

"What was that?" Rainbow asked. "What happened?"

"Bussemi worked her over, too." And Dexx was more than a little relieved. "Caused her to go nuts. Probably didn't even know it herself."

"But she's good now, right? Will she be okay? I feel so bad, I didn't know. I just thought she was being extra Valkyrie. Do you think he did that to me because I don't know, you know? I have to be me. I don't think I could live with myself if he did that to me. Dexx, do you think I'm okay? What do you think?" She cupped Frey's head and gently lifted. She bent down like she wanted to kiss. She just bowed her head to the Valkyrie.

He wasn't sure she was making sense, but he knew the words falling out of her mouth weren't as important as the things she was working through in her heart and mind. "I think there isn't a ward ever invented that could keep up with you and not burn itself out. Pretty sure you're fine."

"But what about Frey? Will she be okay? Dexx, I don't

believe that I felt all that anger at her for being so hard on us. Please be okay. Please?"

"You promise to shut up?" Frey asked with a groan.

Rainbow squeaked and dropped Frey's head.

"Ow." Frey still hadn't opened her eyes, but they squeezed hard at the bump.

Dexx knelt by her other side. "You feel like you again?"

"That depends." She put a hand to her head. "Am I still second lead?"

Dexx chuckled. "Yeah. You get to share. I have reasons."

"Fuck me. I can't even die and get what I want."

"I've been dead before. Never got what I wanted either." Dexx put a hand under her neck, still looking for the ward Bussemi placed in her. "Can you sit up?"

"No. But I'll try. You have my sword?"

That was his Frey. Sword first, alive second. "I missed you. You remember everything?"

"You're still an asshole, and I deserve to be captain, but I don't have the burn to beat you."

"We'll talk about that later." Dexx pulled her up.

She sat up shaky, but she sat up.

Dexx grabbed her sword and placed the pommel in her hand. "Bow, you want to watch her for a minute? I need to talk with Scout."

"Sure thing, boss. Is she fired?" Rainbow's big brown eyes pleaded with Dexx. About what he had no idea.

"Have I fired anyone else today?"

"No?"

"Just stay with her and help." Dexx rose and went into the office.

The harpy sat in the chair across from his desk, not moving. Her eyes were focused somewhere beyond the walls.

"Okay, Scout. Time for the talk."

So, he couldn't sit in his chair, or it would look bad, no

matter what he said. He leaned against his desk instead. "You want to explain it?" Dexx already knew what the cause was, but what did Scout think?

"She didn't even wait for me to explain. She came at me and started yelling for me to clean up the mess and get to the work she had. Went off the deep end. I couldn't defend myself, couldn't talk her down. I don't know if I even want to work here anymore."

"What would you say if I said she was under a curse that made her all sorts of evil crazy. DoDO's work.

"I'd say we shouldn't invite them to the Christmas party." She bared her claws.

"One step ahead there. No party invites. That Frey out there wasn't the one I knew before DoDO. Bussemi is a bad person."

"Okay. So, you want me to apologize to her."

Dexx winced. "No."

"You want me to leave?"

He frowned and shook his head. "No."

"You want me to stay?" she asked in surprise.

He sighed. "No. I want you to figure out what you want. And then make it happen."

She rolled her eyes slightly and made to get up.

Dexx's phone and Scout's beeped at the same time.

Dexx ignored his.

Scout picked hers up. She stared at her phone. Not a good way to impress the boss. "Did you say we were supposed to meet with the Pope?"

"Yeah, why?"

"Things changed a little bit. They're sending another guy in. Some cardinal guy. Bussemi?"

All the blood left Dexx's body.

34

Dexx walked off the plane, surveying the tarmac. It was a little strip in a secluded valley. The flight hadn't been that long, but he still wasn't sure where they'd found "neutral ground." Probably in Canada.

Three black Suburbans waited, drivers behind dark sunglasses in the seats.

The media circus waited beyond them, pictures snapping and location reporters talking into cameras.

He could hear it in his head now. "And here is our first look at the delegation representing the paranormals and defending the actions abroad just a few weeks ago... Yes, they look pretty much normal from here, but we'll get a much closer look at the talks in the days ahead... Sure thing, this is—" insert *any name* of the throngs of reporters, "—signing off."

At least Bussemi got the message and hadn't so much as *brushed* his mind in the last week. Too and the reporters wouldn't be so accommodating. Baby steps.

Dexx grinned in frustration and turned back to Jake Shirley and Alwyn. "So much for a quiet talk. They pulled out all the stops." In all the preparation for the talks, nobody had said they'd have to contend with public opinion. He should have guessed, though. The church didn't so much as make a sandwich without alerting the media. They'd been trying to raise their image in recent years after receiving so many black eyes in rapid succession.

How much of that had been caused by the demon influences infiltrating their organization?

Rainbow brought up the last of their delegation. Merry Eastwood and her entourage wouldn't be arriving until later. She wanted the press all to herself.

Should have known she'd showboat. Maybe that would keep some of the attention away from Dexx.

He led his team to the first Suburban in line. He pulled on the handle.

Locked.

He looked at the driver, who was pointing to the next one in line. What the hell? Dexx tried the handle again.

The window rolled down. "This is a decoy, sir. You're in the next one."

"A decoy? You've got to be kidding me." A decoy meant there were people trying to kill them. "You should let me drive, then. I got experience."

"Can't do that, sir. Yours is the next one."

Dammit. "Sure. Sure. Drive well." Dexx lifted a hand to wave and strode to the next oh-so-obvious target in line.

The door opened, and Dexx let Alwyn, Rainbow, and Shirley–Jake in the back. He scooted around the back and slipped in the passenger seat.

Luggage went into the rear vehicle.

The driver stared at Dexx as he sat in the seat.

Dexx stared back. "What?"

"Usually, the dignitary sits in the back and enjoys the ride."

"Well, when the dignitary shows up, they can sit in the back. We're just people."

The driver nodded once, and they waited for the line to move.

Dexx recognized the high gate and stone wall they pulled up to. It would encircle the entire compound. He'd been told they'd be meeting on neutral ground. "What did you say this place was?"

"I didn't, sir. I'm told it's a cooperative sponsored by the church, living off the land, communing with God and such."

No, it wasn't. This was the Montana branch of DoDO. He twisted behind him.

Alwyn saw it, too. "I think we're in trouble."

Jake tensed, searching for a gun that wasn't there. "What's up?"

"Bastards took us to the Montana DoDO compound. This is where they brought me when they kidnapped me."

Rainbow's eyes flashed with fear. "You don't think—"

The driver frowned. "You're sure, sir?"

Dexx grunted with a nod. Yeah, he was damned sure. "I don't know what they have planned. Not with all the news hanging around." If they had kept it quiet, Dexx would have blown the whole place into a crater. He might have enough magick in him to do that.

The gate opened to the unwelcome and familiar. Wide tracts of perfectly manicured landscape opened up. Old statues of long-dead people stared out over the grounds. Trees dotted the lawns, creating shade perfect for picnics that never happened. A thick spruce forest sat beyond the medical building and the old-structure house.

This had been his home for a long time. Not that he remembered most of it. Even with the continual memory wipes, this still felt... wildly familiar.

"Fill me in here." Jake looked everywhere at once, for the first time, his face showing concern.

"What's going on?"

"This is the place the bastards took me when they kidnapped me. I'd love to say I have fond memories of the place, but I don't." Dexx's stomach dropped and kept going. The world started to spin as his anxiety and fear rode higher and higher. The cab went hot. He couldn't breathe. "Sop. Sop te rtruff." He yanked on the handle, and nothing happened. He slapped at the door controls and yanked the handle again, this time the door opened, and he fell out to the ground.

The driver skidded the Suburban to a stop, and the other doors opened.

Dexx wasn't ready to fight Bussemi on his own ground. He didn't have his answer. He didn't have the key to unlock the crystal he forgot in his office desk in order to keep it safe. He'd traveled around for nothing, learning nothing. He was going to lose.

He sprawled out on the ground, trying to breathe, trying to cool off.

A single spell floated to him, but it didn't quite make sense. The only thing he really understood was "escape."

He took it. He whispered the incantation and closed his eyes, hoping it'd work as his panic attack worsened.

Sickness roiled in his belly, the feel of the grass and gravel falling far away in his mind.

Thoughts swirled with images and feelings that didn't belong. People's castings he now recognized. Spells to implant suggestive memories. Others to forget people and situations. More to plant seeds of hate.

All of them together would have worked, but not on Dexx, not the way they wanted.

More images broke in. Cardinal Bussemi parading around as a doctor. Alwyn being installed to keep him under observation. The "promotion" to get him into line. Mario, Hopkirk, Sayyid, all of them manipulating his head.

Cool hands touched him. Too late. He was burning up, the fever sending his vision to pinpricks of light.

Words were being spoken to him. They had to be words, but they were only noises that had no meaning.

Hattie, where are you? Answer me. You...

The thought faded. The desire faded as the searing swallowed him. The noise, the pressure, the vision all faded into a jumble too chaotic to set right.

A different heat sparked in him—hotter, more concentrated, burning his mind with a white-hot pinprick of light.

The light darkened in places and became shades. Images formed slowly.

He lay on his back, the flat cobbles of fine paving pressing into him. Buildings solidified around him, stretching high into the sky. This wasn't New York or Los Angeles. This was modern only in that it was a city. The buildings weren't made of glass and steel. It reminded him of the past, but... when?

He looked to the surrounding buildings that flowed from one to the next. His hand gripped a fistful of grass. Manicured grass cut longer than most parks, but not too long to be patchy. He recognized the architecture. It reminded him of Kupul, but as it might have looked when it was a new city. He lay in a park of sorts. Two young girls played with toys balanced in the air by blasts of wind the two called.

Dexx sat up, confused. Where was he?

The parents of the two girls stared in his direction. The man stood up and began walking his way to Dexx. He looked familiar. Too familiar.

Dekskulta... but younger. Lots younger. He had a full head of long, dark hair that would have made Paige jealous. He stopped twenty feet away.

What... in the hell? "Son of a bitch." Dexx stood. Or he

would have, but things were too unsettled to make his feet do what he wanted.

"*Shenesae? Te Unnum ahsa tuun. Dekskulta.*" The other guy pointed to himself.

Why couldn't Dexx understand him now like he had before? "Yeah. You're Dekskulta." Dexx stumbled to his feet, wondering why his spell would bring him here as an escape.

Deskulta cast a spell Dexx could read; a translation spell that unraveled words into a growing and living dictionary, but it had to be fed words to form a context matrix.

Shit. Dexx understood what all of that meant. "You know, I ought to clean your clock. You son of a bitch. You *knew* she was going away. Fuck you."

"Ekks use me? How know you, I?"

What? "I'm you, asshole." Dexx advanced on him. "You're me. But from a long time ago. What are you? One of the first recycling of my lives? I know you have that crystal of power somewhere. But if you have the *kadu* or *shamiyir,* you have to hide them *forever.* Bussemi found them."

"No crystal. No *kadu.* Should not have those. Too dangerous." Dekskutla took three slow steps forward.

"No shit. You didn't hide anything." Dexx stumbled and caught himself on the paw of a lion statue. He stopped himself as he fell backward, looking at it.

This was the statue of the griffin and the manticore, fighting each other. The one he'd seen in Kupul. Okay. He didn't have time to be a bumbling idiot. What was going on here? Where was he? He wasn't in Montana anymore. That was for sure. He looked to the sky, but that only made the vertigo worse.

"How are you here?" Dekskulta looked as confused as Dexx was. "You are me, but not."

What if... this spinning world thing was a side-effect of

him falling through a temporary temporal shift? What if "escape" had been a translation of "fall through time?"

That brought more questions, and that could actually turn into answers. Answers to questions he'd had for a *while* now. Like, how had Dekskulta *known* to create a power crystal? Or that he'd be able to use it? Or that it'd be the answer to taking out Bussemi? And why hadn't he given that crystal to a former version of himself?

The answers to all those questions hit him the face like Dr. Strange.

His past lives had known *he'd* be stepping through the temporal shift to... tell all the versions of himself what was needed.

Shit. So, what did he need?

"If you have something I left for you," Dekskulta said, glancing back at his daughters, "you must have visited an older self."

"Stop, stop." How much time did he have? It had to be enough. "You need to listen to me very carefully."

The younger Dekskulta frowned but nodded.

"I'm from the future."

"Yes. I see." But the look on his face said he didn't really.

"My name is Dexx Colt."

"Dekskulta," the other guy said, putting his hand to his chest.

Dear God. It was like talking to a child. "I know. Bussemi, First Brother, is trying to kill us."

"He's very bad. Big shadow. Lost brother."

"Yeah, yeah." Dexx remembered the story. "He's going to bond with a bahlrok."

Dekskulta's dark eyes widened in alarm. "That is very bad."

"Yeah." Thank goodness for small favors. The world whipped him again with a wave of dizziness. He had to have enough time to give his full message. "I came into this life with no magick."

"Why?"

"I don't' know. But I'm pretty sure one of us thought it was needed. I can…" He didn't know. "Think on my feet better, I guess. I also bond with Hattie pretty strong."

"Good. That is good. Very good."

"Should be. But to get *here*, I had to sacrifice her."

Shock and disbelief crashed over Dekskulta's face. "You did not."

"I… hope not. I don't have her." This wasn't time for him to pour out his soul. "Look, the reason I'm telling you this is because you have to create a weapon I can use. My magick is… kinda back without her?"

Understanding crashed over the other guy's face. "Oh."

Dexx had to hope that meant he understood *why* that was a thing. "I'm going to face him. I need the weapon to unlock my magick, and I need it to be a power stone I can then use to kill Bussemi and his bahlrok."

"Of course." "And another thing," Dexx said as a wave of dizziness ripped through him. He was running out of time. "Bussemi—First Brother finds you. Here. He destroys the city. So you have to trap it in time. The city."

Dekskulta frowned in sorrow and turned to his wife, who glanced at them in worry but focused mostly on their kids. He turned back to Dexx. "I understand."

"Good. I'm going to give you the password to unlock that crystal. Okay."

"Of course," the other guy said.

The world tipped and threw Dexx to the side. He needed a good password Bussemi wouldn't be able to guess through the lifetimes just in case he got his hands on it. *Darkwing Duck* had a great password. He'd use that because there was no way anyone would guess it. "Bathering blatherskite."

Dekskulta's face folded in confusion. "That does not make sense."

The world shook Dexx. He was running out of time. He needed a code that was unique to him that no one else could guess. He'd be in the room with Bussemi. He'd have his chance to get his hand on Dexx's crystal. It couldn't be easy. "Setec Astronomy!" That was a great *Sneakers* reference that meant too many secrets. What better password.

But the look on Dekskulta's face said otherwise.

A force pulled Dexx back. Damn it! He needed a password that would withstand the test of time. What—"Open, Sesame!" he shouted.

Then Kupul was yanked away and replaced with the stomach-twisting assault of returning memories from his stay at the Montana facility.

Sounds came back slowly—warbling and nasal at first. Then light permeated through in stabbing pinpricks.

"—he's okay? Come on, boss." A female. Who did he know— oh, yes. Rainbow.

Coolness on his face came through. Not just cool, but cold. The cold-of-the-grave kind.

Dexx waved his arm to avoid the freezing touch, but it was more like flailing. That spell had taken a lot of energy.

Gravel crunched as feet shuffled away. "We got incoming. News crews steaming hard for us." Jake Shirley. He was taking the personal protection gig seriously.

"F...nor...lap." Dexx pushed out some words. Never mind, they meant nothing...in *any* language.

"He's coming around." Alwyn passed his athame over Dexx's face and torso again. "I think the worst is over."

Sight, sound, and motor control crashed back into Dexx. He slapped at everyone, needing space.

"What happened?" Alwyn reached a hand to help Dexx up.

News cameras surrounded the Suburban. Crowding reporters pressed microphones into his face and shot off inane questions.

"Are you all right—"

"Did you collapse—"

"Can you respond—"

Dexx stood and turned to the crews with a smile. "Just so glad to be back in my captor's compound. Makes me feel like a Jew in the forties."

That silenced all of them.

He had exactly three seconds of total silence as he reclaimed the passenger seat and slammed the door. "Let's go." He had to hope that the message had gotten through. That Dekskulta understood his situation and had installed the right message. But now? He just had to find a way to get the crystal.

Maybe he could call Leah and ask her to bring it to him. Not that... he didn't want her anywhere near Bussemi, but... he needed that crystal. This was the big fight. He had to win.

Everyone piled in the back, silent and still. Their nerves had to be thin.

"What happened?" Rainbow asked quietly.

He should tell the team, but he didn't know his driver. "Went back to Kupul." That should be code enough for the driver not to pick up anything.

The driver didn't blink. He just took off, leaving the reporters behind in the dust.

"Okay. Did—was it... good?" Rainbow smiled, but weak, not her normal blazing smile of happiness.

"Yeah. Got what we needed."

"Oh." She glanced at the driver, then Alwyn to her right, then her eyes went wide. "Oh."

At least one member of his team understood.

"Huh, that's weird." The driver leaned forward.

"What?" Dexx looked out to the main house, the one that looked more like the X-men mansion than a para-military base.

A crowd of suited figures surrounded just one diminutive person dressed all in red.

The driver stopped at a red carpet leading to the front of the house. "That." He gave Dexx that said good-luck-buddy and shrugged.

The crowd slowly parted as a valet opened the doors for Dexx and his crew.

Dexx waited for the rear door to open and felt the pull he never wanted to feel again. It was something sweeter than breath.

His *kadu* called from the crowd.

Every one of the bodyguards peeled back to form a semi-circle around Bussemi was a demon. Strong ones.

Dexx felt the radiating of each one, and a spell emerged from his mind. A light, easy one to see the demons inside the hosts. He cast it, not even checking to see if he had the juice to make it work. The area was lit with demons in meat suits.

Most of the news crews were human, although a few had touches of demonic influence tainting their aura.

The demons in front of him had names. Uastiel. Jurviel. Duur. Huanniel. The list went on for seventeen names.

Dexx had walked his team into a trap.

Fear held him nailed to the spot. Bussemi had him, and his friends pinned down where they couldn't run and, while he *had* the key to unlock his magick, he'd left his power crystal at home where it would be safe.

Rainbow swiveled in her seat, just extending her foot to get out.

Dexx slid out of the vehicle and hurled a gust of air, slamming the door shut and sealing the big Chevy. A second, heavier blast skidded it across the gravel and away from the demons. Distantly, he heard his team's screams and yells from inside, but Bussemi had his attention.

I told you you'd come to me, Bussemi-voice said as the cardinal's piercing gaze stabbed him through the windshield. *And now you are mine.*

Fuck you. Before Dexx took a step forward, six demons threw containment shields at Dexx, the air crackling with golden light.

Child's play—if he was at full strength. That time spell should have drained him, but he severed the source of the magicks with a mix of earth and air elements, spearing out a response.

He lit life energy from the ground and called seeds of the plants on a gust of wind. He hit the six with the seeds available, mostly grass, and hyper-motivated their growth. The growth of the plants sickened their hosts to uselessness, with stomach cramps doubling them over in pain as the plants literally grew out of their pores.

The meat suits might recover, with a little care, and if the demons didn't kill them first.

The demons left the hosts in a swelling of black smoke that covered the ground.

Bussemi smiled, the hunger in his eyes turning his grandfatherly face demonic. "My power," he breathed. He reached up and tugged at Dexx's *kadu*.

Dexx pulled out his *ma'a'shed* and extended the blade.

Somewhere in the back of his mind, he knew the news crews were rolling cameras. He might not be able to explain what was happening. Shit, he'd probably be dead way before then. He felt the smallest pang of regret at not marrying Paige, but he didn't have time for that. He *knew* he wasn't going to survive this. He'd left his one good weapon at home. He didn't have time for regret.

Nine Hells, if this was his end, he'd go down swinging.

Bussemi'd tortured him and his team. His friends. Altered at least one of them to the point of attempting to kill him and hounding him relentlessly. Fuck that old guy.

Dexx waded into the converging demons. Lesser demons. They must not have been told about Dexx and his *mavet ma'a'shed*. The blade went through them with barely a tug.

The rest of the greater demons hesitated for a second.

The second was too long for them.

The blue crystal he'd made when he almost fried Stef Lovejoy floated from his pocket at the smallest mental tug.

Oh. That's how he'd repowered himself. Great.

He swung the *mavet,* slicing the crystal cleanly in two, and in that instant, he gathered the bolt of power trapped inside and cast it wide into the demons in front of him.

The cascade of lightning from the sword would have impressed Thor. Maybe.

The demons fried as the bolts touched them, but Bussemi took the bolt aimed at him and stood up to the attack. Dexx focused the slivers of power into a single blinding jagged bolt and poured the last of the energy into the cardinal.

He went down in a ball of red smoking robes and lay still.

Did he just kill Bussemi? Without Dekskulta's power crystal?

"Nice work." A black door opened to his left, and Mario Kester stepped out. "You killed the old man finally. Not bad. Now you can give me the crystal, and I'll let you live."

Dexx didn't have it. Maybe that *had* been a good thing.

"Come and take it from my cold dead fingers."

Mario smiled. "All right. I will."

Dexx felt the magick roil up from Mario. Not a killing spell. A snare and a cage. It formed a golden yellow network, reaching around Dexx in a sphere.

Dexx pulled a severing magick and formed it from the ley line pulsing dully at his feet. He cut the cage away and jumped back.

Where the nine Hells had Mario come from? Dexx didn't think for more than one instant that he'd managed to *kill* Bussemi with one shot. Not this easily after so many lifetimes of fleeing? No. He didn't need Bussemi to wake up and join this battle. So, this—whatever this was—needed to go quickly.

"Give me..." Mario threw more magick toward Dexx. "... the crystal."

Dexx bounced it back at him.

Mario erupted into dust. As the cloud diminished, he stepped out, his clothes charred, his shirt only tatters. Magick built in Mario, but it pooled ready.

Dexx needed a plan. He was more than a little amazed

that he still had his power. His reserves didn't seem spent even in the least. What did that mean? Where was he getting the power boost from? He'd destroyed the crystal he'd made. "You haven't said please at all." Dexx could return fire, but he didn't know Mario's full abilities, his weakness, or how to find out without dying.

"You should cooperate. I just came back from beating Paige." He took a step forward.

Dexx took a step back. No. What did he mean by that? Killed or captured? It didn't matter. He'd gone after Paige. She wasn't here, so he had to assume the worst.

That made the decision to kill Mario easier. He lifted his sword. "You should have left Paige out of it." He swung the sword toward Mario, but he wasn't close enough to hit. He didn't want to be.

The lightning he'd threatened Lovejoy with danced from his energy core, down his arm, and raced through the *mavet ma'a'shed*, launching itself at Mario.

The bolt crackled over the other man's pale head, jabbing into him. Mario stood there, taking the punishment. The rest of his shirt turned into smoke.

Oh… shit.

Mario raised fists, crackling with lightning. "You have no idea what I am, what I can do. Give me the crystal."

Not likely. "This should be fun." This was going to suck balls. Dexx pulled the sword back into a ready position. He'd seen Frey use the move, and it looked cool. As his body fell into the stance, he understood why and carefully adjusted, locating his center of gravity, shifting it to the balls of his feet for better agility.

"You know nothing." Mario grabbed the pool of magick he'd collected and threw it.

Dexx didn't have time to react. Not well, anyway. The spell wasn't really a spell. It was just raw magickal energy that hit him like a club. He flew through the air, his sword falling to the ground as he hit. He needed a tether on that thing. He skidded to a halt only a few feet away from the black Suburban his team was in.

Rainbow pounded on the window, pleading with Dexx to open the door.

No. He wasn't going to lose anyone else, and he had a personal score to settle with Mario.

Dexx sat up and shook his head. Damn, that hurt. "So what are you?"

"More than you can imagine." Mario twirled more of the magick in the air with a finger. "I thought I was dead back in your spirit world. You and your little bitch of a girl destroyed the containment circle, but this? This is better. *Much* better."

Dexx rose to his feet, pulling at anything that might help him. One looked particularly pleasing, but the cost was more than he had if it didn't work the first time. It would incinerate the host human and the possessing demon from existence, but it took time and required the human to stand still. Mario didn't seem the type to do what Dexx wanted.

He spared a glance at the damaged and sealed SUV. "My terrible manners. Should we invite your friends to play our game, too?"

This wasn't the first time Dexx had danced with this asshole. "Sure." Wasn't happening.

Mario gave him a surprised smile. "You *are* learning sacrifice. Aren't you? Too bad Paige isn't."

Dexx called elemental energy and pulled the wind to carry seeds to Mario. The wind answered, pelting Mario with whatever was left in the area. Life energy followed the seeds in, and as soon as they made contact, they sprouted.

Mario screamed, pulling at the persistent seedlings burrowing into his skin, but Dexx poured more life energy into them, not knowing what he was doing. His magick did.

It felt like going to the gym and remembering how to properly curl. He commanded them to grow as fast as they could. The hundreds of seeds sprouted colorful flowers in a radically fast time-lapse.

Mario's screams quieted and became less pained. He took a step and fell forward, just a clump of grass on the perfectly manicured grounds.

The pounding on the window gained volume in Dexx's head as the wind quieted. The end of the spell thanked the wind with reverence.

He turned to Rainbow, still making noise by slapping the windows. "What?" Dexx had just taken out his two biggest enemies in the shortest fight he'd ever had. He hooked a thumb behind him. "He's starting to grow on me."

Rainbow slammed the window with both hands screaming his name.

She was... rather insistent. Both of his enemies were down... for the moment. While they were out, though, he, Alwyn, and Rainbow could finish them off. He'd need Jake to get the reporters out of there for that, though. They didn't need that on video.

Dexx lifted his hand to pop the seal on the door when a blast of wind knocked him to the side. He fell as he lost his balance.

"What the—" Dexx pushed off the ground but stopped as he saw a black spear where he'd stood just a second before. He spun to see Mario, a malevolent glare in his eye, swaying in place.

The spear stuck through the window... and Rainbow.

The look on her face was filled with surprise as she looked at Dexx. She raised her hand and signed to him. *Stay strong.*

Wait. No. He scrambled for a spell that would stabilize her, keep her alive.

Life left her face, and she sagged on the deep black spear.

"No." Dexx blinked several times, time spreading itself so thin it might have stopped, forever or for an instant. Not again.

The flash in his head somehow encompassed every single second he'd ever spent with Rainbow Blu, Bruna, and Doxy. Hattie.

His rage boiled over.

With every bit of magick he had in him and every offensive spell that came up, he turned and spun them all out, all targeting Mario.

He raised his defenses in time to deflect most of them but not all. Several of the *thousand cut* spells hit Mario, blood running down his arms. Legs. And torso.

The larger assault spells bore down on the ex-DoDO agent only to be deflected harmlessly into the earth.

Mario wasn't attacking.

He couldn't. Dexx continued to feed every offensive spell he'd learned over *lifetimes* at this demon-possessed asshole.

Dexx kept up the magickal attack until his tank finally started draining. Each spell was as powerful as he'd ever seen, but Mario kept deflecting most of them, taking little damage.

Dexx needed a solution fast.

He called the wind and tried the seed trick again.

Mario called his own wind with ley magick and fire.

The two winds collided and spun into a fire funnel. The seeds burned to less than ash before they ever had a chance to land.

Dexx pushed at the fire with more elemental magick and the full force of his *rage*.

The inferno raced high in the sky, scorching the leaves of the surrounding trees and threatening a wildfire.

Dexx called on water, forcing it into the fire funnel, creating intensely hot steam, and shoved it at Mario.

He howled with pain, but the fire didn't falter.

Shit, Mario didn't even act wounded, but he'd felt the pain of the superheated steam.

Fog filled the area, obscuring Mario from view.

Dexx let up, scouring the grounds.

Something from the corner of his eye caught his attention. A rock the size of his fist sailed through the air right at his head. He ducked, surprise ending every active spell he had.

Just as he went to cast a severing at the incoming capture spell, the ground leapt up and pounded the breath out of him.

He saw the remnants of the from deep in the ground. Mario had sent the spell deep and had brought it back when Dexx had been distracted.

Mario had outclassed him.

While Dexx still struggled for air, Mario closed in on him. He grabbed Dexx by the hair and lifted him off the ground.

Crap, that demon was making that pasty bastard strong. Dexx gripped Mario's hand as his toes scraped the ground.

"I killed your people," Mario said through bloodied teeth. "Give me the crystal, and you die quickly like them. Refuse me, and you go slow, like your girlfriend."

Was Paige still alive?

Dexx reached for his pool, but he couldn't touch it. A wall of smooth force kept him out and away from his magick.

Why *had* Dexx come back without his magick this time?

Because maybe he'd become too reliant on it? He'd been using his magick with the muscle memory of experience. A lot of it. What would a guy without powers do in a situation like this?

He kicked Mario in the mommy-daddy button.

Mario dropped and curled in on himself, backing away slowly.

That's why. Magick *wasn't* always the answer. Dexx stumbled to his *ma'a'shed* and grabbed the hilt.

The knife sang in his ears, demanding Mario's blood. It became the *mavet ma'a'shed* with nothing more than Dexx's permission. He'd be *glad* to give the sword Mario's blood.

Dexx stood up to lop Mario's head off.

Mario cut open a door and stumbled through, the door closing behind him. That still left Bussemi, but he was still out cold on the ground.

Where were the other DoDO agents? Why weren't they attacking?

They weren't, and that's all that mattered. Mario would be back, and Dexx had to take care of Bussemi. But he had to do something else first. "Bow."

Dexx slashed the spear of the dark, rock-like substance. If smoke could be solid, this might be it.

The sword clanged against the spear, but chips flew from away. Screams from the sword filled his head, and deafened him. Whatever that thing was, it had hurt the sword, and him along with it. A few more hacks and a length fell to the ground and dissipated. His head rang with pain, but at least the scream ended.

He slashed the door like passing a hot knife through butter. Rainbow fell forward a few inches, pulling Alwyn with her.

Officer Shirley was unconscious, his shoulder pierced with the sharp, hardened smoke spear. Alwyn didn't look like he'd made it either.

Crushing guilt filled Dexx. How had they all died while remaining protected inside a bullet-proof vehicle?

A change in the air was the only warning he had.

He ducked a club of air that could have taken his head off.

Dexx swung the sword behind him without taking the time to see whatever was there. Of course, he hit nothing, but he was on the move, keeping the *ma'a'shed* between him and Mario.

No, not Mario. That was the feel of a demon. Where had he been hiding?

A demon materialized from the black smoke swirling around Bussemi.

Kusere, a big player in the minor demon leagues, stepped toward Dexx. "How to make you pay for that stunt at the trial? I'm going to enjoy this."

It must have hurt a lot. "Cash or charge. My favorite is cash."

Kusere stopped like he hit an invisible wall, or the ground refused to let him go further. His eyes went wide and bulged as he struggled. His head whipped back and forth in a silent scream. He flaked away to ash and smoke.

"Dexx Colt belongs to me." Mario walked through the remaining floating demon bits.

"Fuck," Dexx muttered. He'd drawn on his reservoir of magick too much. It filled, but too slow to be any use in *this* fight. Without Hattie and her strength and speed, he was just a human with a sword. He didn't need more. Not for Mario.

Big words. Big *empty* words.

"No quick wit for me?" Mario sneered.

A list of spells pulled up, but without the energy, they were useless. So, Dexx kept them to himself, waiting, holding onto what energy he had.

Just a few more steps, and Mario'd be in range.

Dexx sent a weak death spell toward Mario, careful not to fill it with too much energy. It wasn't going to work anyway. It was just something to keep Mario from using his own.

Mario flicked it away and took one more step. "Pathetic. You aren't worth more effort than what I came for. Now, where is the crystal?"

Dexx let his sword drop slowly to the ground. "You're

awfully interested in it." He swayed on his feet. He *was* tired, but he wanted Mario's defenses *down*. Dexx was the bait.

Mario reached out and grabbed Dexx by the neck. "I want it for... my benefactor."

Dexx whipped the sword out and released the one spell he had that only required minimal energy to fill.

Mario let go of Dexx and danced back out of the way. Straight back.

Into Dexx's wall of spears.

Mario howled as points of spears poked through parts of his body, one of them off-center from the middle of his skull. The howls turned into less than human screams.

"Both of you can go to hell." Dexx raised the *mavet ma'a'shed*.

Mario vibrated, slipping from the spears, leaving dark stains on the needle-like stones. They smoked like they'd been sprayed with acid. "Mine."

The voice that came out of him wasn't Mario's. It was deep and guttural and felt like pure fear.

Dexx nearly dropped the sword from weak fingers, but he held on. Whatever inhabited Mario wasn't a regular demon. Not a regular *anything*. He glanced over at Bussemi, but that guy was still out.

"You are nothing." The demon looked like Mario, but the blood seeping through the wounds wasn't human. Nearly black and acidic, it disintegrated anything it touched. It acted like the demon tears Tarik given them, but way more potent.

Dexx went for the demon while it was still... weak.

It shivered. Sucking sounds came from the body as Dexx closed the distance.

A small silver device fell from the remnants of Mario-demon's pants.

Dexx didn't wait to find out what that was. He turned to

run, crashing into an invisible wall. Dexx'd seen what Mario-demon could do with this thing.

"Nothing at all." Mario advanced.

Who was he trying to tell? "I must be *something*." Dexx really didn't feel like it.

But he needed to remember that the real villain in this battle was Bussemi. He needed to kill *Bussemi*.

Black ghost-like hands exploded from Mario and gripped Dexx's throat, squeezing. Spells filled Dexx's vision. He didn't have the energy left to fill any of them.

Mario-demon was eating Dexx's magick, taking everything. He tried lifting the sword to cut Mario in half, but it was too heavy. The sword fell to the ground, the sound clunking like poor steel. The blade turned from midnight black to lead grey.

One at a time, his spell list disappeared. At first, only the most powerful, but then in entire bunches, depending on the difficulty level. They zipped from his mind, lost forever.

Mario-demon was devouring his knowledge.

Only a few of the weakest and most innate abilities remained when a wall of ice slammed into Mario, breaking the hold of the ghost hand on Dexx.

Rainbow Blu stood in full currents glory, her hair blue and billowing as if she stood underwater. She held the ends of tendrils of pure elemental water in her hands like whips. She whipped the water and ice so fast, the sounds of the impact on Mario sounded like one extended hit.

Water surrounded Mario and solidified into a prison ice ball. Inside the ice, lightning crackled and struck at the Mario-demon. He quivered as screams gushed from him.

Dexx fell to the ground, unable to stand or move. His magick had kept him up before, and now he had none. None at all.

"The Dexx will stand." Rainbow spoke with the Blue Lady's voice.

Dexx tried. He sincerely did, but he was... out of juice.

"The Dexx will stand. Now."

The words didn't just command. They controlled. They overrode his weakness.

How?

Did it matter? Dexx stood, barely. A fart could knock him over again.

"The Dexx was given charge of our child's welfare."

Oh, shit.

"Our child is dead, but our child still has claims of attachment to the Dexx. We are in a quandary."

"I'm sorry." Dexx closed his weary eyes. "I tried to—"

Mario's ice prison shattered.

Mario advanced on the currents. "Mine. Yours will be mine."

The back of Dexx's neck tingled. He'd only ever felt that once before. Many lifetimes ago. A memory less than a dream. A presence stronger than Earth.

The currents whipped the elemental water into a frenzy

Mario-demon cast his own frenzy of spells back at the currents.

Spears and knives of ice hacked into Mario-demon, lopping off large chunks of the man.

Dexx understood just enough to realize that the currents had taken over Rainbow, and they were fighting Mario. That gave Dexx the opportunity to take out Bussemi while he slept. Dexx would make this fight worth it.

He grabbed his dead and drained knife and crawled painfully across the asphalt and concrete to where Bussemi still lay.

Mario-demon threw fire and earth at Blue Lady Rainbow.

Pieces of his friend were blasted away to nothing.

Dexx breathed, struggling to find the energy to do what he had to. He couldn't make it this far to fail.

The tingle strengthened. He wouldn't believe it. *Couldn't* believe it. The pain would be too much if he was wrong.

A group of DoDO agents ran toward them.

Finally, but this wasn't a great time. Dexx didn't know if they were headed for him or Bussemi. Whichever, he needed to hurry.

Quinn ran in the back, her eyes on Dexx. They flashed with warning, but warning of what?

He crawled faster, trying to get to Bussemi. All he had to do was to lop off the man's head while he was down, make sure Bussemi never got up again.

He risked a look back at the Blue Lady and Mario.

A lash of elemental water and lightning caught Mario-demon around the neck like a whip of burning rock pinned Rainbow's arms down. The force rattled the ground under Dexx and the on-coming team.

They hesitated.

He did too, but mostly because he'd fought a demon battle. They hadn't. He crawled faster, trying to make up the time he'd lost.

They beat him to the fallen cardinal, grabbed him, and then opened a portal.

Damn it! Quinn paused, frowned at Dexx, then glanced at the raging fight, her eyes widening in alarm. She ducked through the door, and it closed behind her.

Something crashed hard behind Dexx.

He turned, rage fueling him a little more, his batteries charging slightly.

Blue Lady Rainbow's glowing ice-blue eyes turned to Dexx and went a warm brown, filling with tears. "Stay strong, boss. I have to go."

The two monsters held each other in place, both trying to gain the upper hand on the other.

What could he do? He had no magick, just a lot of rage and nothing to do with it.

No, that wasn't true. He gripped his knife. It needed blood to feed on. Dexx'd give it blood. "Mother fucker. You die." He picked up the lead-colored sword and stood. It was heavier than it had been, its magick depleted. Dexx felt weak, but he pressed on, gaining speed with each step. He almost made a trot when he stabbed Mario in the heart.

Or where his heart should have been.

"Die ass hat."

Mario-demon latched his gaze onto Dexx's. Something pulled at Dexx's spirit. The thing that made him live. His soul?

Dexx yanked back. "Mine is mine." This was an energy vampire from hell, leaching magic, energy, and soul?

Blue Lady Rainbow's body weakened as it became little more than an upright pile of flesh.

"Give me back my friend," Dexx growled. He twisted the sword in the monster's chest and pulled at his essence now draining away into Mario-demon.

The flow slowed and stopped.

Very slowly, Dexx pulled something back. "I said, give me my friend."

Mario-Demon's mouth moved, but no sounds came out.

Dexx felt a push. Something like the alpha push commanding obedience. He resisted and pushed his own will at the creature.

A distant memory came back to him—something from a long time in the past when he only wanted to be a loner.

We are powerful and strong of will, Hattie had said.

Strong enough to overcome the siren's will?

Strong enough to overcome anyone's *will.* Something in the tone of her voice had said she'd known something.

She'd known something. How much?

Hattie, if I go now, this is for you.

Be the alpha, the memory of her voice said.

Dexx sneered, pulling his lips back and showing his teeth. "I *am* the alpha." He pushed his will out, removing his now black and red blade out of the demon's body. "Die, you bitch." Dexx raised his foot and kicked Mario's chest.

Mario-demon fell back several steps, a look of surprise filtering over what was left of Mario's face.

The blade of the *mavet ma'a'shed* and screamed in Dexx's mind for the blood of the creature.

No problem. Dexx took two steps forward and swung the sword at Mario's neck.

The blade connected with the neck and sliced through neatly, the acidic blood pumping out and into the blade itself.

Power built like a volcano getting ready to blow. The ground shook.

Blue Lady Rainbow's eyes widened and came to life for a moment.

Dexx felt the explosion in a distant part of his mind. This was his end. Not a bad way to die. Inside a nuclear blast sending the biggest, not demon creature back to the hell it came from.

I'm coming, Hattie.

I'm already here, cub.

How many times had Dexx been unconscious in the past month? Ten? Twelve? None of those times had he felt swaddled in comfort or felt truly safe.

Dexx sat with Mah'se at his side on the bluff overlooking the plains and animals below.

Hattie sat on the other.

Relief pummeled him. "I'm not sure what happened. Do *you?*"

You have taken your alpha back. Hattie nudged him playfully.

"Yeah, so?" Good. If he was still alive. But he'd been in the middle of that blast. "Don't know what that means. Am I shifter again or shifter witch? Or shifter mage? That sounds kind of cool." He called his list of spells. Nothing. But he didn't have an intent either.

He felt for the pool of magick. It was full, but that wasn't saying much. He used to have a one hundred fifty-thousand gallon tank of gas, and what he was looking at now had been crushed to a single gallon, with a restricted flow.

He didn't have enough magick ability to do more than light a candle or blow a kiss.

You have always been a shifter, Hattie said. *You needed to be the alpha. You* became *the alpha.*

"Bussemi's curse?"

She shook her head. *That was you.*

He still didn't understand. "I missed you."

"How did I get here?" He turned to Hattie, then Mah'se.

You arrived here. Mah'se swiveled his head to look at Dexx then out to the plains.

What was the last thing he remembered? He'd been… with someone? The memory was too fuzzy.

He had no magick, that much he knew. It was almost a relief. He felt its loss because it was so useful and as much a part of him as Hattie. But *why* had he lost it?

Cub.

Dexx looked at Hattie. *Yes, dear?*

We are still not one. We need to become one. Hattie nudged him again, this time with something that felt closer to urgency.

"Oooh, that sounds naughty." He wasn't still in DoDO agents' hands, that much he knew.

We need to be one. Hattie generally wasn't insistent like this —repeating the same words as if thinking they had different meanings each time. She still looked haggard and thin. "Be one. Like I shift-and-poof-you're-there kind of one, or… biblically?" That was going to be awkward.

She looked hungry, her green eyes boring into his. *As we were the first time.* Hattie stuck a paw out and rested it on Dexx's leg. The paw was enormous.

"I'm getting the feeling this isn't the standard spirit agrees to inhabit clause."

We made a pact in that first life. I would do that again. For as many lifetimes you come back.

If it meant having her back? For the next life? "Well, sounds good to me, I guess?" What else could he say?

Without the memory of *how* they'd become shifter spirit and host, he'd just agree. It couldn't be that—

Hattie attacked.

Dexx's eyes shot open to destruction. Smoke. Bodies littering the sidewalk and roadway.

Dexx sat up, smoke rolling off his body. That could be steam, actually. There were several small fires lazily burning in random spots in the area.

A few of the reporters were out, covering the situation, looking scorched but okay.

Devastation wasn't exactly the word he'd put to the DoDO campus. *Extreme devastation* might work better.

The mansion was kindling and rubble. The larger medical facility and training building had entire wings missing. The SUV's were blown all over the street.

Amazingly, two cone-shaped areas of un-disaster survived —one behind him and one where the Mario-demon had stood.

Dexx checked his extremities. Hands felt normal. Feet, still present. Pain spread through the rest of his body, but it faded fast. He put his hands to the grass and felt a small smooth object. The little silver fob Mario lost. If he had it, it must be important. But what did it do?

Hattie happy-pawed in his mind. *Hattie, why in* hell—

Cub. That was a small taste of what I will do if you separate us again.

Relief bum-rushed him, bringing tears to his eyes and shutting him up for a long, long moment where he just enjoyed her voice back in his mind. *Okay. You got a deal.*

Dexx stood over Rainbow's grave two weeks later. The fresh

dirt mingled with the older dirt of Boot's graves and Alma's headstone. "Thanks, kid. For everything. You deserved a better friend than me. I disregarded your importance. Your *value*. I couldn't keep you safe, and I couldn't keep Alma safe, and I couldn't keep Boot safe." Failure? He knew and understood. This though? This was... hard. "I'm truly sorry. To all of you."

The air changed. He wasn't alone. The smell of death and life and repulsion and desire and hundreds of contradictions wafted into his nose.

"The Dexx has completed the action we asked of the Dexx."

Dexx looked up at the Blue Lady with a sad sigh. "Not the best time, lady," he said as respectfully as he could manage. "I'm mourning my friend. She was like the sister I never had. My cheerleader and confidant and personal challenge all rolled into one."

The Blue Lady stepped closer to him.

He took a step away, not ready for whatever else she had to throw at him.

"The child is ours. We asked the Dexx to take an action, and the Dexx did." The currents walked toward him, dipping to capture his gaze, holding it. "We shall grant a boon to the Dexx."

When he tried to speak, he couldn't talk past the lump. He tried again, and all he managed was a whisper. "I want my friend back."

Fuck. His eyes were definitely wet.

"I want them *all* back." He gestured weakly to the graves in front of him.

"The Dexx asks more than can be granted." The Blue Lady turned to look on Rainbow's grave.

"Can I talk to her one more time?"

"The Dexx asks more than can be granted."

The air changed, and the scent of pure cleanliness wafted over him. It changed again, and deep earthiness followed.

Roxxie and Furiel had joined them. They were silent, as they, too, mourned Rainbow's passing. She deserved no less.

"You're a good friend, Dexx." Roxxie put a light hand on his shoulder.

That was a crock. "I'm a suck-ass friend. A real friend would have made sure she lived, would have kept her where she'd be safe."

You kept your littermate as safe as you had access to, cub. Not even the great Dexx Colt can save everyone every time. Hattie had never chided him like that before. But she held a sadness too.

Rainbow's eternal optimism had affected her too.

Mah'se says he will miss the sheneshae. She was not like the others.

"Where have you two been? You might have been able to help us fight Mario, and whatever was possessing him." Dexx was past accusing them of anything. Angels and demons were always going to be too late or too busy to count on.

Furiel clasped his hands behind him. "Other things needed our attention. I was unaware of... Mario and what inhabited him."

"I cannot help as I have in the past." At least Roxxie *sounded* sad. "I am far too weak."

"I get it. The humans are in a mess. Let them stop digging deeper and figure out how to fill it in." This wasn't their fight.

"It's not like that. But I admit, it *feels* like it."

He should cut Roxxie some slack. She'd done amazing things for them in the past. She'd very nearly died for them.

"Sorry for being an ass. My heart hurts. I shouldn't take it out on you." Dexx had his shift back. He had Paige. He had his kids and Jackie. He even had Red Star, and things were running. Not smooth, but they'd moved forward.

"Blue Lady?" He was *not* going to call her the currents.

"The Dexx has a boon to request?" She tipped her water-haired head to the side as if listening to something far away.

"I do." He really didn't, but he still had to take care of Bussemi, and, with his memories of his past lives returned, Dexx realized what he had this time that he hadn't had before. It was more than a power crystal. He had the Whiskeys, Troutdale, his pack. And the Blue Lady. "I'm going to need something in the future, but I don't know what that is yet. When I ask, I want it, no questions asked."

"The Dexx will know the dead cannot be raised."

Roxxie twitched her head but said nothing.

Furiel shifted his feet.

Maybe the dead could be raised, but either she would not or could not. "Yeah, the Dexx knows you won't. What I want will be important. And I want it without question."

"The boon will be only what is in our ability. The Dexx will have one chance to ask this boon in the future. The Dexx has held the Dexx's end of the act. We will hold ours." She disappeared without another word.

"Damn, I wish I could do that." Dexx shook his head.

He stood in numb silence for a while longer, his mind settling into his grief and wallowing in it. He dragged his gaze to Furiel. "He's dead, right? Mario and whatever the fuck he became is gone?"

"He is." Roxxie put a hand on her angel blade. "Your blade... devoured him in a way we have not seen before."

Dexx wasn't sure what he'd done could ever be replayed. He'd had a starved blood blade and had reforged his alpha bond as his blade had reacquired life by consuming energy-zapping blood. Dexx wasn't sure what kind of lasting effects that would have on his blade. It... seemed to be sleeping.

"We are here because there is word." Furiel turned to the house.

Dexx glanced once to Rainbow's grave. At least she hadn't died for nothing. He shifted on the spot and ran the short distance on four massive paws, reveling in the form of the ancient cat. He might have also been running from his broken heart.

He shifted back as he reached the door, his clothes intact and not even a little ruffled. *That* was cause for some celebration. The clothing bill would fall dramatically. His magick might only hold a single gallon of the energy he was used to, but it was enough. Just enough. The silkies were safe.

Furiel and Roxxie stepped through an angel teleportation doorway to the porch.

Dexx opened the sliding glass door for the two and closed it behind them.

Paige and Leslie waited for them in the living room, the TV controller in Leslie's hand.

Mandy, Leah, and Tyler sat on the couch, quiet and still.

That wasn't a good sign. "What did Walton say?" Dexx stopped next to Paige, his arm lightly around her waist. President Flynn had been removed from office, leaving Vice President Walton to step in as the acting president. Turned out he wasn't a paranormal ally.

"Nothing, yet," Paige said quietly, quivering slightly. "He just started."

Dexx touched her arm, trying to see if she was okay.

She glanced at him, rage dancing in her eyes.

Oh. Shit.

The TV showed Acting President Walton standing at the edge of a stage, waving at the crowd in a stadium somewhere. Camera flashes went off, and people waved and cheered behind the news crews and security forces. "Ladies and gentlemen, the President of the United States." An announcer said, and Walton walked across the stage, still smiling and waving.

"They're putting on a fuckin show," Leslie growled. Robin shared her anger, which Dexx could feel through the alpha bond, but since Dexx had taken his alpha back, the griffin was firmly under control and content.

"I can't believe he dismissed us all." Paige dug her fingernails into her upper arm. "He needs us."

Dexx knew they were headed toward another battle, but he didn't know what this one would even look like. Civil war was something that only happened in history.

Walton waved for silence. He started before the last adoring person stopped cheering. "My fellow Americans. The time has come for all good people to stand up to the threat in our midst. These so-called paranormals are a plague to our good, God-fearing nation. We came under existential and material attack two weeks ago at the peace talks in the great State of Montana. The inhuman act of treachery and terrorism killed Cardinal Bussemi and seventeen of his guards. Thank God no other humans were hurt in the surprise attack."

"Damn. It. All. To. Hell." Dexx scrubbed his hands through his hair. "He attacked *me*. As soon as I got out of that truck, he was waving the *kadu*. It was a fight whether I wanted it or not. The camera crews were there."

"I know," Paige quietly, her tone hinting at experience in dealing with this situation.

Walton was speaking again. "I have disbanded the illegal post of the Paranormal Relations Cabinet. The world isn't prepared for those *things* out there. It's meant for good, honest folk. Like us. Like the ones who fought in the second world war to free the world of another black smudge on humanity. And like them, we *will win*."

The crowd exploded into applause.

Acting President Walton went on for another half hour,

riling up the mundanes, calling for worse fates of the paranormals with every other sentence.

The Whiskey clan sat through the sham in ever-increasing
disbelief, the living room filling with more of them as the
speech went on.

A doorway opened, and Derek Blackman stepped through.
"I've been asked to collect you," he said grimly.

Paige wrinkled her eyebrows. "By who?"

Derrick glanced at the TV and grimaced, then looked at
Paige with a raised eyebrow, dipping his head with a shrug.

Why did Paige have to keep going on these stupid
summons every hour on the hour?

She turned to Dexx, her eyes beady, her jaw clenched, her
shoulders tight. "Sorry, babe. I gotta go."

Would she be safe? "Yeah, I know. Head on out." He'd be
here, keeping the kids safe.

And maybe working on Jackie. She was complete, sort of.
A small but important part had been forgotten when they'd
sent the new crate engine—an oil galley plug. Oil had shot all
over as soon as he'd primed the system.

Derrick waved a finger at waist level. "Actually, I was sent
for *both* of you."

Now Dexx had a chance to lift a lip in confusion. "Me?"

"Just doing what I was told." Derek clamped his lips shut
and sneered at the screen with distaste.

"Okay." Paige blew out her cheeks. "Lee, you have the
kids. No burning down the house."

"Got it, Mom," Leah said with a quiet fire in her blue
eyes. "I'll run their lives like a benevolent queen."

Paige thinned her lips. "How about more like a good
sister."

"I think I just said that. Now go. My subjects await."

Dexx turned Paige around. He didn't know what would
happen next if they'd have a moment for this. But everyone

was here, so. "Hey, there's something I've been meaning to ask."

"Hold that thought," Paige said and looked to Derrick. "Where are we going?"

Derrick turned his dark gaze to his sister. "I don't know. Just got coordinates."

"Open the door."

The black lines of the door opened to someplace else, and Paige led them through.

Well, he had to hope they made it through this so he *could* get his question out. They were always so damned busy. He held back a step. *We'll be okay, right?* He couldn't *smell* any ill intent on Derek, but that didn't mean it wasn't there.

We will meet it with tooth, claw, and power. Hattie was always confident. She was a cat after his own heart.

Dexx turned to Roxxie and Furiel. "You guys good?"

"We are," Furiel answered for them both.

Dexx stepped through the door with Paige.

The room they walked into was posh in the way that a volcano was warm. And this was only an entry. The white marble tile floor had gold for grout, and the walls were a slightly different marble. White pedestals held vases that looked expensive, but they didn't have flowers. The hallway had bright but not harsh lighting, and the smells were clean but not clinical.

"Wow, this place is money," Dexx said low. "Like the liquid sort. There's more money in two steps in this hall than we'll make... ever."

"Yeah," Paige said, leaning back slightly. "Now hush. Don't talk unless they ask a question. This ain't your kind of fight."

Ouch. That hurt.

But she wasn't wrong.

"Just in there." Derrick waved his arm down the hall. "I'll just be... waiting."

Paige led them to the doorway and stopped before going in. She recognized the people inside and didn't appear to be the least bit surprised.

Dexx recognized only two. Balnore and Bastet.

The rest were a mix of humans and... not humans. Were those... elves?

Balnore saw them standing in the doorway and raised a well-dressed arm. "Please come in, peanut. I'm glad to see you, Dexx. I heard of your... adventures. Leading an international team of mystery." His lip curled up in humor.

That was a catchy name. "I didn't... have a lot of fun." Dexx didn't feel any humor.

"I wouldn't think so. Please come in." Balnore walked toward them with a drink he offered to Paige.

She turned to Dexx, taking the drink. "Fairy whiskey. Drink very slowly."

"I prefer beer." If it was that kind of meeting.

While a beverage was fetched for him, Paige led the way to a set of empty chairs with... faces. It looked like something out of *Harry Potter*. Only, these monster chairs weren't even a thing there. Were they? Dexx sat, keeping his booted feet away from the chair's teeth.

It breathed around him and worked his shoulders.

Oh, nice chair. Good chair. He needed one of these.

Opposite them was a very impressive man with dark hair and eyes sat with no emotion on his face.

Hattie took notice but did not urge him to fight. He was an alpha. The blonde woman who sat beside him was another one. Hattie *did* want a chance at her. They stared at Dexx.

The man spoke to Dexx, not Paige. "The rumor is true?"

Dexx shook his head. "Sorry. What rumor?"

"The one who claimed the greatest of the first lived."

Dexx hated riddle names. "Yeah, sure." What was he getting at? If he wanted a story, he wasn't going to get it. "Who told you?"

"We have ways of gathering information. I would steer clear of any djinn you find around. They didn't appreciate your... hasty departure. Word is there was a small fight because of you."

Dexx bet. "Fuck 'em. They deserve what they got." And more.

"Believe me." The man raised a blonde eyebrow and turned to his mate. "There is no love lost there. I was interested in seeing it first-hand. Welcome back, Shedim Patesh."

"Yeah. Good to be back." Dexx was ready for this show to be on the road.

A man with dark hair, pristine clothing, and slitted eyes raised his hand for silence.

What is he? Dexx asked.

Dragon, Hattie answered with no small amount of respect.

No shit.

She didn't answer him.

"The main purpose of bringing you here is not to talk of rumors or issue warnings. The time for that is past."

Paige leaned in and whispered to Dexx, "These are the guys who really run the countries. This is the highest order of the paranormal council." She released a long sigh. "The most powerful, richest, most influential."

"Great. Why am I here?" She took a sip of her fairy whiskey and leaned back into her back-rubbing chair.

The dragon nodded to the woman and the man. "Dexx Colt, this is your first time here. This is Kat and her husband, Hadwin. They are the North American high alphas."

"Congratulations." Why would they ask him to be here? "So you're Chuck's boss?"

The woman—Kat smiled. "That is simplistic, but yes."

A servant appeared out of thin air with Dexx's beer.

He took it, and the servant disappeared again.

"Drink slowly," Paige said quietly. "It's probably fairy beer. Fuckin' put you down."

Dexx turned his attention back to Kat and Hadwin. "So you should be talking to Chuck, not me."

Kat smiled and nodded as though she agreed. "You still have a vote."

Dexx exhaled through his nose. "Vote on what?"

"You and the Whiskey clan have been under uncommon attack," the dragon said. "Today, we vote again to go to war."

Paige told him a few states had wanted to secede. The courts had struck down the petition, Though. The only way to break away from the states would be through war.

Break the Union.

"So, this is…" This was *really* huge. "This is really happening."

There were several nods around the room, and none seemed to feel the burden of it, the decision.

But Dexx'd been at war. He *knew* what that meant.

He also realized his vote really wouldn't count. They already knew what they wanted.

Well, Dexx wanted to eradicate DoDO. And the acting president had just made his children outlaws. So… yeah. Maybe he wanted this too.

But if they were making an empty vote to find an answer they already had, then he was taking the time to finalize something before shit went to hell.

Dexx slid out of his chair, setting down his beer on a table that ran up to him.

He needed one of those, too.

He went to a knee and took Paige's hand. "Location sucks. Timing sucks. I know all this."

She closed her eyes and smiled as she shook her head. "Now?"

He shrugged as she opened her eyes again. "One thing kept me going this last year... or so—the thought of coming home to you. I hated being away from my kids and you. And Jackie, too."

She chuckled. "Mostly her."

"Shut up," he grouched and squeezed her hand tighter. "The things I went through were at times more than I could bear, but with you, I'd do it all again. I love you, and I want to be with you for as long as I can. If this goes the way I think it is, I won't do it without you. Not again. Paige Whiskey, would you be my wife?"

She wriggled her hand out of his and cupped his face. "Yes," she whispered and then claimed more than her lips with hers.

She claimed his soul.

He met Kat's cat-green gaze from around Paige's head. "You have my vote." They were going to war anyway. Might as well be on his own terms.

PRE-ORDER SLIPPING ON KARMA PEELS

Join us in *Slipping on Karma Peels* as Wynona Hunts races to save Paige's life from a treacherous demon, and Paige and Dexx lead the nation to civil war.

Pick up *Slipping on Karma Peels*:
https://www.fjblooding.com/pre-order-wwmr-book-5

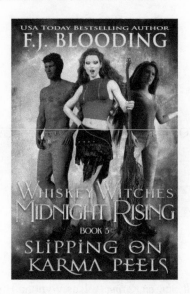

Don't forget to leave reviews! Let us know what you think!

SNEAK PEAK AT SLIPPING ON
KARMA PEELS

I have few fears in life.

Kids are one of them.

So, okay. I realized in that moment that, as a full-grown thirty-something woman, a preteen shouldn't scare me in the slightest. I was still bigger than that little punk. I was definitely smarter than him, and I smelled better.

But this little... a-hole didn't know when to f-ing *stop*. And *that?* That annoyed the piss out of me.

Time for a little karmic placement.

That eyeroll-worthy little twerp picked up yet another one of my bars of soap, scraped it across his snotty nose, and then put it back. That was the third one in a matter of minutes. His mom had told him to stop being a brat three times and he just got progressively worse.

Look, I'm not allergic to a little snot. I know that the shelf-life on "gross" isn't long, but when you're just nasty because you can get away with it, I'm going to punch you in the face with your own karma.

With pleasure.

"You want to stop wiping your nose on my soaps, kid?" I

asked, saddling up to him with a likeable enough smile. I'm pretty, even at the ripe old age of thirty-two—maybe even because of it—and I know how to sweep men and women off their feet. No matter their age.

But this kid? He glanced at me, shrugged flippantly, then grabbed another soap out of one of the boxes and wiped it up his nose. Then, he looked directly at me with a what-you-going-to-do-about-it smile and put it back.

I just smiled back and winked at him. You know why? Because f-him that's why. I sashayed back to the counter near the side of the occult shop I ran with my girlfriend and grabbed one of my karmic blessing stamped cards. Walking back to him, I palmed the card so he couldn't see it.

His eyes flared as he watched me, maybe taking in my full appearance. Like I said. I'm not bad to look at and I own my sass with my biker boots, fishnets, and ragged black skirt. I like my t-shirts sassy and tight and I definitely wear the bras that make my not-as-young-as-they-used be but-still-not-that-old-so-stop-judging tits to stand at attention. I have just enough control over air to be able to manipulate men a *little* more, so I employed that, pushing my wavy dark hair around me.

Yeah. The kid was a little slack-jawed.

I walked past him, leaning in to whisper, "Maybe don't be a complete asshat." I slipped the karmic blessing into his back pocket and kept walking. "Okay?"

Whomper, my personality-enhanced broom, met me at the end of the aisle, peaking around as if he could *actually see.* Though, could he? I didn't know. I'd imbued him with a personality and the ability to walk and move on his own. I hadn't given him eyes or ears. He just somehow managed not to run into things. Magick, man. It was awesome.

I pushed my broom out of the way and back into his hidey-corner near the window. There was a coat rack stashed there with some material I changed out to suit my moods and the changing seasons and sometimes holidays if I felt like entertaining the notion of celebrating them. It wasn't for coats though. It was so Whomper had a place to watch people and not get lonely. A lonely broom was a bad, bad broom.

"Stop it," I hissed at him.

He "wagged" his handle, which meant he bashed it around like it was a tail, except in his case, it was his head-body.

Yeah, giving my broom life hadn't been the *brightest* move of all time.

After getting Whomper stashed back behind the violet material draped coat rack, I turned to survey my handy work and prepared to laugh my butt off.

The kid grabbed one of my soaps, looking around to see if I was there. He kinda saw me. I know how to hide in my own darned store, all right? Then he smiled and proceeded to wipe that soap up his nose.

I just waited. He'd been karmically marked. I didn't need to do anything else.

He returned the soap to the box and turned toward his mom.

She bumped into the glass tower candle display and a large black candle fell and whacked him on the head, cracking and breaking on the floor.

"Jerimiah Anderson," his mother screeched.

I could be judgmental about that. She'd bumped the table. She'd made the candle fall and hit her kid. But I *knew* she hadn't *really* been what had knocked the candle onto the kid's —Jerimiah's—head. His karma had.

The kid's face turned red. "It wasn't me, you cow. You hit me."

I glanced at Whomper with an excited grin because things

were about to get good. That kid was putting out some *nasty* karmic actions.

My broom quivered in what I took as excitement and then poked his stick out around the material for a better view.

"You do *not* get to call me that," she said, gripping her purse straps and looking around worried.

That wasn't a good sign. That typically said "abuse in the home," or even that she was scared of her own son. Huh. I had a spell for that.

It could also just mean that she'd raised a walking temper tantrum and didn't want to get judged. Yeah. I had a spell for that, too.

"I'll call you whatever I want. Now, pick that up." Jerimiah took a step back, his foot finding one of my geode balls. He twisted his ankle and stumbled into the basket that held them. They then rolled out, making it even more messy. He bent down to catch himself as he tipped but put his hands on the soap box shelf.

And dumped them all over him and the floor.

His eyes lit up with bristling anger as he held up his arm. "You cut me!"

Definitely abuse in the house. I'd step in and handle this soon, but not quite yet. I wanted that blessing to kick him around just a *little* longer first.

"How could I have," his mother asked, her voice small yet assertive, "when I was standing over here. Now, clean up your mess before—" She glanced around and leaned in. "—people see."

"I am *not* cleaning this up," he said belligerently.

And then proceeded to step on one of my bars of soap—a black and yellow bar that had been imbued with elderberry and five finger grass. Yeah, my karmically blessed customer had just slipped on my Fuck You Karmically soap bar.

He slipped and fell on his ass, on top of the geodes and

bars of soap and the broken candle.

The mother took a step back, her eyes widening in what I read as fear.

Okay. *Now* it was time to step in. "Watch my back," I whispered to my broom.

His excitement died and he was now *very* solid as he stood on bristles of anger.

I stepped around the corner as Jerimiah growled low and long and got to his feet. "Oh, my," I exclaimed with a chipper smile. "What a mess." I wanted to rub that in.

Jerimiah spun on me, his face angry. But it melted away a little as he brushed off his pants. "Yeah, uh, Linda hit me with a candle and I fell."

"Linda, huh?" So, maybe not his mom. Step-mom? Rough. I looked down at the candle in question. The thing was *huge*. "You broke my karma candle, dude. Do you realize what that means?"

He frowned, staring down at it. "Linda owes you a lot of money? She broke it."

"On your head, obviously," I muttered, but screwed my smile back in place. "You've been blessed. Congratulations." I wiggled my fingers and did a little dance.

Narrowing his eyes, he looked around at the mess, his hands out.

"I know, it doesn't *feel* like a blessing right now, but it is." And if I'd managed to catch him at *this* point in his little asshole life, I might have saved him a little. "And this?" I reached down to pick up the soap he'd slid on. "This is my karmic soap. And this?" I knelt down to pull some of the soaps that had fallen to the floor. "This is a karmic soap. I believe you wiped your snot all over it. And this one? One of my favorites." I handed him the blue and grey bar. "The karmic scrub? So good. Looks like karma came a callin' for ya, kid."

His hands fisted on either side of his body and he glared at me, obviously at a loss for words.

I'm not saying that because I *knew* he couldn't speak. I'm saying that because he *actually* didn't speak. I'm not a mind reader. I'm just, seriously, not stupid.

I rose to my biker-booted feet and gave him an alluring smile, cocking one hip flirtatiously—not like I was *actually* flirting with the jailbait boy. I've learned that an easy way to diffuse a situation is through straight up sex appeal. And when you've *got* that sex appeal? Yeah. It's a weapon my arsenal. Bet your butt I'm going to use it. I don't care if the receiver is jailbait or not. "All of this soap is ruined, unfortunately." I shrugged helplessly. "Especially now that you've spilled it all over the floor. I don't know which ones are carrying your literal snot."

Linda's eyes widened. "I can pay for the damages."

And then Linda would never be back, and I had a feeling I'd be one of her last chances as her situation degraded. I often was. "Nah. I've got a way for him to pay me back."

"I'm not paying for this," the jackass boy said.

I chuckled. He seriously was. I tipped my head to the side. "May you be blessed." I *loved* handing that out, though I had to be careful because of the law of return. Yeah. Sometimes, that came back and bit me in the ass. "However, the payment will be...easy."

Linda shook her head and reached into her purse. "Just tell me how much I owe you."

"You owe me nothing." Though the woman would be paying later, but not to me. That's kinda how karma worked even *if* I wasn't the one throwing it around like a dish best served cold. "But this sweet little thing?" But what did I want from him?

Hmm...service would mean I'd actually have to employ

this little asshole and then deal with him. No. I didn't like that idea at all.

Toenail or fingernail clippings came to mind. Those *could* be useful, especially since the boy was *obviously* filled with rage. I could think of at least three potions I could infuse with those alone. But they were *easy* to give and I wasn't looking for ease.

The kid had lustrous long locks of dark brown hair. Taking *those* would serve three purposes: I'd humiliate him by shaving them off *in the store*, I'd have a lot of product to use for potions—though I *would* have to hurry as hair didn't keep its potency as long as nails did—and it would have a bigger karmic impact on him.

Linda had continued to talk. She was babbling now, and I hadn't listened to any of it. Okay. I was *kinda* listening and the only thing I really gleaned was that she was well-versed in talking herself out of situations that would break her bones. She was a bruise-is-better mitigator. Which, by my experience, meant the kid's father was probably the abuser and the kid was probably a fantastic student.

I met her gaze and held it, ignoring the whiny voice of the boy as he complained about how none of this was his fault and how he should be blameless. "You want to save him?" I asked in a tone that was *below* the volume of the kid.

See, that's something that people who have been abused excel at, being able to hear small sounds in the wake of world-shattering noise.

Linda clamped her lips shut and nodded.

"You're going to let me," I said under the kid who'd actually started getting *louder*, "take all of his hair."

Thanks to the kid, we now had a small audience. I'd had, I don't know, maybe five customers before? Now, they were all peaking around the shelves and there were *more* of them as if the tantrum was actually drawing them in.

Yeah. That's another reason why I'm not big into the "worship the customer" and thinking they were always right. Sure. I like money. Paying the bills is great. But I'm not going to turn in a dick-licker just to make a buck. I've already got some pretty low morals. They don't need to *that* low.

Also, sometimes, I can make a small mint on the pity-buys. Commerce works in mysterious ways.

The kid squeaked a startled, "What?!" and shut up finally.

I smiled at Linda. "I don't want your money. I just want his hair."

Linda raised her chin, blinking several times as she thought about this. Glancing over at Jerimiah, she pulled her empty hand out of her purse which settled under her arm. "And that will cover the cost to replace all of this?"

And then some. "I'll even throw something in there to help with your...situation."

Linda met my gaze with the fierceness of the warrior spirit the people in her life had beaten down and broken. "Deal," she whispered.

See? I don't just own and operate an occult shop in New Orleans, which is cool by any right. I'm this person. I'm the last resort. I'm the worst "good" choice left.

I give people the power to build themselves up.

And this kid's hair was going to help a lot of people. And make me a crap-ton of cash for the business.

"Excellent." I smiled at the other customers on my way back to my cash register and grabbed the clippers I had stashed there—not because I did this often but because Jerry, the guy who owned the *other* occult shop, had a dog and I was the only one who could actually get him shaved every month. I pulled out my behind-the-counter bar stool and set it out right there in the front window. "Take a seat."

I spent the next probably fifteen minutes sheering that kid's hair. He was *silent* the entire time. But *as* I was doing that, I also turned on my mini-burner and a single serve candle. I had those encased so I could create candle spells for people as needed. You'd be amazed at how much people would pay for a "real" spell that only asked for them to light a candle.

When I was done, a few of the customers had managed to clean up the mess Jerimiah had made, stacking it up on the counter as neatly as possible and they—and about five or so *more* customers—were now perusing my book section and trying to figure out what to do with chicken feet. A lot of people thought they were "dark." Look, seriously? I could make a *spoon* dark. Chicken feet were just another protection method. But, damn if they didn't bring in a lot of money. About half of it was spent by people who had no earthly idea what to do with them.

And I was okay with that.

But I took a clump of the much quieter Jerimiah's hair off his shoulders—because I was keeping as much as I could— and took it over to the counter. Now, okay. Here's where I go a bit over the top for commercial reasons. Sure, magick needs a little show and tell—not super really, but okay. And certain spells need words—for energy focus, not because the magick itself needs it. But when you're running an occult shop, you want to *find* reasons to *inspire* people to spend money and the *best* way to do that if they think you're a real witch.

You know, which I am.

So, I chanted some mumbo-jumbo—it was more of an instruction manual for Linda—and then shoved the hair by strand into the soft, black wax. I then reached under the counter and pulled out some wolfsbane, shoving a little bit of that—because, you didn't want to overburn that--, some devil's shoestring, and some basil into it using my metal chopstick. I removed it from the mini-burner and turned to Jerimiah. "While this is setting, how about you go get that broom over by that window over there and clean up all this hair." I smiled sweetly at him. "I want all of it."

Jerimiah glowered—at the floor—and trudged in the direction I'd shown.

One of the wandering customers actually helped him locate Whomper. Well, the broom helped a little, too.

Linda was a bundle of fiery nerves as she gripped her purse straps and then released them.

So, I told her to go look through the store and find one thing that called to her. "It doesn't have to make sense to you, but if it calls to you, bring it here."

Nodding, Linda walked away.

A man sidled up to the counter with a devilish smile and a flirtatious twinkle in his eye. "I'll pay for the damages."

Oh, the pockets of chivalrous men. "You wanna know how much it costs first?"

He shook his head and offered me a credit card. "I'll take your number."

Okay. So you might have heard that I had a girlfriend earlier, but here's the thing. My barndoor swings both ways and Veronica is fine with an open relationship. I wished I was. So, I just smiled and dropped my eyelids as a refusal to his proposal. "My girlfriend wouldn't understand."

He chuckled good naturedly. "I had to try. But I'll still pay for that." He gestured to the pile on the counter.

So, I went through and tallied it all up, and gave him the bill.

He didn't even blink. He just paid for it.

I reached down and pulled out an amulet I kept for those rare customers who deserved a special kick of karma. It works both ways. Sometimes, it's a slap in the face—and a punch to the gut. But sometimes—like in this case—it was a pat on the back. I'm not totally *evil*. Judgmental? Oh, yeah. Definitely that.

He accepted it and draped it over his head. "I'll be back later when it's less busy."

Oh. "You needed something special?"

He glanced at the candle I'd made for Linda, then nodded. "Something like that."

"Okay." I smiled. I enjoyed it when customers knew what they needed and wanted. "I'll be here."

He saluted with his receipt and left.

The rest of the day flew by. Two *other* customers offered to pay for the damages, but I told them it was already covered. Jerimiah—thanks to Whomper who was a *very* good broom—cleaned up his hair which I stowed away for a rainy day.

And the customers just kept flooding in.

I didn't even realize the sun had set until I felt soft, warm lips caress the back of my neck as Veronica's arms slid around my abdomen, tucking me in close.

Smiling, I finished that transaction, the customer beaming at us.

New Orleans was a special, *special* place and I *loved* it.

I turned in her arms, allowing my fingertips to trail along her shoulders before clasping behind her head. "Hey, baby."

"Hey." Veronica pulled her head back to survey the store before turning her swoon-worthy brown eyes to me. "Looks like you've been hit."

Let me just show you my gorgeous Veronica. I won't say she's the love of my life. Someone already took that spot, but this woman sure is a close second. She's tall and curvy in *all* the right places. She loves flowy skirts that would totally get tangled up in *my* legs, and she has the most perfect toes for her open sandals. I've got ugly feet. Always have. Her skin is just that shade of brown that reflects light back at a person, making her look like she's softly glowing all the time. And her hair? Damn, that woman makes most people jealous. It's long and full and utterly luxurious. Is it extensions? A weave? I don't know and I don't care. My woman is physically beautiful.

And her soul is too, which is how she claimed my heart.

I released her and moved around the counter. If she was here, it was *past* closing time. So, I made a pass to make sure the store was empty and locked the door, flipping the sign closed. "Yeah. Pretty much. Don't know what got into everyone."

"I do," Veronica said, her voice tight.

Oh, bad sign. I flipped the middle switch to take out most of the lights and turned around. "What happened?"

The look on her face was grim, like grim reaper grim as she raked her full top lip with her teeth. "The vice president is moving to ratify the Registration Act."

"But I thought Paige had stopped that."

Veronica nodded and then closed her eyes with a sigh. "And she was doin' good, near as I can tell. But... he dissolved her position."

Oh... crap. "He did what?"

Veronica opened her eyes and nodded.

"Shit." What were we—"What do we do?"

"We're meeting."

That was something I heard a ton before, but these "meetings" just meant that she'd be home late and that I shouldn't worry. Which I typically didn't. Much.

"Come with me," she said quietly, offering her hand.

I paused as that one request settled over me like a blanket. I met her halfway and took her hand. "You bet." I had no idea what was in store, but I was finally going to get one step closer to figuring it out.

Pick up *Slipping on Karma Peels*:
https://www.fjblooding.com/pre-order-wwmr-book-5

ALSO BY S.S. WOLFRAM

Whiskey Witches Universe

Whiskey Witches

Whiskey Witches

Blood Moon Magick

Barrel of Whiskey

Witches of the West

Whiskey Witches: Ancients

Desert Shaman

Big Bad Djinn

Lizard Wizard

Whiskey on the Rocks

Double-Double Demon Trouble

Mirror, Mirror Demon Rubble

Dead Demon Die

Whiskey Witches: Para Wars

Whiskey Storm

London Bridge Down

Midnight Whiskey

International Team of Mystery

Slipping on Karma Peels

Pre-order now at: https://www.fjblooding.com/preorder

Other Books in the Whiskey-Verse

Shifting Heart Romances

by Hattie Hunt & F.J. Blooding

Bear Moon

Grizzly Attraction

Here's the reading order to make it even easier to catch up!

https://www.fjblooding.com/reading-order

Other Books by F.J. Blooding

Devices of War Trilogy

Fall of Sky City

Sky Games

Whispers of the Skyborne

Discover more, sign up for updates and gifts, and join the forum discussions at www.fjblooding.com.

WHISKEY MAGICK & MENTAL HEALTH

S ign up to learn more about our books and receive this free e-zine about Whiskey Magick and Mental Health. https://www.fjblooding.com/books-lp

ABOUT THE AUTHOR

Shane Wolfram lives in his hometown with his amazing wife F.J. Blooding. Frankie let him take over Dexx's story one deadline-ridden night and he's never looked back since. He hadn't quite realized what he'd be jumping into when he volunteered, but he's grown as an author and is enjoying the journey.

They live with his twin brother, his wife, their two kids, and during their long summer days, he gets to spend time with his two amazing daughters. He loves working on cars and letting my bestselling wife write his bios, newsletters, and articles for him while he crafts amazing Dexx books and naps with the cat.

Enjoy!

Follow us on Bookbub!

https://www.bookbub.com/authors/f-j-blooding